CHARLES DICKENS

COMPLETE
WORKS

CENTENNIAL EDITION

Charles Dickens

CHARLES DICKENS

CHRISTMAS STORIES

II

Illustrations
by
Arthur Jules Goodman

Edito-Service S.A., Geneva, Publishers

CONTENTS

Mrs. Lirriper's Lodgings 1

Mrs. Lirriper's Legacy 43

Doctor Marigold 79

Mugby Junction 127

No Thoroughfare 205

The Lazy Tour of Two Idle Apprentices 353

LIST OF ILLUSTRATIONS

DOCTOR MARIGOLD 92

MUGBY JUNCTION 148

NO THOROUGHFARE 322

LAZY TOUR OF TWO IDLE APPRENTICES 438

MRS. LIRRIPER'S LODGINGS

[1863]

CHAPTER I

WHOEVER would begin to be worried with letting Lodgings that wasn't a lone woman with a living to get is a thing inconceivable to me, my dear; excuse the familiarity, but it comes natural to me in my own little room, when wishing to open my mind to those that I can trust, and I should be truly thankful if they were all mankind, but such is not so, for have but a Furnished bill in the window and your watch on the mantelpiece, and farewell to it if you turn your back for but a second, however gentlemanly the manners; nor is being of your own sex any safeguard, as I have reason, in the form of sugar-tongs to know, for that lady (and a fine woman she was) got me to run for a glass of water, on the plea of going to be confined, which certainly turned out true, but it was in the Station-house.

Number Eighty-one Norfolk Street, Strand—situated midway between the City and St. James's, and within five minutes' walk of the principal places of public amusement—is my address. I have rented this house many years, as the parish rate-books will testify; and I could wish my landlord was as

3

alive to the fact as I am myself; but no, bless you, not a half a pound of paint to save his life, nor so much, my dear, as a tile upon the roof, though on your bended knees.

My dear, you never have found Number Eighty-one Norfolk Street Strand advertised in Bradshaw's *Railway Guide*, and with the blessing of Heaven you never will or shall so find it. Some there are who do not think it lowering themselves to make their names that cheap, and even going the lengths of a portrait of the house not like it with a blot in every window and a coach and four at the door, but what will suit Wozenham's lower down on the other side of the way will not suit me, Miss Wozenham having her opinions and me having mine, though when it comes to systematic underbidding capable of being proved on oath in a court of justice and taking the form of "If Mrs. Lirriper names eighteen shillings a week, I name fifteen and six," it then comes to a settlement between yourself and your conscience, supposing for the sake of argument your name to be Wozenham, which I am well aware it is not or my opinion of you would be greatly lowered, and as to airy bedrooms and a night-porter in constant attendance the less said the better, the bedrooms being stuffy and the porter stuff.

It is forty years ago since me and my poor Lirriper got married at St. Clement's Danes, where I now have a sitting in a very pleasant pew with genteel company and my own hassock, and being partial to evening service not too crowded. My poor Lirriper was a handsome figure of a man, with a beaming eye and a voice as mellow as a musical instrument made of honey and steel, but he had ever been a free liver being in the commercial travelling line and travelling what he called a limekiln road—"a dry road, Emma my dear," my poor Lirriper says to me, "where I have to lay the dust with one drink or another all day long and half the night, and it wears me Emma"—and this led to his running through a good deal and might have run through the turnpike too when that dreadful horse that never would stand still for a

4

single instant set off, but for its being night and the gate shut, and consequently took his wheel, my poor Lirriper and the gig smashed to atoms and never spoke afterwards. He was a handsome figure of a man, and a man with a jovial heart and a sweet temper; but if they had come up then they never could have given you the mellowness of his voice, and indeed I consider photographs wanting in mellowness as a general rule and making you look like a new-ploughed field.

My poor Lirriper being behindhand with the world and being buried at Hatfield church in Hertfordshire, not that it was his native place but that he had a liking for the Salisbury Arms where we went upon our wedding-day and passed as happy a fortnight as ever happy was, I went round to the creditors and I says "Gentlemen I am acquainted with the fact that I am not answerable for my late husband's debts but I wish to pay them for I am his lawful wife and his good name is dear to me. I am going into the Lodgings gentlemen as a business and if I prosper every farthing that my late husband owed shall be paid for the sake of the love I bore him, by this right hand." It took a long time to do but it was done, and the silver cream-jug which is between ourselves and the bed and the mattress in my room up-stairs (or it would have found legs so sure as ever the Furnished bill was up) being presented by the gentlemen engraved "To Mrs. Lirriper a mark of grateful respect for her honourable conduct" gave me a turn which was too much for my feelings, till Mr. Betley which at that time had the parlours and loved his joke says "Cheer up Mrs. Lirriper, you should feel as if it was only your christening and they were your godfathers and godmothers which did promise for you." And it brought me round, and I don't mind confessing to you my dear that I then put a sandwich and a drop of sherry in a little basket and went down to Hatfield churchyard outside the coach and kissed my hand and laid it with a kind of proud and swelling love on my husband's grave, though bless you it had taken me so long to clear his name

MRS. LIRRIPER'S LODGINGS

that my wedding-ring was worn quite fine and smooth when I laid it on the green green waving grass.

I am an old woman now and my good looks are gone but that's me my dear over the plate-warmer and considered like in the times when you used to pay two guineas on ivory and took your chance pretty much how you came out, which made you very careful how you left it about afterwards because people were turned so red and uncomfortable by mostly guessing it was somebody else quite different, and there was once a certain person that had put his money in a hop business that came in one morning to pay his rent and his respects being the second floor that would have taken it down from its hook and put it in his breast-pocket—you understand my dear—for the L, he says of the original—only there was no mellowness in *his* voice and I wouldn't let him, but his opinion of it you may gather from his saying to it "Speak to me Emma!" which was far from a rational observation no doubt but still a tribute to its being a likeness, and I think myself it *was* like me when I was young and wore that sort of stays.

But it was about the Lodgings that I was intending to hold forth and certainly I ought to know something of the business having been in it so long, for it was early in the second year of my married life that I lost my poor Lirriper and I set up at Islington directly afterwards and afterwards came here, being two houses and eight-and-thirty years and some losses and a deal of experience.

Girls are your first trial after fixtures and they try you even worse than what I call the Wandering Christians, though why *they* should roam the earth looking for bills and then coming in and viewing the apartments and stickling about terms and never at all wanting them or dreaming of taking them being already provided, is a mystery I should be thankful to have explained if by any miracle it could be. It's wonderful they live so long and thrive so on it but I suppose the exercise makes it healthy, knocking so much and

6

going from house to house and up and down stairs all day, and then their pretending to be so particular and punctual is a most astonishing thing, looking at their watches and saying " Could you give me the refusal of the rooms till twenty minutes past eleven the day after to-morrow in the forenoon, and supposing it to be considered essential by my friend from the country could there be a small iron bedstead put in the little room upon the stairs?" Why when I was new to it my dear I used to consider before I promised and to make my mind anxious with calculations and to get quite wearied out with disappointments, but now I says " Certainly by all means" well knowing it's a Wandering Christian and I shall hear no more about it, indeed by this time I know most of the Wandering Christians by sight as well as they know me, it being the habit of each individual revolving round London in that capacity to come back about twice a year, and it's very remarkable that it runs in families and the children grow up to it, but even were it otherwise I should no sooner hear of the friend from the country which is a certain sign than I should nod and say to myself You're a Wandering Christian, though whether they are (as I *have* heard) persons of small property with a taste for regular employment and frequent change of scene I cannot undertake to tell you.

Girls as I was beginning to remark are one of your first and your lasting troubles, being like your teeth which begin with convulsions and never cease tormenting you from the time you cut them till they cut you, and then you don't want to part with them which seems hard but we must all succumb or buy artificial, and even where you get a will nine times out of ten you'll get a dirty face with it and naturally lodgers do not like good society to be shown in with a smear of black across the nose or a smudgy eyebrow. Where they pick the black up is a mystery I cannot solve, as in the case of the willingest girl that ever came into a house half-starved poor thing, a girl so willing that I called her Willing Sophy down upon her knees scrubbing early and late and ever cheerful but always smiling with a black face. And I says to Sophy, "Now Sophy my good girl have a regular day for your stoves and keep the width of the Airy between yourself and the blacking and do not brush your hair with the bottoms of the saucepans and do not meddle with the snuffs of the candles and it stands to reason that it can no longer be" yet there it was and always on her nose, which turning up and being broad at the end seemed to boast of it and caused warning from a steady gentleman and excellent lodger with breakfast by the week but a little irritable and use of a sitting-room when required, his words being "Mrs. Lirriper I have arrived at the point of admitting that the Black is a man and a brother, but only in a natural form and when it can't be got off." Well consequently I put poor Sophy on to other work and forbid her answering the door or answering a bell on any account but she was so unfortunately willing that nothing would stop her flying up the kitchen-stairs whenever a bell was heard to tingle. I put it to her "O Sophy Sophy for goodness' goodness' sake where does it come from?" To which that poor unlucky willing mortal bursting out crying to see me so vexed replied "I took a deal of black into me ma'am when I was a small child being much neglected and I think it must be, that it works out," so it continuing to work out of that poor thing and not having another fault to find with her I says "Sophy what do you seriously think of my helping you away to New South Wales where it might not be noticed?" Nor did I ever repent the money which was well spent, for she married the ship's cook on the voyage (himself a Mulotter) and did well and lived happy, and so far as ever I heard it was *not* noticed in a new state of society to her dying day.

In what way Miss Wozenham lower down on the other side of the way reconciled it to her feelings as a lady (which she is not) to entice Mary Anne Perkinsop from my service is best known to herself, I do not know and I do not wish to

know how opinions are formed at Wozenham s on any point.
But Mary Anne Perkinsop although I behaved handsomely
to her and she behaved unhandsomely to me was worth her
weight in gold as overawing lodgers without driving them
away, for lodgers would be far more sparing of their bells
with Mary Anne than I ever knew them to be with Maid
or Mistress, which is a great triumph especially when accompanied with a cast in the eye and a bag of bones, but it was
the steadiness of her way with them through her father's
having failed in Pork. It was Mary Anne's looking so
respectable in her person and being so strict in her spirits
that conquered the tea-and-sugarest gentleman (for he weighed
them both in a pair of scales every morning) that I have
ever had to deal with and no lamb grew meeker, still it
afterwards came round to me that Miss Wozenham happening
to pass and seeing Mary Anne take in the milk of a milkman
that made free in a rosy-faced way (I think no worse of him)
with every girl in the street but was quite frozen up like the
statue at Charing-cross by her, saw Mary Anne's value in
the lodging business and went as high as one pound per
quarter more, consequently Mary Anne with not a word
betwixt us says "If *you* will provide yourself Mrs. Lirriper
in a month from this day *I* have already done the same,"
which hurt me and I said so, and she then hurt me more
by insinuating that her father having failed in Pork had laid
her open to it.

My dear I do assure you it's a harassing thing to know
what kind of girls to give the preference to, for if they are
lively they get bell'd off their legs and if they are sluggish
you suffer from it yourself in complaints and if they are
sparkling-eyed they get made love to, and if they are smart
in their persons they try on your Lodgers' bonnets and if
they are musical I defy you to keep them away from bands
and organs, and allowing for any difference you like in their
heads their heads will be always out of window just the same.
And then what the gentlemen like in girls the ladies don't,

9

which is fruitful hot water for all parties, and then there's temper though such a temper as Caroline Maxey's I hope not often. A good-looking black-eyed girl was Caroline and a comely-made girl to your cost when she did break out and laid about her, as took place first and last through a new-married couple come to see London in the first floor and the lady very high and it *was* supposed not liking the good looks of Caroline having none of her own to spare, but anyhow she did try Caroline though that was no excuse. So one afternoon Caroline comes down into the kitchen flushed and flashing, and she says to me "Mrs. Lirriper that woman in the first has aggravated me past bearing," I says "Caroline keep your temper," Caroline says with a curdling laugh "Keep my temper? You're right Mrs. Lirriper, so I will. Capital D her!" bursts out Caroline (you might have struck me into the centre of the earth with a feather when she said it) "I'll give her a touch of the temper that *I* keep!" Caroline downs with her hair my dear, screeches and rushes up-stairs, I following as fast as my trembling legs could bear me, but before I got into the room the dinner-cloth and pink-and-white service all dragged off upon the floor with a crash and the new-married couple on their backs in the firegrate, him with the shovel and tongs and a dish of cucumber across him and a mercy it was summer-time. "Caroline" I says "be calm," but she catches off my cap and tears it in her teeth as she passes me, then pounces on the new-married lady makes her a bundle of ribbons takes her by the two ears and knocks the back of her head upon the carpet Murder screaming all the time Policemen running down the street and Wozenham's windows (judge of my feelings when I came to know it) thrown up and Miss Wozenham calling out from the balcony with crocodile's tears "It's Mrs. Lirriper been overcharging somebody to madness —she'll be murdered—I always thought so—Pleeseman save her!" My dear four of them and Caroline behind the chiffoniere attacking with the poker and when disarmed

prize-fighting with her double fists, and down and up and
up and down and dreadful! But I couldn't bear to see the
poor young creature roughly handled and her hair torn when
they got the better of her, and I says " Gentlemen Policemen
pray remember that her sex is the sex of your mothers and
sisters and your sweethearts, and God bless them and you ! "
And there she was sitting down on the ground handcuffed,
taking breath against the skirting-board and them cool with
their coats in strips, and all she says was " Mrs. Lirriper I'm
sorry as ever I touched *you*, for you're a kind motherly old
thing," and it made me think that I had often wished I had
been a mother indeed and how would my heart have felt if I
had been the mother of that girl! Well you know it turned
out at the Police-office that she had done it before, and she
had her clothes away and was sent to prison, and when she
was to come out I trotted off to the gate in the evening with
just a morsel of jelly in that little basket of mine to give
her a mite of strength to face the world again, and there I
met with a very decent mother waiting for her son through
bad company and a stubborn one he was with his half-boots
not laced. So out came Caroline and I says " Caroline come
along with me and sit down under the wall where it's retired
and eat a little trifle that I have brought with me to do you
good," and she throws her arms round my neck and says
sobbing " O why were you never a mother when there are such
mothers as there are ! " she says, and in half a minute more
she begins to laugh and says " Did I really tear your cap to
shreds ? " and when I told her " You certainly did so Caroline "
she laughed again and said while she patted my face " Then
why do you wear such queer old caps you dear old thing?
If you hadn't worn such queer old caps I don't think I should
have done it even then." Fancy the girl! Nothing could
get out of her what she was going to do except O she would
do well enough, and we parted she being very thankful and
kissing my hands, and I nevermore saw or heard of that girl,
except that I shall always believe that a very genteel cap

which was brought anonymous to me one Saturday night in an oilskin basket by a most impertinent young sparrow of a monkey whistling with dirty shoes on the clean steps and playing the harp on the Airy railings with a hoop-stick came from Caroline.

What you lay yourself open to my dear in the way of being the object of uncharitable suspicions when you go into the Lodging business I have not the words to tell you, but never was I so dishonourable as to have two keys nor would I willingly think it even of Miss Wozenham lower down on the other side of the way sincerely hoping that it may not be, though doubtless at the same time money cannot come from nowhere and it is not reason to suppose that Bradshaws put it in for love be it blotty as it may. It *is* a hardship hurting to the feelings that Lodgers open their minds so wide to the idea that you are trying to get the better of them and shut their minds so close to the idea that they are trying to get the better of you, but as Major Jackman says to me "I know the ways of this circular world Mrs. Lirriper, and that's one of 'em all round it" and many is the little ruffle in my mind that the Major has smoothed, for he is a clever man who has seen much. Dear dear, thirteen years have passed though it seems but yesterday since I was sitting with my glasses on at the open front parlour window one evening in August (the parlours being then vacant) reading yesterday's paper my eyes for print being poor though still I am thankful to say a long sight at a distance, when I hear a gentleman come posting across the road and up the street in a dreadful rage talking to himself in a fury and d'ing and c'ing somebody. "By George!" says he out loud and clutching his walking-stick, "I'll go to Mrs. Lirriper's. Which is Mrs. Lirriper's?" Then looking round and seeing me he flourishes his hat right off his head as if I had been the queen and he says, "Excuse the intrusion Madam, but pray Madam can you tell me at what number in this street there resides a well-known and much-respected lady by the name of Lirriper?" A little flustered though I must say gratified I took off my glasses and courtesied and said "Sir, Mrs. Lirriper is your humble servant." "Astonishing!" says he. "A million pardons! Madam, may I ask you to have the kindness to direct one of your domestics to open the door to a gentleman in search of apartments, by the name of Jackman?" I had never heard the name but a politer gentleman I never hope to see, for says he "Madam I am shocked at your opening the door yourself to no worthier a fellow than Jemmy Jackman. After you Madam. I never precede a lady." Then he comes into the parlours and he sniffs, and he says "Hah! These are parlours! Not musty cupboards" he says "but parlours, and no smell of coal-sacks." Now my dear it having been remarked by some inimical to the whole neighbourhood that it always smells of coal-sacks which might prove a drawback to Lodgers if encouraged, I says to the Major gently though firmly that I think he is referring to Arundel or Surrey or Howard but not Norfolk. "Madam" says he "I refer to Wozenham's lower down over the way—Madam you can form no notion what Wozenham's is—Madam it is a vast coal-sack, and Miss Wozenham has the principles and manners of a female heaver—Madam from the manner in which I have heard her mention you I know she has no appreciation of a lady, and from the manner in which she has conducted herself towards me I know she has no appreciation of a gentleman—Madam my name is Jackman—should you require any other reference than what I have already said, I name the Bank of England—perhaps you know it!" Such was the beginning of the Major's occupying the parlours and from that hour to this the same and a most obliging Lodger and punctual in all respects except one irregular which I need not particularly specify, but made up for by his being a protection and at all times ready to fill in the papers of the Assessed Taxes and Juries and that, and once collared a young man with the drawing-room clock under his coat, and once on the parapets with his own hands and blankets put out the kitchen chimney and afterwards attending the summons made a most eloquent speech against the Parish before the magistrates and saved the engine, and ever quite the gentleman though passionate. And certainly Miss Wozenham's detaining the trunks and umbrella was not in a liberal spirit though it may have been according to her rights in law or an act *I* would myself have stooped to, the Major being so much the gentleman that though he is far from tall he seems almost so when he has his shirt-frill out and his frock-coat on and his hat with the curly brims, and in what service he was I cannot truly tell you my dear whether Militia or Foreign, for I never heard him even name himself as Major but always simple "Jemmy Jackman" and once soon after he came when I felt it my duty to let him know that Miss Wozenham had put it about that he was no Major and I took the liberty of adding "which you are sir" his words were "Madam at any rate I am not a Minor, and sufficient for the day is the evil thereof" which cannot be denied to be the sacred truth, nor yet his military ways of having his boots with only the dirt brushed off taken to him in the front parlour every morning on a clean plate and varnishing them himself with a little sponge and a saucer and a whistle in a whisper so sure as ever his breakfast is ended, and so neat his ways that it never soils his linen which is scrupulous though more in quality than quantity, neither that nor his mustachios which to the best of my belief are done at the same time and which are as black and shining as his boots, his head of hair being a lovely white.

It was the third year nearly up of the Major's being in the parlours that early one morning in the month of February when Parliament was coming on and you may therefore suppose a number of impostors were about ready to take hold of anything they could get, a gentleman and a lady from the country came in to view the Second, and I well remember that I had been looking out of window and had watched them and the heavy sleet driving down the street together looking for bills. I did not quite take to the face of the gentleman though he was good-looking too but the lady was a very pretty young thing and delicate, and it seemed too rough for her to be out at all though she had only come from the Adelphi Hotel which would not have been much above a quarter of a mile if the weather had been less severe. Now it did so happen my dear that I had been forced to put five shillings weekly additional on the second in consequence of a loss from running away full dressed as if going out to a dinner-party, which was very artful and had made me rather suspicious taking it along with Parliament, so when the gentleman proposed three months certain and the money in advance and leave then reserved to renew on the same terms for six months more, I says I was not quite certain but that I might have engaged myself to another party but would step down-stairs and look into it if they would take a seat. They took a seat and I went down to the handle of the Major's door that I had already began to consult finding it a great blessing, and I knew by his whistling in a whisper that he was varnishing his boots which was generally considered private, however he kindly calls out "If it's you, Madam, come in," and I went in and told him.

"Well, Madam," says the Major rubbing his nose—as I did fear at the moment with the black sponge but it was only his knuckle, he being always neat and dexterous with his fingers—"well, Madam, I suppose you would be glad of the money?"

I was delicate of saying "Yes" too out, for a little extra colour rose into the Major's cheeks and there was irregularity which I will not particularly specify in a quarter which I will not name.

"I am of opinion, Madam," says the Major "that when money is ready for you—when it is ready for you, Mrs. Lirriper—you ought to take it. What is there against it, Madam, in this case up-stairs?"

15

"I really cannot say there is anything against it sir, still I thought I would consult you."

"You said a newly-married couple, I think, Madam?" says the Major.

I says "Ye-es. Evidently. And indeed the young lady mentioned to me in a casual way that she had not been married many months."

The Major rubbed his nose again and stirred the varnish round and round in its little saucer with his piece of sponge and took to his whistling in a whisper for a few moments. Then he says "You would call it a Good Let, Madam?"

"O certainly a Good Let sir."

"Say they renew for the additional six months. Would it put you about very much Madam if—if the worst was to come to the worst?" said the Major.

"Well I hardly know," I says to the Major. "It depends upon circumstances. Would *you* object Sir for instance?"

"I?" says the Major. "Object? Jemmy Jackman? Mrs. Lirriper close with the proposal."

So I went up-stairs and accepted, and they came in next day which was Saturday and the Major was so good as to draw up a Memorandum of an agreement in a beautiful round hand and expressions that sounded to me equally legal and military, and Mr. Edson signed it on the Monday morning and the Major called upon Mr. Edson on the Tuesday and Mr. Edson called upon the Major on the Wednesday and the Second and the parlours were as friendly as could be wished.

The three months paid for had run out and we had got without any fresh overtures as to payment into May my dear, when there came an obligation upon Mr. Edson to go a business expedition right across the Isle of Man, which fell quite unexpected upon that pretty little thing and is not a place that according to my views is particularly in the way to anywhere at any time but that may be a matter of opinion. So short a notice was it that he was to go next day, and dreadfully she cried poor pretty, and I am sure I cried too when I saw her on the cold pavement in the sharp east wind —it being a very backward spring that year—taking a last leave of him with her pretty bright hair blowing this way and that and her arms clinging round his neck and him saying "There there there. Now let me go Peggy." And by that time it was plain that what the Major had been so accommodating as to say he would not object to happening in the house, would happen in it, and I told her as much when he was gone while I comforted her with my arm up the staircase, for I says "You will soon have others to keep up for my pretty and you must think of that."

His letter never came when it ought to have come and what she went through morning after morning when the postman brought none for her the very postman himself compassionated when she ran down to the door, and yet we cannot wonder at its being calculated to blunt the feelings to have all the trouble of other people's letters and none of the pleasure and doing it oftener in the mud and mizzle than not and at a rate of wages more resembling Little Britain than Great. But at last one morning when she was too poorly to come running down-stairs he says to me with a pleased look in his face that made me next to love the man in his uniform coat though he was dripping wet "I have taken you first in the street this morning Mrs. Lirriper, for here's the one for Mrs. Edson." I went up to her bed-room with it as fast as ever I could go, and she sat up in bed when she saw it and kissed it and tore it open and then a blank stare came upon her. "It's very short!" she says lifting her large eyes to my face. "O Mrs. Lirriper it's very short!" I says "My dear Mrs. Edson no doubt that's because your husband hadn't time to write more just at that time." "No doubt, no doubt," says she, and puts her two hands on her face and turns round in her bed.

I shut her softly in and I crept down-stairs and I tapped at the Major's door, and when the Major having his thin slices of bacon in his own Dutch oven saw me he came out of his chair and put me down on the sofa. "Hush!" says he, "I see something's the matter. Don't speak—take time." I says "O Major I'm afraid there's cruel work up-stairs." "Yes yes," says he "I had begun to be afraid of it—take time." And then in opposition to his own words he rages out frightfully, and says "I shall never forgive myself Madam, that I, Jemmy Jackman, didn't see it all that morning—didn't go straight up-stairs when my boot-sponge was in my hand —didn't force it down his throat—and choke him dead with it on the spot!"

The Major and me agreed when we came to ourselves that just at present we could do no more than take on to suspect nothing and use our best endeavours to keep that poor young creature quiet, and what I ever should have done without the Major when it got about among the organ-men that quiet was our object is unknown, for he made lion and tiger war upon them to that degree that without seeing it I could not have believed it was in any gentleman to have such a power of bursting out with fire-irons walking-sticks water-jugs coals potatoes off his table the very hat off his head, and at the same time so furious in foreign languages that they would stand with their handles half-turned fixed like the Sleeping Ugly—for I cannot say Beauty.

Ever to see the postman come near the house now gave me such a fear that it was a reprieve when he went by, but in about another ten days or a fortnight he says again, "Here's one for Mrs. Edson.—Is she pretty well?" "She is pretty well postman, but not well enough to rise so early as she used" which was so far gospel-truth.

I carried the letter in to the Major at his breakfast and I says tottering "Major I have not the courage to take it up to her."

"It's an ill-looking villain of a letter," says the Major.

"I have not the courage Major" I says again in a tremble "to take it up to her."

A DREADFUL LETTER

After seeming lost in consideration for some moments the Major says, raising his head as if something new and useful had occurred to his mind "Mrs. Lirriper, I shall never forgive myself that I, Jemmy Jackman, didn't go straight up-stairs that morning when my boot-sponge was in my hand—and force it down his throat—and choke him dead with it."

"Major" I says a little hasty "you didn't do it which is a blessing, for it would have done no good and I think your sponge was better employed on your own honourable boots."

So we got to be rational, and planned that I should tap at her bedroom door and lay the letter on the mat outside and wait on the upper landing for what might happen, and never was gunpowder cannon-balls or shells or rockets more dreaded than that dreadful letter was by me as I took it to the second floor.

A terrible loud scream sounded through the house the minute after she had opened it, and I found her on the floor lying as if her life was gone. My dear I never looked at the face of the letter which was lying open by her, for there was no occasion.

Everything I needed to bring her round the Major brought up with his own hands, besides running out to the chemist's for what was not in the house and likewise having the fiercest of all his many skirmishes with a musical instrument representing a ball-room I do not know in what particular country and company waltzing in and out at folding-doors with rolling eyes. When after a long time I saw her coming to, I slipped on the landing till I heard her cry, and then I went in and says cheerily "Mrs. Edson you're not well my dear and it's not to be wondered at," as if I had not been in before. Whether she believed or disbelieved I cannot say and it would signify nothing if I could, but I stayed by her for hours and then she God ever blesses me! and says she will try to rest for her head is bad.

"Major," I whispers, looking in at the parlours, "I beg and pray of you don't go out."

19

MRS. LIRRIPER'S LODGINGS

The Major whispers, " Madam, trust me I will do no such a thing. How is she ? "

I says " Major the good Lord above us only knows what burns and rages in her poor mind. I left her sitting at her window. I am going to sit at mine.'

It came on afternoon and it came on evening. Norfolk is a delightful street to lodge in—provided you don't go lower down—but of a summer evening when the dust and waste paper lie in it and stray children play in it and a kind of a gritty calm and bake settles on it and a peal of church-bells is practising in the neighbourhood it is a trifle dull, and never have I seen it since at such a time and never shall I see it evermore at such a time without seeing the dull June evening when that forlorn young creature sat at her open corner window on the second and me at my open corner window (the other corner) on the third. Something merciful, something wiser and better far than my own self, had moved me while it was yet light to sit in my bonnet and shawl, and as the shadows fell and the tide rose I could sometimes—when I put out my head and looked at her window below—see that she leaned out a little looking down the street. It was just settling dark when I saw *her* in the street.

So fearful of losing sight of her that it almost stops my breath while I tell it, I went down-stairs faster than I ever moved in all my life and only tapped with my hand at the Major's door in passing it and slipping out. She was gone already. I made the same speed down the street and when I came to the corner of Howard-street I saw that she had turned it and was there plain before me going towards the west. O with what a thankful heart I saw her going along!

She was quite unacquainted with London and had very seldom been out for more than an airing in our own street where she knew two or three little children belonging to neighbours and had sometimes stood among them at the street looking at the water. She must be going at hazard I knew, still she kept the bye-streets quite correctly as long as they would serve her, and then turned up into the Strand. But at every corner I could see her head turned one way, and that way was always the river way.

It may have been only the darkness and quiet of the Adelphi that caused her to strike into it but she struck into it much as readily as if she had set out to go there, which perhaps was the case. She went straight down to the Terrace and along it and looked over the iron rail, and I often woke afterwards in my own bed with the horror of seeing her do it. The desertion of the wharf below and the flowing of the high water there seemed to settle her purpose. She looked about as if to make out the way down, and she struck out the right way or the wrong way—I don't know which, for I don't know the place before or since—and I followed her the way she went.

It was noticeable that all this time she never once looked back. But there was now a great change in the manner of her going, and instead of going at a steady quick walk with her arms folded before her,—among the dark dismal arches she went in a wild way with her arms opened wide, as if they were wings and she was flying to her death.

We were on the wharf and she stopped. I stopped. I saw her hands at her bonnet-strings, and I rushed between her and the brink and took her round the waist with both my arms. She might have drowned me, I felt then, but she could never have got quit of me.

Down to that moment my mind had been all in a maze and not half an idea had I had in it what I should say to her, but the instant I touched her it came to me like magic and I had my natural voice and my senses and even almost my breath.

"Mrs. Edson!" I says "My dear! Take care. How ever did you lose your way and stumble on a dangerous place like this? Why you must have come here by the most perplexing streets in all London. No wonder you are lost, I'm sure.

And this place too! Why I thought nobody ever got here, except me to order my coals and the Major in the parlours to smoke his cigar!"—for I saw that blessed man close by, pretending to it.

"Hah—Hah—Hum!" coughs the Major.

"And good gracious me" I says, "why here he is!"

"Halloa! who goes there?" says the Major in a military manner.

"Well!" I says, "if this don't beat everything! Don't you know us Major Jackman?"

"Halloa!" says the Major. "Who calls on Jemmy Jackman?" (and more out of breath he was, and did it less like life than I should have expected.)

"Why here's Mrs. Edson Major" I says, "strolling out to cool her poor head which has been very bad, has missed her way and got lost, and Goodness knows where she might have got to but for me coming here to drop an order into my coal merchant's letter-box and you coming here to smoke your cigar!—And you really are not well enough my dear" I says to her "to be half so far from home without me.—And your arm will be very acceptable I am sure Major" I says to him "and I know she may lean upon it as heavy as she likes." And now we had both got her—thanks be Above! —one on each side.

She was all in a cold shiver and she so continued till I laid her on her own bed, and up to the early morning she held me by the hand and moaned and moaned "O wicked, wicked, wicked!" But when at last I made believe to droop my head and be overpowered with a dead sleep, I heard that poor young creature give such touching and such humble thanks for being preserved from taking her own life in her madness that I thought I should have cried my eyes out on the counterpane and I knew she was safe.

Being well enough to do and able to afford it, me and the Major laid our little plans next day while she was asleep worn out, and so I says to her as soon as I could do it nicely:

"Mrs. Edson my dear, when Mr. Edson paid me the rent for these farther six months——"

She gave a start and I felt her large eyes look at me, but I went on with it and with my needlework.

"——I can't say that I am quite sure I dated the receipt right. Could you let me look at it?"

She laid her frozen cold hand upon mine and she looked through me when I was forced to look up from my needlework, but I had taken the precaution of having on my spectacles.

"I have no receipt" says she.

"Ah! Then he has got it" I says in a careless way. "It's of no great consequence. A receipt's a receipt."

From that time she always had hold of my hand when I could spare it which was generally only when I read to her, for of course she and me had our bits of needlework to plod at and neither of us was very handy at those little things, though I am still rather proud of my share in them too considering. And though she took to all I read to her, I used to fancy that next to what was taught upon the Mount she took most of all to His gentle compassion for us poor women and to His young life and to how His mother was proud of Him and treasured His sayings in her heart. She had a grateful look in her eyes that never never never will be out of mine until they are closed in my last sleep, and when I chanced to look at her without thinking of it I would always meet that look, and she would often offer me her trembling lip to kiss, much more like a little affectionate half broken-hearted child than ever I can imagine any grown person.

One time the trembling of this poor lip was so strong and her tears ran down so fast that I thought she was going to tell me all her woe, so I takes her two hands in mine and I says:

"No my dear not now, you had best not try to do it now. Wait for better times when you have got over this and are strong, and then you shall tell me whatever you will. Shall it be agreed?"

With our hands still joined she nodded her head many times, and she lifted my hands and put them to her lips and to her bosom.

"Only one word now my dear" I says. "Is there any one?"

She looked inquiringly "Any one?"

"That I can go to?"

She shook her head.

"No one that I can bring?"

She shook her head.

"No one is wanted by *me* my dear. Now that may be considered past and gone."

Not much more than a week afterwards—for this was far on in the time of our being so together—I was bending over at her bedside with my ear down to her lips, by turns listening for her breath and looking for a sign of life in her face. At last it came in a solemn way—not in a flash but like a kind of pale faint light brought very slow to the face.

She said something to me that had no sound in it, but I saw she asked me:

"Is this death?"

And I says:

"Poor dear poor dear, I think it is."

Knowing somehow that she wanted me to move her weak right hand, I took it and laid it on her breast and then folded her other hand upon it, and she prayed a good good prayer and I joined in it poor me though there were no words spoke. Then I brought the baby in its wrappers from where it lay, and I says:

"My dear this is sent to a childless old woman. This is for me to take care of."

The trembling lip was put up towards my face for the last time, and I dearly kissed it.

"Yes my dear," I says. "Please God! Me and the Major."

I don't know how to tell it right, but I saw her soul brighten and leap up, and get free and fly away in the grateful look.

So this is the why and wherefore of its coming to pass my dear that we called him Jemmy, being after the Major his own godfather with Lirriper for a surname being after myself, and never was a dear child such a brightening thing in a Lodgings or such a playmate to his grandmother as Jemmy to this house and me, and always good and minding what he was told (upon the whole) and soothing for the temper and making everything pleasanter except when he grew old enough to drop his cap down Wozenham's Airy and they wouldn't hand it up to him, and being worked into a state I put on my best bonnet and gloves and parasol with the child in my hand and I says "Miss Wozenham I little thought ever to have entered *your* house but unless my grandson's cap is instantly restored, the laws of this country regulating the property of the Subject shall at length decide betwixt yourself and me, cost what it may." With a sneer upon her face which did strike me I must say as being expressive of two keys but it may have been a mistake and if there is any doubt let Miss Wozenham have the full benefit of it as is but right, she rang the bell and she says "Jane, is there a street-child's old cap down our Airy?" I says "Miss Wozenham before your housemaid answers that question you must allow me to inform you to your face that my grandson is *not* a street-child and is *not* in the habit of wearing old caps. In fact" I says "Miss Wozenham I am far from sure that my grandson's cap may not be newer than your own" which was perfectly savage in me, her lace being the commonest machine-make washed and torn besides, but I had been put into a state to begin with fomented by impertinence. Miss

Wozenham says red in the face "Jane you heard my question, is there any child's cap down our Airy?" "Yes Ma'am" says Jane "I think I did see some such rubbish a-lying there." "Then" says Miss Wozenham "let these visitors out, and then throw up that worthless article out of my premises." But here the child who had been staring at Miss Wozenham with all his eyes and more, frowns down his little eyebrows purses up his little mouth puts his chubby legs far apart turns his little dimpled fists round and round slowly over one another like a little coffee-mill, and says to her "Oo impdent to mi Gran, me tut oor hi!" "O!" says Miss Wozenham looking down scornfully at the Mite "this is not a street-child is it not! Really!" I bursts out laughing and I says "Miss Wozenham if this ain't a pretty sight to you I don't envy your feelings and I wish you good-day. Jemmy come along with Gran." And I was still in the best of humours though his cap came flying up into the street as if it had been just turned on out of the water-plug, and I went home laughing all the way, all owing to that dear boy.

The miles and miles that me and the Major have travelled with Jemmy in the dusk between the lights are not to be calculated, Jemmy driving on the coach-box which is the Major's brass-bound writing desk on the table, me inside in the easy-chair and the Major Guard up behind with a brown-paper horn doing it really wonderful. I do assure you my dear that sometimes when I have taken a few winks in my place inside the coach and have come half awake by the flashing light of the fire and have heard that precious pet driving and the Major blowing up behind to have the change of horses ready when we got to the Inn, I have half believed we were on the old North Road that my poor Lirriper knew so well. Then to see that child and the Major both wrapped up getting down to warm their feet and going stamping about and having glasses of ale out of the paper match-boxes on the chimney-piece is to see the Major enjoying it fully as much as the child I am very sure, and it's equal to any play when Coachee opens the coach-door to look in at me inside and say " Wery 'past that 'tage.—'Prightened old lady ? "

But what my inexpressible feelings were when we lost that child can only be compared to the Major's which were not a shade better, through his straying out at five years old and eleven o'clock in the forenoon and never heard of by word or sign or deed till half-past nine at night, when the Major had gone to the Editor of the *Times* newspaper to put in an advertisement, which came out next day four-and-twenty hours after he was found, and which I mean always carefully to keep in my lavender drawer as the first printed account of him. The more the day got on, the more I got distracted and the Major too and both of us made worse by the composed ways of the police though very civil and obliging and what I must call their obstinacy in not entertaining the idea that he was stolen. " We mostly find Mum " says the sergeant who came round to comfort me, which he didn't at all and he had been one of the private constables in Caroline's time to which he referred in his opening words when he said " Don't give way to uneasiness in your mind Mum, it'll all come as right as my nose did when I got the same barked by that young woman in your second floor "—says this sergeant " we mostly find Mum as people ain't over-anxious to have what I may call second-hand children. *You'll* get him back Mum." " O but my dear good sir " I says clasping my hands and wringing them and clasping them again " he is such an uncommon child ! " " Yes Mum " says the sergeant, " we mostly find that too Mum. The question is what his clothes were worth." " His clothes " I says " were not worth much sir for he had only got his playing-dress on, but the dear child !— " " All right Mum " says the sergeant. " *You'll* get him back Mum. And even if he'd had his best clothes on, it wouldn't come to worse than his being found wrapped up in a cabbage-leaf, a shivering in a lane." His words pierced my heart like daggers and daggers, and me

27

gs

and the Major ran in and out like wild things all day long till the Major returning from his interview with the Editor of the *Times* at night rushes into my little room hysterical and squeezes my hand and wipes his eyes and says "Joy joy—officer in plain clothes came up on the steps as I was letting myself in—compose your feelings—Jemmy's found." Consequently I fainted away and when I came to, embraced the legs of the officer in plain clothes who seemed to be taking a kind of a quiet inventory in his mind of the property in my little room with brown whiskers, and I says "Blessings on you sir where is the Darling!" and he says "In Kennington Station House." I was dropping at his feet Stone at the image of that Innocence in cells with murderers when he adds "He followed the Monkey." I says deeming it slang language "O sir explain for a loving grandmother what Monkey!" He says "Him in the spangled cap with the strap under the chin, as won't keep on—him as sweeps the crossings on a round table and don't want to draw his sabre more than he can help." Then I understood it all and most thankfully thanked him, and me and the Major and him drove over to Kennington and there we found our boy lying quite comfortable before a blazing fire having sweetly played himself to sleep upon a small accordion nothing like so big as a flat-iron which they had been so kind as to lend him for the purpose and which it appeared had been stopped upon a very young person.

My dear the system upon which the Major commenced and as I may say perfected Jemmy's learning when he was so small that if the dear was on the other side of the table you had to look under it instead of over it to see him with his mother's own bright hair in beautiful curls, is a thing that ought to be known to the Throne and Lords and Commons and then might obtain some promotion for the Major which he well deserves and would be none the worse for (speaking between friends) L. S. D.-ically. When the Major first undertook his learning he says to me:

28

"I'm going Madam," he says "to make our child a Calculating Boy."

"Major," I says, "you terrify me and may do the pet a permanent injury you would never forgive yourself."

"Madam," says the Major, "next to my regret that when I had my boot-sponge in my hand, I didn't choke that scoundrel with it—on the spot——"

"There! For Gracious' sake," I interrupts, "let his conscience find him without sponges."

"—I say next to that regret, Madam," says the Major "would be the regret with which my breast," which he tapped, "would be surcharged if this fine mind was not early cultivated. But mark me Madam," says the Major holding up his forefinger "cultivated on a principle that will make it a delight."

"Major" I says "I will be candid with you and tell you openly that if ever I find the dear child fall off in his appetite I shall know it is his calculations and shall put a stop to them at two minutes' notice. Or if I find them mounting to his head" I says, "or striking anyways cold to his stomach or leading to anything approaching flabbiness in his legs, the result will be the same, but Major you are a clever man and have seen much and you love the child and are his own godfather, and if you feel a confidence in trying try."

"Spoken Madam" says the Major "like Emma Lirriper. All I have to ask, Madam, is that you will leave my godson and myself to make a week or two's preparations for surprising you, and that you will give me leave to have up and down any small articles not actually in use that I may require from the kitchen."

"From the kitchen Major?" I says half feeling as if he had a mind to cook the child.

"From the kitchen" says the Major, and smiles and swells, and at the same time looks taller.

So I passed my word and the Major and the dear boy were shut up together for half an hour at a time through a certain while, and never could I hear anything going on betwixt them but talking and laughing and Jemmy clapping his hands and screaming out numbers, so I says to myself "it has not harmed him yet" nor could I on examining the dear find any signs of it anywhere about him which was likewise a great relief. At last one day Jemmy brings me a card in joke in the Major's neat writing "The Messrs. Jemmy Jackman" for we had given him the Major's other name too "request the honour of Mrs. Lirriper's company at the Jackman Institution in the front parlour this evening at five, military time, to witness a few slight feats of elementary arithmetic." And if you'll believe me there in the front parlour at five punctual to the moment was the Major behind the Pembroke table with both leaves up and a lot of things from the kitchen tidily set out on old newspapers spread atop of it, and there was the Mite stood up on a chair with his rosy cheeks flushing and his eyes sparkling clusters of diamonds.

"Now Gran" says he, "oo tit down and don't oo touch ler poople"—for he saw with every one of those diamonds of his that I was going to give him a squeeze.

"Very well sir" I says "I am obedient in this good company I am sure." And I sits down in the easy-chair that was put for me, shaking my sides.

But picture my admiration when the Major going on almost as quick as if he was conjuring sets out all the articles he names, and says "Three saucepans, an Italian iron, a hand-bell, a toasting-fork, a nutmeg-grater, four potlids, a spice-box, two egg-cups, and a chopping-board—how many?" and when that Mite instantly cries "Tifteen, tut down tive and carry ler 'toppin-board" and then claps his hands draws up his legs and dances on his chair.

My dear with the same astonishing ease and correctness him and the Major added up the tables chairs and sofy, the picters fenders and fire-irons their own selves me and the cat and the eyes in Miss Wozenham's head, and whenever the

30

sum was done Young Roses and Diamonds claps his hands
and draws up his legs and dances on his chair.

The pride of the Major! ("*Here's* a mind, Ma'am!" he
says to me behind his hand.)

Then he says aloud, "We now come to the next elementary
rule,—which is called——"

"Umtraction!" cries Jemmy.

"Right," says the Major. "We have here a toasting-
fork, a potato in its natural state, two potlids, one egg-cup,
a wooden spoon, and two skewers, from which it is necessary
for commercial purposes to subtract a sprat-gridiron, a small
pickle-jar, two lemons, one pepper-castor, a blackbeetle-trap,
and a knob of the dresser-drawer—what remains?"

"Toatin-fork!" cries Jemmy.

"In numbers how many?" says the Major.

"One!" cries Jemmy.

("*Here's* a boy, Ma'am!" says the Major to me behind his
hand.)

Then the Major goes on:

"We now approach the next elementary rule,—which is
entitled——"

"Tickleication" cries Jemmy.

"Correct" says the Major.

But my dear to relate to you in detail the way in which
they multiplied fourteen sticks of firewood by two bits of
ginger and a larding-needle, or divided pretty well everything
else there was on the table by the heater of the Italian iron
and a chamber candlestick, and got a lemon over, would
make my head spin round and round and round as it did at
the time. So I says "if you'll excuse my addressing the
chair Professor Jackman I think the period of the lecture has
now arrived when it becomes necessary that I should take a
good hug of this young scholar." Upon which Jemmy calls
out from his station on the chair, "Gran oo open oor arms
and me'll make a 'pring into 'em." So I opened my arms
to him as I had opened my sorrowful heart when his poor

young mother lay a dying, and he had his jump and we had a good long hug together and the Major prouder than any peacock says to me behind his hand, "You need not let him know it Madam" (which I certainly need not for the Major was quite audible) "but he is a boy!"

In this way Jemmy grew and grew and went to day-school and continued under the Major too, and in summer we were as happy as the days were long, and in winter we were as happy as the days were short and there seemed to rest a Blessing on the Lodgings for they as good as Let themselves and would have done it if there had been twice the accommodation, when sore and hard against my will I one day says to the Major:

"Major you know what I am going to break to you. Our boy must go to boarding-school."

It was a sad sight to see the Major's countenance drop, and I pitied the good soul with all my heart.

"Yes Major" I says, "though he is as popular with the Lodgers as you are yourself and though he is to you and me what only you and me know, still it is in the course of things and Life is made of partings and we must part with our Pet."

Bold as I spoke, I saw two Majors and half-a-dozen fire-places, and when the poor Major put one of his neat bright-varnished boots upon the fender and his elbow on his knee and his head upon his hand and rocked himself a little to and fro, I was dreadfully cut up.

"But" says I clearing my throat "you have so well prepared him Major—he has had such a Tutor in you—that he will have none of the first drudgery to go through. And he is so clever besides that he'll soon make his way to the front rank."

"He is a boy" says the Major—having sniffed—"that has not his like on the face of the earth."

"True as you say Major, and it is not for us merely for our own sakes to do anything to keep him back from being a credit and an ornament wherever he goes and perhaps even rising to be a great man, is it Major? He will have all my little savings when my work is done (being all the world to me) and we must try to make him a wise man and a good man, mustn't we Major?"

"Madam" says the Major rising "Jemmy Jackman is becoming an older file than I was aware of, and you put him to shame. You are thoroughly right Madam. You are simply and undeniably right.—And if you'll excuse me, I'll take a walk."

So the Major being gone out and Jemmy being at home, I got the child into my little room here and I stood him by my chair and I took his mother's own curls in my hand and I spoke to him loving and serious. And when I had reminded the darling how that he was now in his tenth year and when I had said to him about his getting on in life pretty much what I had said to the Major I broke to him how that we must have this same parting, and there I was forced to stop for there I saw of a sudden the well-remembered lip with its tremble, and it so brought back that time! But with the spirit that was in him he controlled it soon and he says gravely nodding through his tears, "I understand Gran—I know it *must* be, Gran,—go on Gran, don't be afraid of *me*." And when I had said all that ever I could think of, he turned his bright steady face to mine and he says just a little broken here and there "You shall see Gran that I can be a man and that I can do anything that is grateful and loving to you—and if I don't grow up to be what you would like to have me—I hope it will be—because I shall die." And with that he sat down by me and I went on to tell him of the school of which I had excellent recommendations and where it was and how many scholars and what games they played as I had heard and what length of holidays, to all of which he listened bright and clear. And so it came that at last he says "And now dear Gran let me kneel down here where I have been used to say my prayers and let me fold my face for just a minute in your gown and let me cry

33

for you have been more than father—more than mother—
more than brothers sisters friends—to me!" And so he did
cry and I too and we were both much the better for it.

From that time forth he was true to his word and ever
blithe and ready, and even when me and the Major took him
down into Lincolnshire he was far the gayest of the party
though for sure and certain he might easily have been that,
but he really was and put life into us only when it came to
the last Good-bye, he says with a wistful look, "You wouldn't
have me not really sorry would you Gran?" and when I says
"No dear, Lord forbid!" he says "I am glad of that!" and
ran in out of sight.

But now that the child was gone out of the Lodgings the
Major fell into a regularly moping state. It was taken notice
of by all the Lodgers that the Major moped. He hadn't
even the same air of being rather tall that he used to have,
and if he varnished his boots with a single gleam of interest
it was as much as he did.

One evening the Major came into my little room to take
a cup of tea and a morsel of buttered toast and to read
Jemmy's newest letter which had arrived that afternoon (by
the very same postman more than middle-aged upon the
Beat now), and the letter raising him up a little I says to
the Major:

"Major you mustn't get into a moping way."

The Major shook his head. "Jemmy Jackman Madam,"
he says with a deep sigh, "is an older file than I thought
him."

"Moping is not the way to grow younger Major."

"My dear Madam," says the Major, "is there *any* way of
growing younger?"

Feeling that the Major was getting rather the best of that
point I made a diversion to another.

"Thirteen years! Thir-teen years! Many Lodgers have
come and gone, in the thirteen years that you have lived in
the parlours Major."

34

"Hah!" says the Major warming. "Many Madam, many."

"And I should say you have been familiar with them all?"

"As a rule (with its exceptions like all rules) my dear Madam" says the Major, "they have honoured me with their acquaintance, and not unfrequently with their confidence."

Watching the Major as he drooped his white head and stroked his black mustachios and moped again, a thought which I think must have been going about looking for an owner somewhere dropped into my old noddle if you will excuse the expression.

"The walls of my Lodgings" I says in a casual way—for my dear it is of no use going straight at a man who mopes—"might have something to tell if they could tell it."

The Major neither moved nor said anything but I saw he was attending with his shoulders my dear—attending with his shoulders to what I said. In fact I saw that his shoulders were struck by it.

"The dear boy was always fond of story-books" I went on, like as if I was talking to myself. "I am sure this house—his own home—might write a story or two for his reading one day or another."

The Major's shoulders gave a dip and a curve and his head came up in his shirt-collar. The Major's head came up in his shirt-collar as I hadn't seen it come up since Jemmy went to school.

"It is unquestionable that in intervals of cribbage and a friendly rubber, my dear Madam," says the Major, "and also over what used to be called in my young times—in the salad days of Jemmy Jackman—the social glass, I have exchanged many a reminiscence with your Lodgers."

My remark was—I confess I made it with the deepest and artfullest of intentions—"I wish our dear boy had heard them!"

"Are you serious Madam?" asks the Major starting and turning full round.

"Why not Major?"

"Madam" says the Major, turning up one of his cuffs, "they shall be written for him."

"Ah! Now you speak" I says giving my hands a pleased clap. "Now you are in a way out of moping Major!"

"Between this and my holidays—I mean the dear boy's" says the Major turning up his other cuff, "a good deal may be done towards it."

"Major you are a clever man and you have seen much and not a doubt of it."

"I'll begin," says the Major looking as tall as ever he did, "to-morrow."

My dear the Major was another man in three days and he was himself again in a week and he wrote and wrote and wrote with his pen scratching like rats behind the wainscot, and whether he had many grounds to go upon or whether he did at all romance I cannot tell you, but what he has written is in the left-hand glass closet of the little bookcase close behind you.

CHAPTER II

I HAVE the honour of presenting myself by the name of Jack-man. I esteem it a proud privilege to go down to posterity through the instrumentality of the most remarkable boy that ever lived,—by the name of JEMMY JACKMAN LIRRIPER,—and of my most worthy and most highly respected friend, Mrs. Emma Lirriper, of Eighty-one, Norfolk Street, Strand, in the County of Middlesex, in the United Kingdom of Great Britain and Ireland.

It is not for me to express the rapture with which we received that dear and eminently remarkable boy, on the occurrence of his first Christmas holidays. Suffice it to observe that when he came flying into the house with two splendid prizes (Arithmetic, and Exemplary Conduct), Mrs. Lirriper and myself embraced with emotion, and instantly took him to the Play, where we were all three admirably entertained.

Nor is it to render homage to the virtues of the best of her good and honoured sex—whom, in deference to her un-assuming worth, I will only here designate by the initials E. L.—that I add this record to the bundle of papers with which our, in a most distinguished degree, remarkable boy has expressed himself delighted, before reconsigning the same to the left-hand glass closet of Mrs. Lirriper's little bookcase.

Neither is it to obtrude the name of the old original super-annuated obscure Jemmy Jackman, once (to his degradation) of Wozenham's, long (to his elevation) of Lirriper's. If I could be consciously guilty of that piece of bad taste, it would indeed be a work of supererogation, now that the name is borne by JEMMY JACKMAN LIRRIPER.

No, I take up my humble pen to register a little record of our strikingly remarkable boy, which my poor capacity regards as presenting a pleasant little picture of the dear boy's mind. The picture may be interesting to himself when he is a man.

Our first reunited Christmas-day was the most delightful one we have ever passed together. Jemmy was never silent for five minutes, except in church-time. He talked as we sat by the fire, he talked when we were out walking, he talked as we sat by the fire again, he talked incessantly at dinner, though he made a dinner almost as remarkable as himself. It was the spring of happiness in his fresh young heart flowing and flowing, and it fertilised (if I may be allowed so bold a figure) my much-esteemed friend, and J. J. the present writer.

There were only we three. We dined in my esteemed friend's little room, and our entertainment was perfect. But everything in the establishment is, in neatness, order, and comfort, always perfect. After dinner our boy slipped away to his old stool at my esteemed friend's knee, and there, with his hot chestnuts and his glass of brown sherry (really, a most excellent wine!) on a chair for a table, his face outshone the apples in the dish.

We talked of these jottings of mine, which Jemmy had read through and through by that time; and so it came about that my esteemed friend remarked, as she sat smoothing Jemmy's curls:

"And as you belong to the house too, Jemmy,—and so much more than the Lodgers, having been born in it,—why, your story ought to be added to the rest, I think, one of these days."

Jemmy's eyes sparkled at this, and he said, "So *I* think. Gran."

Then he sat looking at the fire, and then he began to laugh in a sort of confidence with the fire, and then he said, folding his arms across my esteemed friend's lap, and raising his bright face to hers: " Would you like to hear a boy's story, Gran ? "

" Of all things," replied my esteemed friend.

" Would you, godfather ? "

" Of all things," I too replied.

" Well, then," said Jemmy, " I'll tell you one."

Here our indisputably remarkable boy gave himself a hug, and laughed again, musically, at the idea of his coming out in that new line. Then he once more took the fire into the same sort of confidence as before, and began :

" Once upon a time, When pigs drank wine, And monkeys chewed tobaccer, 'Twas neither in your time nor mine, But that's no macker—— "

" Bless the child ! " cried my esteemed friend, " what's amiss with his brain ? "

" It's poetry, Gran," returned Jemmy, shouting with laughter. " We always begin stories that way at school."

" Gave me quite a turn, Major," said my esteemed friend, fanning herself with a plate. " Thought he was light-headed ! "

" In those remarkable times, Gran and godfather, there was once a boy,—not me, you know."

" No, no," says my respected friend, " not you. Not him, Major, you understand ? "

" No, no," says I.

" And he went to school in Rutlandshire—— "

" Why not Lincolnshire ? " says my respected friend.

" Why not, you dear old Gran ? Because I go to school in Lincolnshire, don't I ? "

" Ah, to be sure ! " says my respected friend. " And it's not Jemmy, you understand, Major ? "

" No, no," says I.

" Well ! " our boy proceeded, hugging himself comfortably,

39

and laughing merrily (again in confidence with the fire), before he again looked up in Mrs. Lirriper's face, " and so he was tremendously in love with his schoolmaster's daughter, and she was the most beautiful creature that ever was seen, and she had brown eyes, and she had brown hair all curling beautifully, and she had a delicious voice, and she was delicious altogether, and her name was Seraphina."

" What's the name of *your* schoolmaster's daughter, Jemmy ? " asks my respected friend.

" Polly ! " replied Jemmy, pointing his forefinger at her. " There now ! Caught you ! Ha, ha, ha ! "

When he and my respected friend had had a laugh and a hug together, our admittedly remarkable boy resumed with a great relish :

" Well ! And so he loved her. And so he thought about her, and dreamed about her, and made her presents of oranges and nuts, and would have made her presents of pearls and diamonds if he could have afforded it out of his pocket-money, but he couldn't. And so her father—O, he was a Tartar ! Keeping the boys up to the mark, holding examinations once a month, lecturing upon all sorts of subjects at all sorts of times, and knowing everything in the world out of book. And so this boy—— "

" Had he any name ? " asks my respected friend.

" No, he hadn't, Gran. Ha, ha ! There now ! Caught you again ! "

After this, they had another laugh and another hug, and then our boy went on.

" Well ! And so this boy, he had a friend about as old as himself at the same school, and his name (for He *had* a name, as it happened) was—let me remember—was Bobbo."

" Not Bob," says my respected friend.

" Of course not," says Jemmy. " What made you think it was, Gran ? Well ! And so this friend was the cleverest and bravest and best-looking and most generous of all the friends that ever were, and so he was in love with Seraphina's sister, and so Seraphina's sister was in love with him, and so they all grew up."

"Bless us!" says my respected friend. "They were very sudden about it."

"So they all grew up," our boy repeated, laughing heartily, "and Bobbo and this boy went away together on horseback to seek their fortunes, and they partly got their horses by favour, and partly in a bargain; that is to say, they had saved up between them seven and fourpence, and the two horses, being Arabs, were worth more, only the man said he would take that, to favour them. Well! And so they made their fortunes and came prancing back to the school, with their pockets full of gold, enough to last for ever. And so they rang at the parents' and visitors' bell (not the back gate), and when the bell was answered they proclaimed 'The same as if it was scarlet fever! Every boy goes home for an indefinite period!' And then there was great hurrahing, and then they kissed Seraphina and her sister,—each his own love, and not the other's on any account,—and then they ordered the Tartar into instant confinement."

"Poor man!" said my respected friend.

"Into instant confinement, Gran," repeated Jemmy, trying to look severe and roaring with laughter; "and he was to have nothing to eat but the boys' dinners, and was to drink half a cask of their beer every day. And so then the preparations were made for the two weddings, and there were hampers, and potted things, and sweet things, and nuts, and postage-stamps, and all manner of things. And so they were so jolly, that they let the Tartar out, and he was jolly too."

"I am glad they let him out," says my respected friend, "because he had only done his duty."

"O, but hadn't he overdone it, though!" cried Jemmy. "Well! And so then this boy mounted his horse, with his bride in his arms, and cantered away, and cantered on and on till he came to a certain place where he had a certain Gran and a certain godfather,—not you two, you know."

41

"No, no," we both said.

"And there he was received with great rejoicings, and he filled the cupboard and the bookcase with gold, and he showered it out on his Gran and his godfather because they were the two kindest and dearest people that ever lived in this world. And so while they were sitting up to their knees in gold, a knocking was heard at the street door, and who should it be but Bobbo, also on horseback with his bride in his arms, and what had he come to say but that he would take (at double rent) all the Lodgings for ever, that were not wanted by this boy and this Gran and this godfather, and that they would all live together, and all be happy! And so they were, and so it never ended!"

"And was there no quarrelling?" asked my respected friend, as Jemmy sat upon her lap and hugged her.

"No! Nobody ever quarrelled."

"And did the money never melt away?"

"No! Nobody could ever spend it all."

"And did none of them ever grow older?"

"No! Nobody ever grew older after that."

"And did none of them ever die?"

"O, no, no, no, Gran!" exclaimed our dear boy, laying his cheek upon her breast, and drawing her closer to him. "Nobody ever died."

"Ah, Major, Major!" says my respected friend, smiling benignly upon me, "this beats our stories. Let us end with the Boy's story, Major, for the Boy's story is the best that is ever told!"

In submission to which request on the part of the best of women, I have here noted it down as faithfully as my best abilities, coupled with my best intentions, would admit, subscribing it with my name,

J. JACKMAN.

The Parlours.
Mrs. Lirriper's Lodgings.

MRS. LIRRIPER'S LEGACY

[1864]

CHAPTER I

AH! It's pleasant to drop into my own easy-chair my dear though a little palpitating what with trotting up-stairs and what with trotting down, and why kitchen stairs should all be corner stairs is for the builders to justify though I do not think they fully understand their trade and never did, else why the sameness and why not more conveniences and fewer draughts and likewise making a practice of laying the plaster on too thick I am well convinced which holds the damp, and as to chimney-pots putting them on by guess-work like hats at a party and no more knowing what their effect will be upon the smoke bless you than I do if so much, except that it will mostly be either to send it down your throat in a straight form or give it a twist before it goes there. And what I says speaking as I find of those new metal chimneys all manner of shapes (there's a row of 'em at Miss Wozenham's lodging-house lower down on the other side of the way) is that they only work your smoke into artificial patterns for you before you swallow it and that I'd quite as soon swallow mine plain, the flavour being the same, not to mention the conceit of putting up signs on the top of your house to show the forms in which you take your smoke into your inside.

Being here before your eyes my dear in my own easy-chair in my own quiet room in my own Lodging-House Number Eighty-one Norfolk Street Strand London situated midway between the city and St. James's—if anything is where it used to be with these hotels calling themselves Limited but called unlimited by Major Jackman rising up everywhere and rising up into flagstaffs where they can't go any higher, but my mind of those monsters is give me a landlord's or landlady's wholesome face when I come off a journey and not a brass plate with an electrified number clicking out of it which it's not in nature can be glad to see me and to which I don't want to be hoisted like molasses at the Docks and left there telegraphing for help with the most ingenious instruments but quite in vain—being here my dear I have no call to mention that I am still in the Lodgings as a business hoping to die in the same and if agreeable to the clergy partly read over at Saint Clement's Danes and concluded in Hatfield churchyard when lying once again by my poor Lirriper ashes to ashes and dust to dust.

Neither should I tell you any news my dear in telling you that the Major is still a fixture in the Parlours quite as much so as the roof of the house, and that Jemmy is of boys the best and brightest and has ever had kept from him the cruel story of his poor pretty young mother Mrs. Edson being deserted in the second floor and dying in my arms, fully believing that I am his born Gran and him an orphan, though what with engineering since he took a taste for it and him and the Major making Locomotives out of parasols broken iron pots and cotton-reels and them absolutely a getting off the line and falling over the table and injuring the passengers almost equal to the originals it really is quite wonderful. And when I says to the Major, "Major can't you by *any* means give us a communication with the guard?" the Major says quite huffy, "No madam it's not

46

to be done," and when I says " Why not ? " the Major says,
" That is between us who are in the Railway Interest madam
and our friend the Right Honourable Vice-President of the
Board of Trade " and if you'll believe me my dear the Major
wrote to Jemmy at school to consult him on the answer
I should have before I could get even that amount of
unsatisfactoriness out of the mah, the reason being that
when we first began with the little model and the working
signals beautiful and perfect (being in general as wrong as
the real) and when I says laughing " What appointment am
I to hold in this undertaking gentlemen ? " Jemmy hugs me
round the neck and tells me dancing, " You shall be the
Public Gran " and consequently they put upon me just as
much as ever they like and I sit a growling in my easy-chair.

My dear whether it is that a grown man as clever as the
Major cannot give half his heart and mind to anything—even
a plaything—but must get into right down earnest with it,
whether it is so or whether it is not so I do not undertake to
say, but Jemmy is far outdone by the serious and believing
ways of the Major in the management of the United Grand
Junction Lirriper and Jackman Great Norfolk Parlour Line,
" For " says my Jemmy with the sparkling eyes when it was
christened, " we must have a whole mouthful of name Gran
or our dear old Public " and there the young rogue kissed
me, " won't stump up." So, the Public took the shares—
ten at ninepence, and immediately when that was spent
twelve Preference at one and sixpence—and they were all
signed by Jemmy and countersigned by the Major, and
between ourselves much better worth the money than some
shares I have paid for in my time. In the same holidays
the line was made and worked and opened and ran excursions
and had collisions and burst its boilers and all sorts of
accidents and offences all most regular correct and pretty.
The sense of responsibility entertained by the Major as a
military style of station-master my dear starting the down
train behind time and ringing one of those little bells that

you buy with the little coal-scuttles off the tray round the man's neck in the street did him honour, but noticing the Major of a night when he is writing out his monthly report to Jemmy at school of the state of the Rolling Stock and the Permanent Way and all the rest of it (the whole kept upon the Major's sideboard and dusted with his own hands every morning before varnishing his boots) I notice him as full of thought and care as full can be and frowning in a fearful manner, but indeed the Major does nothing by halves as witness his great delight in going out surveying with Jemmy when he has Jemmy to go with, carrying a chain and a measuring-tape and driving I don't know what improvements right through Westminster Abbey and fully believed in the streets to be knocking everything upside down by Act of Parliament. As please Heaven will come to pass when Jemmy takes to that as a profession!

Mentioning my poor Lirriper brings into my head his own youngest brother the Doctor though Doctor of what I am sure it would be hard to say unless Liquor, for neither Physic nor Music nor yet Law does Joshua Lirriper know a morsel of except continually being summoned to the County Court and having orders made upon him which he runs away from, and once was taken in the passage of this very house with an umbrella up and the Major's hat on, giving his name with the door-mat round him as Sir Johnson Jones, K.C.B. in spectacles residing at the Horse Guards. On which occasion he had got into the house not a minute before, through the girl letting him on the mat when he sent in a piece of paper twisted more like one of those spills for lighting candles than a note, offering me the choice between thirty shillings in hand and his brains on the premises marked immediate and waiting for an answer. My dear it gave me such a dreadful turn to think of the brains of my poor dear Lirriper's own flesh and blood flying about the new oilcloth however unworthy to be so assisted, that I went out of my room here to ask him what he would take once for all not to do it for life when I found him in the custody of two gentlemen that I should have judged to be in the feather-bed trade if they had not announced the law, so fluffy were their personal appearance. "Bring your chains, sir," says Joshua to the littlest of the two in the biggest hat, "rivet on my fetters!" Imagine my feelings when I pictered him clanking up Norfolk-street in irons and Miss Wozenham looking out of window! "Gentlemen," I says all of a tremble and ready to drop "please to bring him into Major Jackman's apartments." So they brought him into the Parlours, and when the Major spies his own curly-brimmed hat on him which Joshua Lirriper had whipped off its peg in the passage for a military disguise he goes into such a tearing passion that he tips it off his head with his hand and kicks it up to the ceiling with his foot where it grazed long afterwards. "Major" I says "be cool and advise me what to do with Joshua my dead and gone Lirriper's own youngest brother." "Madam" says the Major "my advice is that you board and lodge him in a Powder Mill, with a handsome gratuity to the proprietor when exploded." "Major" I says "as a Christian you cannot mean your words." "Madam" says the Major "by the Lord I do!" and indeed the Major besides being with all his merits a very passionate man for his size had a bad opinion of Joshua on account of former troubles even unattended by liberties taken with his apparel. When Joshua Lirriper hears this conversation betwixt us he turns upon the littlest one with the biggest hat and says "Come sir! Remove me to my vile dungeon. Where is my mouldy straw?" My dear at the picter of him rising in my mind dressed almost entirely in padlocks like Baron Trenck in Jemmy's book I was so overcome that I burst into tears and I says to the Major, "Major take my keys and settle with these gentlemen or I shall never know a happy minute more," which was done several times both before and since, but still I must remember that Joshua Lirriper has his good feelings and shows them in being always so troubled in his mind when he cannot wear mourning for his brother. Many a long year have I left off my widow's mourning not being wishful to intrude, but the tender point in Joshua that I cannot help a little yielding to is when he writes "One single sovereign would enable me to wear a decent suit of mourning for my much-loved brother. I vowed at the time of his lamented death that I would ever wear sables in memory of him but Alas how short-sighted is man, How keep that vow when penniless!" It says a good deal for the strength of his feelings that he couldn't have been seven year old when my poor Lirriper died and to have kept to it ever since is highly creditable. But we know there's good in all of us,—if we only knew where it was in some of us,—and though it was far from delicate in Joshua to work upon the dear child's feelings when first sent to school and write down into Lincolnshire for his pocket-money by return of post and got it, still he is my poor Lirriper's own youngest brother and mightn't have meant not paying his bill at the Salisbury Arms when his affection took him down to stay a fortnight at Hatfield churchyard and might have meant to keep sober but for bad company. Consequently if the Major *had* played on him with the garden-engine which he got privately into his room without my knowing of it, I think that much as I should have regretted it there would have been words betwixt the Major and me. Therefore my dear though he played on Mr. Buffle by mistake being hot in his head, and though it might have been misrepresented down at Wozenham's into not being ready for Mr. Buffle in other respects he being the Assessed Taxes, still I do not so much regret it as perhaps I ought. And whether Joshua Lirriper will yet do well in life I cannot say, but I did hear of his coming out at a Private Theatre in the character of a Bandit without receiving any offers afterwards from the regular managers.

Mentioning Mr. Buffle gives an instance of there being good in persons where good is not expected, for it cannot be denied that Mr. Buffle's manners when engaged in his business were not agreeable. To collect is one thing, and to look about as if suspicious of the goods being gradually removing in the dead of the night by a back door is another, over taxing you have no control but suspecting is voluntary. Allowances too must ever be made for a gentleman of the Major's warmth not relishing being spoke to with a pen in the mouth, and while I do not know that it is more irritable to my own feelings to have a low-crowned hat with a broad brim kept on in doors than any other hat still I can appreciate the Major's, besides which without bearing malice or vengeance the Major is a man that scores up arrears as his habit always was with Joshua Lirriper. So at last my dear the Major lay in wait for Mr. Buffle and it worrited me a good deal. Mr. Buffle gives his rap of two sharp knocks one day and the Major bounces to the door. "Collector has called for two quarters' Assessed Taxes" says Mr. Buffle. "They are ready for him" says the Major and brings him in here. But on the way Mr. Buffle looks about him in his usual suspicious manner and the Major fires and asks him "Do you see a Ghost sir?" "No sir" says Mr. Buffle. "Because I have before noticed you" says the Major "apparently looking for a spectre very hard beneath the roof of my respected friend. When you find that supernatural agent, be so good as point him out sir." Mr. Buffle stares at the Major and then nods at me. "Mrs. Lirriper sir" says the Major going off into a perfect steam and introducing me with his hand. "Pleasure of knowing her" says Mr. Buffle. "A—hum!—Jemmy Jackman sir!" says the Major introducing himself. "Honour of knowing you by sight" says Mr. Buffle. "Jemmy Jackman sir" says the Major wagging his head sideways in a sort of obstinate fury "presents to you his esteemed friend that lady Mrs. Emma Lirriper of Eighty-one Norfolk Street Strand London in the County of Middlesex in the United Kingdom of Great Britain and Ireland. Upon which occasion sir," says the Major, "Jemmy Jackman takes your hat off." Mr. Buffle looks at his hat where the Major drops it on the floor, and he picks it up and puts it on again. "Sir" says the Major very red and looking him full in the face "there are two quarters of the Gallantry Taxes due and the Collector has called." Upon which if you can believe my words my dear the Major drops Mr. Buffle's hat off again. "This——" Mr. Buffle begins very angry with his pen in his mouth, when the Major steaming more and more says "Take your bit out sir! Or by the whole infernal system of Taxation of this country and every individual figure in the National Debt, I'll get upon your back and ride you like a horse!" which it's my belief he would have done and even actually jerking his neat little legs ready for a spring as it was. "This," says Mr. Buffle without his pen "is an assault and I'll have the law of you." "Sir" replies the Major "if you are a man of honour, your Collector of whatever may be due on the Honourable Assessment by applying to Major Jackman at the Parlours Mrs. Lirriper's Lodgings, may obtain what he wants in full at any moment."

When the Major glared at Mr. Buffle with those meaning words my dear I literally gasped for a teaspoonful of salvolatile in a wineglass of water, and I says "Pray let it go no farther gentlemen I beg and beseech of you!" But the Major could be got to do nothing else but snort long after Mr. Buffle was gone, and the effect it had upon my whole mass of blood when on the next day of Mr. Buffle's rounds the Major spruced himself up and went humming a tune up and down the street with one eye almost obliterated by his hat there are not expressions in Johnson's dictionary to state. But I safely put the street door on the jar and got behind the Major's blinds with my shawl on and my mind made up the moment I saw danger to rush out screeching till my voice failed me and catch the Major round the neck till my strength went and have all parties bound. I had not been behind the blinds a quarter of an hour when I saw Mr. Buffle approaching with his Collecting-books in his hand. The Major likewise saw him approaching and hummed louder and himself approached. They met before the Airy railings. The Major takes off his hat at arm's length and says " Mr. Buffle I believe?" Mr. Buffle takes off *his* hat at arm's length and says "That is my name sir." Says the Major "Have you any commands for me, Mr. Buffle?" Says Mr. Buffle "Not any sir." Then my dear both of 'em bowed very low and haughty and parted, and whenever Mr. Buffle made his rounds in future him and the Major always met and bowed before the Airy railings, putting me much in mind of Hamlet and the other gentleman in mourning before killing one another, though I could have wished the other gentleman had done it fairer and even if less polite no poison.

Mr. Buffle's family were not liked in this neighbourhood, for when you are a householder my dear you'll find it does not come by nature to like the Assessed, and it was considered besides that a one-horse pheayton ought not to have elevated Mrs. Buffle to that height especially when purloined from the Taxes which I myself did consider uncharitable. But they were *not* liked and there was that domestic unhappiness in the family in consequence of their both being very hard with Miss Buffle and one another on account of Miss Buffle's favouring Mr. Buffle's articled young gentleman, that it *was* whispered that Miss Buffle would go either into a consumption or a convent she being so very thin and off her appetite and two close-shaved gentlemen with white bands round their necks peeping round the corner whenever she went out in waistcoats resembling black pinafores. So things stood towards Mr. Buffle when one night I was woke by a frightful noise and a smell of burning, and going to my bedroom window saw the whole street in a glow. Fortunately we had two sets empty just then and before I could hurry on some clothes I heard the Major hammering at the attics' doors and calling out " Dress yourselves!—Fire ! Don't be frightened ! —Fire! Collect your presence of mind!—Fire ! All right —Fire !" most tremenjously. As I opened my bedroom door the Major came tumbling in over himself and me, and caught me in his arms. "Major" I says breathless "where is it?" "I don't know dearest madam" says the Major—"Fire! Jemmy Jackman will defend you to the last drop of his blood —Fire! If the dear boy was at home what a treat this would be for him—Fire!" and altogether very collected and bold except that he couldn't say a single sentence without shaking me to the very centre with roaring Fire. We ran down to the drawing-room and put our heads out of window, and the Major calls to an unfeeling young monkey, scampering by be joyful and ready to split "Where is it?—Fire!" The monkey answers without stopping "O here's a lark! Old Buffle's been setting his house alight to prevent its being found out that he boned the Taxes. Hurrah! Fire!" And then the sparks came flying up and the smoke came pouring down and the crackling of flames and spatting of water and banging of engines and hacking of axes and breaking of glass and knocking at doors and the shouting and crying and hurrying and the heat and altogether gave me a dreadful palpitation. "Don't be frightened dearest madam," says the Major, "—Fire! There's nothing to be alarmed at—Fire! Don't open the street door till I come back—Fire! I'll go and see if I can be of any service—Fire! You're quite composed and comfortable ain't you?—Fire, Fire, Fire!" It was in vain for me to hold the man and tell him he'd be galloped to death by the engines—pumped to death by his over-exertions—wet-feeted to death by the slop and mess— flattened to death when the roofs fell in—his spirit was up and he went scampering off after the young monkey with all the breath he had and none to spare, and me and the girls huddled together at the parlour windows looking at the dreadful flames above the houses over the way, Mr. Buffle's being round the corner. Presently what should we see but some people running down the street straight to our door, and then the Major directing operations in the busiest way, and then some more people and then—carried in a chair similar to Guy Fawkes—Mr. Buffle in a blanket!

GALLANT CONDUCT OF THE MAJOR

My dear the Major has Mr. Buffle brought up our steps and whisked into the parlour and carted out on the sofy, and then he and all the rest of them without so much as a word burst away again full speed, leaving the impression of a vision except for Mr. Buffle awful in his blanket with his eyes a rolling. In a twinkling they all burst back again with Mrs. Buffle in another blanket, which whisked in and carted out on the sofy they all burst off again and all burst back again with Miss Buffle in another blanket, which again whisked in and carted out they all burst off again and all burst back again with Mr. Buffle's articled young gentleman in another blanket—him a holding round the necks of two men carrying him by the legs, similar to the picter of the disgraceful creetur who has lost the fight (but where the chair I do not know) and his hair having the appearance of newly played upon. When all four of a row, the Major rubs his hands and whispers me with what little hoarseness he can get together, "If our dear remarkable boy was only at home what a delightful treat this would be for him!"

My dear we made them some hot tea and toast and some hot brandy-and-water with a little comfortable nutmeg in it, and at first they were scared and low in their spirits but being fully insured got sociable. And the first use Mr. Buffle made of his tongue was to call the Major his Preserver and his best of friends and to say "My for ever dearest sir let me make you known to Mrs. Buffle" which also addressed him as her Preserver and her best of friends and was fully as cordial as the blanket would admit of. Also Miss Buffle. The articled young gentleman's head was a little light and he sat a moaning "Robina is reduced to cinders, Robina is reduced to cinders!" Which went more to the heart on account of his having got wrapped in his blanket as if he was looking out of a violinceller case, until Mr. Buffle says "Robina speak to him!" Miss Buffle says "Dear George!" and but for the Major's pouring down brandy-and-water on the instant which caused a catching in his throat owing to

55

the nutmeg and a violent fit of coughing it might have proved too much for his strength. When the articled young gentleman got the better of it Mr. Buffle leaned up against Mrs. Buffle being two bundles, a little while in confidence, and then says with tears in his eyes which the Major noticing wiped, "We have not been a united family, let us after this danger become so, take her George." The young gentleman could not put his arm out far to do it, but his spoken expressions were very beautiful though of a wandering class. And I do not know that I ever had a much pleasanter meal than the breakfast we took together after we had all dozed, when Miss Buffle made tea very sweetly in quite the Roman style as depicted formerly at Covent Garden Theatre and when the whole family was most agreeable, as they have ever proved since that night when the Major stood at the foot of the Fire-Escape and claimed them as they came down—the young gentleman head-foremost, which accounts. And though I do not say that we should be less liable to think ill of one another if strictly limited to blankets, still I do say that we might most of us come to a better understanding if we kept one another less at a distance.

Why there's Wozenham's lower down on the other side of the street. I had a feeling of much soreness several years respecting what I must still ever call Miss Wozenham's systematic underbidding and the likeness of the house in Bradshaw having far too many windows and a most um-brageous and outrageous Oak which never yet was seen in Norfolk-street nor yet a carriage and four at Wozenham's door, which it would have been far more to Bradshaw's credit to have drawn a cab. This frame of mind continued bitter down to the very afternoon in January last when one of my girls, Sally Rairyganoo which I still suspect of Irish extraction though family represented Cambridge, else why abscond with a bricklayer of the Limerick persuasion and be married in pattens not waiting till his black eye was decently got round with all the company fourteen in number

and one horse fighting outside on the roof of the vehicle,—
I repeat my dear my ill-regulated state of mind towards
Miss Wozenham continued down to the very afternoon of
January last past when Sally Rairyganoo came banging (I
can use no milder expression) into my room with a jump
which may be Cambridge and may not, and said "Hurroo
Missis! Miss Wozenham's sold up!" My dear when I had
it thrown in my face and conscience that the girl Sally had
reason to think I could be glad of the ruin of a fellow-creeter,
I burst into tears and dropped back in my chair and I says
"I am ashamed of myself!"

Well! I tried to settle to my tea but I could not do it
what with thinking of Miss Wozenham and her distresses.
It was a wretched night and I went up to a front window
and looked over at Wozenham's and as well as I could make
it out down the street in the fog it was the dismallest of
the dismal and not a light to be seen. So at last I says to
myself "This will not do," and I puts on my oldest bonnet
and shawl not wishing Miss Wozenham to be reminded of
my best at such a time, and lo and behold you I goes over
to Wozenham's and knocks. "Miss Wozenham at home?"
I says turning my head when I heard the door go. And
then I saw it was Miss Wozenham herself who had opened
it and sadly worn she was poor thing and her eyes all swelled
and swelled with crying. "Miss Wozenham" I says "it is
several years since there was a little unpleasantness betwixt
us on the subject of my grandson's cap being down your
Airy. I have overlooked it and I hope you have done the
same." "Yes Mrs. Lirriper" she says in a surprise "I have."
"Then my dear" I says "I should be glad to come in and
speak a word to you." Upon my calling her my dear Miss
Wozenham breaks out a crying most pitiful, and a not
unfeeling elderly person that might have been better shaved
in a nightcap with a hat over it offering a polite apology
for the mumps having worked themselves into his constitution,
and also for sending home to his wife on the bellows which

57

was in his hand as a writing-desk, looks out of the back
parlour and says "The lady wants a word of comfort" and
goes in again. So I was able to say quite natural "Wants
a word of comfort does she sir? Then please the pigs she
shall have it!" And Miss Wozenham and me we go into
the front room with a wretched light that seemed to have
been crying too and was sputtering out, and I says "Now
my dear, tell me all," and she wrings her hands and says
"O Mrs. Lirriper that man is in possession here, and I have
not a friend in the world who is able to help me with a
shilling."

It doesn't signify a bit what a talkative old body like me
said to Miss Wozenham when she said that, and so I'll tell
you instead my dear that I'd have given thirty shillings to
have taken her over to tea, only I durstn't on account of
the Major. Not you see but what I knew I could draw
the Major out like thread and wind him round my finger
on most subjects and perhaps even on that if I was to set
myself to it, but him and me had so often belied Miss
Wozenham to one another that I was shamefaced, and I
knew she had offended his pride and never mine, and likewise
I felt timid that that Rairyganoo girl might make things
awkward. So I says "My dear if you could give me a cup of
tea to clear my muddle of a head I should better understand
your affairs." And we had the tea and the affairs too and
after all it was but forty pound, and—— There! she's as
industrious and straight a creeter as ever lived and has paid
back half of it already, and where's the use of saying more,
particularly when it ain't the point? For the point is that
when she was a kissing my hands and holding them in hers
and kissing them again and blessing blessing blessing, I
cheered up at last and I says "Why what a waddling old
goose I have been my dear to take you for something so
very different!" "Ah but I too" says she "how have *I*
mistaken *you*!" "Come for goodness' sake tell me" I says
"what you thought of me?" "O" says she "I thought

58

you had no feeling for such a hard hand-to-mouth life as mine, and were rolling in affluence." I says shaking my sides (and very glad to do it for I had been a choking quite long enough) "Only look at my figure my dear and give me your opinion whether if I was in affluence I should be likely to roll in it?" That did it! We got as merry as grigs (whatever *they* are, if you happen to know my dear—*I* don't) and I went home to my blessed home as happy and as thankful as could be. But before I make an end of it, think even of my having misunderstood the Major! Yes! For next forenoon the Major came into my little room with his brushed hat in his hand and he begins "My dearest madam——" and then put his face in his hat as if he had just come into church. As I sat all in a maze he came out of his hat and began again. "My esteemed and beloved friend——" and then went into his hat again. "Major," I cries out frightened "has anything happened to our darling boy?" "No, no, no" says the Major "but Miss Wozenham has been here this morning to make her excuses to me, and by the Lord I can't get over what she told me." "Hoity toity, Major," I says "you don't know yet that I was afraid of you last night and didn't think half as well of you as I ought! So come out of church Major and forgive me like a dear old friend and I'll never do so any more." And I leave you to judge my dear whether I ever did or will. And how affecting to think of Miss Wozenham out of her small income and her losses doing so much for her poor old father, and keeping a brother that had had the misfortune to soften his brain against the hard mathematics as neat as a new pin in the three back represented to lodgers as a lumber-room and consuming a whole shoulder of mutton whenever provided!

And now my dear I really am a going to tell you about my Legacy if you're inclined to favour me with your attention, and I did fully intend to have come straight to it only one thing does so bring up another. It was the month of June and the day before Midsummer Day when my girl Winifred

Madgers—she was what is termed a Plymouth Sister, and the Plymouth Brother that made away with her was quite right, for a tidier young woman for a wife never came into a house and afterwards called with the beautifullest Plymouth Twins —it was the day before Midsummer Day when Winifred Madgers comes and says to me " A gentleman from the Consul's wishes particular to speak to Mrs. Lirriper." If you'll believe me my dear the Consols at the bank where I have a little matter for Jemmy got into my head, and I says " Good gracious I hope he ain't had any dreadful fall!" Says Winifred " He don't look as if he had ma'am." And I says " Show him in."

The gentleman came in dark and with his hair cropped what I should consider too close, and he says very polite " Madame Lirrwiper!" I says " Yes sir. Take a chair." " I come," says he " frrwom the Frrwench Consul's." So I saw at once that it wasn't the Bank of England. " We have rrweceived," says the gentleman turning his r's very curious and skilful, " frrwom the Mairrwie at Sens, a communication which I will have the honour to rrwead. Madame Lirrwiper understands Frrwench?" " O dear no sir!" says I. " Madame Lirriper don't understand anything of the sort." " It matters not," says the gentleman, " I will trrwanslate."

With that my dear the gentleman after reading something about a Department and a Marie (which Lord forgive me I supposed till the Major came home was Mary, and never was I more puzzled than to think how that young woman came to have so much to do with it) translated a lot with the most obliging pains, and it came to this:—That in the town of Sens in France an unknown Englishman lay a dying. That he was speechless and without motion. That in his lodging there was a gold watch and a purse containing such and such money and a trunk containing such and such clothes, but no passport and no papers, except that on his table was a pack of cards and that he had written in pencil on the back of the ace of hearts: " To the authorities.

A VISITOR FROM THE FRENCH CONSULATE

When I am dead, pray send what is left, as a last Legacy, to Mrs. Lirriper Eighty-one Norfolk Street Strand London." When the gentleman had explained all this, which seemed to be drawn up much more methodical than I should have given the French credit for, not at that time knowing the nation, he put the document into my hand. And much the wiser I was for that you may be sure, except that it had the look of being made out upon grocery paper and was stamped all over with eagles.

"Does Madame Lirrwiper" says the gentleman, "believe she rrwecognises her unfortunate compatrrwiot?"

You may imagine the flurry it put me into my dear to be talked to about my compatriots.

I says "Excuse me. Would you have the kindness sir to make your language as simple as you can?"

"This Englishman unhappy, at the point of death. This compatrrwiot afflicted," says the gentleman.

"Thank you sir," I says "I understand you now. No sir I have not the least idea who this can be."

"Has Madame Lirrwiper no son, no nephew, no godson, no frrwiend, no acquaintance of any kind in Frrwance?"

"To my certain knowledge" says I "no relation or friend, and to the best of my belief no acquaintance."

"Pardon me. You take Locataires?" says the gentleman.

My dear fully believing he was offering me something with his obliging foreign manners,—snuff for anything I knew,—I gave a little bend of my head and I says if you'll credit it, "No I thank you. I have not contracted the habit."

The gentleman looks perplexed and says "Lodgers!"

"Oh!" says I laughing. "Bless the man! Why yes to be sure!"

"May it not be a former lodger?" says the gentleman. "Some lodger that you pardoned some rrwent? You have pardoned lodgers some rrwent?"

"Hem! It has happened sir" says I, "but I assure you

61

I can call to mind no gentleman of that description that this is at all likely to be."

In short my dear, we could make nothing of it, and the gentleman noted down what I said and went away. But he left me the paper of which he had two with him, and when the Major came in I says to the Major as I put it in his hand "Major here's Old Moore's Almanac with the hieroglyphic complete, for your opinion."

It took the Major a little longer to read than I should have thought, judging from the copious flow with which he seemed to be gifted when attacking the organ-men, but at last he got through it, and stood a gazing at me in amazement.

"Major" I says "you're paralysed."

"Madam" says the Major, "Jemmy Jackman is doubled up."

Now it did so happen that the Major had been out to get a little information about railroads and steamboats, as our boy was coming home for his Midsummer holidays next day and we were going to take him somewhere for a treat and a change. So while the Major stood a gazing it came into my head to say to him "Major I wish you'd go and look at some of your books and maps, and see whereabouts this same town of Sens is in France."

The Major he roused himself and he went into the Parlours and he poked about a little, and he came back to me and he says, "Sens my dearest madam is seventy-odd miles south of Paris."

With what I may truly call a desperate effort "Major," I says "we'll go there with our blessed boy."

If ever the Major was beside himself it was at the thoughts of that journey. All day long he was like the wild man of the woods after meeting with an advertisement in the papers telling him something to his advantage, and early next morning hours before Jemmy could possibly come home he was outside in the street ready to call out to him that we was all a going to France. Young Rosycheeks you may believe was as wild as the Major, and they did carry on to that degree that I says "If you two children ain't more orderly I'll pack you both off to bed." And then they fell to cleaning up the Major's telescope to see France with, and went out and bought a leather bag with a snap to hang round Jemmy, and him to carry the money like a little Fortunatus with his purse.

If I hadn't passed my word and raised their hopes, I doubt if I could have gone through with the undertaking but it was too late to go back now. So on the second day after Midsummer Day we went off by the morning mail. And when we came to the sea which I had never seen but once in my life and that when my poor Lirriper was courting me, the freshness of it and the deepness and the airiness and to think that it had been rolling ever since and that it was always a rolling and so few of us minding, made me feel quite serious. But I felt happy too and so did Jemmy and the Major and not much motion on the whole, though me with a swimming in the head and a sinking but able to take notice that the foreign insides appear to be constructed hollower than the English, leading to much more tremenjous noises when bad sailors.

But my dear the blueness and the lightness and the coloured look of everything and the very sentry-boxes striped and the shining rattling drums and the little soldiers with their waists and tidy gaiters, when we got across to the Continent—it made me feel as if I don't know what—as if the atmosphere had been lifted off me. And as to lunch why bless you if I kept a man-cook and two kitchen-maids I couldn't get it done for twice the money, and no injured young woman a glaring at you and grudging you and acknowledging your patronage by wishing that your food might choke you, but so civil and so hot and attentive and every way comfortable except Jemmy pouring wine down his throat by tumblers-full and me expecting to see him drop under the table.

And the way in which Jemmy spoke his French was a real charm. It was often wanted of him, for whenever anybody spoke a syllable to me I says "Non-comprenny, you're very kind, but it's no use—Now Jemmy!" and then Jemmy he fires away at 'em lovely, the only thing wanting in Jemmy's French being as it appeared to me that he hardly ever understood a word of what they said to him which made it scarcely of the use it might have been though in other respects a perfect Native, and regarding the Major's fluency I should have been of the opinion judging French by English that there might have been a greater choice of words in the language though still I must admit that if I hadn't known him when he asked a military gentleman in a gray cloak what o'clock it was I should have took him for a Frenchman born.

Before going on to look after my Legacy we were to make one regular day in Paris, and I leave you to judge my dear what a day *that* was with Jemmy and the Major and the telescope and me and the prowling young man at the inn door (but very civil too) that went along with us to show the sights. All along the railway to Paris Jemmy and the Major had been frightening me to death by stooping down on the platforms at stations to inspect the engines underneath their mechanical stomachs, and by creeping in and out I don't know where all, to find improvements for the United Grand Junction Parlour, but when we got out into the brilliant streets on a bright morning they gave up all their London improvements as a bad job and gave their minds to Paris. Says the prowling young man to me "Will I speak Inglis No?" So I says "If you can young man I shall take it as a favour," but after half-an-hour of it when I fully believed the man had gone mad and me too I says "Be so good as fall back on your French sir," knowing that then I shouldn't have the agonies of trying to understand him, which was a happy release. Not that I lost much more than the rest either, for I generally noticed that when he had

64

described something very long indeed and I says to Jemmy "What does he say Jemmy?" Jemmy says looking with vengeance in his eye "He is so jolly indistinct!" and that when he had described it longer all over again and I says to Jemmy "Well Jemmy what's it all about?" Jemmy says "He says the building was repaired in seventeen hundred and four, Gran."

Wherever that prowling young man formed his prowling habits I cannot be expected to know, but the way in which he went round the corner while we had our breakfasts and was there again when we swallowed the last crumb was most marvellous, and just the same at dinner and at night, prowling equally at the theatre and the inn gateway and the shop doors when we bought a trifle or two and everywhere else but troubled with a tendency to spit. And of Paris I can tell you no more my dear than that it's town and country both in one, and carved stone and long streets of high houses and gardens and fountains and statues and trees and gold, and immensely big soldiers and immensely little soldiers and the pleasantest nurses with the whitest caps a playing at skipping-rope with the bunchiest babies in the flattest caps, and clean table-cloths spread everywhere for dinner and people sitting out of doors smoking and sipping all day long and little plays being acted in the open air for little people and every shop a complete and elegant room, and everybody seeming to play at everything in this world. And as to the sparkling lights my dear after dark, glittering high up and low down and on before and on behind and all round, and the crowd of theatres and the crowd of people and the crowd of all sorts, it's pure enchantment. And pretty well the only thing that grated on me was that whether you pay your fare at the railway or whether you change your money at a money-dealer's or whether you take your ticket at the theatre, the lady or gentleman is caged up (I suppose by government) behind the strongest iron bars having more of a Zoological appearance than a free country.

Well to be sure when I did after all get my precious bones to bed that night, and my Young Rogue came in to kiss me and asks "What do you think of this lovely lovely Paris, Gran?" I says "Jemmy I feel as if it was beautiful fireworks being let off in my head." And very cool and refreshing the pleasant country was next day when we went on to look after my Legacy, and rested me much and did me a deal of good.

So at length and at last my dear we come to Sens, a pretty little town with a great two-towered cathedral and the rooks flying in and out of the loopholes and another tower atop of one of the towers like a sort of a stone pulpit. In which pulpit with the birds skimming below him if you'll believe me, I saw a speck while I was resting at the inn before dinner which they made signs to me was Jemmy and which really was. I had been a fancying as I sat in the balcony of the hotel that an Angel might light there and call down to the people to be good, but I little thought what Jemmy all unknown to himself was a calling down from that high place to some one in the town.

The pleasantest-situated inn my dear! Right under the two towers, with their shadows a changing upon it all day like a kind of a sundial, and country people driving in and out of the courtyard in carts and hooded cabriolets and such like, and a market outside in front of the cathedral, and all so quaint and like a picter. The Major and me agreed that whatever came of my Legacy this was the place to stay in for our holiday, and we also agreed that our dear boy had best not be checked in his joy that night by the sight of the Englishman if he was still alive, but that we would go together and alone. For you are to understand that the Major not feeling himself quite equal in his wind to the height to which Jemmy had climbed, had come back to me and left him with the Guide.

So after dinner when Jemmy had set off to see the river, the Major went down to the Mairie, and presently came back with a military character in a sword and spurs and a cocked hat and a yellow shoulder-belt and long tags about him that he must have found inconvenient. And the Major says "The Englishman still lies in the same state dearest madam. This gentleman will conduct us to his lodging." Upon which the military character pulled off his cocked hat to me, and I took notice that he had shaved his forehead in imitation of Napoleon Bonaparte but not like.

We went out at the courtyard gate and past the great doors of the cathedral and down a narrow High-street where the people were sitting chatting at their shop doors and the children were at play. The military character went in front and he stopped at a pork-shop with a little statue of a pig sitting up, in the window, and a private door that a donkey was looking out of.

When the donkey saw the military character he came slipping out on the pavement to turn round and then clattered along the passage into a back yard. So the coast being clear, the Major and me were conducted up the common stair and into the front room on the second, a bare room with a red tiled floor and the outside lattice blinds pulled close to darken it. As the military character opened the blinds I saw the tower where I had seen Jemmy, darkening as the sun got low, and I turned to the bed by the wall and saw the Englishman.

It was some kind of brain fever he had had, and his hair was all gone, and some wetted folded linen lay upon his head. I looked at him very attentive as he lay there all wasted away with his eyes closed, and I says to the Major:

"I never saw this face before."

The Major looked at him very attentive too, and he says:

"*I* never saw this face before."

When the Major explained our words to the military character, that gentleman shrugged his shoulders and showed the Major the card on which it was written about the Legacy for me. It had been written with a weak and trembling

67

hand in bed, and I knew no more of the writing than of the face. Neither did the Major.

Though lying there alone, the poor creetur was as well taken care of as could be hoped, and would have been quite unconscious of any one's sitting by him then. I got the Major to say that we were not going away at present and that I would come back to-morrow and watch a bit by the bedside. But I got him to add—and I shook my head hard to make it stronger—"We agree that we never saw this face before."

Our boy was greatly surprised when we told him sitting out in the balcony in the starlight, and he ran over some of those stories of former Lodgers, of the Major's putting down, and asked wasn't it possible that it might be this lodger or that lodger. It was not possible, and we went to bed.

In the morning just at breakfast-time the military character came jingling round, and said that the doctor thought from the signs he saw there might be some rally before the end. So I says to the Major and Jemmy, "You two boys go and enjoy yourselves, and I'll take my Prayer Book and go sit by the bed." So I went, and I sat there some hours, reading a prayer for him poor soul now and then, and it was quite on in the day when he moved his hand.

He had been so still, that the moment he moved I knew of it, and I pulled off my spectacles and laid down my book and rose and looked at him. From moving one hand he began to move both, and then his action was the action of a person groping in the dark. Long after his eyes had opened, there was a film over them and he still felt for his way out into light. But by slow degrees his sight cleared and his hands stopped. He saw the ceiling, he saw the wall, he saw me. As his sight cleared, mine cleared too, and when at last we looked in one another's faces, I started back and I cries passionately :

"O you wicked wicked man ! Your sin has found you out !"

For I knew him, the moment life looked out of his eyes,

to be Mr. Edson, Jemmy's father who had so cruelly deserted Jemmy's young unmarried mother who had died in my arms, poor tender creetur, and left Jemmy to me.

"You cruel wicked man! You bad black traitor!"

With the little strength he had, he made an attempt to turn over on his wretched face to hide it. His arm dropped out of the bed and his head with it, and there he lay before me crushed in body and in mind. Surely the miserablest sight under the summer sun!

"O blessed Heaven," I says a crying, "teach me what to say to this broken mortal! I am a poor sinful creetur, and the Judgment is not mine."

As I lifted my eyes up to the clear bright sky, I saw the high tower where Jemmy had stood above the birds, seeing that very window; and the last look of that poor pretty young mother when her soul brightened and got free, seemed to shine down from it.

"O man, man, man!" I says, and I went on my knees beside the bed; "if your heart is rent asunder and you are truly penitent for what you did, Our Saviour will have mercy on you yet!"

As I leaned my face against the bed, his feeble hand could just move itself enough to touch me. I hope the touch was penitent. It tried to hold my dress and keep hold, but the fingers were too weak to close.

I lifted him back upon the pillows and I says to him:

"Can you hear me?"

He looked yes.

"Do you know me?"

He looked yes, even yet more plainly.

"I am not here alone. The Major is with me. You recollect the Major?"

Yes. That is to say he made out yes, in the same way as before.

"And even the Major and I are not alone. My grandson —his godson—is with us. Do you hear? My grandson."

The fingers made another trial to catch at my sleeve, but could only creep near it and fall.

"Do you know who my grandson is?"

Yes.

"I pitied and loved his lonely mother. When his mother lay a dying I said to her, 'My dear, this baby is sent to a childless old woman.' He has been my pride and joy ever since. I love him as dearly as if he had drunk from my breast. Do you ask to see my grandson before you die?"

Yes.

"Show me, when I leave off speaking, if you correctly understand what I say. He has been kept unacquainted with the story of his birth. He has no knowledge of it. No suspicion of it. If I bring him here to the side of this bed, he will suppose you to be a perfect stranger. It is more than I can do to keep from him the knowledge that there is such wrong and misery in the world; but that it was ever so near him in his innocent cradle I have kept from him, and I do keep from him, and I ever will keep from him, for his mother's sake, and for his own."

He showed me that he distinctly understood, and the tears fell from his eyes.

"Now rest, and you shall see him."

So I got him a little wine and some brandy, and I put things straight about his bed. But I began to be troubled in my mind lest Jemmy and the Major might be too long of coming back. What with this occupation for my thoughts and hands, I didn't hear a foot upon the stairs, and was startled when I saw the Major stopped short in the middle of the room by the eyes of the man upon the bed, and knowing him then, as I had known him a little while ago.

There was anger in the Major's face, and there was horror and repugnance and I don't know what. So I went up to him and I led him to the bedside, and when I clasped my hands and lifted of them up, the Major did the like.

"O Lord" I says "Thou knowest what we two saw together

70

of the sufferings and sorrows of that young creetur now with
Thee. If this dying man is truly penitent, we two together
humbly pray Thee to have mercy on him!"

The Major says "Amen!" and then after a little stop I
whispers him, "Dear old friend fetch our beloved boy."
And the Major, so clever as to have got to understand it all
without being told a word, went away and brought him.

Never never never shall I forget the fair bright face of our
boy when he stood at the foot of the bed, looking at his unknown father. And O so like his dear young mother then!

"Jemmy." I says, "I have found out all about this poor
gentleman who is so ill, and he did lodge in the old house
once. And as he wants to see all belonging to it, now that
he is passing away, I sent for you."

"Ah poor man!" says Jemmy stepping forward and touching one of his hands with great gentleness. "My heart
melts for him. Poor, poor man!"

The eyes that were so soon to close for ever turned to me,
and I was not that strong in the pride of my strength that
I could resist them.

"My darling boy, there is a reason in the secret history of
this fellow-creetur lying as the best and worst of us must all
lie one day, which I think would ease his spirit in his last
hour if you would lay your cheek against his forehead and
say, 'May God forgive you!'"

"O Gran," says Jemmy with a full heart "I am not
worthy!" But he leaned down and did it. Then the falter-
ing fingers made out to catch hold of my sleeve at last, and
I believe he was a-trying to kiss me when he died.

There my dear! There you have the story of my Legacy
in full, and it's worth ten times the trouble I have spent
upon it if you are pleased to like it.

You might suppose that it set us against the little French
town of Sens, but no we didn't find that. I found myself
that I never looked up at the high tower atop of the other

tower, but the days came back again when that fair young creetur with her pretty bright hair trusted in me like a mother, and the recollection made the place so peaceful to me as I can't express. And every soul about the hotel down to the pigeons in the courtyard made friends with Jemmy and the Major, and went lumbering away with them on all sorts of expeditions in all sorts of vehicles drawn by rampagious cart-horses—with heads and without,—mud for paint and ropes for harness,—and every new friend dressed in blue like a butcher, and every new horse standing on his hind legs wanting to devour and consume every other horse, and every man that had a whip to crack crack-crack-crack-crack-cracking it as if it was a schoolboy with his first. As to the Major my dear that man lived the greater part of his time with a little tumbler in one hand and a bottle of small wine in the other, and whenever he saw anybody else with a little tumbler, no matter who it was,—the military character with the tags, or the inn-servants at their supper in the courtyard, or townspeople a chatting on a bench, or country people a starting home after Market,—down rushes the Major to clink his glass against their glasses and cry,—Hola! Vive Somebody! or Vive Something! as if he was beside himself. And though I could not quite approve of the Major's doing it, still the ways of the world are the ways of the world varying according to the different parts of it, and dancing at all in the open Square with a lady that kept a barber's shop my opinion is that the Major was right to dance his best and to lead off with a power that I did not think was in him, though I was a little uneasy at the Barricading sound of the cries that were set up by the other dancers and the rest of the company, until when I says "What are they ever calling out Jemmy?" Jemmy says, "They're calling out Gran, Bravo the Military English! Bravo the Military English!" which was very gratifying to my feelings as a Briton and became the name the Major was known by.

But every evening at a regular time we all three sat out in the balcony of the hotel at the end of the courtyard, looking up at the golden and rosy light as it changed on the great towers, and looking at the shadows of the towers as they changed on all about us ourselves included, and what do you think we did there? My dear, if Jemmy hadn't brought some other of those stories of the Major's taking down from the telling of former lodgers at Eighty-one Norfolk-street, and if he didn't bring 'em out with this speech:

"Here you are Gran! Here you are godfather! More of 'em! I'll read. And though you wrote 'em for me, godfather, I know you won't disapprove of my making 'em over to Gran; will you?"

"No, my dear boy," says the Major. "Everything we have is hers, and we are hers."

"Hers ever affectionately and devotedly J. Jackman, and J. Jackman Lirriper," cries the Young Rogue giving me a close hug. "Very well then godfather. Look here. As Gran is in the Legacy way just now, I shall make these stories a part of Gran's Legacy. I'll leave 'em to her. What do you say godfather?"

"Hip hip Hurrah!" says the Major.

"Very well then," cries Jemmy all in a bustle. "Vive the Military English! Vive the Lady Lirriper! Vive the Jemmy Jackman Ditto! Vive the Legacy! Now, you look out, Gran. And you look out, godfather. I'll read! And I'll tell you what I'll do besides. On the last night of our holiday here when we are all packed and going away, I'll top up with something of my own."

"Mind you do sir" says I.

CHAPTER II

WELL my dear and so the evening readings of those jottings of the Major's brought us round at last to the evening when we were all packed and going away next day, and I do assure you that by that time though it was deliciously comfortable to look forward to the dear old house in Norfolk-street again, I had formed quite a high opinion of the French nation and had noticed them to be much more homely and domestic in their families and far more simple and amiable in their lives than I had ever been led to expect, and it did strike me between ourselves that in one particular they might be imitated to advantage by another nation which I will not mention, and that is in the courage with which they take their little enjoyments on little means and with little things and don't let solemn big-wigs stare them out of countenance or speechify them dull, of which said solemn big-wigs I have ever had the one opinion that I wish they were all made comfortable separately in coppers with the lids on and never let out any more.

"Now young man," I says to Jemmy when we brought our chairs into the balcony that last evening, "you please to remember who was to 'top up.'"

"All right Gran" says Jemmy. "I am the illustrious personage."

But he looked so serious after he had made me that light

74

answer, that the Major raised his eyebrows at me and I raised mine at the Major.

" Gran and godfather," says Jemmy, " you can hardly think how much my mind has run on Mr. Edson's death."

It gave me a little check. " Ah ! it was a sad scene my love " I says, " and sad remembrances come back stronger than merry. But this " I says after a little silence, to rouse myself and the Major and Jemmy all together, " is not topping up. Tell us your story my dear."

" I will " says Jemmy.

" What is the date sir ? " says I. " Once upon a time when pigs drank wine ? "

" No Gran," says Jemmy, still serious ; " once upon a time when the French drank wine."

Again I glanced at the Major, and the Major glanced at me.

" In short, Gran and godfather," says Jemmy, looking up, " the date is this time, and I'm going to tell you Mr. Edson's story."

The flutter that it threw me into. The change of colour on the part of the Major !

" That is to say, you understand," our bright-eyed boy says, " I am going to give you my version of it. I shall not ask whether it's right or not, firstly because you said you knew very little about it, Gran, and secondly because what little you did know was a secret."

I folded my hands in my lap and I never took my eyes off Jemmy as he went running on.

" The unfortunate gentleman " Jemmy commences, " who is the subject of our present narrative was the son of Somebody, and was born Somewhere, and chose a profession Somehow. It is not with those parts of his career that we have to deal ; but with his early attachment to a young and beautiful lady."

I thought I should have dropped. I durstn't look at the Major ; but I knew what his state was, without looking at him.

"The father of our ill-starred hero" says Jemmy, copying as it seemed to me the style of some of his story-books, " was a worldly man who entertained ambitious views for his only son and who firmly set his face against the contemplated alliance with a virtuous but penniless orphan. Indeed he went so far as roundly to assure our hero that unless he weaned his thoughts from the object of his devoted affection, he would disinherit him. At the same time, he proposed as a suitable match the daughter of a neighbouring gentleman of a good estate, who was neither ill-favoured nor unamiable, and whose eligibility in a pecuniary point of view could not be disputed. But young Mr. Edson, true to the first and only love that had inflamed his breast, rejected all considerations of self-advancement, and, deprecating his father's anger in a respectful letter, ran away with her."

My dear I had begun to take a turn for the better, but when it come to running away I began to take another turn for the worse.

"The lovers" says Jemmy "fled to London and were united at the altar of Saint Clement's Danes. And it is at this period of their simple but touching story that we find them inmates of the dwelling of a highly-respected and beloved lady of the name of Gran, residing within a hundred miles of Norfolk-street."

I felt that we were almost safe now, I felt that the dear boy had no suspicion of the bitter truth, and I looked at the Major for the first time and drew a long breath. The Major gave me a nod.

"Our hero's father" Jemmy goes on "proving implacable and carrying his threat into unrelenting execution, the struggles of the young couple in London were severe, and would have been far more so, but for their good angel's having conducted them to the abode of Mrs. Gran; who, divining their poverty (in spite of their endeavours to conceal it from her), by a thousand delicate arts smoothed their rough way, and alleviated the sharpness of their first distress."

Here Jemmy took one of my hands in one of his, and began a marking the turns of his story by making me give a beat from time to time upon his other hand.

"After a while, they left the house of Mrs. Gran, and pursued their fortunes through a variety of successes and failures elsewhere. But in all reverses, whether for good or evil, the words of Mr. Edson to the fair young partner of his life were, 'Unchanging Love and Truth will carry us through all!'"

My hand trembled in the dear boy's, those words so wofully unlike the fact.

"Unchanging Love and Truth" says Jemmy over again, as if he had a proud kind of a noble pleasure in it, "will carry us through all! Those were his words. And so they fought their way, poor but gallant and happy, until Mrs. Edson gave birth to a child."

"A daughter," I says.

"No," says Jemmy, "a son. And the father was so proud of it that he could hardly bear it out of his sight. But a dark cloud overspread the scene. Mrs. Edson sickened, drooped, and died."

"Ah! Sickened, drooped, and died!" I says.

"And so Mr. Edson's only comfort, only hope on earth, and only stimulus to action, was his darling boy. As the child grew older, he grew so like his mother that he was her living picture. It used to make him wonder why his father cried when he kissed him. But unhappily he was like his mother in constitution as well as in face, and he died too before he had grown out of childhood. Then Mr. Edson, who had good abilities, in his forlornness and despair, threw them all to the winds. He became apathetic, reckless, lost. Little by little he sank down, down, down, down, until at last he almost lived (I think) by gaming. And so sickness overtook him in the town of Sens in France, and he lay down to die. But now that he laid him down when all was done, and looked back upon the green Past beyond the time

77

when he had covered it with ashes, he thought gratefully of the good Mrs. Gran long lost sight of, who had been so kind to him and his young wife in the early days of their marriage, and he left the little that he had as a last Legacy to her. And she, being brought to see him, at first no more knew him than she would know from seeing the ruin of a Greek or Roman Temple, what it used to be before it fell; but at length she remembered him. And then he told her, with tears, of his regret for the misspent part of his life, and besought her to think as mildly of it as she could, because it was the poor fallen Angel of his unchanging Love and Constancy after all. And because she had her grandson with her, and he fancied that his own boy, if he had lived, might have grown to be something like him, he asked her to let him touch his forehead with his cheek and say certain parting words."

Jemmy's voice sank low when it got to that, and tears filled my eyes, and filled the Major's.

"You little Conjurer" I says, "how did you ever make it all out? Go in and write it every word down, for it's a wonder."

Which Jemmy did, and I have repeated it to you my dear from his writing.

Then the Major took my hand and kissed it, and said, "Dearest madam all has prospered with us."

"Ah Major" I says drying my eyes, "we needn't have been afraid. We might have known it. Treachery don't come natural to beaming youth; but trust and pity, love and constancy,—they do, thank God!"

DOCTOR MARIGOLD

[1865]

I

TO BE TAKEN IMMEDIATELY

I AM a Cheap Jack, and my own father's name was Willum Marigold. It was in his lifetime supposed by some that his name was William, but my own father always consistently said, No, it was Willum. On which point I content myself with looking at the argument this way: If a man is not allowed to know his own name in a free country, how much is he allowed to know in a land of slavery? As to looking at the argument through the medium of the Register, Willum Marigold come into the world before Registers come up much,—and went out of it too. They wouldn't have been greatly in his line neither, if they had chanced to come up before him.

I was born on the Queen's highway, but it was the King's at that time. A doctor was fetched to my own mother by my own father, when it took place on a common; and in consequence of his being a very kind gentleman, and accepting no fee but a tea-tray, I was named Doctor, out of gratitude and compliment to him. There you have me. Doctor Marigold.

DOCTOR MARIGOLD

I am at present a middle-aged man of a broadish build, in cords, leggings, and a sleeved waistcoat the strings of which is always gone behind. Repair them how you will, they go like fiddle-strings. You have been to the theatre, and you have seen one of the wiolin-players screw up his wiolin, after listening to it as if it had been whispering the secret to him that it feared it was out of order, and then you have heard it snap. That's as exactly similar to my waistcoat as a waistcoat and a wiolin can be like one another.

I am partial to a white hat, and I like a shawl round my neck wore loose and easy. Sitting down is my favourite posture. If I have a taste in point of personal jewelry, it is mother-of-pearl buttons. There you have me again, as large as life.

The doctor having accepted a tea-tray, you'll guess that my father was a Cheap Jack before me. You are right. He was. It was a pretty tray. It represented a large lady going along a serpentining up-hill gravel-walk, to attend a little church. Two swans had likewise come astray with the same intentions. When I call her a large lady, I don't mean in point of breadth, for there she fell below my views, but she more than made it up in heighth; her heighth and slimness was—in short THE heighth of both.

I often saw that tray, after I was the innocently smiling cause (or more likely screeching one) of the doctor's standing it up on a table against the wall in his consulting-room. Whenever my own father and mother were in that part of the country, I used to put my head (I have heard my own mother say it was flaxen curls at that time, though you wouldn't know an old hearth-broom from it now till you come to the handle, and found it wasn't me) in at the doctor's door, and the doctor was always glad to see me, and said, "Aha, my brother practitioner! Come in, little M.D. How are your inclinations as to sixpence?"

You can't go on for ever, you'll find, nor yet could my father nor yet my mother. If you don't go off as a whole when you are about due, you're liable to go off in part, and two to one your head's the part. Gradually my father went off his, and my mother went off hers. It was in a harmless way, but it put out the family where I boarded them. The old couple, though retired, got to be wholly and solely devoted to the Cheap Jack business, and were always selling the family off. Whenever the cloth was laid for dinner, my father began rattling the plates and dishes, as we do in our line when we put up crockery for a bid, only he had lost the trick of it, and mostly let 'em drop and broke 'em. As the old lady had been used to sit in the cart, and hand the articles out one by one to the old gentleman on the footboard to sell, just in the same way she handed him every item of the family's property, and they disposed of it in their own imaginations from morning to night. At last the old gentleman, lying bedridden in the same room with the old lady, cries out in the old patter, fluent, after having been silent for two days and nights : " Now here, my jolly companions every one,—which the Nightingale club in a village was held, At the sign of the Cabbage and Shears, Where the singers no doubt would have greatly excelled, But for want of taste, voices, and ears,—now, here, my jolly companions, every one, is a working model of a used-up old Cheap Jack, without a tooth in his head, and with a pain in every bone : so like life that it would be just as good if it wasn't better, just as bad if it wasn't worse, and just as new if it wasn't worn out. Bid for the working model of the old Cheap Jack, who has drunk more gunpowder-tea with the ladies in his time than would blow the lid off a washerwoman's copper, and carry it as many thousands of miles higher than the moon as naught nix naught, divided by the national debt, carry nothing to the poor-rates, three under, and two over. Now, my hearts of oak and men of straw, what do you say for the lot? Two shillings, a shilling, tenpence, eightpence, sixpence, fourpence. Twopence? Who said twopence? The gentleman in the scarecrow's hat? I am ashamed of the

gentleman in the scarecrow's hat. I really am ashamed of
him for his want of public spirit. Now I'll tell you what I'll
do with you. Come! I'll throw you in a working model of
a old woman that was married to the old Cheap Jack so long
ago that upon my word and honour it took place in Noah's
Ark, before the Unicorn could get in to forbid the banns
by blowing a tune upon his horn. There now! Come!
What do you say for both? I'll tell you what I'll do with
you. I don't bear you malice for being so backward. Here!
If you make me a bid that'll only reflect a little credit on
your town, I'll throw you in a warming-pan for nothing, and
lend you a toasting-fork for life. Now come; what do you
say after that splendid offer? Say two pound, say thirty
shillings, say a pound, say ten shillings, say five, say two and
six. You don't say even two and six? You say two and
three? No. You shan't have the lot for two and three. I'd
sooner give it to you, if you was good-looking enough.
Here! Missis! Chuck the old man and woman into the
cart, put the horse to, and drive 'em away and bury 'em!'"
Such were the last words of Willum Marigold, my own
father, and they were carried out, by him and by his wife,
my own mother, on one and the same day, as I ought to
know, having followed as mourner.

My father had been a lovely one in his time at the Cheap
Jack work, as his dying observations went to prove. But I
top him. I don't say it because it's myself, but because it
has been universally acknowledged by all that has had the
means of comparison. I have worked at it. I have measured
myself against other public speakers,—Members of Parliament,
Platforms, Pulpits, Counsel learned in the law,—and where I
have found 'em good, I have took a bit of imagination from
'em, and where I have found 'em bad, I have let 'em alone.
Now I'll tell you what. I mean to go down into my grave
declaring that of all the callings ill used in Great Britain,
the Cheap Jack calling is the worst used. Why ain't we a
profession? Why ain't we endowed with privileges? Why

are we forced to take out a hawker's license, when no such thing is expected of the political hawkers? Where's the difference betwixt us? Except that we are Cheap Jacks, and they are Dear Jacks, *I* don't see any difference but what's in our favour.

For look here! Say it's election time. I am on the footboard of my cart in the market-place, on a Saturday night. I put up a general miscellaneous lot. I say: "Now here, my free and independent woters, I'm a going to give you such a chance as you never had in all your born days, nor yet the days preceding. Now I'll show you what I am a going to do with you. Here's a pair of razors that'll shave you closer than the Board of Guardians; here's a flat-iron worth its weight in gold; here's a frying-pan artificially flavoured with essence of beefsteaks to that degree that you've only got for the rest of your lives to fry bread and dripping in it and there you are replete with animal food; here's a genuine chronometer watch in such a solid silver case that you may knock at the door with it when you come home late from a social meeting, and rouse your wife and family, and save up your knocker for the postman; and here's half-a-dozen dinner plates that you may play the cymbals with to charm the baby when it's fractious. Stop! I'll throw you in another article, and I'll give you that, and it's a rolling-pin; and if the baby can only get it well into its mouth when its teeth is coming and rub the gums once with it, they'll come through double, in a fit of laughter equal to being tickled. Stop again! I'll throw you in another article, because I don't like the looks of you, for you haven't the appearance of buyers unless I lose by you, and because I'd rather lose than not take money to-night, and that's a looking-glass in which you may see how ugly you look when you don't bid. What do you say now? Come! Do you say a pound? Not you, for you haven't got it. Do you say ten shillings? Not you, for you owe more to the tallyman. Well then, I'll tell you what I'll do with you. I'll heap 'em all on the footboard of the cart,—there they are! razors, flat-iron, frying-pan, chrono-meter watch, dinner plates, rolling-pin, and looking-glass,—take 'em all away for four shillings, and I'll give you sixpence for your trouble!" This is me, the Cheap Jack. But on the Monday morning, in the same market-place, comes the Dear Jack on the hustings—*his* cart—and what does *he* say? "Now my free and independent woters, I am a going to give you such a chance" (he begins just like me) "as you never had in all your born days, and that's the chance of sending Myself to Parliament. Now I'll tell you what I am a going to do for you. Here's the interests of this magnificent town promoted above all the rest of the civilised and uncivilised earth. Here's your railways carried, and your neighbours' railways jockeyed. Here's all your sons in the Post-office. Here's Britannia smiling on you. Here's the eyes of Europe on you. Here's uniwersal prosperity for you, repletion of animal food, golden cornfields, gladsome homesteads, and rounds of applause from your own hearts, all in one lot, and that's myself. Will you take me as I stand? You won't? Well, then, I'll tell you what I'll do with you. Come now! I'll throw you in anything you ask for. There! Church-rates, abolition of church-rates, more malt tax, no malt tax, uniwersal education to the highest mark, or uniwersal ignor-ance to the lowest, total abolition of flogging in the army or a dozen for every private once a month all round. Wrongs of Men or Rights of Women—only say which it shall be, take 'em or leave 'em, and I'm of your opinion altogether, and the lot's your own on your own terms. There! You won't take it yet! Well, then, I'll tell you what I'll do with you. Come! You *are* such free and independent woters, and I *am* so proud of you,—you *are* such a noble and enlightened constituency, and I *am* so ambitious of the honour and dignity of being your member, which is by far the highest level to which the wings of the human mind can soar,—that I'll tell you what I'll do with you. I'll throw you in all the public-houses in your magnificent town for nothing. Will that content you ? It won't ? You won't take the lot yet ? Well, then, before I put the horse in and drive away, and make the offer to the next most magnificent town that can be discovered, I'll tell you what I'll do. Take the lot, and I'll drop two thousand pound in the streets of your magnificent town for them to pick up that can. Not enough ? Now look here. This is the very furthest that I'm a going to. I'll make it two thousand five hundred. And still you won't ? Here, missis ! Put the horse—no, stop half a moment, I shouldn't like to turn my back upon you neither for a trifle, I'll make it two· thousand seven hundred and fifty pound. There ! Take the lot on your own terms, and I'll count out two thousand seven hundred and fifty pound on the foot-board of the cart, to be dropped in the streets of your magnificent town for them to pick up that can. What do you say ? Come now ! You won't do better, and you may do worse. You take it ? Hooray ! Sold again, and got the seat !"

These Dear Jacks soap the people shameful, but we Cheap Jacks don't. We tell 'em the truth about themselves to their faces, and scorn to court 'em. As to wenturesomeness in the way of puffing up the lots, the Dear Jacks beats us hollow. It is considered in the Cheap Jack calling, that better patter can be made out of a gun than any article we put up from the cart, except a pair of spectacles. I often hold forth about a gun for a quarter of an hour, and feel as if I need never leave off. But when I tell 'em what the gun can do, and what the gun has brought down, I never go half so far as the Dear Jacks do when they make speeches in praise of *their* guns—their great guns that set 'em on to do it. Besides, I'm in business for myself : I ain't sent down into the market-place to order, as they are. Besides, again, my guns don't know what I say in their laudation, and their guns do, and the whole concern of 'em have reason to be sick and ashamed all round. These are some of my arguments for declaring that the Cheap Jack calling is treated ill in Great

Britain, and for turning warm when I think of the other Jacks in question setting themselves up to pretend to look down upon it.

I courted my wife from the footboard of the cart. I did indeed. She was a Suffolk young woman, and it was in Ipswich market-place right opposite the corn-chandler's shop. I had noticed her up at a window last Saturday that was, appreciating highly. I had took to her, and I had said to myself, "If not already disposed of, I'll have that lot." Next Saturday that come, I pitched the cart on the same pitch, and I was in very high feather indeed, keeping 'em laughing the whole of the time, and getting off the goods briskly. At last I took out of my waistcoat-pocket a small lot wrapped in soft paper, and I put it this way (looking up at the window where she was). "Now here, my blooming English maidens, is an article, the last article of the present evening's sale, which I offer to only you, the lovely Suffolk Dumplings biling over with beauty, and I won't take a bid of a thousand pounds for from any man alive. Now what is it? Why, I'll tell you what it is. It's made of fine gold, and it's not broke, though there's a hole in the middle of it, and it's stronger than any fetter that ever was forged, though it's smaller than any finger in my set of ten. Why ten? Because, when my parents made over my property to me, I tell you true, there was twelve sheets, twelve towels, twelve table-cloths, twelve knives, twelve forks, twelve tablespoons, and twelve teaspoons, but my set of fingers was two short of a dozen, and could never since be matched. Now what else is it? Come, I'll tell you. It's a hoop of solid gold, wrapped in a silver curl-paper, that I myself took off the shining locks of the ever beautiful old lady in Threadneedle-street, London city; I wouldn't tell you so if I hadn't the paper to show, or you mightn't believe it even of me. Now what else is it? It's a man-trap and a handcuff, the parish stocks and a leg-lock, all in gold and all in one. Now what else is it? It's a wedding-ring. Now I'll tell you what I'm a going to do with it. I'm not a going to offer this lot for money; but I mean to give it to the next of you beauties that laughs, and I'll pay her a visit to-morrow morning at exactly half after nine o'clock as the chimes go, and I'll take her out for a walk to put up the banns." *She* laughed, and got the ring handed up to her. When I called in the morning, she says, "O dear! It's never you, and you never mean it?" "It's ever me," says I, "and I am ever yours, and I ever mean it." So we got married, after being put up three times—which, by the bye, is quite in the Cheap Jack way again, and shows once more how the Cheap Jack customs pervade society.

She wasn't a bad wife, but she had a temper. If she could have parted with that one article at a sacrifice, I wouldn't have swopped her away in exchange for any other woman in England. Not that I ever did swop her away, for we lived together till she died, and that was thirteen year. Now, my lords and ladies and gentlefolks all, I'll let you into a secret, though you won't believe it. Thirteen year of temper in a Palace would try the worst of you, but thirteen year of temper in a Cart would try the best of you. You are kept so very close to it in a cart, you see. There's thousands of couples among you getting on like sweet ile upon a whetstone in houses five and six pairs of stairs high, that would go to the Divorce Court in a cart. Whether the jolting makes it worse, I don't undertake to decide; but in a cart it does come home to you, and stick to you. Wiolence in a cart is *so* wiolent, and aggrawation in a cart is *so* aggrawating.

We might have had such a pleasant life! A roomy cart, with the large goods hung outside, and the bed slung underneath it when on the road, an iron pot and a kettle, a fireplace for the cold weather, a chimney for the smoke, a hanging-shelf and a cupboard, a dog and a horse. What more do you want? You draw off upon a bit of turf in a green lane or by the roadside, you hobble your old horse and turn him grazing, you light your fire upon the ashes of the last visitors, you cook your stew, and you wouldn't call the

Emperor of France your father. But have a temper in the cart, flinging language and the hardest goods in stock at you, and where are you then? Put a name to your feelings.

My dog knew as well when she was on the turn as I did. Before she broke out, he would give a howl, and bolt. How he knew it, was a mystery to me; but the sure and certain knowledge of it would wake him up out of his soundest sleep, and he would give a howl, and bolt. At such times I wished I was him.

The worst of it was, we had a daughter born to us, and I love children with all my heart. When she was in her furies she beat the child. This got to be so shocking, as the child got to be four or five year old, that I have many a time gone on with my whip over my shoulder, at the old horse's head, sobbing and crying worse than ever little Sophy did. For how could I prevent it? Such a thing is not to be tried with such a temper—in a cart—without coming to a fight. It's in the natural size and formation of a cart to bring it to a fight. And then the poor child got worse terrified than before, as well as worse hurt generally, and her mother made complaints to the next people we lighted on, and the word went round, " Here's a wretch of a Cheap Jack been a beating his wife."

Little Sophy was such a brave child! She grew to be quite devoted to her poor father, though he could do so little to help her. She had a wonderful quantity of shining dark hair, all curling natural about her. It is quite astonishing to me now, that I didn't go tearing mad when I used to see her run from her mother before the cart, and her mother catch her by this hair, and pull her down by it, and beat her.

Such a brave child I said she was! Ah! with reason.

" Don't you mind next time, father dear," she would whisper to me, with her little face still flushed, and her bright eyes still wet; " if I don't cry out, you may know I am not much hurt. And even if I do cry out, it will only

90

be to get mother to let go and leave off." What I have seen the little spirit bear—for me—without crying out!

Yet in other respects her mother took great care of her. Her clothes were always clean and neat, and her mother was never tired of working at 'em. Such is the inconsistency in things. Our being down in the marsh country in unhealthy weather, I consider the cause of Sophy's taking bad low fever; but however she took it, once she got it she turned away from her mother for evermore, and nothing would persuade her to be touched by her mother's hand. She would shiver and say, "No, no, no," when it was offered at, and would hide her face on my shoulder, and hold me tighter round the neck.

The Cheap Jack business had been worse than ever I had known it, what with one thing and what with another (and not least with railroads, which will cut it all to pieces, I expect, at last), and I was run dry of money. For which reason, one night at that period of little Sophy's being so bad, either we must have come to a dead-lock for victuals and drink, or I must have pitched the cart as I did.

I couldn't get the dear child to lie down or leave go of me, and indeed I hadn't the heart to try, so I stepped out on the footboard with her holding round my neck. They all set up a laugh when they see us, and one chuckle-headed Joskin (that I hated for it) made the bidding, "Tuppence for her!"

"Now, you country boobies," says I, feeling as if my heart was a heavy weight at the end of a broken sashline, "I give you notice that I am a going to charm the money out of your pockets, and to give you so much more than your money's worth that you'll only persuade yourselves to draw your Saturday night's wages ever again arterwards by the hopes of meeting me to lay 'em out with, which you never will, and why not? Because I've made my fortune by selling my goods on a large scale for seventy-five per cent. less than I give for 'em, and I am consequently to be elevated to the

91

House of Peers next week, by the title of the Duke of Cheap and Markis Jackaloorul. Now let's know what you want to-night, and you shall have it. But first of all, shall I tell you why I have got this little girl round my neck? You don't want to know? Then you shall. She belongs to the Fairies. She's a fortune-teller. She can tell me all about you in a whisper, and can put me up to whether you're going to buy a lot or leave it. Now do you want a saw? No, she says you don't, because you're too clumsy to use one. Else here's a saw which would be a lifelong blessing to a handy man, at four shillings, at three and six, at three, at two and six, at two, at eighteen-pence. But none of you shall have it at any price, on account of your well-known awkwardness, which would make it manslaughter. The same objection applies to this set of three planes which I won't let you have neither, so don't bid for 'em. Now I am a going to ask her what you do want." (Then I whispered, "Your head burns so, that I am afraid it hurts you bad, my pet," and she answered, without opening her heavy eyes, "Just a little, father.") "O! This little fortune-teller says it's a memorandum-book you want. Then why didn't you mention it? Here it is. Look at it. Two hundred superfine hot-pressed wire-wove pages—if you don't believe me, count 'em—ready ruled for your expenses, an everlastingly pointed pencil to put 'em down with, a double-bladed penknife to scratch 'em out with, a book of printed tables to calculate your income with, and a camp-stool to sit down upon while you give your mind to it! Stop! And an umbrella to keep the moon off when you give your mind to it on a pitch dark night. Now I won't ask you how much for the lot, but how little? How little are you thinking of? Don't be ashamed to mention it, because my fortune-teller knows already." (Then making believe to whisper, I kissed her, and she kissed me.) "Why, she says you are thinking of as little as three and threepence! I couldn't have believed it, even of you, unless she told me. Three and

Doctor Marigold

threepence! And a set of printed tables in the lot that'll calculate your income up to forty thousand a year! With an income of forty thousand a year, you grudge three and sixpence. Well then, I'll tell you my opinion. I so despise the threepence, that I'd sooner take three shillings. There. For three shillings, three shillings, three shillings! Gone. Hand 'em over to the lucky man."

As there had been no bid at all, everybody looked about and grinned at everybody, while I touched little Sophy's face and asked her if she felt faint, or giddy. "Not very, father. It will soon be over." Then turning from the pretty patient eyes, which were opened now, and seeing nothing but grins across my lighted grease-pot, I went on again in my Cheap Jack style. "Where's the butcher?" (My sorrowful eye had just caught sight of a fat young butcher on the outside of the crowd.) "She says the good luck is the butcher's. Where is he?" Everybody handed on the blushing butcher to the front, and there was a roar, and the butcher felt himself obliged to put his hand in his pocket, and take the lot. The party so picked out, in general, does feel obliged to take the lot—good four times out of six. Then we had another lot, the counterpart of that one, and sold it sixpence cheaper, which is always wery much enjoyed. Then we had the spectacles. It ain't a special profitable lot, but I put 'em on, and I see what the Chancellor of the Exchequer is going to take off the taxes, and I see what the sweetheart of the young woman in the shawl is doing at home, and I see what the Bishops has got for dinner, and a deal more that seldom fails to fetch 'em up in their spirits; and the better their spirits, the better their bids. Then we had the ladies' lot,—the teapot, tea-caddy, glass sugar-basin, half-a-dozen spoons, and caudle-cup—and all the time I was making similar excuses to give a look or two and say a word or two to my poor child. It was while the second ladies' lot was holding 'em enchained that I felt her lift herself a little on my shoulder, to look across the dark street. "What troubles you, darling?" "Nothing 'troubles me, father. I am not at all troubled. But don't I see a pretty churchyard over there?" "Yes, my dear." "Kiss me twice, dear father, and lay me down to rest upon that churchyard grass so soft and green." I staggered back into the cart with her head dropped on my shoulder, and I says to her mother, "Quick. Shut the door! Don't let those laughing people see!" "What's the matter?" she cries. "O woman, woman," I tells her, "you'll never catch my little Sophy by her hair again, for she has flown away from you!"

Maybe those were harder words than I meant 'em; but from that time forth my wife took to brooding, and would sit in the cart or walk beside it, hours at a stretch, with her arms crossed, and her eyes looking on the ground. When her furies took her (which was rather seldomer than before) they took her in a new way, and she banged herself about to that extent that I was forced to hold her. She got none the better for a little drink now and then, and through some years I used to wonder, as I plodded along at the old horse's head, whether there was many carts upon the road that held so much dreariness as mine, for all my being looked up to as the King of the Cheap Jacks. So sad our lives went on till one summer evening, when, as we were coming into Exeter, out of the farther West of England, we saw a woman beating a child in a cruel manner, who screamed, "Don't beat me! O mother, mother, mother!" Then my wife stopped her ears, and ran away like a wild thing, and next day she was found in the river.

Me and my dog were all the company left in the cart now; and the dog learned to give a short bark when they wouldn't bid, and to give another and a nod of his head when I asked him, "Who said half a crown? Are you the gentleman, sir, that offered half a crown?" He attained to an immense height of popularity, and I shall always believe taught himself entirely out of his own head to growl at any person in the crowd that bid as low as sixpence. But he got to be well on in years, and one night when I was conwulsing York with the spectacles, he took a conwulsion on his own account upon the very footboard by me, and it finished him.

Being naturally of a tender turn, I had dreadful lonely feelings on me arter this. I conquered 'em at selling times, having a reputation to keep (not to mention keeping myself), but they got me down in private, and rolled upon me. That's often the way with us public characters. See us on the footboard, and you'd give pretty well anything you possess to be us. See us off the footboard, and you'd add a trifle to be off your bargain. It was under those circumstances that I come acquainted with a giant. I might have been too high to fall into conversation with him, had it not been for my lonely feelings. For the general rule is, going round the country, to draw the line at dressing up. When a man can't trust his getting a living to his undisguised abilities, you consider him below your sort. And this giant when on view figured as a Roman.

He was a languid young man, which I attribute to the distance betwixt his extremities. He had a little head and less in it, he had weak eyes and weak knees, and altogether you couldn't look at him without feeling that there was greatly too much of him both for his joints and his mind. But he was an amiable though timid young man (his mother let him out, and spent the money), and we come acquainted when he was walking to ease the horse betwixt two fairs. He was called Rinaldo di Velasco, his name being Pickleson.

This giant, otherwise Pickleson, mentioned to me under the seal of confidence that, beyond his being a burden to himself, his life was made a burden to him by the cruelty of his master towards a step-daughter who was deaf and dumb. Her mother was dead, and she had no living soul to take her part, and was used most hard. She travelled with his master's caravan only because there was nowhere to leave her, and this giant, otherwise Pickleson, did go so far as to believe that his master often tried to lose her. He was such a very

95

languid young man, that I don't know how long it didn't take him to get this story out, but it passed through his defective circulation to his top extremity in course of time.

When I heard this account from the giant, otherwise Pickleson, and likewise that the poor girl had beautiful long dark hair, and was often pulled down by it and beaten, I couldn't see the giant through what stood in my eyes. Having wiped 'em, I give him sixpence (for he was kept as short as he was long), and he laid it out in two threepenn'orths of gin-and-water, which so brisked him up, that he sang the Favourite Comic of Shivery Shakey, ain't it cold?—a popular effect which his master had tried every other means to get out of him as a Roman wholly in vain.

His master's name was Mim, a wery hoarse man, and I knew him to speak to. I went to that Fair as a mere civilian, leaving the cart outside the town, and I looked about the back of the Vans while the performing was going on, and at last, sitting dozing against a muddy cart-wheel, I come upon the poor girl who was deaf and dumb. At the first look I might almost have judged that she had escaped from the Wild Beast Show; but at the second I thought better of her, and thought that if she was more cared for and more kindly used she would be like my child. She was just the same age that my own daughter would have been, if her pretty head had not fell down upon my shoulder that unfortunate night.

To cut it short, I spoke confidential to Mim while he was beating the gong outside betwixt two lots of Pickleson's publics, and I put it to him, "She lies heavy on your own hands; what'll you take for her?" Mim was a most ferocious swearer. Suppressing that part of his reply which was much the longest part, his reply was, "A pair of braces." "Now I'll tell you," says I, "what I'm a going to do with you. I'm a going to fetch you half-a-dozen pair of the primest braces in the cart, and then to take her away with me." Says Mim (again ferocious), "I'll believe it when I've got the goods, and no sooner." I made all the haste I could,

lest he should think twice of it, and the bargain was completed, which Pickleson he was thereby so relieved in his
mind that he come out at his little back door, longways like
a serpent, and give us Shivery Shakey in a whisper among
the wheels at parting.

It was happy days for both of us when Sophy and me
began to travel in the cart. I at once give her the name of
Sophy, to put her ever towards me in the attitude of my
own daughter. We soon made out to begin to understand
one another, through the goodness of the Heavens, when she
knowed that I meant true and kind by her. In a very little
time she was wonderful fond of me. You have no idea what
it is to have anybody wonderful fond of you, unless you
have been got down and rolled upon by the lonely feelings
that I have mentioned as having once got the better of me.

You'd have laughed—or the reverse—it's according to
your disposition—if you could have seen me trying to teach
Sophy. At first I was helped—you'd never guess by what
—milestones. I got some large alphabets in a box, all the
letters separate on bits of bone, and saying we was going to
WINDSOR, I give her those letters in that order, and then at
every milestone I showed her those same letters in that
same order again, and pointed towards the abode of royalty.
Another time I give her CART, and then chalked the same
upon the cart. Another time I give her DOCTOR MARI-
GOLD, and hung a corresponding inscription outside my
waistcoat. People that met us might stare a bit and laugh,
but what did *I* care, if she caught the idea? She caught it
after long patience and trouble, and then we did begin to
get on swimmingly, I believe you! At first she was a little
given to consider me the cart, and the cart the abode of
royalty, but that soon wore off.

We had our signs, too, and they was hundreds in number.
Sometimes she would sit looking at me and considering hard
how to communicate with me about something fresh,—how
to ask me what she wanted explained,—and then she was

97

(or I thought she was; what does it signify?) so like my child with those years added to her, that I half-believed it was herself, trying to tell me where she had been to up in the skies, and what she had seen since that unhappy night when she flied away. She had a pretty face, and now that there was no one to drag at her bright dark hair, and it was all in order, there was a something touching in her looks that made the cart most peaceful and most quiet, though not at all melancholy. [N.B. In the Cheap Jack patter, we generally sound it lemonjolly, and it gets a laugh.]

The way she learnt to understand any look of mine was truly surprising. When I sold of a night, she would sit in the cart unseen by them outside, and would give a eager look into my eyes when I looked in, and would hand me straight the precise article or articles I wanted. And then she would clap her hands, and laugh for joy. And as for me, seeing her so bright, and remembering what she was when I first lighted on her, starved and beaten and ragged, leaning asleep against the muddy cart-wheel, it give me such heart that I gained a greater heighth of reputation than ever, and I put Pickleson down (by the name of Mim's Travelling Giant otherwise Pickleson) for a fypunnote in my will.

This happiness went on in the cart till she was sixteen year old. By which time I began to feel not satisfied that I had done my whole duty by her, and to consider that she ought to have better teaching than I could give her. It drew a many tears on both sides when I commenced explaining my views to her; but what's right is right, and you can't neither by tears nor laughter do away with its character.

So I took her hand in mine, and I went with her one day to the Deaf and Dumb Establishment in London, and when the gentleman come to speak to us, I says to him: "Now I'll tell you what I'll do with you, sir. I am nothing but a Cheap Jack, but of late years I have laid by for a rainy day notwithstanding. This is my only daughter (adopted), and you can't produce a deafer nor a dumber. Teach her the

98

most that can be taught her in the shortest separation that can be named,—state the figure for it,—and I am game to put the money down. I won't bate you a single farthing, sir, but I'll put down the money here and now, and I'll thankfully throw you in a pound to take it. There!" The gentleman smiled, and then, "Well, well," says he, "I must first know what she has learned already. How do you communicate with her?" Then I showed him, and she wrote in printed writing many names of things and so forth; and we held some sprightly conversation, Sophy and me, about a little story in a book which the gentleman showed her, and which she was able to read. "This is most extraordinary," says the gentleman; "is it possible that you have been her only teacher?" "I have been her only teacher, sir," I says, "besides herself." "Then," says the gentleman, and more acceptable words was never spoke to me, "you're a clever fellow, and a good fellow." This he makes known to Sophy, who kisses his hands, claps her own, and laughs and cries upon it.

We saw the gentleman four times in all, and when he took down my name and asked how in the world it ever chanced to be Doctor, it come out that he was own nephew by the sister's side, if you'll believe me, to the very Doctor that I was called after. This made our footing still easier, and he says to me:

"Now, Marigold, tell me what more do you want your adopted daughter to know?"

"I want her, sir, to be cut off from the world as little as can be, considering her deprivations, and therefore to be able to read whatever is wrote with perfect ease and pleasure."

"My good fellow," urges the gentleman, opening his eyes wide, "why *I* can't do that myself!"

I took his joke, and gave him a laugh (knowing by experience how flat you fall without it), and I mended my words accordingly.

"What do you mean to do with her afterwards?" asks

the gentleman, with a sort of a doubtful eye. "To take her about the country?"

"In the cart, sir, but only in the cart. She will live a private life, you understand, in the cart. I should never think of bringing her infirmities before the public. I wouldn't make a show of her for any money."

The gentleman nodded, and seemed to approve.

"Well," says he, "can you part with her for two years?"

"To do her that good,—yes, sir."

"There's another question," says the gentleman, looking towards her,—"can she part with you for two years?"

I don't know that it was a harder matter of itself (for the other was hard enough to me), but it was harder to get over. However, she was pacified to it at last, and the separation betwixt us was settled. How it cut up both of us when it took place, and when I left her at the door in the dark of an evening, I don't tell. But I know this ; remembering that night, I shall never pass that same establishment without a heartache and a swelling in the throat ; and I couldn't put you up the best of lots in sight of it with my usual spirit, —no, not even the gun, nor the pair of spectacles,—for five hundred pound reward from the Secretary of State for the Home Department, and throw in the honour of putting my legs under his mahogany arterwards.

Still, the loneliness that followed in the cart was not the old loneliness, because there was a term put to it, however long to look forward to ; and because I could think, when I was anyways down, that she belonged to me and I belonged to her. Always planning for her coming back, I bought in a few months' time another cart, and what do you think I planned to do with it? I'll tell you. I planned to fit it up with shelves and books for her reading, and to have a seat in it where I could sit and see her read, and think that I had been her first teacher. Not hurrying over the job, I had the fittings knocked together in contriving ways under my own inspection, and here was her bed in a berth with curtains, and there was her reading-table, and here was her writing-desk, and elsewhere was her books in rows upon rows, picters and no picters, bindings and no bindings, gilt-edged and plain, just as I could pick 'em up for her in lots up and down the country, North and South and West and East, Winds liked best and winds liked least, Here and there and gone astray, Over the hills and far away. And when I had got together pretty well as many books as the cart would neatly hold, a new scheme come into my head, which, as it turned out, kept my time and attention a good deal employed, and helped me over the two years' stile.

Without being of an awaricious temper, I like to be the owner of things. I shouldn't wish, for instance, to go partners with yourself in the Cheap Jack cart. It's not that I mistrust you, but that I'd rather know it was mine. Similarly, very likely you'd rather know it was yours. Well! A kind of a jealousy began to creep into my mind when I reflected that all those books would have been read by other people long before they was read by her. It seemed to take away from her being the owner of 'em like. In this way, the question got into my head: Couldn't I have a book new-made express for her, which she should be the first to read?

It pleased me, that thought did; and as I never was a man to let a thought sleep (you must wake up all the whole family of thoughts you've got and burn their nightcaps, or you won't do in the Cheap Jack line), I set to work at it. Considering that I was in the habit of changing so much about the country, and that I should have to find out a literary character here to make a deal with, and another literary character there to make a deal with, as opportunities presented, I hit on the plan that this same book should be a general miscellaneous lot,—like the razors, flat-iron, chronometer watch, dinner plates, rolling-pin, and looking-glass,— and shouldn't be offered as a single indiwidual article, like the spectacles or the gun. When I had come to that conclusion, I come to another, which shall likewise be yours.

101

Often had I regretted that she never had heard me on the footboard, and that she never could hear me. It ain't that *I* am vain, but that *you* don't like to put your own light under a bushel. What's the worth of your reputation, if you can't convey the reason for it to the person you most wish to value it? Now I'll put it to you. Is it worth sixpence, fippence, fourpence, threepence, twopence, a penny, a halfpenny, a farthing? No, it ain't. Not worth a farthing. Very well, then. My conclusion was that I would begin her book with some account of myself. So that, through reading a specimen or two of me on the footboard, she might form an idea of my merits there. I was aware that I couldn't do myself justice. A man can't write his eye (at least *I* don't know how to), nor yet can a man write his voice, nor the rate of his talk, nor the quickness of his action, nor his general spicy way. But he can write his turns of speech, when he is a public speaker,—and indeed I have heard that he very often does, before he speaks 'em.

Well! Having formed that resolution, then come the question of a name. How did I hammer that hot iron into shape? This way. The most difficult explanation I had ever had with her was, how I come to be called Doctor, and yet was no Doctor. After all, I felt that I had failed of getting it correctly into her mind, with my utmost pains. But trusting to her improvement in the two years, I thought that I might trust to her understanding it when she should come to read it as put down by my own hand: Then I thought I would try a joke with her and watch how it took, by which of itself I might fully judge of her understanding it. We had first discovered the mistake we had dropped into, through her having asked me to prescribe for her when she had supposed me to be a Doctor in a medical point of view; so thinks I, "Now, if I give this book the name of my Prescriptions, and if she catches the idea that my only Prescriptions are for her amusement and interest,—to make her laugh in a pleasant way, or to make her cry in a pleasant way,—it will be a delightful proof to both of us that we have got over our difficulty." It fell out to absolute perfection. For when she saw the book, as I had it got up, —the printed and pressed book,—lying on her desk in her cart, and saw the title, DOCTOR MARIGOLD's PRESCRIPTIONS, she looked at me for a moment with astonishment, then fluttered the leaves, then broke out a laughing in the charmingest way, then felt her pulse and shook her head, then turned the pages pretending to read them most attentive, then kissed the book to me, and put it to her bosom with both her hands. I never was better pleased in all my life!

But let me not anticipate. (I take that expression out of a lot of romances I bought for her. I never opened a single one of 'em—and I have opened many—but I found the romancer saying "let me not anticipate." Which being so, I wonder why he did anticipate, or who asked him to it.) Let me not, I say, anticipate. This same book took up all my spare time. It was no play to get the other articles together in the general miscellaneous lot, but when it come to my own article! There! I couldn't have believed the blotting, nor yet the buckling to at it, nor the patience over it. Which again is like the footboard. The public have no idea.

At last it was done, and the two years' time was gone after all the other time before it, and where it's all gone to, who knows? The new cart was finished,—yellow outside, relieved with vermilion and brass fittings,—the old horse was put in it, a new 'un and a boy being laid on for the Cheap Jack cart, and I cleaned myself up to go and fetch her. Bright cold weather it was, cart-chimneys smoking, carts pitched private on a piece of waste ground over at Wandsworth, where you may see 'em from the Sou'western Railway when not upon the road. (Look out of the right-hand window going down.)

"Marigold," says the gentleman, giving his hand hearty, "I am very glad to see you."

"Yet I have my doubts, sir," says I, "if you can be half as glad to see me as I am to see you."

"The time has appeared so long,—has it, Marigold?"

"I won't say that, sir, considering its real length; but——"

"What a start, my good fellow!"

Ah! I should think it was! Grown such a woman, so pretty, so intelligent, so expressive! I knew then that she must be really like my child, or I could never have known her, standing quiet by the door.

"You are affected," says the gentleman in a kindly manner.

"I feel, sir," says I, "that I am but a rough chap in a sleeved waistcoat."

"I feel," says the gentleman, "that it was you who raised her from misery and degradation, and brought her into communication with her kind. But why do we converse alone together, when we can converse so well with her? Address her in your own way."

"I am such a rough chap in a sleeved waistcoat, sir," says I, "and she is such a graceful woman, and she stands so quiet at the door!"

"Try if she moves at the old sign," says the gentleman.

They had got it up together o' purpose to please me! For when I give her the old sign, she rushed to my feet, and dropped upon her knees, holding up her hands to me with pouring tears of love and joy; and when I took her hands and lifted her, she clasped me round the neck, and lay there; and I don't know what a fool I didn't make of myself, until we all three settled down into talking without sound, as if there was a something soft and pleasant spread over the whole world for us.

[A portion is here omitted from the text, having reference to the sketches contributed by other writers; but the reader will be pleased to have what follows retained in a note:

"Now I'll tell you what I am a-going to do with you.

104

A FINAL PRESCRIPTION ADDED

I am a-going to offer you the general miscellaneous lot, her own book, never read by anybody else but me, added to and completed by me after her first reading of it, eight-and-forty printed pages, six-and-ninety columns, Whiting's own work, Beaufort House to wit, thrown off by the steam-ingine, best of paper, beautiful green wrapper, folded like clean linen come home from the clear-starcher's, and so exquisitely stitched that, regarded as a piece of needlework alone, it's better than the sampler of a seamstress undergoing a Competitive examination for Starvation before the Civil Service Commissioners—and I offer the lot for what? For eight pound? Not so much. For six pound? Less. For four pound. Why, I hardly expect you to believe me, but that's the sum. Four pound! The stitching alone cost half as much again. Here's forty-eight original pages, ninety-six original columns, for four pound. You want more for the money? Take it. Three whole pages of advertisements of thrilling interest thrown in for nothing. Read 'em and believe 'em. More? My best of wishes for your merry Christmases and your happy New Years, your long lives and your true prosperities. Worth twenty pound good if they are delivered as I send them. Remember! Here's a final prescription added, "To be taken for life," which will tell you how the cart broke down, and where the journey ended. You think Four Pound too much? And still you think so? Come! I'll tell you what then. Say Four Pence, and keep the secret."]

TO BE TAKEN WITH A GRAIN OF SALT

I HAVE always noticed a prevalent want of courage, even among persons of superior intelligence and culture, as to imparting their own psychological experiences when those have been of a strange sort. Almost all men are afraid that what they could relate in such wise would find no parallel or response in a listener's internal life, and might be suspected or laughed at. A truthful traveller, who should have seen some extraordinary creature in the likeness of a sea-serpent, would have no fear of mentioning it; but the same traveller, having had some singular presentiment, impulse, vagary of thought, vision (so called), dream, or other remarkable mental impression, would hesitate considerably before he would own to it. To this reticence I attribute much of the obscurity in which such subjects are involved. We do not habitually communicate our experiences of these subjective things as we do our experiences of objective creation. The consequence is, that the general stock of experience in this regard appears exceptional, and really is so, in respect of being miserably imperfect.

In what I am going to relate, I have no intention of setting up, opposing, or supporting, any theory whatever. I know the history of the Bookseller of Berlin, I have studied the case of the wife of a late Astronomer Royal as related by Sir David Brewster, and I have followed the minutest details of a much more remarkable case of Spectral Illusion occurring within my private circle of friends. It may be necessary to state as to this last, that the sufferer (a lady) was in no degree, however distant, related to me. A mistaken assumption on that head might suggest an explanation of a part of my own case,—but only a part,—which would be wholly without foundation. It cannot be referred to my inheritance of any developed peculiarity, nor had I ever before any at all similar experience, nor have I ever had any at all similar experience since.

It does not signify how many years ago, or how few, a certain murder was committed in England, which attracted great attention. We hear more than enough of murderers as they rise in succession to their atrocious eminence, and I would bury the memory of this particular brute, if I could, as his body was buried, in Newgate Jail. I purposely abstain from giving any direct clue to the criminal's individuality.

When the murder was first discovered, no suspicion fell—or I ought rather to say, for I cannot be too precise in my facts, it was nowhere publicly hinted that any suspicion fell—on the man who was afterwards brought to trial. As no reference was at that time made to him in the newspapers, it is obviously impossible that any description of him can at that time have been given in the newspapers. It is essential that this fact be remembered.

Unfolding at breakfast my morning paper, containing the account of that first discovery, I found it to be deeply interesting, and I read it with close attention. I read it twice, if not three times. The discovery had been made in a bedroom, and, when I laid down the paper, I was aware of a flash—rush—flow—I do not know what to call it,— no word I can find is satisfactorily descriptive,—in which I seemed to see that bedroom passing through my room, like a picture impossibly painted on a running river. Though almost instantaneous in its passing, it was perfectly clear; so clear that I distinctly, and with a sense of relief, observed the absence of the dead body from the bed.

It was in no romantic place that I had this curious sensation, but in chambers in Piccadilly, very near to the corner of St. James's-street. It was entirely new to me. I was in my easy-chair at the moment, and the sensation was accompanied with a peculiar shiver which started the chair from its position. (But it is to be noted that the chair ran easily on castors.) I went to one of the windows (there are two in the room, and the room is on the second floor) to refresh my eyes with the moving objects down in Piccadilly. It was a bright autumn morning, and the street was sparkling and cheerful. The wind was high. As I looked out, it brought down from the Park a quantity of fallen leaves, which a gust took, and whirled into a spiral pillar. As the pillar fell and the leaves dispersed, I saw two men on the opposite side of the way, going from West to East. They were one behind the other. The foremost man often looked back over his shoulder. The second man followed him, at a distance of some thirty paces, with his right hand menacingly raised. First, the singularity and steadiness of this threatening gesture in so public a thoroughfare attracted my attention; and next, the more remarkable circumstance that nobody heeded it. Both men threaded their way among the other passengers with a smoothness hardly consistent even with the action of walking on a pavement; and no single creature, that I could see, gave them place, touched them, or looked after them. In passing before my windows, they both stared up at me. I saw their two faces very distinctly, and I knew that I could recognise them anywhere. Not that I had consciously noticed anything very remarkable in either face, except that the man who went first had an unusually lowering appearance, and that the face of the man who followed him was of the colour of impure wax.

I am a bachelor, and my valet and his wife constitute my whole establishment. My occupation is in a certain Branch Bank, and I wish that my duties as head of a Department were as light as they are popularly supposed to be. They kept me in town that autumn, when I stood in need of change. I was not ill, but I was not well. My reader is to make the most that can be reasonably made of my feeling jaded, having a depressing sense upon me of a monotonous life, and being "slightly dyspeptic." I am assured by my renowned doctor that my real state of health at that time justifies no stronger description, and I quote his own from his written answer to my request for it.

As the circumstances of the murder, gradually unravelling, took stronger and stronger possession of the public mind, I kept them away from mine by knowing as little about them as was possible ·in the midst of the universal excitement. But I knew that a verdict of Wilful Murder had been found against the suspected murderer, and that he had been committed to Newgate for trial. I also knew that his trial had been postponed over one Sessions of the Central Criminal Court, on the ground of general prejudice and want of time for the preparation of the defence. I may further have known, but I believe I did not, when, or about when, the Sessions to which his trial stood postponed would come on.

My sitting-room, bedroom, and dressing-room, are all on one floor. With the last there is no communication but through the bedroom. True, there is a door in it, once communicating with the staircase; but a part of the fitting of my bath has been—and had then been for some years—fixed across it. At the same period, and as a part of the same arrangement, the door had been nailed up and canvased over.

I was standing in my bedroom late one night, giving some directions to my servant before he went to bed. My face was towards the only available door of communication with the dressing-room, and it was closed. My servant's back was towards that door. While I was speaking to him, I saw it open, and a man look in, who very earnestly and mysteriously beckoned to me. That man was the man who had gone second of the two along Piccadilly, and whose face was of the colour of impure wax.

The figure, having beckoned, drew back, and closed the door. With no longer pause than was made by my crossing the bedroom, I opened the dressing-room door, and looked in. I had a lighted candle already in my hand. I felt no inward expectation of seeing the figure in the dressing-room, and I did not see it there.

Conscious that my servant stood amazed, I turned round to him, and said: "Derrick, could you believe that in my cool senses I fancied I saw a——" As I there laid my hand upon his breast, with a sudden start he trembled violently, and said, "O Lord, yes, sir! A dead man beckoning!"

Now I do not believe that this John Derrick, my trusty and attached servant for more than twenty years, had any impression whatever of having seen any such figure, until I touched him. The change in him was so startling, when I touched him, that I fully believe he derived his impression in some occult manner from me at that instant.

I bade John Derrick bring some brandy, and I gave him a dram, and was glad to take one myself. Of what had preceded that night's phenomenon, I told him not a single word. Reflecting on it, I was absolutely certain that I had never seen that face before, except on the one occasion in Piccadilly. Comparing its expression when beckoning at the door with its expression when it had stared up at me as I stood at my window, I came to the conclusion that on the first occasion it had sought to fasten itself upon my memory, and that on the second occasion it had made sure of being immediately remembered.

I was not very comfortable that night, though I felt a certainty, difficult to explain, that the figure would not return. At daylight I fell into a heavy sleep, from which I was awakened by John Derrick's coming to my bedside with a paper in his hand.

This paper, it appeared, had been the subject of an altercation at the door between its bearer and my servant. It was a summons to me to serve upon a Jury at the forthcoming

Sessions of the Central Criminal Court at the Old Bailey. I had never before been summoned on such a Jury, as John Derrick well knew. He believed—I am not certain at this hour whether with reason or otherwise—that that class of Jurors were customarily chosen on a lower qualification than mine, and he had at first refused to accept the summons. The man who served it had taken the matter very coolly. He had said that my attendance or non-attendance was nothing to him; there the summons was; and I should deal with it at my own peril, and not at his.

For a day or two I was undecided whether to respond to this call, or take no notice of it. I was not conscious of the slightest mysterious bias, influence, or attraction, one way or other. Of that I am as strictly sure as of every other statement that I make here. Ultimately I decided, as a break in the monotony of my life, that I would go.

The appointed morning was a raw morning in the month of November. There was a dense brown fog in Piccadilly, and it became positively black and in the last degree oppressive East of Temple Bar. I found the passages and staircases of the Court-House flaringly lighted with gas, and the Court itself similarly illuminated. I *think* that, until I was conducted by officers into the Old Court and saw its crowded state, I did not know that the Murderer was to be tried that day. I *think* that, until I was so helped into the Old Court with considerable difficulty, I did not know into which of the two Courts sitting my summons would take me. But this must not be received as a positive assertion, for I am not completely satisfied in my mind on either point.

I took my seat in the place appropriated to Jurors in waiting, and I looked about the Court as well as I could through the cloud of fog and breath that was heavy in it. I noticed the black vapour hanging like a murky curtain outside the great windows, and I noticed the stifled sound of wheels on the straw or tan that was littered in the street; also, the hum of the people gathered there, which a shrill whistle, or a louder song or hail than the rest, occasionally pierced. Soon afterwards the Judges, two in number, entered, and took their seats. The buzz in the Court was awfully hushed. The direction was given to put the Murderer to the bar. He appeared there. And in that same instant I recognised in him the first of the two men who had gone down Piccadilly.

If my name had been called then, I doubt if I could have answered to it audibly. But it was called about sixth or eighth in the panel, and I was by that time able to say "Here!" Now, observe. As I stepped into the box, the prisoner, who had been looking on attentively, but with no sign of concern, became violently agitated, and beckoned to his attorney. The prisoner's wish to challenge me was so manifest, that it occasioned a pause, during which the attorney, with his hand upon the dock, whispered with his client, and shook his head. I afterwards had it from that gentleman, that the prisoner's first affrighted words to him were, "*At all hazards, challenge that man!*" But that, as he would give no reason for it, and admitted that he had not even known my name until he heard it called and I appeared, it was not done.

Both on the ground already explained, that I wish to avoid reviving the unwholesome memory of that Murderer, and also because a detailed account of his long trial is by no means indispensable to my narrative, I shall confine myself closely to such incidents in the ten days and nights during which we, the Jury, were kept together, as directly bear on my own curious personal experience. It is in that, and not in the Murderer, that I seek to interest my reader. It is to that, and not to a page of the Newgate Calendar, that I beg attention.

I was chosen Foreman of the Jury. On the second morning of the trial, after evidence had been taken for two hours (I heard the church clocks strike), happening to cast my eyes over my brother jurymen, I found an inexplicable difficulty in counting them. I counted them several times, yet always with the same difficulty. In short, I made them one too many.

I touched the brother juryman whose place was next me, and I whispered to him, "Oblige me by counting us." He looked surprised by the request, but turned his head and counted. "Why," says he, suddenly, "we are Thirt—; but no, it's not possible. No. We are twelve."

According to my counting that day, we were always right in detail, but in the gross we were always one too many. There was no appearance—no figure—to account for it; but I had now an inward foreshadowing of the figure that was surely coming.

The Jury were housed at the London Tavern. We all slept in one large room on separate tables, and we were constantly in the charge and under the eye of the officer sworn to hold us in safe-keeping. I see no reason for suppressing the real name of that officer. He was intelligent, highly polite, and obliging, and (I was glad to hear) much respected in the City. He had an agreeable presence, good eyes, enviable black whiskers, and a fine sonorous voice. His name was Mr. Harker.

When we turned into our twelve beds at night, Mr. Harker's bed was drawn across the door. On the night of the second day, not being disposed to lie down, and seeing Mr. Harker sitting on his bed, I went and sat beside him, and offered him a pinch of snuff. As Mr. Harker's hand touched mine in taking it from my box, a peculiar shiver crossed him, and he said, "Who is this?"

Following Mr. Harker's eyes, and looking along the room, I saw again the figure I expected,—the second of the two men who had gone down Piccadilly. I rose, and advanced a few steps; then stopped, and looked round at Mr. Harker. He was quite unconcerned, laughed, and said in a pleasant way, "I thought for a moment we had a thirteenth juryman, without a bed. But I see it is the moonlight."

Making no revelation to Mr. Harker, but inviting him to

take a walk with me to the end of the room, I watched what the figure did. It stood for a few moments by the bedside of each of my eleven brother jurymen, close to the pillow. It always went to the right-hand side of the bed, and always passed out crossing the foot of the next bed. It seemed, from the action of the head, merely to look down pensively at each recumbent figure. It took no notice of me, or of my bed, which was that nearest to Mr. Harker's. It seemed to go out where the moonlight came in, through a high window, as by an aërial flight of stairs.

Next morning at breakfast, it appeared that everybody present had dreamed of the murdered man last night, except myself and Mr. Harker.

I now felt as convinced that the second man who had gone down Piccadilly was the murdered man (so to speak), as if it had been borne into my comprehension by his immediate testimony. But even this took place, and in a manner for which I was not at all prepared.

On the fifth day of the trial, when the case for the prosecution was drawing to a close, a miniature of the murdered man, missing from his bedroom upon the discovery of the deed, and afterwards found in a hiding-place where the Murderer had been seen digging, was put in evidence. Having been identified by the witness under examination, it was handed up to the Bench, and thence handed down to be inspected by the Jury. As an officer in a black gown was making his way with it across to me, the figure of the second man who had gone down Piccadilly impetuously started from the crowd, caught the miniature from the officer, and gave it to me with his own hands, at the same time saying, in a low and hollow tone,—before I saw the miniature, which was in a locket,— "*I was younger then, and my face was not then drained of blood.*" It also came between me and the brother juryman to whom I would have given the miniature, and between him and the brother juryman to whom he would have given it, and so passed it on through the whole of our number, and back into my possession. Not one of them, however, detected this.

At table, and generally when we were shut up together in Mr. Harker's custody, we had from the first naturally discussed the day's proceedings a good deal. On that fifth day, the case for the prosecution being closed, and we having that side of the question in a completed shape before us, our discussion was more animated and serious. Among our number was a vestryman,—the densest idiot I have ever seen at large, —who met the plainest evidence with the most preposterous objections, and who was sided with by two flabby parochial parasites; all the three impanelled from a district so delivered over to Fever that they ought to have been upon their own trial for five hundred Murders. When these mischievous blockheads were at their loudest, which was towards midnight, while some of us were already preparing for bed, I again saw the murdered man. He stood grimly behind them, beckoning to me. On my going towards them, and striking into the conversation, he immediately retired. This was the beginning of a separate series of appearances, confined to that long room in which *we* were confined. Whenever a knot of my brother jurymen laid their heads together, I saw the head of the murdered man among theirs. Whenever their comparison of notes was going against him, he would solemnly and irresistibly beckon to me.

It will be borne in mind that down to the production of the miniature, on the fifth day of the trial, I had never seen the Appearance in Court. Three changes occurred now that we entered on the case for the defence. Two of them I will mention together, first. The figure was now in Court continually, and it never there addressed itself to me, but always to the person who was speaking at the time. For instance : the throat of the murdered man had been cut straight across. In the opening speech for the defence, it was suggested that the deceased might have cut his own throat. At that very moment, the figure, with its throat in the dreadful condition

115

referred to (this it had concealed before), stood at the speaker's elbow, motioning across and across its windpipe, now with the right hand, now with the left, vigorously suggesting to the speaker himself the impossibility of such a wound having been self-inflicted by either hand. For another instance : a witness to character, a woman, deposed to the prisoner's being the most amiable of mankind. The figure at that instant stood on the floor before her, looking her full in the face, and pointing out the prisoner's evil countenance with an extended arm and an outstretched finger.

The third change now to be added impressed me strongly as the most marked and striking of all. I do not theorise upon it ; I accurately state it, and there leave it. Although the Appearance was not itself perceived by those whom it addressed, its coming close to such persons was invariably attended by some trepidation or disturbance on their part. It seemed to me as if it were prevented, by laws to which I was not amenable, from fully revealing itself to others, and yet as if it could invisibly, dumbly, and darkly overshadow their minds. When the leading counsel for the defence suggested that hypothesis of suicide, and the figure stood at the learned gentleman's elbow, frightfully sawing at its severed throat, it is undeniable that the counsel faltered in his speech, lost for a few seconds the thread of his ingenious discourse, wiped his forehead with his handkerchief, and turned extremely pale. When the witness to character was confronted by the Appearance, her eyes most certainly did follow the direction of its pointed finger, and rest in great hesitation and trouble upon the prisoner's face. Two additional illustrations will suffice. On the eighth day of the trial, after the pause which was every day made early in the afternoon for a few minutes' rest and refreshment, I came back into court with the rest of the Jury some little time before the return of the Judges. Standing up in the box and looking about me, I thought the figure was not there, until, chancing to raise my eyes to the gallery, I saw it bending forward, and leaning over a very decent woman, as if to assure itself whether the Judges had resumed their seats or not. Immediately afterwards that woman screamed, fainted, and was carried out. So with the venerable, sagacious, and patient Judge who conducted the trial. When the case was over, and he settled himself and his papers to sum up, the murdered man, entering by the Judges' door, advanced to his Lordship's desk, and looked eagerly over his shoulder at the pages of his notes which he was turning. A change came over his Lordship's face; his hand stopped; the peculiar shiver, that I knew so well, passed over him; he faltered, "Excuse me, gentlemen, for a few moments. .I am somewhat oppressed by the vitiated air;" and did not recover until he had drunk a glass of water.

Through all the monotony of six of those interminable ten days,—the same Judges and others on the bench, the same Murderer in the dock, the same lawyers at the table, the same tones of question and answer rising to the roof of the court, the same scratching of the Judge's pen, the same ushers going in and out, the same lights kindled at the same hour when there had been any natural light of day, the same foggy curtain outside the great windows when it was foggy, the same rain pattering and dripping when it was rainy, the same footmarks of turnkeys and prisoner day after day on the same sawdust, the same keys locking and un-locking the same heavy doors,—through all the wearisome monotony which made me feel as if I had been Foreman of the Jury for a vast period of time, and Piccadilly had flourished coevally with Babylon, the murdered man never lost one trace of his distinctness in my eyes, nor was he at any moment less distinct than anybody else. I must not omit, as a matter of fact, that I never once saw the Appearance which I call by the name of the murdered man look at the Murderer. Again and again I wondered, "Why does he not?" But he never did.

Nor did he look at me, after the production of the miniature, until the last closing minutes of the trial arrived.

We retired to consider, at seven minutes before ten at night. The idiotic vestryman and his two parochial parasites gave us so much trouble that we twice returned into Court to beg to have certain extracts from the Judge's notes re-read. Nine of us had not the smallest doubt about those passages, neither, I believe, had any one in the Court; the dunder-headed triumvirate, however, having no idea but obstruction, disputed them for that very reason. At length we prevailed, and finally the Jury returned into Court at ten minutes past twelve.

The murdered man at that time stood directly opposite the Jury-box, on the other side of the Court. As I took my place, his eyes rested on me with great attention; he seemed satisfied, and slowly shook a great gray veil, which he carried on his arm for the first time, over his head and whole form. As I gave in our verdict, "Guilty," the veil collapsed, all was gone, and his place was empty.

The Murderer, being asked by the Judge, according to usage, whether he had anything to say before sentence of Death should be passed upon him, indistinctly muttered something which was described in the leading newspapers of the following day as "a few rambling, incoherent, and half-audible words, in which he was understood to complain that he had not had a fair trial, because the Foreman of the Jury was prepossessed against him." The remarkable declaration that he really made was this: "*My Lord, I knew I was a doomed man, when the Foreman of my Jury came into the box. My Lord, I knew he would never let me off, because, before I was taken, he somehow got to my bedside in the night, woke me, and put a rope round my neck.*"

III

So every item of my plan was crowned with success. Our re-united life was more than all that we had looked forward to. Content and joy went with us as the wheels of the two carts went round, and the same stopped with us when the two carts stopped. I was as pleased and as proud as a Pug-Dog with his muzzle black-leaded for a evening party, and his tail extra curled by machinery.

But I had left something out of my calculations. Now, what had I left out? To help you to guess I'll say, a figure. Come. Make a guess and guess right. Nought? No. Nine? No. Eight? No. Seven? No. Six? No. Five? No. Four? No. Three? No. Two? No. One? No. Now I'll tell you what I'll do with you. I'll say it's another sort of figure altogether. There. Why then, says you, it's a mortal figure. No, nor yet a mortal figure. By such means you get yourself penned into a corner, and you can't help guessing a *im*mortal figure. That's about it. Why didn't you say so sooner?

Yes. It was a immortal figure that I had altogether left out of my calculations. Neither man's, nor woman's, but a child's. Girl's or boy's? Boy's. "I, says the sparrow, with my bow and arrow." Now you have got it.

We were down at Lancaster, and I had done two nights more than fair average business (though I cannot in honour

119

recommend them as a quick audience) in the open square there, near the end of the street where Mr. Sly's King's Arms and Royal Hotel stands. Mim's travelling giant, otherwise Pickleson, happened at the self-same time to be trying it on in the town. The genteel lay was adopted with him. No hint of a van. Green baize alcove leading up to Pickleson in a Auction Room. Printed poster, "Free list suspended, with the exception of that proud boast of an enlightened country, a free press. Schools admitted by private arrangement. Nothing to raise a blush in the cheek of youth or shock the most fastidious." Mim swearing most horrible and terrific, in a pink calico pay-place, at the slackness of the public. Serious handbill in the shops, importing that it was all but impossible to come to a right understanding of the history of David without seeing Pickleson.

I went to the Auction Room in question, and I found it entirely empty of everything but echoes and mouldiness, with the single exception of Pickleson on a piece of red drugget. This suited my purpose, as I wanted a private and confidential word with him, which was: "Pickleson. Owing much happiness to you, I put you in my will for a fypunnote; but, to save trouble, here's fourpunten down, which may equally suit your views, and let us so conclude the transaction." Pickleson, who up to that remark had had the dejected appearance of a long Roman rushlight that couldn't anyhow get lighted, brightened up at his top extremity, and made his acknowledgments in a way which (for him) was parliamentary eloquence. He likewise did add, that, having ceased to draw as a Roman, Mim had made proposals for his going in as a converted Indian Giant worked upon by The Dairyman's Daughter. This, Pickleson, having no acquaintance with the tract named after that young woman, and not being willing to couple gag with his serious views, had declined to do, thereby leading to words and the total stoppage of the unfortunate young man's beer. All of which, during the whole of the interview, was confirmed by the ferocious growling

120

of Mim down below in the pay-place, which shook the giant like a leaf.

But what was to the present point in the remarks of the travelling giant, otherwise Pickleson, was this: "Doctor Marigold,"—I give his words without a hope of conveying their feebleness,—"who is the strange young man that hangs about your carts?"—"The strange young *man?*" I gives him back, thinking that he meant her, and his languid circulation had dropped a syllable. "Doctor," he returns, with a pathos calculated to draw a tear from even a manly eye, "I am weak, but not so weak yet as that I don't know my words. I repeat them, Doctor. The strange young man." It then appeared that Pickleson, being forced to stretch his legs (not that they wanted it) only at times when he couldn't be seen for nothing, to wit in the dead of the night and towards daybreak, had twice seen hanging about my carts, in that same town of Lancaster where I had been only two nights, this same unknown young man.

It put me rather out of sorts. What it meant as to particulars I no more foreboded then than you forebode now, but it put me rather out of sorts. Howsoever, I made light of it to Pickleson, and I took leave of Pickleson, advising him to spend his legacy in getting up his stamina, and to continue to stand by his religion. Towards morning I kept a look out for the strange young man, and—what was more—I saw the strange young man. He was well dressed and well looking. He loitered very nigh my carts, watching them like as if he was taking care of them, and soon after daybreak turned and went away. I sent a hail after him, but he never started or looked round, or took the smallest notice.

We left Lancaster within an hour or two, on our way towards Carlisle. Next morning, at daybreak, I looked out again for the strange young man. I did not see him. But next morning I looked out again, and there he was once more. I sent another hail after him, but as before he gave not the slightest sign of being anyways disturbed. This put

121

a thought into my head. Acting on it I watched him in different manners and at different times not necessary to enter into, till I found that this strange young man was deaf and dumb.

The discovery turned me over, because I knew that a part of that establishment where she had been was allotted to young men (some of them well off), and I thought to myself, "If she favours him, where am I? and where is all that I have worked and planned for?" Hoping—I must confess to the selfishness—that she might *not* favour him, I set myself to find out. At last I was by accident present at a meeting between them in the open air, looking on leaning behind a fir-tree without their knowing of it. It was a moving meeting for all the three parties concerned. I knew every syllable that passed between them as well as they did. I listened with my eyes, which had come to be as quick and true with deaf and dumb conversation as my ears with the talk of people that can speak. He was a-going out to China as clerk in a merchant's house, which his father had been before him. He was in circumstances to keep a wife, and he wanted her to marry him and go along with him. She persisted, no. He asked if she didn't love him. Yes, she loved him dearly, dearly; but she could never disappoint her beloved, good, noble, generous, and I-don't-know-what-all father (meaning me, the Cheap Jack in the sleeved waistcoat), and she would stay with him, Heaven bless him! though it was to break her heart. Then she cried most bitterly, and that made up my mind.

While my mind had been in an unsettled state about her favouring this young man, I had felt that unreasonable towards Pickleson, that it was well for him he had got his legacy down. For I often thought, "If it hadn't been for this same weak-minded giant, I might never have come to trouble my head and wex my soul about the young man." But, once that I knew she loved him,—once that I had seen her weep for him,—it was a different thing. I made it right in my mind with Pickleson on the spot, and I shook myself together to do what was right by all.

She had left the young man by that time (for it took a few minutes to get me thoroughly well shook together), and the young man was leaning against another of the fir-trees,—of which there was a cluster,—with his face upon his arm. I touched him on the back. Looking up and seeing me, he says, in our deaf-and-dumb talk, "Do not be angry."

"I am not angry, good boy. I am your friend. Come with me."

I left him at the foot of the steps of the Library Cart, and I went up alone. She was drying her eyes.

"You have been crying, my dear."

"Yes, father."

"Why?"

"A headache."

"Not a heartache?"

"I said a headache, father."

"Doctor Marigold must prescribe for that headache."

She took up the book of my Prescriptions, and held it up with a forced smile; but seeing me keep still and look earnest, she softly laid it down again, and her eyes were very attentive.

"The Prescription is not there, Sophy."

"Where is it?",

"Here, my dear."

I brought her young husband in, and I put her hand in his, and my only farther words to both of them were these: "Doctor Marigold's last Prescription. To be taken for life." After which I bolted.

When the wedding come off, I mounted a coat (blue, and bright buttons), for the first and last time in all my days, and I give Sophy away with my own hand. There were only us three and the gentleman who had had charge of her for those two years. I give the wedding dinner of four in the Library Cart. Pigeon-pie, a leg of pickled pork, a pair of fowls, and suitable garden stuff. The best of drinks. I give them a speech, and the gentleman give us a speech, and all our jokes told, and the whole went off like a sky-rocket. In the course of the entertainment I explained to Sophy that I should keep the Library Cart as my living-cart when not upon the road, and that I should keep all her books for her just as they stood, till she come back to claim them. So she went to China with her young husband, and it was a parting sorrowful and heavy, and I got the boy I had another service; and so as of old, when my child and wife were gone, I went plodding along alone, with my whip over my shoulder, at the old horse's head.

Sophy wrote me many letters, and I wrote her many letters. About the end of the first year she sent me one in an unsteady hand: "Dearest father, not a week ago I had a darling little daughter, but I am so well that they let me write these words to you. Dearest and best father, I hope my child may not be deaf and dumb, but I do not yet know." When I wrote back, I hinted the question; but as Sophy never answered that question, I felt it to be a sad one, and I never repeated it. For a long time our letters were regular, but then they got irregular, through Sophy's husband being moved to another station, and through my being always on the move. But we were in one another's thoughts, I was equally sure, letters or no letters.

Five years, odd months, had gone since Sophy went away. I was still the King of the Cheap Jacks, and at a greater height of popularity than ever. I had had a first-rate autumn of it, and on the twenty-third of December, one thousand eight hundred and sixty-four, I found myself at Uxbridge, Middlesex, clean sold out. So I jogged up to London with the old horse, light and easy, to have my Christmas-eve and Christmas-day alone by the fire in the Library Cart, and then to buy a regular new stock of goods all round, to sell 'em again and get the money.

I am a neat hand at cookery, and I'll tell you what

VISION AND REALITY

I knocked up for my Christmas-eve dinner in the Library Cart. I knocked up a beefsteak-pudding for one, with two kidneys, a dozen oysters, and a couple of mushrooms thrown in. It's a pudding to put a man in good humour with everything, except the two bottom buttons of his waistcoat. Having relished that pudding and cleared away, I turned the lamp low, and sat down by the light of the fire, watching it as it shone upon the backs of Sophy's books.

Sophy's books so brought up Sophy's self, that I saw her touching face quite plainly, before I dropped off dozing by the fire. This may be a reason why Sophy, with her deaf-and-dumb child in her arms, seemed to stand silent by me all through my nap. I was on the road, off the road, in all sorts of places, North and South and West and East, Winds liked best and winds liked least, Here and there and gone astray, Over the hills and far away, and still she stood silent by me, with her silent child in her arms. Even when I woke with a start, she seemed to vanish, as if she had stood by me in that very place only a single instant before.

I had started at a real sound, and the sound was on the steps of the cart. It was the light hurried tread of a child, coming clambering up. That tread of a child had once been so familiar to me, that for half a moment I believed I was a-going to see a little ghost.

But the touch of a real child was laid upon the outer handle of the door, and the handle turned, and the door opened a little way, and a real child peeped in. A bright little comely girl with large dark eyes.

Looking full at me, the tiny creature took off her mite of a straw hat, and a quantity of dark curls fell all about her face. Then she opened her lips, and said in a pretty voice,

" Grandfather ! "

" Ah, my God ! " I cries out. " She can speak ! "

" Yes, dear grandfather. And I am to ask you whether there was ever any one that I remind you of ? "

In a moment Sophy was round my neck, as well as the

child, and her husband was a-wringing my hand with his face hid, and we all had to shake ourselves together before we could get over it. And when we did begin to get over it, and I saw the pretty child a-talking, pleased and quick and eager and busy, to her mother, in the signs that I had first taught her mother, the happy and yet pitying tears fell rolling down my face.

MUGBY JUNCTION

[1866]

CHAPTER I

I

'Guard! What place is this?"

"Mugby Junction, sir."

"A windy place!"

"Yes, it mostly is, sir."

"And looks comfortless indeed!"

"Yes, it generally does, sir."

"Is it a rainy night still?"

"Pours, sir."

"Open the door. I'll get out."

"You'll have, sir," said the guard, glistening with drops of wet, and looking at the tearful face of his watch by the light of his lantern as the traveller descended, "three minutes here."

"More, I think.—For I am not going on."

"Thought you had a through ticket, sir?"

"So I have, but I shall sacrifice the rest of it. I want my luggage."

"Please to come to the van and point it out, sir. Be good enough to look very sharp, sir. Not a moment to spare."

The guard hurried to the luggage van, and the traveller hurried after him. The guard got into it, and the traveller looked into it.

"Those two large black portmanteaus in the corner where your light shines. Those are mine."

"Name upon 'em, sir?"

"Barbox Brothers."

"Stand clear, sir, if you please. One. Two. Right!" Lamp waved. Signal lights ahead already changing. Shriek from engine. Train gone.

"Mugby Junction!" said the traveller, pulling up the woollen muffler round his throat with both hands. "At past three o'clock of a tempestuous morning! So!"

He spoke to himself. There was no one else to speak to. Perhaps, though there had been any one else to speak to, he would have preferred to speak to himself. Speaking to himself he spoke to a man within five years of fifty either way, who had turned grey too soon, like a neglected fire; a man of pondering habit, brooding carriage of the head, and suppressed internal voice; a man with many indications on him of having been much alone.

He stood unnoticed on the dreary platform, except by the rain and by the wind. Those two vigilant assailants made a rush at him. "Very well," said he, yielding. "It signifies nothing to me to what quarter I turn my face."

Thus, at Mugby Junction, at past three o'clock of a tempestuous morning, the traveller went where the weather drove him.

Not but what he could make a stand when he was so minded, for, coming to the end of the roofed shelter (it is of considerable extent at Mugby Junction), and looking out upon the dark night, with a yet darker spirit-wing of storm beating its wild way through it, he faced about, and held his own as ruggedly in the difficult direction as he had held it in the easier one. Thus, with a steady step, the traveller went up and down, up and down, up and down, seeking nothing and finding it.

A place replete with shadowy shapes, this Mugby Junction in the black hours of the four-and-twenty. Mysterious goods trains, covered with palls and gliding on like vast weird funerals, conveying themselves guiltily away from the presence of the few lighted lamps, as if their freight had come to a secret and unlawful end. Half-miles of coal pursuing in a Detective manner, following when they lead, stopping when they stop, backing when they back. Red-hot embers showering out upon the ground, down this dark avenue, and down the other, as if torturing fires were being raked clear; concurrently, shrieks and groans and grinds invading the ear, as if the tortured were at the height of their suffering. Iron-barred cages full of cattle jangling by midway, the drooping beasts with horns entangled, eyes frozen with terror, and mouths too: at least they have long icicles (or what seem so) hanging from their lips. Unknown languages in the air, conspiring in red, green, and white characters. An earthquake, accompanied with thunder and lightning, going up express to London. Now, all quiet, all rusty, wind and rain in possession, lamps extinguished, Mugby Junction dead and indistinct, with its robe drawn over its head, like Cæsar.

Now, too, as the belated traveller plodded up and down, a shadowy train went by him in the gloom which was no other than the train of a life. From whatsoever intangible deep cutting or dark tunnel it emerged, here it came, unsummoned and unannounced, stealing upon him, and passing away into obscurity. Here mournfully went by a child who had never had a childhood or known a parent, inseparable from a youth with a bitter sense of his nameless-ness, coupled to a man the enforced business of whose best years had been distasteful and oppressive, linked to an un-grateful friend, dragging after him a woman once beloved.

Attendant, with many a clank and wrench, were lumbering cares, dark meditations, huge, dim disappointments, monotonous years, a long jarring line of the discords of a solitary and unhappy existence.

" —Yours, sir?"

The traveller recalled his eyes from the waste into which they had been staring, and fell back a step or so under the abruptness, and perhaps the chance appropriateness, of the question.

" Oh! My thoughts were not here for the moment. Yes. Yes. Those two portmanteaus are mine. Are you a Porter?"

" On Porter's wages, sir. But I am Lamps."

The traveller looked a little confused.

" Who did you say you are?"

" Lamps, sir," showing an oily cloth in his hand, as further explanation.

" Surely, surely. Is there any hotel or tavern here?"

" Not exactly here, sir. There is a Refreshment Room here, but——" Lamps, with a mighty serious look, gave his head a warning roll that plainly added—" but it's a blessed circumstance for you that it's not open."

" You couldn't recommend it, I see, if it was available?"

" Ask your pardon, sir. If it was——?"

" Open?"

" It ain't my place, as a paid servant of the company, to give my opinion on any of the company's toepics,"—he pronounced it more like toothpicks,—" beyond lamp-ile and cottons," returned Lamps in a confidential tone; " but, speaking as a man, I wouldn't recommend my father (if he was to come to life again) to go and try how he'd be treated at the Refreshment Room. Not speaking as a man, no, I would *not*."

The traveller nodded conviction. " I suppose I can put up in the town? There is a town here?" For the traveller (though a stay-at-home compared with most travellers) had been, like many others, carried on the steam winds and the iron tides through that Junction before, without having ever, as one might say, gone ashore there.

"Oh yes, there's a town, sir ! Anyways, there's town enough to put up in. But," following the glance of the other at his luggage, "this is a very dead time of the night with us, sir. The deadest time. I might a'most call it our deadest and buriedest time."

"No porters about?"

"Well, sir, you see," returned Lamps, confidential again, "they in general goes off with the gas. That's how it is. And they seem to have overlooked you, through your walking to the furder end of the platform. But, in about twelve minutes or so, she may be up."

"Who may be up?"

"The three forty-two, sir. She goes off in a sidin' till the Up X passes, and then she"—here an air of hopeful vagueness pervaded Lamps — "does all as lays in her power."

"I doubt if I comprehend the arrangement."

"I doubt if anybody do, sir. She's a Parliamentary, sir. And, you see, a Parliamentary, or a Skirmishun——"

"Do you mean an Excursion?"

"That's it, sir. —A Parliamentary or a Skirmishun, she mostly *doos* go off into a sidin'. But, when she *can* get a chance, she's whistled out of it, and she's whistled up into doin' all as,"—Lamps again wore the air of a highly sanguine man who hoped for the best,—"all as lays in her power."

He then explained that porters on duty, being required to be in attendance on the Parliamentary matron in question, would doubtless turn up with the gas. In the meantime, if the gentleman would not very much object to the smell of lamp-oil, and would accept the warmth of his little room——
The gentleman, being by this time very cold, instantly closed with the proposal.

A greasy little cabin it was, suggestive, to the sense of smell, of a cabin in a Whaler. But there was a bright fire burning in its rusty grate, and on the floor there stood a wooden stand of newly trimmed and lighted lamps, ready for carriage service. They made a bright show, and their light, and the warmth, accounted for the popularity of the room, as borne witness to by many impressions of velveteen trousers on a form by the fire, and many rounded smears and smudges of stooping velveteen shoulders on the adjacent wall. Various untidy shelves accommodated a quantity of lamps and oil-cans, and also a fragrant collection of what looked like the pocket-handkerchiefs of the whole lamp family.

As Barbox Brothers (so to call the traveller on the warranty of his luggage) took his seat upon the form, and warmed his now ungloved hands at the fire, he glanced aside at a little deal desk, much blotched with ink, which his elbow touched. Upon it were some scraps of coarse paper, and a superannuated steel pen in very reduced and gritty circumstances.

From glancing at the scraps of paper, he turned involuntarily to his host, and said, with some roughness :

" Why, you are never a poet, man ? "

Lamps had certainly not the conventional appearance of one, as he stood modestly rubbing his squab nose with a handkerchief so exceedingly oily, that he might have been in the act of mistaking himself for one of his charges. He was a spare man of about the Barbox Brothers time of life, with his features whimsically drawn upward as if they were attracted by the roots of his hair. He had a peculiarly shining, transparent complexion, probably occasioned by constant oleaginous application; and his attractive hair, being cut short, and being grizzled, and standing straight up on end as if it in its turn were attracted by some invisible magnet above it, the top of his head was not very unlike a lamp-wick.

" But, to be sure, it's no business of mine," said Barbox

Brothers. "That was an impertinent observation on my part. Be what you like."

"Some people, sir," remarked Lamps in a tone of apology, "are sometimes what they don't like."

"Nobody knows that better than I do," sighed the other. "I have been what I don't like, all my life."

"When I first took, sir," resumed Lamps, "to composing little Comic-Songs-like—— "

Barbox Brothers eyed him with great disfavour.

"—To composing little Comic-Songs-like—and what was more hard—to singing 'em afterwards," said Lamps, "it went against the grain at that time, it did indeed."

Something that was not all oil here shining in Lamps's eye, Barbox Brothers withdrew his own a little disconcerted, looked at the fire, and put a foot on the top bar. "Why did you do it, then?" he asked after a short pause; abruptly enough, but in a softer tone. "If you didn't want to do it, why did you do it? Where did you sing them? Public-house?"

To which Mr. Lamps returned the curious reply: "Bed-side."

At this moment, while the traveller looked at him for elucidation, Mugby Junction started suddenly, trembled violently, and opened its gas eyes. "She's got up!" Lamps announced, excited. "What lays in her power is sometimes more, and sometimes less; but it's laid in her power to get up to-night, by George!"

The legend "Barbox Brothers," in large white letters on two black surfaces, was very soon afterwards trundling on a truck through a silent street, and, when the owner of the legend had shivered on the pavement half an hour, what time the porter's knocks at the Inn Door knocked up the whole town first, and the Inn last, he groped his way into the close air of a shut-up house, and so groped between the sheets of a shut-up bed that seemed to have been expressly refrigerated for him when last made.

II

"You remember me, Young Jackson?"

"What do I remember if not you? You are my first remembrance. It was you who told me that was my name. It was you who told me that on every twentieth of December my life had a penitential anniversary in it called a birthday. I suppose the last communication was truer than the first!"

"What am I like, Young Jackson?"

"You are like a blight all through the year to me. You hard-lined, thin-lipped, repressive, changeless woman with a wax mask on. You are like the Devil to me; most of all when you teach me religious things, for you make me abhor them."

"You remember me, Mr. Young Jackson?" In another voice from another quarter.

"Most gratefully, sir. You were the ray of hope and prospering ambition in my life. When I attended your course, I believed that I should come to be a great healer, and I felt almost happy—even though I was still the one boarder in the house with that horrible mask, and ate and drank in silence and constraint with the mask before me, every day. As I had done every, every, every day, through my school-time and from my earliest recollection."

"What am I like, Mr. Young Jackson?"

"You are like a Superior Being to me. You are like Nature beginning to reveal herself to me. I hear you again, as one of the hushed crowd of young men kindling under the power of your presence and knowledge, and you bring into my eyes the only exultant tears that ever stood in them."

"You remember Me, Mr. Young Jackson?" In a grating voice from quite another quarter.

"Too well. You made your ghostly appearance in my

136

life one day, and announced that its course was to be
suddenly and wholly changed. You showed me which was
my wearisome seat in the Galley of Barbox Brothers.
(When *they* were, if they ever were, is unknown to me;
there was nothing of them but the name when I bent to
the oar.) You told me what I was to do, and what to be
paid; you told me afterwards, at intervals of years, when I
was to sign for the Firm, when I became a partner, when I
became the Firm. I know no more of it, or of myself."

"What am I like, Mr. Young Jackson?"

"You are like my father, I sometimes think. You are
hard enough and cold enough so to have brought up an
acknowledged son. I see your scanty figure, your close brown
suit, and your tight brown wig; but you, too, wear a wax
mask to your death. You never by a chance remove it—it
never by a chance falls off—and I know no more of you."

Throughout this dialogue, the traveller spoke to himself at
his window in the morning, as he had spoken to himself at
the Junction overnight. And as he had then looked in the
darkness, a man who had turned grey too soon, like a neglected
fire: so he now looked in the sunlight, an ashier grey, like
a fire which the brightness of the sun put out.

The firm of Barbox Brothers had been some offshoot or
irregular branch of the Public Notary and bill-broking tree.
It had gained for itself a griping reputation before the days
of Young Jackson, and the reputation had stuck to it and
to him. As he had imperceptibly come into possession of
the dim den up in the corner of a court off Lombard Street,
on whose grimy windows the inscription Barbox Brothers had
for many long years daily interposed itself between him and
the sky, so he had insensibly found himself a personage
held in chronic distrust, whom it was essential to screw tight
to every transaction in which he engaged, whose word was
never to be taken without his attested bond, whom all dealers
openly set up guards and wards against. This character
had come upon him through no act of his own. It was as

if the original Barbox had stretched himself down upon the office floor, and had thither caused to be conveyed Young Jackson in his sleep, and had there effected a metempsychosis and exchange of persons with him. The discovery—aided in its turn by the deceit of the only woman he had ever loved, and the deceit of the only friend he had ever made: who eloped from him to be married together—the discovery, so followed up, completed what his earliest rearing had begun. He shrank, abashed, within the form of Barbox, and lifted up his head and heart no more.

But he did at last effect one great release in his condition. He broke the oar he had plied so long, and he scuttled and sank the galley. He prevented the gradual retirement of an old conventional business from him, by taking the initiative and retiring from it. With enough to live on (though, after all, with not too much), he obliterated the firm of Barbox Brothers from the pages of the Post-Office Directory and the face of the earth, leaving nothing of it but its name on two portmanteaus.

"For one must have some name in going about, for people to pick up," he explained to Mugby High Street, through the Inn window, "and that name at least was real once. Whereas, Young Jackson!—Not to mention its being a sadly satirical misnomer for Old Jackson."

He took up his hat and walked out, just in time to see, passing along on the opposite side of the way, a velveteen man, carrying his day's dinner in a small bundle that might have been larger without suspicion of gluttony, and pelting away towards the Junction at a great pace.

"There's Lamps!" said Barbox Brothers. "And by-the-bye——"

Ridiculous, surely, that a man so serious, so self-contained, and not yet three days emancipated from a routine of drudgery, should stand rubbing his chin in the street, in a brown study about Comic Songs.

"Bedside?" said Barbox Brothers testily. "Sings them

at the bedside? Why at the bedside, unless he goes to bed drunk? Does, I shouldn't wonder. But it's no business of mine. Let me see. Mugby Junction, Mugby Junction. Where shall I go next? As it came into my head last night when I woke from an uneasy sleep in the carriage and found myself here, I can go anywhere from here. Where shall I go? I'll go and look at the Junction by daylight. There's no hurry, and I may like the look of one Line better than another."

But there were so many Lines. Gazing down upon them from a bridge at the Junction, it was as if the concentrating Companies formed a great Industrial Exhibition of the works of extraordinary ground spiders that spun iron. And then so many of the Lines went such wonderful ways, so crossing and curving among one another, that the eye lost them. And then some of them appeared to start with the fixed intention of going five hundred miles, and all of a sudden gave it up at an insignificant barrier, or turned off into a workshop. And then others, like intoxicated men, went a little way very straight, and surprisingly slued round and came back again. And then others were so chock-full of trucks of coal, others were so blocked with trucks of casks, others were so gorged with trucks of ballast, others were so set apart for wheeled objects like immense iron cotton-reels: while others were so bright and clear, and others were so delivered over to rust and ashes and idle wheelbarrows out of work, with their legs in the air (looking much like their masters on strike), that there was no beginning, middle, or end to the bewilderment.

Barbox Brothers stood puzzled on the bridge, passing his right hand across the lines on his forehead, which multiplied while he looked down, as if the railway Lines were getting themselves photographed on that sensitive plate. Then was heard a distant ringing of bells and blowing of whistles. Then, puppet-looking heads of men popped out of boxes in perspective, and popped in again. Then, prodigious wooden

139

razors, set up on end, began shaving the atmosphere. Then, several locomotive engines in several directions began to scream and be agitated. Then, along one avenue a train came in. Then, along another two trains appeared that didn't come in, but stopped without. Then, bits of trains broke off. Then, a struggling horse became involved with them. Then, the locomotives shared the bits of trains, and ran away with the whole.

"I have not made my next move much clearer by this. No hurry. No need to make up my mind to-day, or to-morrow, nor yet the day after. I'll take a walk."

It fell out somehow (perhaps he meant it should) that the walk tended to the platform at which he had alighted, and to Lamps's room. But Lamps was not in his room. A pair of velveteen shoulders were adapting themselves to one of the impressions on the wall by Lamps's fireplace, but otherwise the room was void. In passing back to get out of the station again, he learnt the cause of this vacancy, by catching sight of Lamps on the opposite line of railway, skipping along the top of a train, from carriage to carriage, and catching lighted namesakes thrown up to him by a coadjutor.

"He is busy. He has not much time for composing or singing Comic Songs this morning, I take it."

The direction he pursued now was into the country, keeping very near to the side of one great Line of railway, and within easy view of others. "I have half a mind," he said, glancing around, "to settle the question from this point, by saying, 'I'll take this set of rails, or that, or t'other, and stick to it.' They separate themselves from the confusion, out here, and go their ways."

Ascending a gentle hill of some extent, he came to a few cottages. There, looking about him as a very reserved man might who had never looked about him in his life before, he saw some six or eight young children come merrily trooping and whooping from one of the cottages, and disperse. But not until they had all turned at the little garden-gate, and kissed their hands to a face at the upper window: a low window enough, although the upper, for the cottage had but a story of one room above the ground.

Now, that the children should do this was nothing; but that they should do this to a face lying on the sill of the open window, turned towards them in a horizontal position, and apparently only a face, was something noticeable. He looked up at the window again. Could only see a very fragile, though a very bright face, lying on one cheek on the window-sill. The delicate smiling face of a girl or woman. Framed in long bright brown hair, round which was tied a light blue band or fillet, passing under the chin.

He walked on, turned back, passed the window again, shyly glanced up again. No change. He struck off by a winding branch-road at the top of the hill—which he must otherwise have descended—kept the cottages in view, worked his way round at a distance so as to come out once more into the main road, and be obliged to pass the cottages again. The face still lay on the window-sill, but not so much inclined towards him. And now there were a pair of delicate hands too. They had the action of performing on some musical instrument, and yet it produced no sound that reached his ears.

"Mugby Junction must be the maddest place in England," said Barbox Brothers, pursuing his way down the hill. "The first thing I find here is a Railway Porter who composes comic songs to sing at his bedside. The second thing I find here is a face, and a pair of hands playing a musical instrument that *don't* play!"

The day was a fine bright day in the early beginning of November, the air was clear and inspiriting, and the landscape was rich in beautiful colours. The prevailing colours in the court off Lombard Street, London city, had been few and sombre. Sometimes, when the weather elsewhere was very bright indeed, the dwellers in those tents enjoyed a pepper-

and-salt-coloured day or two, but their atmosphere's usual wear was slate or snuff coloured.

He relished his walk so well that he repeated it next day. He was a little earlier at the cottage than on the day before, and he could hear the children up-stairs singing to a regular measure, and clapping out the time with their hands:

"Still, there is no sound of any musical instrument," he said, listening at the corner, "and yet I saw the performing hands again as I came by. What are the children singing? Why, good Lord, they can never be singing the multiplication table?"

They were, though, and with infinite enjoyment. The mysterious face had a voice attached to it, which occasionally led or set the children right. Its musical cheerfulness was delightful. The measure at length stopped, and was succeeded by a murmuring of young voices, and then by a short song which he made out to be about the current month of the year, and about what work it yielded to the labourers in the fields and farmyards. Then there was a stir of little feet, and the children came trooping and whooping out, as on the previous day. And again, as on the previous day, they all turned at the garden-gate, and kissed their hands—evidently to the face on the window-sill, though Barbox Brothers from his retired post of disadvantage at the corner could not see it.

But, as the children dispersed, he cut off one small straggler —a brown-faced boy with flaxen hair—and said to him:

"Come here, little one. Tell me, whose house is that?"

The child, with one swarthy arm held up across his eyes, half in shyness, and half ready for defence, said from behind the inside of his elbow:

"Phœbe's."

"And who," said Barbox Brothers, quite as much embarrassed by his part in the dialogue as the child could possibly be by his, "is Phœbe?"

To which the child made answer: "Why, Phœbe, of course."

The small but sharp observer had eyed his questioner closely, and had taken his moral measure. He lowered his guard, and rather assumed a tone with him : as having discovered him to be an unaccustomed person in the art of polite conversation.

"Phœbe," said the child, "can't be anybobby else but Phœbe. Can she?"

"No, I suppose not."

"Well," returned the child, "then why did you ask me?"

Deeming it prudent to shift his ground, Barbox Brothers took up a new position.

"What do you do there? Up there in that room where the open window is. What do you do there?"

"Cool," said the child.

"Eh?"

"Co-ò-ol," the child repeated in a louder voice, lengthening out the word with a fixed look and great emphasis, as much as to say: "What's the use of your having grown up, if you're such a donkey as not to understand me?"

"Ah! School, school," said Barbox Brothers. "Yes, yes, yes. And Phœbe teaches you?"

The child nodded.

"Good boy."

"Tound it out, have you?" said the child.

"Yes, I have found it out. What would you do with twopence, if I gave it you?"

"Pend it."

The knock-down promptitude of this reply leaving him not a leg to stand upon, Barbox Brothers produced the twopence with great lameness, and withdrew in a state of humiliation.

But, seeing the face on the window-sill as he passed the cottage, he acknowledged its presence there with a gesture, which was not a nod, not a bow, not a removal of his hat from his head, but was a diffident compromise between or struggle with all three. The eyes in the face seemed amused, or cheered, or both, and the lips modestly said: "Good day to you, sir."

143

"I find I must stick for a time to Mugby Junction," said Barbox Brothers with much gravity, after once more stopping on his return road to look at the Lines where they went their several ways so quietly. "I can't make up my mind yet which iron road to take. In fact, I must get a little accustomed to the Junction before I can decide."

So, he announced at the Inn that he was "going to stay on for the present," and improved his acquaintance with the Junction that night, and again next morning, and again next night and morning: going down to the station, mingling with the people there, looking about him down all the avenues of railway, and beginning to take an interest in the incomings and outgoings of the trains. At first, he often put his head into Lamps's little room, but he never found Lamps there. A pair or two of velveteen shoulders he usually found there, stooping over the fire, sometimes in connection with a clasped knife and a piece of bread and meat; but the answer to his inquiry, "Where's Lamps?" was, either that he was "t'other side the line," or, that it was his off-time, or (in the latter case) his own personal introduction to another Lamps who was not his lamps. However, he was not so desperately set upon seeing Lamps now, but he bore the disappointment. Nor did he so wholly devote himself to his severe application to the study of Mugby Junction as to neglect exercise. On the contrary, he took a walk every day, and always the same walk. But the weather turned cold and wet again, and the window was never open.

III

At length, after a lapse of some days, there came another streak of fine bright, hardy autumn weather. It was a Saturday. The window was open, and the children were gone. Not surprising, this, for he had patiently watched and waited at the corner until they *were* gone.

"Good day," he said to the face; absolutely getting his hat clear off his head this time.

"Good day to you, sir."

"I am glad you have a fine sky again to look at."

"Thank you, sir. It is kind of you."

"You are an invalid, I fear?"

"No, sir. I have very good health."

"But are you not always lying down?"

"Oh yes, I am always lying down, because I cannot sit up! But I am not an invalid."

The laughing eyes seemed highly to enjoy his great mistake.

"Would you mind taking the trouble to come in, sir? There is a beautiful view from this window. And you would see that I am not at all ill—being so good as to care."

It was said to help him, as he stood irresolute, but evidently desiring to enter, with his diffident hand on the latch of the garden-gate. It did help him, and he went in.

The room up-stairs was a very clean white room with a low roof. Its only inmate lay on a couch that brought her face to a level with the window. The couch was white too; and her simple dress or wrapper being light blue, like the band around her hair, she had an ethereal look, and a fanciful appearance of lying among clouds. He felt that she instinctively perceived him to be by habit a downcast, taciturn man; it was another help to him to have established that understanding so easily, and got it over.

There was an awkward constraint upon him, nevertheless, as he touched her hand, and took a chair at the side of her couch.

"I see now," he began, not at all fluently, "how you occupy your hand. Only seeing you from the path outside, I thought you were playing upon something."

She was engaged in very nimbly and dexterously making lace. A lace-pillow lay upon her breast; and the quick movements and changes of her hands upon it, as she worked, had given them the action he had misinterpreted.

"That is curious," she answered with a bright smile. "For I often fancy, myself, that I play tunes while I am at work."

"Have you any musical knowledge?"

She shook her head.

"I think I could pick out tunes, if I had any instrument, which could be made as handy to me as my lace-pillow. But I dare say I deceive myself. At all events, I shall never know."

"You have a musical voice. Excuse me; I have heard you sing."

"With the children?" she answered, slightly colouring. "Oh yes. I sing with the dear children, if it can be called singing."

Barbox Brothers glanced at the two small forms in the room, and hazarded the speculation that she was fond of children, and that she was learned in new systems of teaching them?

"Very fond of them," she said, shaking her head again; "but I know nothing of teaching, beyond the interest I have in it, and the pleasure it gives me when they learn. Perhaps your overhearing my little scholars sing some of their lessons has led you so far astray as to think me a grand teacher? Ah! I thought so! No, I have only read and been told about that system. It seemed so pretty and pleasant, and to treat them so like the merry Robins they are, that I took up with it in my little way. You don't need to be told what a very little way mine is, sir," she added with a glance at the small forms and round the room.

All this time her hands were busy at her lace-pillow. As they still continued so, and as there was a kind of substitute for conversation in the click and play of its pegs, Barbox Brothers took the opportunity of observing her. He guessed her to be thirty. The charm of her transparent face and large bright brown eyes was, not that they were passively resigned, but that they were actively and thoroughly cheerful.

Even her busy hands, which of their own thinness alone might have besought compassion, plied their task with a gay courage that made mere compassion an unjustifiable assumption of superiority, and an impertinence.

He saw her eyes in the act of rising towards his, and he directed his towards the prospect, saying: "Beautiful, indeed!"

"Most beautiful, sir. I have sometimes had a fancy that I would like to sit up, for once, only to try how it looks to an erect head. But what a foolish fancy that would be to encourage! It cannot look more lovely to any one than it does to me."

Her eyes were turned to it, as she spoke, with most delighted admiration and enjoyment. There was not a trace in it of any sense of deprivation.

"And those threads of railway, with their puffs of smoke and steam changing places so fast, make it so lively for me," she went on. "I think of the number of people who *can* go where they wish, on their business, or their pleasure; I remember that the puffs make signs to me that they are actually going while I look; and that enlivens the prospect with abundance of company, if I want company. There is the great Junction, too. I don't see it under the foot of the hill, but I can very often hear it, and I always know it is there. It seems to join me, in a way, to I don't know how many places and things that *I* shall never see."

With an abashed kind of idea that it might have already joined himself to something he had never seen, he said constrainedly: "Just so."

"And so you see, sir," pursued Phœbe, "I am not the invalid you thought me, and I am very well off indeed."

"You have a happy disposition," said Barbox Brothers: perhaps with a slight excusatory touch for his own disposition.

"Ah! But you should know my father," she replied. "His is the happy disposition!—Don't mind, sir!" For his reserve took the alarm at a step upon the stairs, and he distrusted that he would be set down for a troublesome intruder. "This is my father coming."

The door opened, and the father paused there.

"Why, Lamps!" exclaimed Barbox Brothers, starting from his chair. "How do you DO, Lamps?"

To which Lamps responded: "The gentleman for Nowhere! How do you DO, sir?"

And they shook hands, to the greatest admiration and surprise of Lamps's daughter.

"I have looked you up half-a-dozen times since that night," said Barbox Brothers, "but have never found you."

"So I've heerd on, sir, so I've heerd on," returned Lamps. "It's your being noticed so often down at the Junction, without taking any train, that has begun to get you the name among us of the gentleman for Nowhere. No offence in my having called you by it when took by surprise, I hope, sir?"

"None at all. It's as good a name for me as any other you could call me by. But may I ask you a question in the corner here?"

Lamps suffered himself to be led aside from his daughter's couch by one of the buttons of his velveteen jacket.

"Is this the bedside where you sing your songs?"

Lamps nodded.

The gentleman for Nowhere clapped him on the shoulder, and they faced about again.

"Upon my word, my dear," said Lamps then to his daughter, looking from her to her visitor, "it is such an amaze to me, to find you brought acquainted with this gentleman, that I must (if this gentleman will excuse me) take a rounder."

Mr. Lamps demonstrated in action what this meant, by pulling out his oily handkerchief rolled up in the form of a ball, and giving himself an elaborate smear, from behind the right ear, up the cheek, across the forehead, and down the other cheek to behind his left ear. After this operation he shone exceedingly.

"It's according to my custom when particular warmed up

Mugby Junction

by any agitation, sir," he offered by way of apology. "And really, I am throwed into that state of amaze by finding you brought acquainted with Phœbe, that I—that I think I will, if you'll excuse me, take another rounder." Which he did, seeming to be greatly restored by it.

They were now both standing by the side of her couch, and she was working at her lace-pillow. "Your daughter tells me," said Barbox Brothers, still in a half-reluctant shamefaced way, "that she never sits up."

"No, sir, nor never has done. You see, her mother (who died when she was a year and two months old) was subject to very bad fits, and as she had never mentioned to me that she *was* subject to fits, they couldn't be guarded against. Consequently, she dropped the baby when took, and this happened."

"It was very wrong of her," said Barbox Brothers with a knitted brow, "to marry you, making a secret of her infirmity."

"Well, sir!" pleaded Lamps in behalf of the long-deceased. "You see, Phœbe and me, we have talked that over too. And Lord bless us! Such a number on us has our infirmities, what with fits, and what with misfits, of one sort and another, that if we confessed to 'em all before we got married, most of us might never get married."

"Might not that be for the better?"

"Not in this case, sir," said Phœbe, giving her hand to her father.

"No, not in this case, sir," said her father, patting it between his own.

"You correct me," returned Barbox Brothers with a blush; "and I must look so like a Brute, that at all events it would be superfluous in me to confess to *that* infirmity. I wish you would tell me a little more about yourselves. I hardly know how to ask it of you, for I am conscious that I have a bad stiff manner, a dull discouraging way with me, but I wish you would."

149

"With all our hearts, sir," returned Lamps gaily for both. "And first of all, that you may know my name——"

"Stay!" interposed the visitor with a slight flush. "What signifies your name? Lamps is name enough for me. I like it. It is bright and expressive. What do I want more?"

"Why, to be sure, sir," returned Lamps. "I have in general no other name down at the Junction; but I thought, on account of your being here as a first-class single, in a private character, that you might——"

The visitor waved the thought away with his hand, and Lamps acknowledged the mark of confidence by taking another rounder.

"You are hard-worked, I take for granted?" said Barbox Brothers, when the subject of the rounder came out of it much dirtier than he went into it.

Lamps was beginning, "Not particular so"—when his daughter took him up.

"Oh yes, sir, he is very hard-worked. Fourteen, fifteen, eighteen hours a day. Sometimes twenty-four hours at a time."

"And you," said Barbox Brothers, "what with your school, Phœbe, and what with your lace-making——"

"But my school is a pleasure to me," she interrupted, opening her brown eyes wider, as if surprised to find him so obtuse. "I began it when I was but a child, because it brought me and other children into company, don't you see? *That* was not work. I carry it on still, because it keeps children about me. *That* is not work. I do it as love, not as work. Then my lace-pillow;" her busy hands had stopped, as if her argument required all her cheerful earnestness, but now went on again at the name; "it goes with my thoughts when I think, and it goes with my tunes when I hum any, and *that's* not work. Why, you yourself thought it was music, you know, sir. And so it is to me."

"Everything is!" cried Lamps radiantly. "Everything is music to her, sir."

150

" My father is, at any rate," said Phœbe, exultingly pointing her thin forefinger at him. "'There is more music in my father than there is in a brass band."

"I say! My dear! It's very fillyillially done, you know; but you are flattering your father," he protested, sparkling.

"No, I am not, sir, I assure you. No, I am not. If you could hear my father sing, you would know I am not. But you never will hear him sing, because he never sings to any one but me. However tired he is, he always sings to me when he comes home. When I lay here long ago, quite a poor little broken doll, he used to sing to me. More than that, he used to make songs, bringing in whatever little jokes we had between us. More than that, he often does so to this day. Oh! I'll tell of you, father, as the gentleman has asked about you. He is a poet, sir."

"I shouldn't wish the gentleman, my dear," observed Lamps, for the moment turning grave, "to carry away that opinion of your father, because it might look as if I was given to asking the stars in a molloncolly manner what they was up to. Which I wouldn't at once waste the time, and take the liberty, my dear."

"My father," resumed Phœbe, amending her text, "is always on the bright side, and the good side. You told me, just now, I had a happy disposition. How can I help it?"

"Well; but, my dear," returned Lamps argumentatively, "how can *I* help it? Put it to yourself, sir. Look at her. Always as you see her now. Always working—and after all, sir, for but a very few shillings a week—always contented, always lively, always interested in others, of all sorts. I said, this moment, she was always as you see her now. So she is, with a difference that comes to much the same. For, when it is my Sunday off and the morning bells have done ringing, I hear the prayers and thanks read in the touchingest way, and I have the hymns sung to me—so soft, sir, that you couldn't hear 'em out of this room—in notes that seem to me, I am sure, to come from Heaven and go back to it."

151

It might have been merely through the association of these words with their sacredly quiet time, or it might have been through the larger association of the words with the Redeemer's presence beside the bedridden; but here her dexterous fingers came to a stop on the lace-pillow, and clasped themselves around his neck as he bent down. There was great natural sensibility in both father and daughter, the visitor could easily see; but each made it, for the other's sake, retiring, not demonstrative; and perfect cheerfulness, intuitive or acquired, was either the first or second nature of both. In a very few moments Lamps was taking another rounder with his comical features beaming, while Phœbe's laughing eyes (just a glistening speck or so upon their lashes) were again directed by turns to him, and to her work, and to Barbox Brothers.

"When my father, sir," she said brightly, "tells you about my being interested in other people, even though they know nothing about me—which, by-the-bye, I told you myself—you ought to know how that comes about. That's my father's doing."

"No, it isn't!" he protested.

"Don't you believe him, sir; yes, it is. He tells me of everything he sees down at his work. You would be surprised what a quantity he gets together for me every day. He looks into the carriages, and tells me how the ladies are dressed—so that I know all the fashions! He looks into the carriages, and tells me what pairs of lovers he sees, and what new-married couples on their wedding trip—so that I know all about that! He collects chance newspapers and books—so that I have plenty to read! He tells me about the sick people who are travelling to try to get better—so that I know all about them! In short, as I began by saying, he tells me everything he sees and makes out down at his work, and you can't think what a quantity he does see and make out."

"As to collecting newspapers and books, my dear," said Lamps, "it's clear I can have no merit in that, because they're not my perquisites. You see, sir, it's this way: A Guard, he'll say to me, ' Hallo, here you are, Lamps. I've saved this paper for your daughter. How is she a-going on?' A Head-Porter, he'll say to me, ' Here! Catch hold, Lamps. Here's a couple of wollumes for your daughter. Is she pretty much where she were?' And that's what makes it double welcome, you see. If she had a thousand pound in a box, they wouldn't trouble themselves about her; but being what she is—that is, you understand," Lamps added, somewhat hurriedly, " not having a thousand pound in a box—they take thought for her. And as concerning the young pairs, married and unmarried, it's only natural I should bring home what little I can about *them*, seeing that there's not a Couple of either sort in the neighbourhood that don't come of their own accord to confide in Phœbe."

She raised her eyes triumphantly to Barbox Brothers as she said:

" Indeed, sir, that is true. If I could have got up and gone to church, I don't know how often I should have been a bridesmaid. But, if I could have done that, some girls in love might have been jealous of me, and, as it is, no girl is jealous of me. And my pillow would not have been half as ready to put the piece of cake under, as I always find it," she added, turning her face on it with a light sigh, and a smile at her father.

The arrival of a little girl, the biggest of the scholars, now led to an understanding on the part of Barbox Brothers, that she was the domestic of the cottage, and had come to take active measures in it, attended by a pail that might have extinguished her, and a broom three times her height. He therefore rose to take his leave, and took it; saying that, if Phœbe had no objection, he would come again.

He had muttered that he would come " in the course of his walks." The course of his walks must have been highly favourable to his return, for he returned after an interval of a single day.

"You thought you would never see me any more, I suppose?" he said to Phœbe as he touched her hand, and sat down by her couch.

"Why should I think so?" was her surprised rejoinder.

"I took it for granted you would mistrust me."

"For granted, sir? Have you been so much mistrusted?"

"I think I am justified in answering yes. But I may have mistrusted, too, on my part. No matter just now. We were speaking of the Junction last time. I have passed hours there since the day before yesterday."

"Are you now the gentleman for Somewhere?" she asked with a smile.

"Certainly for Somewhere; but I don't yet know Where. You would never guess what I am travelling from. Shall I tell you? I am travelling from my birthday."

Her hands stopped in her work, and she looked at him with incredulous astonishment.

"Yes," said Barbox Brothers, not quite easy in his chair, "from my birthday. I am, to myself, an unintelligible book with the earlier chapters all torn out, and thrown away. My childhood had no grace of childhood, my youth had no charm of youth, and what can be expected from such a lost beginning?" His eyes meeting hers as they were addressed intently to him, something seemed to stir within his breast, whispering: "Was this bed a place for the graces of childhood and the charms of youth to take to kindly? Oh, shame, shame!"

"It is a disease with me," said Barbox Brothers, checking himself, and making as though he had a difficulty in swallowing something, "to go wrong about that. I don't know how I came to speak of that. I hope it is because of an old misplaced confidence in one of your sex involving an old bitter treachery. I don't know. I am all wrong together."

Her hands quietly and slowly resumed their work. Glancing at her, he saw that her eyes were thoughtfully following them.

"I am travelling from my birthday," he resumed, "because it has always been a dreary day to me. My first free birthday coming round some five or six weeks hence, I am travelling to put its predecessors far behind me, and to try to crush the day—or, at all events, put it out of my sight—by heaping new objects on it.

As he paused, she looked at him; but only shook her head as being quite at a loss.

"This is unintelligible to your happy disposition," he pursued, abiding by his former phrase as if there were some lingering virtue of self-defence in it. "I knew it would be, and am glad it is. However, on this travel of mine (in which I mean to pass the rest of my days, having abandoned all thought of a fixed home), I stopped, as you have heard from your father, at the Junction here. The extent of its ramifications quite confused me as to whither I should go, *from* here. I have not yet settled, being still perplexed among so many roads. What do you think I mean to do? How many of the branching roads can you see from your window?"

Looking out, full of interest, she answered, "Seven."

"Seven," said Barbox Brothers, watching her with a grave smile. "Well! I propose to myself at once to reduce the gross number to those very seven, and gradually to fine them down to one—the most promising for me—and to take that."

"But how will you know, sir, which *is* the most promising?" she asked, with her brightened eyes roving over the view.

"Ah!" said Barbox Brothers with another grave smile, and considerably improving in his ease of speech. "To be sure. In this way. Where your father can pick up so much every day for a good purpose, I may once and again pick up a little for an indifferent purpose. The gentleman for Nowhere must become still better known at the Junction. He shall continue to explore it, until he attaches something that he has seen, heard, or found out, at the head of each of the seven roads, to the road itself. And so his choice of a road shall be determined by his choice among his discoveries."

155

Her hands still busy, she again glanced at the prospect, as if it comprehended something that had not been in it before, and laughed as if it yielded her new pleasure.

"But I must not forget," said Barbox Brothers, "(having got so far) to ask a favour. I want your help in this expedient of mine. I want to bring you what I pick up at the heads of the seven roads that you lie here looking out at, and to compare notes with you about it. May I? They say two heads are better than one. I should say myself that probably depends upon the heads concerned. But I am quite sure, though we are so newly acquainted, that your head and your father's have found out better things, Phœbe, than ever mine of itself discovered."

She gave him her sympathetic right hand, in perfect rapture with his proposal, and eagerly and gratefully thanked him.

"That's well!" said Barbox Brothers. "Again I must not forget (having got so far) to ask a favour. Will you shut your eyes?"

Laughing playfully at the strange nature of the request, she did so.

"Keep them shut," said Barbox Brothers, going softly to the door, and coming back. "You are on your honour, mind, not to open your eyes until I tell you that you may?"

"Yes! On my honour."

"Good. May I take your lace-pillow from you for a minute?"

Still laughing and wondering, she removed her hands from it, and he put it aside.

"Tell me. Did you see the puffs of smoke and steam made by the morning fast-train yesterday on road number seven from here?"

"Behind the elm-trees and the spire?"

"That's the road," said Barbox Brothers, directing his eyes towards it.

"Yes. I watched them melt away."

"Anything unusual in what they expressed?"

A PRESENT FOR PHŒBE

"No!" she answered merrily.

"Not complimentary to me, for I was in that train. I went—don't open your eyes—to fetch you this, from the great ingenious town. It is not half so large as your lace-pillow, and lies easily and lightly in its place. These little keys are like the keys of a miniature piano, and you supply the air required with your left hand. May you pick out delightful music from it, my dear! For the present—you can open your eyes now—good-bye!"

In his embarrassed way, he closed the door upon himself, and only saw, in doing so, that she ecstatically took the present to her bosom and caressed it. The glimpse gladdened his heart, and yet saddened it; for so might she, if her youth had flourished in its natural course, have taken to her breast that day the slumbering music of her own child's voice.

CHAPTER II

WITH good-will and earnest purpose, the gentleman for Nowhere began, on the very next day, his researches at the heads of the seven roads. The results of his researches, as he and Phœbe afterwards set them down in fair writing, hold their due places in this veracious chronicle. But they occupied a much longer time in the getting together than they ever will in the perusal. And this is probably the case with most reading matter, except when it is of that highly beneficial kind (for Posterity) which is "thrown off in a few moments of leisure" by the superior poetic geniuses who scorn to take prose pains.

It must be admitted, however, that Barbox by no means hurried himself. His heart being in his work of good-nature, he revelled in it. There was the joy, too (it was a true joy to him), of sometimes sitting by, listening to Phœbe as she picked out more and more discourse from her musical instrument, and as her natural taste and ear refined daily upon her first discoveries. Besides being a pleasure, this was an occupation, and in the course of weeks it consumed hours. It resulted that his dreaded birthday was close upon him before he had troubled himself any more about it.

The matter was made more pressing by the unforeseen circumstance that the councils held (at which Mr. Lamps, beaming most brilliantly, on a few rare occasions assisted) respecting the road to be selected were, after all, in nowise assisted by his investigations. For, he had connected this interest with this road, or that interest with the other, but could deduce no reason from it for giving any road the preference. Consequently, when the last council was holden, that part of the business stood, in the end, exactly where it had stood in the beginning.

"But, sir," remarked Phœbe, "we have only six roads after all. Is the seventh road dumb?"

"The seventh road? Oh!" said Barbox Brothers, rubbing his chin. "That is the road I took, you know, when I went to get your little present. That is *its* story, Phœbe."

"Would you mind taking that road again, sir?" she asked with hesitation.

"Not in the least; it is a great high-road after all."

"I should like you to take it," returned Phœbe with a persuasive smile, "for the love of that little present which must ever be so dear to me. I should like you to take it, because that road can never be again like any other road to me. I should like you to take it, in remembrance of your having done me so much good: of your having made me so much happier! If you leave me by the road you travelled when you went to do me this great kindness," sounding a faint chord as she spoke, "I shall feel, lying here watching at my window, as if it must conduct you to a prosperous end, and bring you back some day."

"It shall be done, my dear; it shall be done."

So at last the gentleman for Nowhere took a ticket for Somewhere, and his destination was the great ingenious town.

He had loitered so long about the Junction that it was the eighteenth of December when he left it. "High time," he reflected, as he seated himself in the train, "that I started in earnest! Only one clear day remains between me and the day I am running away from. I'll push onward for the hill-country to-morrow. I'll go to Wales."

It was with some pains that he placed before himself the undeniable advantages to be gained in the way of novel occupation for his senses from misty mountains, swollen streams, rain, cold, a wild seashore, and rugged roads. And yet he scarcely made them out as distinctly as he could have wished. Whether the poor girl, in spite of her new resource, her music, would have any feeling of loneliness upon her now—just at first—that she had not had before; whether she saw those very puffs of steam and smoke that he saw, as he sat in the train thinking of her; whether her face would have any pensive shadow on it as they died out of the distant view from her window; whether, in telling him he had done her so much good, she had not unconsciously corrected his old moody bemoaning of his station in life, by setting him thinking that a man might be a great healer, if he would, and yet not be a great doctor; these and other similar meditations got between him and his Welsh picture. There was within him, too, that dull sense of vacuity which follows separation from an object of interest, and cessation of a pleasant pursuit; and this sense, being quite new to him, made him restless. Further, in losing Mugby Junction, he had found himself again; and he was not the more enamoured of himself for having lately passed his time in better company.

But surely here, not far ahead, must be the great ingenious town. This crashing and clashing that the train was undergoing, and this coupling on to it of a multitude of new echoes, could mean nothing less than approach to the great station. It did mean nothing less. After some stormy flashes of town lightning, in the way of swift revelations of red brick blocks of houses, high red brick chimney-shafts, vistas of red brick railway arches, tongues of fire, blocks of smoke, valleys of canal, and hills of coal, there came the thundering in at the journey's end.

Having seen his portmanteaus safely housed in the hotel he chose, and having appointed his dinner hour, Barbox

A MEMORABLE WALK

Brothers went out for a walk in the busy streets. And now it began to be suspected by him that Mugby Junction was a Junction of many branches, invisible as well as visible, and had joined him to an endless number of by-ways. For, whereas he would, but a little while ago, have walked these streets blindly brooding, he now had eyes and thoughts for a new external world. How the many toiling people lived, and loved, and died; how wonderful it was to consider the various trainings of eye and hand, the nice distinctions of sight and touch, that separated them into classes of workers, and even into classes of workers at subdivisions of one complete whole which combined their many intelligences and forces, though of itself but some cheap object of use or ornament in common life; how good it was to know that such assembling in a multitude on their part, and such contribution of their several dexterities towards a civilising end, did not deteriorate them as it was the fashion of the supercilious Mayflies of humanity to pretend, but engendered among them a self-respect, and yet a modest desire to be much wiser than they were (the first evinced in their well-balanced bearing and manner of speech when he stopped to ask a question; the second, in the announcements of their popular studies and amusements on the public walls); these considerations, and a host of such, made his walk a memorable one. "I too am but a little part of a great whole," he began to think; "and to be serviceable to myself and others, or to be happy, I must cast my interest into, and draw it out of, the common stock."

Although he had arrived at his journey's end for the day by noon, he had since insensibly walked about the town so far and so long that the lamp-lighters were now at their work in the streets, and the shops were sparkling up brilliantly. Thus reminded to turn towards his quarters, he was in the act of doing so, when a very little hand crept into his, and a very little voice said:

"Oh! if you please, I am lost!"

He looked down, and saw a very little fair-haired girl.

"Yes," she said, confirming her words with a serious nod. "I am indeed. I am lost!"

Greatly perplexed, he stopped, looked about him for help, descried none, and said, bending low:

"Where do you live, my child?"

"I don't know where I live," she returned. "I am lost."

"What is your name?"

"Polly."

"What is your other name?"

The reply was prompt, but unintelligible.

Imitating the sound as he caught it, he hazarded the guess, "Trivits."

"Oh no!" said the child, shaking her head. "Nothing like that."

"Say it again, little one."

An unpromising business. For this time it had quite a different sound.

He made the venture, "Paddens?"

"Oh no!" said the child. "Nothing like that."

"Once more. Let us try it again, dear."

A most hopeless business. This time it swelled into four syllables. "It can't be Tappitarver?" said Barbox Brothers, rubbing his head with his hat in discomfiture.

"No! It ain't," the child quietly assented.

On her trying this unfortunate name once more, with extraordinary efforts at distinctness, it swelled into eight syllables at least.

"Ah! I think," said Barbox Brothers with a desperate air of resignation, "that we had better give it up."

"But I am lost," said the child, nestling her little hand more closely in his, "and you'll take care of me, won't you?"

If ever a man were disconcerted by division between compassion on the one hand, and the very imbecility of irresolution on the other, here the man was. "Lost!" he repeated,

162

looking down at the child. "I am sure *I* am. What is to be done?"

"Where do *you* live?" asked the child, looking up at him wistfully.

"Over there," he answered, pointing vaguely in the direction of his hotel.

"Hadn't we better go there?" said the child.

"Really," he replied, "I don't know but what we had."

So they set off, hand-in-hand. He, through comparison of himself against his little companion, with a clumsy feeling on him as if he had just developed into a foolish giant. She, clearly elevated in her own tiny opinion by having got him so neatly out of his embarrassment.

"We are going to have dinner when we get there, I suppose?" said Polly.

"Well," he rejoined, "I—— Yes, I suppose we are."

"Do you like your dinner?" asked the child.

"Why, on the whole," said Barbox Brothers, "yes, I think I do."

"I do mine," said Polly. "Have you any brothers and sisters?"

"No. Have you?"

"Mine are dead."

"Oh!" said Barbox Brothers. With that absurd sense of unwieldiness of mind and body weighing him down, he would have not known how to pursue the conversation beyond this curt rejoinder, but that the child was always ready for him.

"What," she asked, turning her soft hand coaxingly in his, "are you going to do to amuse me after dinner?"

"Upon my soul, Polly," exclaimed Barbox Brothers, very much at a loss, "I have not the slightest idea!"

"Then I tell you what," said Polly. "Have you got any cards at your house?"

"Plenty," said Barbox Brothers in a boastful vein.

"Very well. Then I'll build houses, and you shall look at me. You mustn't blow, you know."

163

"Oh no," said Barbox Brothers. "No, no, no. No blowing. Blowing's not fair."

He flattered himself that he had said this pretty well for an idiotic monster; but the child, instantly perceiving the awkwardness of his attempt to adapt himself to her level, utterly destroyed his hopeful opinion of himself by saying compassionately: "What a funny man you are!"

Feeling, after this melancholy failure, as if he every minute grew bigger and heavier in person, and weaker in mind, Barbox gave himself up for a bad job. No giant ever submitted more meekly to be led in triumph by all-conquering Jack than he to be bound in slavery to Polly.

"Do you know any stories?" she asked him.

He was reduced to the humiliating confession: "No."

"What a dunce you must be, mustn't you?" said Polly.

He was reduced to the humiliating confession: "Yes."

"Would you like me to teach you a story? But you must remember it, you know, and be able to tell it right to somebody else afterwards."

He professed that it would afford him the highest mental gratification to be taught a story, and that he would humbly endeavour to retain it in his mind. Whereupon Polly, giving her hand a new little turn in his, expressive of settling down for enjoyment, commenced a long romance, of which every relishing clause began with the words: "So this," or, "And so this." As, "So this boy;" or, "So this fairy;" or, "And so this pie was four yards round, and two yards and a quarter deep." The interest of the romance was derived from the intervention of this fairy to punish this boy for having a greedy appetite. To achieve which purpose, this fairy made this pie, and this boy ate and ate and ate, and his cheeks swelled and swelled and swelled. There were many tributary circumstances, but the forcible interest culminated in the total consumption of this pie, and the bursting of this boy. Truly he was a fine sight, Barbox Brothers, with serious attentive face, and ear bent down, much jostled on the

164

pavements of the busy town, but afraid of losing a single incident of the epic, lest he should be examined in it by-and-by, and found deficient.

Thus they arrived at the hotel. And there he had to say at the bar, and said awkwardly enough: "I have found a little girl!"

The whole establishment turned out to look at the little girl. Nobody knew her; nobody could make out her name, as she set it forth—except one chambermaid, who said it was Constantinople—which it wasn't.

"I will dine with my young friend in a private room," said Barbox Brothers to the hotel authorities, "and perhaps you will be so good as to let the police know that the pretty baby is here. I suppose she is sure to be inquired for soon, if she has not been already. Come along, Polly."

Perfectly at ease and peace, Polly came along, but, finding the stairs rather stiff work, was carried up by Barbox Brothers. The dinner was a most transcendent success, and the Barbox sheepishness, under Polly's directions how to mince her meat for her, and how to diffuse gravy over the plate with a liberal and equal hand, was another fine sight.

"And now," said Polly, "while we are at dinner, you be good, and tell me that story I taught you."

With the tremors of a Civil Service examination upon him, and very uncertain indeed, not only as to the epoch at which the pie appeared in history, but also as to the measurements of that indispensable fact, Barbox Brothers made a shaky beginning, but under encouragement did very fairly. There was a want of breadth observable in his rendering of the cheeks, as well as the appetite, of the boy; and there was a certain tameness in his fairy, referable to an under-current of desire to account for her. Still, as the first lumbering performance of a good-humoured monster, it passed muster.

"I told you to be good," said Polly, "and you are good, ain't you?"

"I hope so," replied Barbox Brothers.

Such was his deference that Polly, elevated on a platform of sofa cushions in a chair at his right hand, encouraged him with a pat or two on the face from the greasy bowl of her spoon, and even with a gracious kiss. In getting on her feet upon her chair, however, to give him this last reward, she toppled forward among the dishes, and caused him to exclaim, as he effected her rescue: "Gracious Angels! Whew! I thought we were in the fire, Polly!"

"What a coward you are, ain't you?" said Polly when replaced.

"Yes, I am rather nervous," he replied. "Whew! Don't, Polly! Don't flourish your spoon, or you'll go over sideways. Don't tilt up your legs when you laugh, Polly, or you'll go over backwards. Whew! Polly, Polly, Polly," said Barbox Brothers, nearly succumbing to despair, "we are environed with dangers!"

Indeed, he could descry no security from the pitfalls that were yawning for Polly, but in proposing to her, after dinner, to sit upon a low stool. "I will, if you will," said Polly. So, as peace of mind should go before all, he begged the waiter to wheel aside the table, bring a pack of cards, a couple of footstools, and a screen, and close in Polly and himself before the fire, as it were in a snug room within the room. Then, finest sight of all, was Barbox Brothers on his footstool, with a pint decanter on the rug, contemplating Polly as she built successfully, and growing blue in the face with holding his breath, lest he should blow the house down.

"How you stare, don't you?" said Polly in a houseless pause.

Detected in the ignoble fact, he felt obliged to admit, apologetically: "I am afraid I was looking rather hard at you, Polly."

"Why do you stare?" asked Polly.

"I cannot," he murmured to himself, "recall why.—I don't know, Polly."

"You must be a simpleton to do things and not know why, mustn't you?" said Polly.

In spite of which reproof, he looked at the child again intently, as she bent her head over her card structure, her rich curls shading her face. "It is impossible," he thought, "that I can ever have seen this pretty baby before. Can I have dreamed of her? In some sorrowful dream?"

He could make nothing of it. So he went into the building trade as a journeyman under Polly, and they built three stories high, four stories high; even five.

"I say! Who do you think is coming?" asked Polly, rubbing her eyes after tea.

He guessed: "The waiter?"

"No," said Polly, "the dustman. I am getting sleepy."

A new embarrassment for Barbox Brothers!

"I don't think I am going to be fetched to-night," said Polly. "What do you think?"

He thought not, either. After another quarter of an hour, the dustman not merely impending, but actually arriving, recourse was had to the Constantinopolitan chambermaid: who cheerily undertook that the child should sleep in a comfortable and wholesome room, which she herself would share.

"And I know you will be careful, won't you," said Barbox Brothers, as a new fear dawned upon him, "that she don't fall out of bed?"

Polly found this so highly entertaining that she was under the necessity of clutching him round the neck with both arms as he sat on his footstool picking up the cards, and rocking him to and fro, with her dimpled chin on his shoulder.

"Oh, what a coward you are, ain't you?" said Polly. "Do *you* fall out of bed?"

"N—not generally, Polly."

"No more do I."

With that, Polly gave him a reassuring hug or two to keep him going, and then giving that confiding mite of a

167

hand of hers to be swallowed up in the hand of the Constantinopolitan chambermaid, trotted off, chattering, without a vestige of anxiety.

He looked after her, had the screen removed and the table and chairs replaced, and still looked after her. He paced the room for half an hour. "A most engaging little creature, but it's not that. A most winning little voice, but it's not that. That has much to do with it, but there is something more. How can it be that I seem to know this child? What was it she imperfectly recalled to me when I felt her touch in the street, and, looking down at her, saw her looking up at me?"

"Mr. Jackson!"

With a start he turned towards the sound of the subdued voice, and saw his answer standing at the door.

"Oh, Mr. Jackson, do not be severe with me! Speak a word of encouragement to me, I beseech you."

"You are Polly's mother."

"Yes."

Yes. Polly herself might come to this, one day. As you see what the rose was in its faded leaves; as you see what the summer growth of the woods was in their wintry branches; so Polly might be traced, one day, in a careworn woman like this, with her hair turned grey. Before him were the ashes of a dead fire that had once burned bright. This was the woman he had loved. This was the woman he had lost. Such had been the constancy of his imagination to her, so had Time spared her under its withholding, that now, seeing how roughly the inexorable hand had struck her, his soul was filled with pity and amazement.

He led her to a chair, and stood leaning on a corner of the chimney-piece, with his head resting on his hand, and his face half averted.

"Did you see me in the street, and show me to your child?" he asked.

"Yes."

"Is the little creature, then, a party to deceit?"

"I hope there is no deceit. I said to her, 'We have lost our way, and I must try to find mine by myself. Go to that gentleman, and tell him you are lost. You shall be fetched by-and-by.' Perhaps you have not thought how very young she is?"

"She is very self-reliant."

"Perhaps because she is so young."

He asked, after a short pause, "Why did you do this?"

"Oh, Mr. Jackson, do you ask me? In the hope that you might see something in my innocent child to soften your heart towards me. Not only towards me, but towards my husband."

He suddenly turned about, and walked to the opposite end of the room. He came back again with a slower step, and resumed his former attitude, saying:

"I thought you had emigrated to America?"

"We did. But life went ill with us there, and we came back."

"Do you live in this town?"

"Yes. I am a daily teacher of music here. My husband is a book-keeper."

"Are you—forgive my asking—poor?"

"We earn enough for our wants. That is not our distress. My husband is very, very ill of a lingering disorder. He will never recover——"

"You check yourself. If it is for want of the encouraging word you spoke of, take it from me. I cannot forget the old time, Beatrice."

"God bless you!" she replied with a burst of tears, and gave him her trembling hand.

"Compose yourself. I cannot be composed if you are not, for to see you weep distresses me beyond expression. Speak freely to me. Trust me."

She shaded her face with her veil, and after a little while spoke calmly. Her voice had the ring of Polly's,

"It is not that my husband's mind is at all impaired by his bodily suffering, for I assure you that is not the case. But in his weakness, and in his knowledge that he is incurably ill, he cannot overcome the ascendency of one idea. It preys upon him, embitters every moment of his painful life, and will shorten it."

She stopping, he said again: "Speak freely to me. Trust me."

"We have had five children before this darling, and they all lie in their little graves. He believes that they have withered away under a curse, and that it will blight this child like the rest."

"Under what curse?"

"Both I and he have it on our conscience that we tried you very heavily, and I do not know but that, if I were as ill as he, I might suffer in my mind as he does. This is the constant burden:—'I believe, Beatrice, I was the only friend that Mr. Jackson ever cared to make, though I was so much his junior. The more influence he acquired in the business, the higher he advanced me, and I was alone in his private confidence. I came between him and you, and I took you from him. We were both secret, and the blow fell when he was wholly unprepared. The anguish it caused a man so compressed must have been terrible; the wrath it awakened inappeasable. So, a curse came to be invoked on our poor pretty little flowers, and they fall.'"

"And you, Beatrice," he asked, when she had ceased to speak, and there had been a silence afterwards, "how say you?"

"Until within these few weeks I was afraid of you, and I believed that you would never, never forgive."

"Until within these few weeks," he repeated. "Have you changed your opinion of me within these few weeks?"

"Yes."

"For what reason?"

"I was getting some pieces of music in a shop in this

town, when, to my terror, you came in. As I veiled my face and stood in the dark end of the shop, I heard you explain that you wanted a musical instrument for a bedridden girl. Your voice and manner were so softened, you showed such interest in its selection, you took it away yourself with so much tenderness of care and pleasure, that I knew you were a man with a most gentle heart. Oh, Mr. Jackson, Mr. Jackson, if you could have felt the refreshing rain of tears that followed for me!"

Was Phœbe playing at that moment on her distant couch? He seemed to hear her.

"I inquired in the shop where you lived, but could get no information. As I had heard you say that you were going back by the next train (but you did not say where), I resolved to visit the station at about that time of day, as often as I could, between my lessons, on the chance of seeing you again. I have been there very often, but saw you no more until to-day. You were meditating as you walked the street, but the calm expression of your face emboldened me to send my child to you. And when I saw you bend your head to speak tenderly to her, I prayed to GOD to forgive me for having ever brought a sorrow on it. I now pray to you to forgive me, and to forgive my husband. I was very young, he was young too, and, in the ignorant hardihood of such a time of life, we don't know what we do to those who have undergone more discipline. You generous man! You good man! So to raise me up and make nothing of my crime against you!"—for he would not see her on her knees, and soothed her as a kind father might have soothed an erring daughter—"thank you, bless you, thank you!"

When he next spoke, it was after having drawn aside the window curtain and looked out awhile. Then he only said:

"Is Polly asleep?"

"Yes. As I came in, I met her going away up-stairs, and put her to bed myself."

"Leave her with me for to-morrow, Beatrice, and write me your address on this leaf of my pocket-book. In the evening I will bring her home to you—and to her father."

"Hallo!" cried Polly, putting her saucy sunny face in at the door next morning when breakfast was ready: "I thought I was fetched last night?"

"So you were, Polly, but I asked leave to keep you here for the day, and to take you home in the evening."

"Upon my word!" said Polly. "You are very cool, ain't you?"

However, Polly seemed to think it a good idea, and added:

"I suppose I must give you a kiss, though you *are* cool."

The kiss given and taken, they sat down to breakfast in a highly conversational tone.

"Of course, you are going to amuse me?" said Polly.

"Oh, of course!" said Barbox Brothers.

In the pleasurable height of her anticipations, Polly found it indispensable to put down her piece of toast, cross one of her little fat knees over the other, and bring her little fat right hand down into her left hand with a business-like slap. After this gathering of herself together, Polly, by that time a mere heap of dimples, asked in a wheedling manner:

"What are we going to do, you dear old thing?"

"Why, I was thinking," said Barbox Brothers, "—but are you fond of horses, Polly?"

"Ponies, I am," said Polly, "especially when their tails are long. But horses—n—no—too big, you know."

"Well," pursued Barbox Brothers, in a spirit of grave mysterious confidence adapted to the importance of the consultation, "I did see yesterday, Polly, on the walls, pictures of two long-tailed ponies, speckled all over——"

"No, no, no!" cried Polly, in an ecstatic desire to linger on the charming details. "Not speckled all over!"

"Speckled all over. Which ponies jump through hoops——"

"No, no, NO!" cried Polly as before. "They never jump through hoops!"

"Yes, they do. Oh, I assure you they do! And eat pie in pinafores——"

"Ponies eating pie in pinafores!" said Polly. "What a story-teller you are, ain't you?"

"Upon my honour. —And fire off guns."

(Polly hardly seemed to see the force of the ponies resorting to fire-arms.)

"And I was thinking," pursued the exemplary Barbox, "that if you and I were to go to the Circus where these ponies are, it would do our constitutions good."

"Does that mean amuse us?" inquired Polly. "What long words you do use, don't you?"

Apologetic for having wandered out of his depth, he replied:

"That means amuse us. That is exactly what it means. There are many other wonders besides the ponies, and we shall see them all. Ladies and gentlemen in spangled dresses, and elephants and lions and tigers."

Polly became observant of the teapot, with a curled-up nose indicating some uneasiness of mind.

"They never get out, of course," she remarked as a mere truism.

"The elephants and lions and tigers? Oh, dear no!"

"Oh, dear no!" said Polly. "And of course nobody's afraid of the ponies shooting anybody."

"Not the least in the world."

"No, no, not the least in the world," said Polly.

"I was also thinking," proceeded Barbox, "that if we were to look in at the toy-shop, to choose a doll——"

"Not dressed!" cried Polly with a clap of her hands. "No, no, NO, not dressed!"

"Full-dressed. Together with a house, and all things necessary for house-keeping——"

Polly gave a little scream, and seemed in danger of falling into a swoon of bliss.

"What a darling you are!" she languidly exclaimed, leaning back in her chair. "Come and be hugged, or I must come and hug you."

This resplendent programme was carried into execution with the utmost rigour of the law. It being essential to make the purchase of the doll its first feature—or that lady would have lost the ponies—the toy-shop expedition took precedence. Polly in the magic warehouse, with a doll as large as herself under each arm, and a neat assortment of some twenty more on view upon the counter, did indeed present a spectacle of indecision not quite compatible with unalloyed happiness, but the light cloud passed. The lovely specimen oftenest chosen, oftenest rejected, and finally abided by, was of Circassian descent, possessing as much boldness of beauty as was reconcilable with extreme feebleness of mouth, and combining a sky-blue silk pelisse with rose-coloured satin trousers, and a black velvet hat: which this fair stranger to our northern shores would seem to have founded on the portraits of the late Duchess of Kent. The name this distinguished foreigner brought with her from beneath the glowing skies of a sunny clime was (on Polly's authority) Miss Melluka, and the costly nature of her outfit as a housekeeper, from the Barbox coffers, may be inferred from the two facts that her silver tea-spoons were as large as her kitchen poker, and that the proportions of her watch exceeded those of her frying-pan. Miss Melluka was graciously pleased to express her entire approbation of the Circus, and so was Polly; for the ponies *were* speckled, and brought down nobody when they fired, and the savagery of the wild beasts appeared to be mere smoke—which article, in fact, they did produce in large quantities from their insides. The Barbox absorption in the general subject throughout the realisation of these delights was again a sight to see, nor was it less worthy to behold at dinner, when he drank to Miss Melluka, tied stiff in a chair opposite to Polly (the fair Circassian possessing an unbendable spine), and even induced the waiter to assist in carrying out with due decorum the prevailing glorious idea. To wind up, there came the agreeable fever of getting Miss Melluka and all her wardrobe and rich possessions into a fly with Polly, to be taken home. But, by that time, Polly had become unable to look upon such accumulated joys with waking eyes, and had withdrawn her consciousness into the wonderful Paradise of a child's sleep. "Sleep, Polly, sleep," said Barbox Brothers, as her head dropped on his shoulder; "you shall not fall out of this bed easily, at any rate!"

What rustling piece of paper he took from his pocket, and carefully folded into the bosom of Polly's frock, shall not be mentioned. He said nothing about it, and nothing shall be said about it. They drove to a modest suburb of the great ingenious town, and stopped at the fore-court of a small house. "Do not wake the child," said Barbox Brothers softly to the driver; "I will carry her in as she is."

Greeting the light at the opened door which was held by Polly's mother, Polly's bearer passed on with mother and child into a ground-floor room. There, stretched on a sofa, lay a sick man, sorely wasted, who covered his eyes with his emaciated hands.

"Tresham," said Barbox in a kindly voice, "I have brought you back your Polly, fast asleep. Give me your hand, and tell me you are better."

The sick man reached forth his right hand, and bowed his head over the hand into which it was taken, and kissed it. "Thank you, thank you! I may say that I am well and happy."

"That's brave," said Barbox. "Tresham, I have a fancy—— Can you make room for me beside you here?"

He sat down on the sofa as he said the words, cherishing the plump, peachy cheek that lay uppermost on his shoulder.

"I have a fancy, Tresham (I am getting quite an old fellow now, you know, and old fellows may take fancies into their heads sometimes), to give up Polly, having found her, to no one but you. Will you take her from me?"

As the father held out his arms for the child, each of the two men looked steadily at the other.

"She is very dear to you, Tresham?"

"Unutterably dear."

"God bless her! It is not much, Polly," he continued, turning his eyes upon her peaceful face as he apostrophized her, "it is not much, Polly, for a blind and sinful man to invoke a blessing on something so far better than himself as a little child is; but it would be much—much upon his cruel head, and much upon his guilty soul—if he could be so wicked as to invoke a curse. He had better have a millstone round his neck, and be cast into the deepest sea. Live and thrive, my pretty baby!" Here he kissed her. "Live and prosper, and become in time the mother of other little children, like the Angels who behold The Father's face!"

He kissed her again, gave her up gently to both her parents, and went out.

But he went not to Wales. No, he never went to Wales. He went straightway for another stroll about the town, and he looked in upon the people at their work, and at their play, here, there, everywhere, and where not. For he was Barbox Brothers and Co. now, and had taken thousands of partners into the solitary firm.

He had at length got back to his hotel room, and was standing before his fire refreshing himself with a glass of hot drink which he had stood upon the chimney-piece, when he heard the town clocks striking, and, referring to his watch, found the evening to have so slipped away, that they were striking twelve. As he put up his watch again, his eyes met those of his reflection in the chimney-glass.

"Why, it's your birthday already," he said, smiling. "You are looking very well. I wish you many happy returns of the day."

He had never before bestowed that wish upon himself.

"By Jupiter!" he discovered, "it alters the whole case of running away from one's birthday! It's a thing to explain to Phœbe. Besides, here is quite a long story to tell her, that has sprung out of the road with no story. I'll go back, instead of going on. I'll go back by my friend Lamps's Up X presently."

He went back to Mugby Junction, and, in point of fact, he established himself at Mugby Junction. It was the convenient place to live in, for brightening Phœbe's life. It was the convenient place to live in, for having her taught music by Beatrice. It was the convenient place to live in, for occasionally borrowing Polly. It was the convenient place to live in, for being joined at will to all sorts of agreeable places and persons. So, he became settled there, and, his house standing in an elevated situation, it is noteworthy of him in conclusion, as Polly herself might (not irreverently) have put it:

> "There was an Old Barbox who lived on a hill,
> And if he ain't gone, he lives there still."

HERE FOLLOWS THE SUBSTANCE OF WHAT WAS SEEN, HEARD, OR OTHERWISE PICKED UP, BY THE GENTLEMAN FOR NOWHERE, IN HIS CAREFUL STUDY OF THE JUNCTION.

CHAPTER III

I am the boy at Mugby. That's about what I am.

You don't know what I mean? What a pity! But I think you do. I think you must. Look here. I am the boy at what is called The Refreshment Room at Mugby Junction, and what's proudest boast is, that it never yet refreshed a mortal being.

Up in a corner of the Down Refreshment Room at Mugby Junction, in the height of twenty-seven cross draughts (I've often counted 'em while they brush the First-Class hair twenty-seven ways), behind the bottles, among the glasses, bounded on the nor'west by the beer, stood pretty far to the right of a metallic object that's at times the tea-urn and at times the soup-tureen, according to the nature of the last twang imparted to its contents which are the same ground-work, fended off from the traveller by a barrier of stale sponge-cakes erected atop of the counter, and lastly exposed sideways to the glare of Our Missis's eye—you ask a Boy so sitiwated, next time you stop in a hurry at Mugby, for anything to drink ; you take particular notice that he'll try to seem not to hear you, that he'll appear in a absent manner to survey the Line through a transparent medium composed of your head and body, and that he won't serve you as long as you can possibly bear it. That's me.

What a lark it is! We are the Model Establishment,

178

we are, at Mugby. Other Refreshment Rooms send their imperfect young ladies up to be finished off by Our Missis. For some of the young ladies, when they're new to the business, come into it mild! Ah! Our Missis, she soon takes that out of 'em. Why, I originally come into the business meek myself. But Our Missis, she soon took that out of *me*.

What a delightful lark it is! I look upon us Refreshmenters as ockipying the only proudly independent footing on the Line. There's Papers, for instance,—my honourable friend, if he will allow me to call him so,—him as belongs to Smith's bookstall. Why, he no more dares to be up to our Refreshmenting games than he dares to jump atop of a locomotive with her steam at full pressure, and cut away upon her alone, driving himself, at limited-mail speed. Papers, he'd get his head punched at every compartment, first, second, and third, the whole length of a train, if he was to ventur to imitate my demeanour. It's the same with the porters, the same with the guards, the same with the ticket clerks, the same the whole way up to the secretary, traffic-manager, or very chairman. There ain't a one among 'em on the nobly independent footing we are. Did you ever catch one of *them*, when you wanted anything of him, making a system of surveying the Line through a transparent medium composed of your head and body? I should hope not.

You should see our Bandolining Room at Mugby Junction. It's led to by the door behind the counter, which you'll notice usually stands ajar, and it's the room where Our Missis and our young ladies Bandolines their hair. You should see 'em at it, betwixt trains, Bandolining away, as if they was anointing themselves for the combat. When you're telegraphed, you should see their noses all a-going up with scorn, as if it was a part of the working of the same Cooke and Wheatstone electrical machinery. You should hear Our Missis give the word, "Here comes the Beast to be Fed!" and then you should see 'em indignantly skipping across the

Line, from the Up to the Down, or Wicer Warsaw, and begin to pitch the stale pastry into the plates, and chuck the sawdust sangwiches under the glass covers, and get out the—ha, ha, ha!—the sherry,—O my eye, my eye!—for your Refreshment.

It's only in the Isle of the Brave and Land of the Free (by which, of course, I mean to say Britannia) that Refreshmenting is so effective, so 'olesome, so constitutional a check upon the public. There was a Foreigner, which having politely, with his hat off, beseeched our young ladies and Our Missis for "a leetel gloss hoff prarndee," and having had the Line surveyed through him by all and no other acknowledgment, was a-proceeding at last to help himself, as seems to be the custom in his own country, when Our Missis, with her hair almost a-coming un-Bandolined with rage, and her eyes omitting sparks, flew at him, cotched the decanter out of his hand, and said, "Put it down! I won't allow that!" The foreigner turned pale, stepped back with his arms stretched out in front of him, his hands clasped, and his shoulders riz, and exclaimed: "Ah! Is it possible, this! That these disdaineous females and this ferocious old woman are placed here by the administration, not only to empoison the voyagers, but to affront them! Great Heaven! How arrives it? The English people. Or is he then a slave? Or idiot?" Another time, a merry, wideawake American gent had tried the sawdust and spit it out, and had tried the Sherry and spit that out, and had tried in vain to sustain exhausted natur upon Butter-Scotch, and had been rather extra Bandolined and Line-surveyed through, when, as the bell was ringing and he paid Our Missis, he says, very loud and good-tempered: "I tell Yew what 'tis, ma'arm. I la'af. Theer! I la'af. I Dew. I oughter ha' seen most things, for I hail from the Onlimited side of the Atlantic Ocean, and I haive travelled right slick over the Limited, head on through Jeerusalemm and the East, and likeways France and Italy, Europe Old World, and am now upon the track to the Chief Europian Village; but such an Institution as Yew, and Yewer young ladies, and Yewer fixin's solid and liquid, afore the glorious Tarnal I never did see yet! And if I hain't found the eighth wonder of monarchical Creation, in finding Yew, and Yewer young ladies, and Yewer fixin's solid and liquid, all as aforesaid, established in a country where the people air not absolute Loo-naticks, I am Extra Double Darned with a Nip and Frizzle to the innermostest grit! Wheerfur—Theer!—I la'af! I Dew, ma'arm. I la'af!" And so he went, stamping and shaking his sides, along the platform all the way to his own compartment.

I think it was her standing up agin the Foreigner as giv' Our Missis the idea of going over to France, and droring a comparison betwixt Refreshmenting as followed among the frog-eaters, and Refreshmenting as triumphant in the Isle of the Brave and Land of the Free (by which, of course, I mean to say agin, Britannia). Our young ladies, Miss Whiff, Miss Piff, and Mrs. Sniff, was unanimous opposed to her going; for, as they says to Our Missis one and all, it is well beknown to the hends of the herth as no other nation except Britain has a idea of anythink, but above all of business. Why then should you tire yourself to prove what is already proved? Our Missis, however (being a teazer at all pints) stood out grim obstinate, and got a return pass by South-eastern Tidal, to go right through, if such should be her dispositions, to Marseilles.

Sniff is husband to Mrs. Sniff, and is a regular insignificant cove. He looks arter the sawdust department in a back room, and is sometimes, when we are very hard put to it, let behind the counter with a corkscrew; but never when it can be helped, his demeanour towards the public being disgusting servile. How Mrs. Sniff ever come so far to lower herself as to marry him, I don't know; but I suppose *he* does, and I should think he wished he didn't, for he leads a awful life. Mrs. Sniff couldn't be much harder with him if he was public. Similarly, Miss Whiff and Miss Piff, taking the tone of Mrs.

Sniff, they shoulder Sniff about when he *is* let in with a
corkscrew, and they whisk things out of his hands when in
his servility he is a-going to let the public have 'em, and they
snap him up when in the crawling baseness of his spirit he
is a-going to answer a public question, and they drore more
tears into his eyes than ever the mustard does which he all
day long lays on to the sawdust. (But it ain't strong.) Once,
when Sniff had the repulsiveness to reach across to get the
milk-pot to hand over for a baby, I see Our Missis in her
rage catch him by both his shoulders, and spin him out
into the Bandolining Room.

But Mrs. Sniff,—how different! She's the one! She's the
one as you'll notice to be always looking another way from
you, when you look at her. She's the one with the small
waist buckled in tight in front, and with the lace cuffs at
her wrists, which she puts on the edge of the counter before
her, and stands a-smoothing while the public foams. This
smoothing the cuffs and looking another way while the public
foams is the last accomplishment taught to the young ladies
as come to Mugby to be finished by Our Missis; and it's
always taught by Mrs. Sniff.

When Our Missis went away upon her journey, Mrs. Sniff
was left in charge. She did hold the public in check most
beautiful! In all my time, I never see half so many cups
of tea given without milk to people as wanted it with, nor
half so many cups of tea with milk given to people as wanted
it without. When foaming ensued, Mrs. Sniff would say:
"Then you'd better settle it among yourselves, and change
with one another." It was a most highly delicious lark. I
enjoyed the Refreshmenting business more than ever, and
was so glad I had took to it when young.

Our Missis returned. It got circulated among the young
ladies, and it as it might be penetrated to me through the
crevices of the Bandolining Room, that she had Orrors to
reveal, if revelations so contemptible could be dignified with
the name. Agitation become awakened. Excitement was

up in the stirrups. Expectation stood a-tiptoe. At length it was put forth that on our slacked evening in the week, and at our slackest time of that evening betwixt trains, Our Missis would give her views of foreign Refreshmenting, in the Bandolining Room.

It was arranged tasteful for the purpose. The Bandolining table and glass was hid in a corner, a arm-chair was elevated on a packing-case for Our Missis's ockypation, a table and a tumbler of water (no sherry in it, thankee) was placed beside it. Two of the pupils, the season being autumn, and holly-hocks and dahlias being in, ornamented the wall with three devices in those flowers. On one might be read, "MAY ALBION NEVER LEARN;" on another, "KEEP THE PUBLIC DOWN;" on another, "OUR REFRESHMENTING CHARTER." The whole had a beautiful appearance, with which the beauty of the sentiments corresponded.

On Our Missis's brow was wrote Severity, as she ascended the fatal platform. (Not that that was anythink new.) Miss Whiff and Miss Piff sat at her feet. Three chairs from the Waiting Room might have been perceived by a average eye, in front of her, on which the pupils was accommodated. Behind them a very close observer might have discerned a Boy. Myself.

"Where," said Our Missis, glancing gloomily around, "is Sniff?"

"I thought it better," answered Mrs. Sniff, "that he should not be let to come in. He is such an Ass."

"No doubt," assented Our Missis. "But for that reason is it not desirable to improve his mind?"

"Oh, nothing will ever improve *him*," said Mrs. Sniff.

"However," pursued Our Missis, "call him in, Ezekiel."

I called him in. The appearance of the low-minded cove was hailed with disapprobation from all sides, on account of his having brought his corkscrew with him. He pleaded "the force of habit."

"The force!" said Mrs. Sniff. "Don't let us have you

talking about force, for Gracious' sake. There! Do stand still where you are, with your back against the wall."

He is a smiling piece of vacancy, and he smiled in the mean way in which he will even smile at the public if he gets a chance (language can say no meaner of him), and he stood upright near the door with the back of his head agin the wall, as if he was a-waiting for somebody to come and measure his heighth for the Army.

"I should not enter, ladies," says Our Missis, "on the revolting disclosures I am about to make, if it was not in the hope that they will cause you to be yet more implacable in the exercise of the power you wield in a constitutional country, and yet more devoted to the constitutional motto which I see before me,"—it was behind her, but the words sounded better so,—"'May Albion never learn!'"

Here the pupils as had made the motto admired it, and cried, "Hear! Hear! Hear!" Sniff, showing an inclination to join in chorus, got himself frowned down by every brow.

"The baseness of the French," pursued Our Missis, "as displayed in the fawning nature of their Refreshmenting, equals, if not surpasses, anythink as was ever heard of the baseness of the celebrated Bonaparte."

Miss Whiff, Miss Piff, and me, we drored a heavy breath, equal to saying, "We thought as much!" Miss Whiff and Miss Piff seeming to object to my droring mine along with theirs, I drored another to aggravate 'em.

"Shall I be believed," says Our Missis, with flashing eyes, "when I tell you that no sooner had I set my foot upon that treacherous shore——"

Here Sniff, either bursting out mad, or thinking aloud, says, in a low voice: "Feet. Plural, you know."

The cowering that come upon him when he was spurned by all eyes, added to his being beneath contempt, was sufficient punishment for a cove so grovelling. In the midst of a silence rendered more impressive by the turned-up female noses with which it was pervaded, Our Missis went on:

184

"Shall I be believed when I tell you, that no sooner had I landed," this word with a killing look at Sniff, "on that treacherous shore, than I was ushered into a Refreshment Room where there were—I do not exaggerate—actually eatable things to eat?"

A groan burst from the ladies. I not only did myself the honour of jining, but also of lengthening it out.

"Where there were," Our Missis added, "not only eatable things to eat, but also drinkable things to drink?"

A murmur, swelling almost into a scream, ariz. Miss Piff, trembling with indignation, called out, "Name?"

"I *will* name," said Our Missis. "There was roast fowls, hot and cold; there was smoking roast veal surrounded with browned potatoes; there was hot soup with (again I ask shall I be credited?) nothing bitter in it, and no flour to choke off the consumer; there was a variety of cold dishes set off with jelly; there was salad; there was—mark me! *fresh* pastry, and that of a light construction; there was a luscious show of fruit; there was bottles and decanters of sound small wine, of every size, and adapted to every pocket; the same odious statement will apply to brandy; and these were set out upon the counter so that all could help themselves."

Our Missis's lips so quivered, that Mrs. Sniff, though scarcely less convulsed than she were, got up and held the tumbler to them.

"This," proceeds Our Missis, "was my first unconstitutional experience. Well would it have been if it had been my last and worst. But no. As I proceeded farther into that enslaved and ignorant land, its aspect became more hideous. I need not explain to this assembly the ingredients and formation of the British Refreshment sangwich?"

Universal laughter,—except from Sniff, who, as sangwich-cutter, shook his head in a state of the utmost dejection as he stood with it agin the wall.

"Well!" said Our Missis, with dilated nostrils. "Take a

fresh, crisp, long, crusty penny loaf made of the whitest and best flour. Cut it longwise through the middle. Insert a fair and nicely fitting slice of ham. Tie a smart piece of ribbon round the middle of the whole to bind it together. Add at one end a neat wrapper of clean white paper by which to hold it. And the universal French Refreshment sangwich busts on your disgusted vision."

A cry of "Shame!" from all—except Sniff, which rubbed his stomach with a soothing hand.

"I need not," said Our Missis, "explain to this assembly the usual formation and fitting of the British Refreshment Room?"

No, no, and laughter. Sniff agin shaking his head in low spirits agin the wall.

"Well," said Our Missis, "what would you say to a general decoration of everythink, to hangings (sometimes elegant), to easy velvet furniture, to abundance of little tables, to abundance of little seats, to brisk bright waiters, to great convenience, to a pervading cleanliness and tastefulness positively addressing the public, and making the Beast thinking itself worth the pains?"

Contemptuous fury on the part of all the ladies. Mrs. Sniff looking as if she wanted somebody to hold her, and everybody else looking as if they'd rayther not.

"Three times," said Our Missis, working herself into a truly terrimenjious state,—"three times did I see these shameful things, only between the coast and Paris, and not counting either: at Hazebroucke, at Arras, at Amiens. But worse remains. Tell me, what would you call a person who should propose in England that there should be kept, say at our own model Mugby Junction, pretty baskets, each holding an assorted cold lunch and dessert for one, each at a certain fixed price, and each within a passenger's power to take away, to empty in the carriage at perfect leisure, and to return at another station fifty or a hundred miles farther on?"

There was disagreement what such a person should be called.

A MALIGNANT MANIAC

Whether revolutionist, atheist, Bright (*I* said him), or Un-English. Miss Piff screeched her shrill opinion last, in the words : " A malignant maniac ! "

" I adopt," says Our Missis, " the brand set upon such a person by the righteous indignation of my friend Miss Piff. A malignant maniac. Know, then, that that malignant maniac has sprung from the congenial soil of France, and that his malignant madness was in unchecked action on this same part of my journey."

I noticed that Sniff was a-rubbing his hands, and that Mrs. Sniff had got her· eye upon him. But I did not take more particular notice, owing to the excited state in which the young ladies was, and to feeling myself called upon to keep it up with a howl.

" On my experience south of Paris," said Our Missis, in a deep tone, " I will not expatiate. Too loathsome were the task ! But fancy this. Fancy a guard coming round, with the train at full speed, to inquire how many for dinner. Fancy his telegraphing forward the number of dinners. Fancy every one expected, and the table elegantly laid for the complete party. Fancy a charming dinner, in a charming room, and the head-cook, concerned for the honour of every dish, superintending in his clean white jacket and cap. Fancy the Beast travelling six hundred miles on end, very fast, and with great punctuality, yet being taught to expect all this to be done for it ! "

A spirited chorus of " The Beast ! "

I noticed that Sniff was agin a-rubbing his stomach with a soothing hand, and that he had drored up one leg. But agin I didn't take particular notice, looking on myself as called upon to stimulate public feeling. It being a lark besides.

" Putting everything together," said Our Missis, " French Refreshmenting comes to this, and oh, it comes to a nice total ! First : eatable things to eat, and drinkable things to drink."

A groan from the young ladies, kep' up by me.

187

"Second : convenience, and even elegance."

Another groan from the young ladies, kep' up by me.

"Third : moderate charges."

This time a groan from me, kep' up by the young ladies.

"Fourth :—and here," says Our Missis, "I claim your angriest sympathy,—attention, common civility, nay, even politeness ! "

Me and the young ladies regularly raging mad all together.

"And I cannot in conclusion," says Our Missis, with her spitefullest sneer, "give you a completer pictur of that despicable nation (after what I have related), than assuring you that they wouldn't bear our constitutional ways and noble independence at Mugby Junction, for a single month, and that they would turn us to the right-about and put another system in our places, as soon as look at us ; perhaps sooner, for I do not believe they have the good taste to care to look at us twice."

The swelling tumult was arrested in its rise. Sniff, bore away by his servile disposition, had drored up his leg with a higher and a higher relish, and was now discovered to be waving his corkscrew over his head. It was at this moment that Mrs. Sniff, who had kep' her eye upon him like the fabled obelisk, descended on her victim. Our Missis followed them both out, and cries was heard in the sawdust department.

You come into the Down Refreshment Room, at the Junction, making believe you don't know me, and I'll pint you out with my right thumb over my shoulder which is Our Missis, and which is Miss Whiff, and which is Miss Piff, and which is Mrs. Sniff. But you won't get a chance to see Sniff, because he disappeared that night. Whether he perished, tore to pieces, I cannot say ; but his corkscrew alone remains, to bear witness to the servility of his disposition.

CHAPTER IV

" HALLOA !   Below there ! "

When he heard a voice thus calling to him, he was standing at the door of his box, with a flag in his hand, furled
round its short pole.   One would have thought, considering
the nature of the ground, that he could not have doubted
from what quarter the voice came ; but instead of looking
up to where I stood on the top of the steep cutting nearly
over his head, he turned himself about, and looked down the
Line.   There was something remarkable in his manner of
doing so, though I could not have said for my life what.
But I know it was remarkable enough to attract my notice,
even though his figure was foreshortened and shadowed, down
in the deep trench, and mine was high above him, so steeped
in the glow of an angry sunset, that I had shaded my eyes
with my hand before I saw him at all.

" Halloa !   Below ! "

From looking down the Line, he turned himself about
again, and, raising his eyes, saw my figure high above him.

" Is there any path by which I can come down and speak
to you ? "

He looked up at me without replying, and I looked down
at him without pressing him too soon with a repetition of
my idle question.   Just then there came a vague vibration
in the earth and air, quickly changing into a violent pulsa-
tion, and an oncoming rush that caused me to start back, as

189

though it had force to draw me down. When such vapour as rose to my height from this rapid train had passed me, and was skimming away over the landscape, I looked down again, and saw him refurling the flag he had shown while the train went by.

I repeated my inquiry. After a pause, during which he seemed to regard me with fixed attention, he motioned with his rolled-up flag towards a point on my level, some two or three hundred yards distant. I called down to him, " All right ! " and made for that point. There, by dint of looking closely about me, I found a rough zigzag descending path notched out, which I followed.

The cutting was extremely deep, and unusually precipitate. It was made through a clammy stone, that became oozier and wetter as I went down. For these reasons, I found the way long enough to give me time to recall a singular air of reluctance or compulsion with which he had pointed out the path.

When I came down low enough upon the zigzag descent to see him again, I saw that he was standing between the rails on the way by which the train had lately passed, in an attitude as if he were waiting for me to appear. He had his left hand at his chin, and that left elbow rested on his right hand, crossed over his breast. His attitude was one of such expectation and watchfulness that I stopped a moment, wondering at it.

I resumed my downward way, and stepping out upon the level of the railroad, and drawing nearer to him, saw that he was a dark, sallow man, with a dark beard and rather heavy eyebrows. His post was in as solitary and dismal a place as ever I saw. On either side, a dripping-wet wall of jagged stone, excluding all view but a strip of sky ; the perspective one way only a crooked prolongation of this great dungeon ; the shorter perspective in the other direction terminating in a gloomy red light, and the gloomier entrance to a black tunnel, in whose massive architecture there was a barbarous, depressing, and forbidding air. So little sunlight ever found its way to this spot, that it had an earthy, deadly smell; and so much cold wind rushed through it, that it struck chill to me, as if I had left the natural world.

Before he stirred, I was near enough to him to have touched him. Not even then removing his eyes from mine, he stepped back one step, and lifted his hand.

This was a lonesome post to occupy (I said), and it had riveted my attention when I looked down from up yonder. A visitor was a rarity, I should suppose; not an unwelcome rarity, I hoped? In me, he merely saw a man who had been shut up within narrow limits all his life, and who, being at last set free, had a newly-awakened interest in these great works. To such purpose I spoke to him; but I am far from sure of the terms I used; for, besides that I am not happy in opening any conversation, there was something in the man that daunted me.

He directed a most curious look towards the red light near the tunnel's mouth, and looked all about it, as if something were missing from it, and then looked at me.

That light was part of his charge? Was it not?

He answered in a low voice,—" Don't you know it is?"

The monstrous thought came into my mind, as I perused the fixed eyes and the saturnine face, that this was a spirit, not a man. I have speculated since, whether there may have been infection in his mind.

In my turn, I stepped back. But in making the action, I detected in his eyes some latent fear of me. This put the monstrous thought to flight.

"You look at me," I said, forcing a smile, "as if you had a dread of me."

"I was doubtful," he returned, "whether I had seen you before."

"Where?"

He pointed to the red light he had looked at.

"There?" I said.

Intently watchful of me, he replied (but without sound), "Yes."

"My good fellow, what should I do there? However, be that as it may, I never was there, you may swear."

"I think I may," he rejoined. "Yes; I am sure I may."

His manner cleared, like my own. He replied to my remarks with readiness, and in well-chosen words. Had he much to do there? Yes; that was to say, he had enough responsibility to bear; but exactness and watchfulness were what was required of him, and of actual work—manual labour—he had next to none. To change that signal, to trim those lights, and to turn this iron handle now and then, was all he had to do under that head. Regarding those many long and lonely hours of which I seemed to make so much, he could only say that the routine of his life had shaped itself into that form, and he had grown used to it. He had taught himself a language down here,—if only to know it by sight, and to have formed his own crude ideas of its pronunciation, could be called learning it. He had also worked at fractions and decimals, and tried a little algebra; but he was, and had been as a boy, a poor hand at figures. Was it necessary for him when on duty always to remain in that channel of damp air, and could he never rise into the sunshine from between those high stone walls? Why, that depended upon times and circumstances. Under some conditions there would be less upon the Line than under others, and the same held good as to certain hours of the day and night. In bright weather, he did choose occasions for getting a little above these lower shadows; but, being at all times liable to be called by his electric bell, and at such times listening for it with redoubled anxiety, the relief was less than I would suppose.

He took me into his box, where there was a fire, a desk for an official book in which he had to make certain entries, a telegraphic instrument with its dial, face, and needles, and the little bell of which he had spoken. On my trusting that he would excuse the remark that he had been well educated, and (I hoped I might say without offence), perhaps educated above that station, he observed that instances of slight incongruity in such wise would rarely be found wanting among large bodies of men; that he had heard it was so in workhouses, in the police force, even in that last desperate resource, the army; and that he knew it was so, more or less, in any great railway staff. He had been, when young (if I could believe it, sitting in that hut,—he scarcely could), a student of natural philosophy, and had attended lectures; but he had run wild, misused his opportunities, gone down, and never risen again. He had no complaint to offer about that. He had made his bed, and he lay upon it. It was far too late to make another.

All that I have here condensed he said in a quiet manner, with his grave, dark regards divided between me and the fire. He threw in the word, " Sir," from time to time, and especially when he referred to his youth,—as though to request me to understand that he claimed to be nothing but what I found him. He was several times interrupted by the little bell, and had to read off messages, and send replies. Once he had to stand without the door, and display a flag as a train passed, and make some verbal communication to the driver. In the discharge of his duties, I observed him to be remarkably exact and vigilant, breaking off his discourse at a syllable, and remaining silent until what he had to do was done.

In a word, I should have set this man down as one of the safest of men to be employed in that capacity, but for the circumstance that while he was speaking to me he twice broke off with a fallen colour, turned his face towards the little bell when it did NOT ring, opened the door of the hut (which was kept shut to exclude the unhealthy damp), and looked out towards the red light near the mouth of the tunnel. On both of those occasions, he came back to the fire with the inexplicable air upon him which I had remarked, without being able to define, when we were so far asunder.

Said I, when I rose to leave him, "You almost make me think that I have met with a contented man."

(I am afraid I must acknowledge that I said it to lead him on.)

"I believe I used to be so," he rejoined, in the low voice in which he had first spoken; "but I am troubled, sir, I am troubled."

He would have recalled the words if he could. He had said them, however, and I took them up quickly.

"With what? What is your trouble?"

"It is very difficult to impart, sir. It is very, very difficult to speak of. If ever you make me another visit, I will try to tell you."

"But I expressly intend to make you another visit. Say, when shall it be?"

"I go off early in the morning, and I shall be on again at ten to-morrow night, sir."

"I will come at eleven."

He thanked me, and went out at the door with me. "I'll show my white light, sir," he said, in his peculiar low voice, "till you have found the way up. When you have found it, don't call out! And when you are at the top, don't call out!"

His manner seemed to make the place strike colder to me, but I said no more than, "Very well."

"And when you come down to-morrow night, don't call out! Let me ask you a parting question. What made you cry, 'Halloa! Below there!' to-night?"

"Heaven knows," said I. "I cried something to that effect——"

"Not to that effect, sir. Those were the very words. I know them well."

"Admit those were the very words. I said them, no doubt, because I saw you below."

"For no other reason?"

"What other reason could I possibly have?"

"You had no feeling that they were conveyed to you in any supernatural way?"

"No."

He wished me good night, and held up his light. I walked by the side of the down Line of rails (with a very disagreeable sensation of a train coming behind me) until I found the path. It was easier to mount than to descend, and I got back to my inn without any adventure.

Punctual to my appointment, I placed my foot on the first notch of the zigzag next night, as the distant clocks were striking eleven. He was waiting for me at the bottom, with his white light on. "I have not called out," I said, when we came close together; "may I speak now?" "By all means, sir." "Good night, then, and here's my hand." "Good night, sir, and here's mine." With that we walked side by side to his box, entered it, closed the door, and sat down by the fire.

"I have made up my mind, sir," he began, bending forward as soon as we were seated, and speaking in a tone but a little above a whisper, "that you shall not have to ask me twice what troubles me. I took you for some one else yesterday evening. That troubles me."

"That mistake?"

"No. That some one else."

"Who is it?"

"I don't know."

"Like me?"

"I don't know. I never saw the face. The left arm is across the face, and the right arm is waved,—violently waved. This way."

I followed his action with my eyes, and it was the action of an arm gesticulating, with the utmost passion and vehemence, "For God's sake, clear the way!"

"One moonlight night," said the man, "I was sitting here, when I heard a voice cry, 'Halloa! Below there!' I started up, looked from that door, and saw this Some one else

195

standing by the red light near the tunnel, waving as I just now showed you. The voice seemed hoarse with shouting, and it cried, 'Look out! Look out!' And then again, 'Halloa! Below there! Look out!' I caught up my lamp, turned it on red, and ran towards the figure, calling, 'What's wrong? What has happened? Where?' It stood just outside the blackness of the tunnel. I advanced so close upon it that I wondered at its keeping the sleeve across its eyes. I ran right up at it, and had my hand stretched out to pull the sleeve away, when it was gone."

"Into the tunnel?" said I.

"No. I ran on into the tunnel, five hundred yards. I stopped, and held my lamp above my head, and saw the figures of the measured distance, and saw the wet stains stealing down the walls and trickling through the arch. I ran out again faster than I had run in (for I had a mortal abhorrence of the place upon me), and I looked all round the red light with my own red light, and I went up the iron ladder to the gallery atop of it, and I came down again, and ran back here. I telegraphed both ways, 'An alarm has been given. Is anything wrong?' The answer came back, both ways, 'All well.'"

Resisting the slow touch of a frozen finger tracing out my spine, I showed him how that this figure must be a deception of his sense of sight; and how that figures, originating in disease of the delicate nerves that minister to the functions of the eye, were known to have often troubled patients, some of whom had become conscious of the nature of their affliction, and had even proved it by experiments upon themselves. "As to an imaginary cry," said I, "do but listen for a moment to the wind in this unnatural valley while we speak so low, and to the wild harp it makes of the telegraph wires."

That was all very well, he returned, after we had sat listening for a while, and he ought to know something of the wind and the wires,—he who so often passed long winter nights there, alone and watching. But he would beg to remark that he had not finished.

I asked his pardon, and he slowly added these words, touching my arm,—

"Within six hours after the Appearance, the memorable accident on this Line happened, and within ten hours the dead and wounded were brought along through the tunnel over the spot where the figure had stood."

A disagreeable shudder crept over me, but I did my best against it. It was not to be denied, I rejoined, that this was a remarkable coincidence, calculated deeply to impress his mind. But it was unquestionable that remarkable coincidences did continually occur, and they must be taken into account in dealing with such a subject. Though to be sure I must admit, I added (for I thought I saw that he was going to bring the objection to bear upon me), men of common sense did not allow much for coincidences in making the ordinary calculations of life.

He again begged to remark that he had not finished.

I again begged his pardon for being betrayed into interruptions.

"This," he said, again laying his hand upon my arm, and glancing over his shoulder with hollow eyes, "was just a year ago. Six or seven months passed, and I had recovered from the surprise and shock, when one morning, as the day was breaking, I, standing at the door, looked towards the red light, and saw the spectre again." He stopped, with a fixed look at me.

"Did it cry out?"

"No. It was silent."

"Did it wave its arm?"

"No. It leaned against the shaft of the light, with both hands before the face. Like this."

Once more I followed his action with my eyes. It was an action of mourning. I have seen such an attitude in stone figures on tombs.

"Did you go up to it?"

"I came in and sat down, partly to collect my thoughts, partly because it had turned me faint. When I went to the door again, daylight was above me, and the ghost was gone."

"But nothing followed? Nothing came of this?"

He touched me on the arm with his forefinger twice or thrice, giving a ghastly nod each time: —

"That very day, as a train came out of the tunnel, I noticed, at a carriage window on my side, what looked like a confusion of hands and heads, and something waved. I saw it just in time to signal the driver, Stop! He shut off, and put his brake on, but the train drifted past here a hundred and fifty yards or more. I ran after it, and, as I went along, heard terrible screams and cries. A beautiful young lady had died instantaneously in one of the compartments, and was brought in here, and laid down on this floor between us."

Involuntarily I pushed my chair back, as I looked from the boards at which he pointed to himself.

"True, sir. True. Precisely as it happened, so I tell it you."

I could think of nothing to say, to any purpose, and my mouth was very dry. The wind and the wires took up the story with a long lamenting wail.

He resumed. "Now, sir, mark this, and judge how my mind is troubled. The spectre came back a week ago. Ever since, it has been there, now and again, by fits and starts."

"At the light?"

"At the Danger-light."

"What does it seem to do?"

He repeated, if possible with increased passion and vehemence, that former gesticulation of, "For God's sake, clear the way!"

Then he went on. "I have no peace or rest for it. It calls to me, for many minutes together, in an agonised manner,

'Below there! Look out! Look out!' It stands waving to me. It rings my little bell——"

I caught at that. "Did it ring your bell yesterday evening when I was here, and you went to the door?"

"Twice."

"Why, see," said I, "how your imagination misleads you. My eyes were on the bell, and my ears were open to the bell, and if I am a living man, it did NOT ring at those times. No, nor at any other time, except when it was rung in the natural course of physical things by the station communicating with you."

He shook his head. "I have never made a mistake as to that yet, sir. I have never confused the spectre's ring with the man's. The ghost's ring is a strange vibration in the bell that it derives from nothing else, and I have not asserted that the bell stirs to the eye. I don't wonder that you failed to hear it. But I heard it."

"And did the spectre seem to be there, when you looked out?"

"It WAS there."

"Both times?"

He repeated firmly: "Both times."

"Will you come to the door with me, and look for it now?"

He bit his under lip as though he were somewhat unwilling, but arose. I opened the door, and stood on the step, while he stood in the doorway. There was the Danger-light. There was the dismal mouth of the tunnel. There were the high, wet stone walls of the cutting. There were the stars above them.

"Do you see it?" I asked him, taking particular note of his face. His eyes were prominent and strained, but not very much more so, perhaps, than my own had been when I had directed them earnestly towards the same spot.

"No," he answered. "It is not there."

"Agreed," said I.

We went in again, shut the door, and resumed our seats. I was thinking how best to improve this advantage, if it might be called one, when he took up the conversation in such a matter-of-course way, so assuming that there could be no serious question of fact between us, that I felt myself placed in the weakest of positions.

"By this time you will fully understand, sir," he said, "that what troubles me so dreadfully is the question, What does the spectre mean?"

I was not sure, I told him, that I did fully understand.

"What is its warning against?" he said, ruminating, with his eyes on the fire, and only by times turning them on me. "What is the danger? Where is the danger? There is danger overhanging somewhere on the Line. Some dreadful calamity will happen. It is not to be doubted this third time, after what has gone before. But surely this is a cruel haunting of *me*. What can *I* do?"

He pulled out his handkerchief, and wiped the drops from his heated forehead.

"If I telegraph Danger, on either side of me, or on both, I can give no reason for it," he went on, wiping the palms of his hands. "I should get into trouble, and do no good. They would think I was mad. This is the way it would work,—Message: 'Danger! Take care!' Answer: 'What Danger? Where?' Message: 'Don't know. But, for God's sake, take care!' They would displace me. What else could they do?"

His pain of mind was most pitiable to see. It was the mental torture of a conscientious man, oppressed beyond endurance by an unintelligible responsibility involving life.

"When it first stood under the Danger-light," he went on, putting his dark hair back from his head, and drawing his hands outward across and across his temples in an extremity of feverish distress, "why not tell me where that accident was to happen,—if it must happen? Why not tell me how it could be averted,—if it could have been averted? When on its second coming it hid its face, why not tell me, instead, 'She is going to die. Let them keep her at home'? If it came, on those two occasions, only to show me that its warnings were true, and so to prepare me for the third, why not warn me plainly now? And I, Lord help me! A mere poor signal-man on this solitary station! Why not go to somebody with credit to be believed, and power to act?"

When I saw him in this state, I saw that for the poor man's sake, as well as for the public safety, what I had to do for the time was to compose his mind. Therefore, setting aside all question of reality or unreality between us, I represented to him that whoever thoroughly discharged his duty must do well, and that at least it was his comfort that he understood his duty, though he did not understand these confounding Appearances. In this effort I succeeded far better than in the attempt to reason him out of his conviction. He became calm; the occupations incidental to his post as the night advanced began to make larger demands on his attention: and I left him at two in the morning. I had offered to stay through the night, but he would not hear of it.

That I more than once looked back at the red light as I ascended the pathway, that I did not like the red light, and that I should have slept but poorly if my bed had been under it, I see no reason to conceal. Nor did I like the two sequences of the accident and the dead girl. I see no reason to conceal that either.

But what ran most in my thoughts was the consideration how ought I to act, having become the recipient of this disclosure? I had proved the man to be intelligent, vigilant, painstaking, and exact; but how long might he remain so, in his state of mind? Though in a subordinate position, still he held a most important trust, and would I (for instance) like to stake my own life on the chances of his continuing to execute it with precision?

Unable to overcome a feeling that there would be something treacherous in my communicating what he had told me to his superiors in the Company, without first being plain with himself and proposing a middle course to him, I ultimately resolved to offer to accompany him (otherwise keeping his secret for the present) to the wisest medical practitioner we could hear of in those parts, and to take his opinion. A change in his time of duty would come round next night, he had apprised me, and he would be off an hour or two after sunrise, and on again soon after sunset. I had appointed to return accordingly.

Next evening was a lovely evening, and I walked out early to enjoy it. The sun was not yet quite down when I traversed the field-path near the top of the deep cutting. I would extend my walk for an hour, I said to myself, half an hour on and half an hour back, and it would then be time to go to my signal-man's box.

Before pursuing my stroll, I stepped to the brink, and mechanically looked down, from the point from which I had first seen him. I cannot describe the thrill that seized upon me, when, close at the mouth of the tunnel, I saw the appearance of a man, with his left sleeve across his eyes, passionately waving his right arm.

The nameless horror that oppressed me passed in a moment, for in a moment I saw that this appearance of a man was a man indeed, and that there was a little group of other men, standing at a short distance, to whom he seemed to be rehearsing the gesture he made. The Danger-light was not yet lighted. Against its shaft, a little low hut, entirely new to me, had been made of some wooden supports and tarpaulin. It looked no bigger than a bed.

With an irresistible sense that something was wrong,—with a flashing self-reproachful fear that fatal mischief had come of my leaving the man there, and causing no one to be sent to overlook or correct what he did,—I descended the notched path with all the speed I could make.

" What is the matter ? " I asked the men.

" Signal-man killed this morning, sir."

" Not the man belonging to that box ? "

" Yes, sir."

" Not the man I know ? "

" You will recognise him, sir, if you knew him," said the man who spoke for the others, solemnly uncovering his own head, and raising an end of the tarpaulin, " for his face is quite composed."

" O, how did this happen, how did this happen ? " I asked, turning from one to another as the hut closed in again.

· " He was cut down by an engine, sir. No man in England knew his work better. But somehow he was not clear of the outer rail. It was just at broad day. He had struck the light, and had the lamp in his hand. As the engine came out of the tunnel, his back was towards her, and she cut him down. That man drove her, and was showing how it happened. Show the gentleman, Tom."

The man, who wore a rough dark dress, stepped back to his former place at the mouth of the tunnel.

" Coming round the curve in the tunnel, sir," he said, " I saw him at the end, like as if I saw him down a perspective-glass. There was no time to check speed, and I knew him to be very careful. As he didn't seem to take heed of the whistle, I shut it off when we were running down upon him, and called to him as loud as I could call."

" What did you say ? "

" I said, ' Below there ! Look out ! Look out ! For God's sake, clear the way ! ' "

I started.

" Ah ! it was a dreadful time, sir. I never left off calling to him. I put this arm before my eyes not to see, and I waved this arm to the last ; but it was no use."

Without prolonging the narrative to dwell on any one of its curious circumstances more than on any other, I may,

203

in closing it, point out the coincidence that the warning of the Engine-Driver included, not only the words which the unfortunate Signal-man had repeated to me as haunting him, but also the words which I myself—not he—had attached, and that only in my own mind, to the gesticulation he had imitated.

NO THOROUGHFARE

[1867]

[This was written by Mr. Wilkie Collins conjointly with Mr. Dickens; the only portions furnished exclusively by Mr. Dickens being the "Overture" and the "Third Act;" Mr. Collins contributing to acts first and fourth, and writing the whole of the second.]

DAY of the month and year, November the thirtieth, one thousand eight hundred and thirty-five. London Time by the great clock of Saint Paul's, ten at night. All the lesser London churches strain their metallic throats. Some, flippantly begin before the heavy bell of the great cathedral; some, tardily begin three, four, half a dozen, strokes behind it; all are in sufficiently near accord, to leave a resonance in the air, as if the winged father who devours his children, had made a sounding sweep with his gigantic scythe in flying over the city.

What is this clock lower than most of the rest, and nearer to the ear, that lags so far behind to-night as to strike into the vibration alone? This is the clock of the Hospital for Foundling Children. Time was, when the Foundlings were received without question in a cradle at the gate. Time is, when inquiries are made respecting them, and they are taken as by favour from the mothers who relinquish all natural knowledge of them and claim to them for evermore.

The moon is at the full, and the night is fair with light clouds. The day has been otherwise than fair, for slush and mud, thickened with the droppings of heavy fog, lie black in the streets. The veiled lady who flutters up and down near the postern-gate of the Hospital for Foundling Children has need to be well shod to-night.

She flutters to and fro, avoiding the stand of hackney-coaches, and often pausing in the shadow of the western end of the great quadrangle wall, with her face turned towards the gate. As above her there is the purity of the moonlit sky, and below her there are the defilements of the pavement, so may she, haply, be divided in her mind between two vistas of reflection or experience. As her footprints crossing and recrossing one another have made a labyrinth in the mire, so may her track in life have involved itself in an intricate and unravellable tangle.

The postern-gate of the Hospital for Foundling Children opens, and a young woman comes out. The lady stands aside, observes closely, sees that the gate is quietly closed again from within, and follows the young woman.

Two or three streets have been traversed in silence before she, following close behind the object of her attention, stretches out her hand and touches her. Then the young woman stops and looks round, startled.

"You touched me last night, and, when I turned my head, you would not speak. Why do you follow me like a silent ghost?"

"It was not," returned the lady, in a low voice, "that I would not speak, but that I could not when I tried."

"What do you want of me? I have never done you any harm?"

"Never."

"Do I know you?"

"No."

"Then what can you want of me?"

"Here are two guineas in this paper. Take my poor little present, and I will tell you."

Into the young woman's face, which is honest and comely, comes a flush as she replies: "There is neither grown person nor child in all the large establishment that I belong to, who

208

hasn't a good word for Sally. I am Sally. Could I be so well thought of, if I was to be bought?"

"I do not mean to buy you; I mean only to reward you very slightly."

Sally firmly, but not ungently, closes and puts back the offering hand. "If there is anything I can do for you, ma'am, that I will not do for its own sake, you are much mistaken in me if you think that I will do it for money. What is it you want?"

"You are one of the nurses or attendants at the Hospital; I saw you leave to-night and last night."

"Yes, I am. I am Sally."

"There is a pleasant patience in your face which makes me believe that very young children would take readily to you."

"God bless 'em! So they do."

The lady lifts her veil, and shows a face no older than the nurse's. A face far more refined and capable than hers, but wild and worn with sorrow.

"I am the miserable mother of a baby lately received under your care. I have a prayer to make to you."

Instinctively respecting the confidence which has drawn aside the veil, Sally—whose ways are all ways of simplicity and spontaneity—replaces it, and begins to cry.

"You will listen to my prayer?" the lady urges. "You will not be deaf to the agonised entreaty of such a broken suppliant as I am?"

"O dear, dear, dear!" cries Sally. "What shall I say, or can I say!, Don't talk of prayers. Prayers are to be put up to the Good Father of All, and not to nurses and such. And there! I am only to hold my place for half a year longer, till another young woman can be trained up to it. I am going to be married. I shouldn't have been out last night, and I shouldn't have been out to-night, but that my Dick (he is the young man I am going to be married to) lies ill, and I help his mother and sister to watch him. Don't take on so, don't take on so!"

209

"O good Sally, dear Sally," moans the lady, catching at her dress entreatingly. "As you are hopeful, and I am hopeless; as a fair way in life is before you, which can never, never, be before me; as you can aspire to become a respected wife, and as you can aspire to become a proud mother, as you are a living loving woman, and must die; for GOD's sake hear my distracted petition!"

"Deary, deary, deary ME!" cries Sally, her desperation culminating in the pronoun, "what am I ever to do? And there! See how you turn my own words back upon me. I tell you I am going to be married, on purpose to make it clearer to you that I am going to leave, and therefore couldn't help you if I would, Poor Thing, and you make it seem to my own self as if I was cruel in going to be married and *not* helping you. It ain't kind. Now, is it kind, Poor Thing?"

"Sally! Hear me, my dear. My entreaty is for no help in the future. It applies to what is past. It is only to be told in two words."

"There! This is worse and worse," cries Sally, "supposing that I understand what two words you mean."

"You do understand. What are the names they have given my poor baby? I ask no more than that. I have read of the customs of the place. He has been christened in the chapel, and registered by some surname in the book. He was received last Monday evening. What have they called him?"

Down upon her knees in the foul mud of the by-way into which they have strayed—an empty street without a thoroughfare giving on the dark gardens of the Hospital—the lady would drop in her passionate entreaty, but that Sally prevents her.

"Don't! Don't! You make me feel as if I was setting myself up to be good. Let me look in your pretty face again. Put your two hands in mine. Now, promise. You will never ask me anything more than the two words?"

" Never ! Never ! "

" You will never put them to a bad use, if I say them ? "

" Never ! Never ! "

" Walter Wilding."

The lady lays her face upon the nurse's breast, draws her close in her embrace with both arms, murmurs a blessing and the words, " Kiss him for me ! " and is gone.

Day of the month and year, the first Sunday in October, one thousand eight hundred and forty-seven. London Time by the great clock of Saint Paul's, half-past one in the afternoon. The clock of the Hospital for Foundling Children is well up with the Cathedral to-day. Service in the chapel is over, and the Foundling children are at dinner.

There are numerous lookers-on at the dinner, as the custom is. There are two or three governors, whole families from the congregation, smaller groups of both sexes, individual stragglers of various degrees. The bright autumnal sun strikes freshly into the wards ; and the heavy-framed windows through which it shines, and the panelled walls on which it strikes, are such windows and such walls as pervade Hogarth's pictures. The girls' refectory (including that of the younger children) is the principal attraction. Neat attendants silently glide about the orderly and silent tables ; the lookers-on move or stop as the fancy takes them ; comments in whispers on face such a number from such a window are not unfrequent ; many of the faces are of a character to fix attention. Some of the visitors from the outside public are accustomed visitors. They have established a speaking acquaintance with the occupants of particular seats at the tables, and halt at those points to bend down and say a word or two. It is no disparagement to their kindness that those points are generally points where personal attractions are. The monotony of the long spacious rooms and the double lines of faces is agreeably relieved by these incidents, although so slight.

A veiled lady, who has no companion, goes among the

company. It would seem that curiosity and opportunity have never brought her there before. She has the air of being a little troubled by the sight, and, as she goes the length of the tables, it is with a hesitating step and an uneasy manner. At length she comes to the refectory of the boys. They are so much less popular than the girls that it is bare of visitors when she looks in at the doorway.

But just within the doorway, chances to stand, inspecting, an elderly female attendant: some order of matron or house-keeper. To whom the lady addresses natural questions: As, how many boys? At what age are they usually put out in life? Do they often take a fancy to the sea? So, lower and lower in tone until the lady puts the question: "Which is Walter Wilding?"

Attendant's head shaken. Against the rules.

"You know which is Walter Wilding?"

So keenly does the attendant feel the closeness with which the lady's eyes examine her face, that she keeps her own eyes fast upon the floor, lest by wandering in the right direction they should betray her.

"I know which is Walter Wilding, but it is not my place, ma'am, to tell names to visitors."

"But you can show me without telling me."

The lady's hand moves quietly to the attendant's hand. Pause and silence.

"I am going to pass round the tables," says the lady's interlocutor, without seeming to address her. "Follow me with your eyes. The boy that I stop at and speak to, will not matter to you. But the boy that I touch, will be Walter Wilding. Say nothing more to me, and move a little away."

Quickly acting on the hint, the lady passes on into the room, and looks about her. After a few moments, the attendant, in a staid official way, walks down outside the line of tables commencing on her left hand. She goes the whole length of the line, turns, and comes back on the inside. Very slightly glancing in the lady's direction, she stops, bends forward, and speaks. The boy whom she addresses, lifts his head and replies. Good humouredly and easily, as she listens to what he says, she lays her hand upon the shoulder of the next boy on his right. That the action may be well noted, she keeps her hand on the shoulder while speaking in return, and pats it twice or thrice before moving away. She completes her tour of the tables, touching no one else, and passes out by a door at the opposite end of the long room.

Dinner is done, and the lady, too, walks down outside the line of tables commencing on her left hand, goes the whole length of the line, turns, and comes back on the inside. Other people have strolled in, fortunately for her, and stand sprinkled about. She lifts her veil, and, stopping at the touched boy, asks how old he is?

"I am twelve, ma'am," he answers, with his bright eyes fixed on hers.

"Are you well and happy?"

"Yes, ma'am."

"May you take these sweetmeats from my hand?"

"If you please to give them to me."

In stooping low for the purpose, the lady touches the boy's face with her forehead and with her hair. Then, lowering her veil again, she passes on, and passes out without looking back.

ACT I

In a court-yard in the City of London, which was No Thoroughfare either for vehicles or foot-passengers; a court-yard diverging from a steep, a slippery, and a winding street connecting Tower-street with the Middlesex shore of the Thames; stood the place of business of Wilding and Co., Wine Merchants. Probably as a jocose acknowledgment of the obstructive character of this main approach, the point nearest to its base at which one could take the river (if so inodorously minded) bore the appellation Break-Neck-Stairs. The court-yard itself had likewise been descriptively entitled in old time, Cripple Corner.

Years before the year one thousand eight hundred and sixty-one, people had left off taking boat at Break-Neck-Stairs, and watermen had ceased to ply there. The slimy little causeway had dropped into the river by a slow process of suicide, and two or three stumps of piles and a rusty iron mooring-ring were all that remained of the departed Break-Neck glories. Sometimes, indeed, a laden coal barge would bump itself into the place, and certain laborious heavers, seemingly mud-engendered, would arise, deliver the cargo in the neighbourhood, shove off, and vanish; but at most times the only commerce of Break-Neck-Stairs arose out of the conveyance of casks and bottles, both full and empty, both to and from the cellars of Wilding and Co., Wine Merchants.

214

Even that commerce was but occasional, and through three-fourths of its rising tides the dirty indecorous drab of a river would come solitarily oozing and lapping at the rusty ring, as if it had heard of the Doge and the Adriatic, and wanted to be married to the great conserver of its filthiness, the Right Honourable the Lord Mayor.

Some two hundred and fifty yards on the right, up the opposite hill (approaching it from the low ground of Break-Neck-Stairs) was Cripple Corner. There was a pump in Cripple Corner, there was a tree in Cripple Corner. All Cripple Corner belonged to Wilding and Co., Wine Merchants. Their cellars burrowed under it, their mansion towered over it. It really had been a mansion in the days when merchants inhabited the City, and had a ceremonious shelter to the doorway without visible support, like the sounding-board over an old pulpit. It had also a number of long narrow strips of window, so disposed in its grave brick front as to render it symmetrically ugly. It had also, on its roof, a cupola with a bell in it.

" When a man at five-and-twenty can put his hat on, and can say 'this hat covers the owner of this property and of the business which is transacted on this property,' I consider, Mr. Bintrey, that, without being boastful, he may be allowed to be deeply thankful. I don't know how it may appear to you, but so it appears to me."

Thus Mr. Walter Wilding to his man of law, in his own counting-house; taking his hat down from its peg to suit the action to the word, and hanging it up again when he had done so, not to overstep the modesty of nature.

An innocent, open-speaking, unused-looking man, Mr. Walter Wilding, with a remarkably pink and white complexion, and a figure much too bulky for so young a man, though of a good stature. With crisply curling brown hair, and amiable bright blue eyes. An extremely communicative man: a man with whom loquacity was the irrestrainable out-pouring of contentment and gratitude. Mr. Bintrey, on the other hand, a cautious man, with twinkling beads of eyes in a large overhanging bald head, who inwardly but intensely enjoyed the comicality of openness of speech, or hand, or heart.

"Yes," said Mr. Bintrey. "Yes. Ha, ha!"

A decanter, two wine-glasses, and a plate of biscuits, stood on the desk.

"You like this forty-five year old port-wine?" said Mr. Wilding.

"Like it?" repeated Mr. Bintrey. "Rather, sir!"

"It's from the best corner of our best forty-five year old bin," said Mr. Wilding.

"Thank you, sir," said Mr. Bintrey. "It's most excellent."

He laughed again, as he held up his glass and ogled it, at the highly ludicrous idea of giving away such wine.

"And now," said Wilding, with a childish enjoyment in the discussion of affairs, "I think we have got everything straight, Mr. Bintrey."

"Everything straight," said Bintrey.

"A partner secured——"

"Partner secured," said Bintrey.

"A housekeeper advertised for——"

"Housekeeper advertised for," said Bintrey, "'apply personally at Cripple Corner, Great Tower-street, from ten to twelve'—to-morrow, by-the-bye."

"My late dear mother's affairs wound up——"

"Wound up," said Bintrey.

"And all charges paid."

"And all charges paid," said Bintrey, with a chuckle: probably occasioned by the droll circumstance that they had been paid without a haggle.

"The mention of my late dear mother," Mr. Wilding continued, his eyes filling with tears and his pocket-handkerchief drying them, "unmans me still, Mr. Bintrey. You know how I loved her; you (her lawyer) know how she loved me. The utmost love of mother and child was cherished between us, and we never experienced one moment's division or unhappiness from the time when she took me under her care. Thirteen years in all! Thirteen years under my late dear mother's care, Mr. Bintrey, and eight of them her confidentially acknowledged son! You know the story, Mr. Bintrey, who but you, sir!" Mr. Wilding sobbed and dried his eyes, without attempt at concealment, during these remarks.

Mr. Bintrey enjoyed his comical port, and said, after rolling it in his mouth: "I know the story."

"My late dear mother, Mr. Bintrey," pursued the wine-merchant, "had been deeply deceived, and had cruelly suffered. But on that subject my late dear mother's lips were for ever sealed. By whom deceived, or under what circumstances, Heaven only knows. My late dear mother never betrayed her betrayer."

"She had made up her mind," said Mr. Bintrey, again turning his wine on his palate, "and she could hold her peace." An amused twinkle in his eyes pretty plainly added —"A devilish deal better than *you* ever will!"

"'Honour,'" said Mr. Wilding, sobbing as he quoted from the Commandments, "'thy father and thy mother, that thy days may be long in the land.' When I was in the Found-ling, Mr. Bintrey, I was at such a loss how to do it, that I apprehended my days would be short in the land. But I afterwards came to honour my mother deeply, profoundly. And I honour and revere her memory. For seven happy years, Mr. Bintrey," pursued Wilding, still with the same innocent catching in his breath, and the same unabashed tears, "did my excellent mother article me to my predecessors in this business, Pebbleson Nephew. Her affectionate fore-thought likewise apprenticed me to the Vintners Company, and made me in time a free Vintner, and—and—everything else that the best of mothers could desire. When I came of age, she bestowed her inherited share in this business upon me; it was her money that afterwards bought out Pebbleson Nephew, and painted in Wilding and Co.; it was she who left me everything she possessed, but the mourning ring you wear. And yet, Mr. Bintrey," with a fresh burst of honest affection, "she is no more. It is little over half a year since she came into the Corner to read on that door-post with her own eyes, WILDING AND CO., WINE MERCHANTS. And yet she is no more!"

"Sad. But the common lot, Mr. Wilding," observed Bintrey. "At some time or other we must all be no more." He placed the forty-five year old port-wine in the universal condition, with a relishing sigh.

"So now, Mr. Bintrey," pursued Wilding, putting away his pocket-handkerchief, and smoothing his eyelids with his fingers, "now that I can no longer show my love and honour for the dear parent to whom my heart was mysteriously turned by Nature when she first spoke to me, a strange lady, I sitting at our Sunday dinner-table in the Foundling, I can at least show that I am not ashamed of having been a Foundling, and that I, who never knew a father of my own, wish to be a father to all in my employment. Therefore," continued Wilding, becoming enthusiastic in his loquacity, "therefore, I want a thoroughly good housekeeper to undertake this dwelling-house of Wilding and Co., Wine Merchants, Cripple Corner, so that I may restore in it some of the old relations betwixt employer and employed! So that I may live in it on the spot where my money is made! So that I may daily sit at the head of the table at which the people in my employment eat together, and may eat of the same roast and boiled, and drink of the same beer! So that the people in my employment may lodge under the same roof with me! So that we may one and all—— I beg your pardon, Mr. Bintrey, but that old singing in my head has suddenly come on, and I shall feel obliged if you will lead me to the pump."

Alarmed by the excessive pinkness of his client, Mr. Bintrey lost not a moment in leading him forth into the court-yard. It was easily done; for the counting-house in which they talked together opened on to it, at one side of the dwelling-house. There the attorney pumped with a will, obedient to a sign from the client, and the client laved his head and face with both hands, and took a hearty drink. After these remedies, he declared himself much better.

"Don't let your good feelings excite you," said Bintrey, as they returned to the counting-house, and Mr. Wilding dried himself on a jack-towel behind an inner door.

"No, no. I won't," he returned, looking out of the towel. "I won't. I have not been confused, have I?"

"Not at all. Perfectly clear."

"Where did I leave off, Mr. Bintrey?"

"Well, you left off—but I wouldn't excite myself, if I was you, by taking it up again just yet."

"I'll take care. I'll take care. The singing in my head, came on at where, Mr. Bintrey?"

"At roast, and boiled, and beer," answered the lawyer, prompting—"lodging under the same roof—and one and all——"

"Ah! And one and all singing in the head together——"

"Do you know, I really *would not* let my good feelings excite me, if I was you," hinted the lawyer again, anxiously. "Try some more pump."

"No occasion, no occasion. All right, Mr. Bintrey. And one and all forming a kind of family! You see, Mr. Bintrey, I was not used in my childhood to that sort of individual existence which most individuals have led, more or less, in their childhood. After that time I became absorbed in my late dear mother. Having lost her, I find that I am more fit for being one of a body than one by myself. To be that, and at the same time to do my duty to those dependent on me, and attach them to me, has a patriarchal and pleasant air about it. I don't know how it may appear to you, Mr. Bintrey, but so it appears to me."

"It is not I who am all-important in the case, but you,"

returned Bintrey. "Consequently, how it may appear to me is of very small importance."

"It appears to *me*," said Mr. Wilding, in a glow, "hopeful, useful, delightful!"

"Do you know," hinted the lawyer again, "I really would not ex—— "

"I am not going to. Then there's Handel."

"There's who?" asked Bintrey.

"Handel, Mozart, Haydn, Kent, Purcell, Doctor Arne, Greene, Mendelssohn. I know the choruses to those anthems by heart. Foundling Chapel Collection. Why shouldn't we learn them together?"

"Who learn them together?" asked the lawyer, rather shortly.

"Employer and employed."

"Ay, ay," returned Bintrey, mollified; as if he had half expected the answer to be, Lawyer and client. "That's another thing."

"Not another thing, Mr. Bintrey! The same thing. A part of the bond among us. We will form a Choir in some quiet church near the Corner here, and, having sung together of a Sunday with a relish, we will come home and take an early dinner together with a relish. The object that I have at heart now is, to get this system well in action without delay, so that my new partner may find it founded when he enters on his partnership."

"All good be with it!" exclaimed Bintrey, rising. "May it prosper! Is Joey Ladle to take a share in Handel, Mozart, Haydn, Kent, Purcell, Doctor Arne, Greene, and Mendelssohn?"

"I hope so."

"I wish them all well out of it," returned Bintrey, with much heartiness. "Good-bye, sir."

They shook hands and parted. Then (first knocking with his knuckles for leave) entered to Mr. Wilding from a door of communication between his private counting-house and that in which his clerks sat, the Head Cellarman of the cellars of Wilding and Co., Wine Merchants, and erst Head Cellarman of the cellars of Pebbleson Nephew. The Joey Ladle in question. A slow and ponderous man, of the drayman order of human architecture, dressed in a corrugated suit and bibbed apron, apparently a composite of door-mat and rhinoceros-hide.

"Respecting this same boarding and lodging, Young Master Wilding," said he.

"Yes, Joey?"

"Speaking for myself, Young Master Wilding—and I never did speak and I never do speak for no one else—*I* don't want no boarding nor yet no lodging. But if you wish to board me and to lodge me, take me. I can peck as well as most men. Where I peck ain't so high a object with me as What I peck. Nor even so high a object with me as How Much I peck. Is all to live in the house, Young Master Wilding? The two other cellarmen, the three porters, the two 'prentices, and the odd men?"

"Yes. I hope we shall all be a united family, Joey."

"Ah!" said Joey. "I hope they may be."

"They? Rather say we, Joey."

Joey Ladle shook his head. "Don't look to me to make we on it, Young Master Wilding, not at my time of life and under the circumstarnces which has formed my disposition. I have said to Pebbleson Nephew many a time, when they have said to me, 'Put a livelier face upon it, Joey'—I have said to them, 'Gentlemen, it is all wery well for you that has been accustomed to take your wine into your systems by the conwivial channel of your throttles, to put a lively face upon it; but,' I says, 'I have been accustomed to take *my* wine in at the pores of the skin, and, took that way, it acts different. It acts depressing. It's one thing, gentlemen,' I says to Pebbleson Nephew, 'to charge your glasses in a dining-room with a Hip Hurrah and a Jolly Companions Every One, and it's another thing to be charged yourself, through the pores, in a low dark cellar and a mouldy atmosphere. It makes all the difference betwixt bubbles and wapours,' I tells Pebbleson Nephew. And so it do. I've been a cellarman my life through, with my mind fully given to the business. What's the consequence? I'm as muddled a man as lives—you won't find a muddleder man than me— nor yet you won't find my equal in molloncolly. Sing of Filling the bumper fair, Every drop you sprinkle, O'er the brow of care, Smooths away a wrinkle? Yes. P'raps so. But try filling yourself through the pores, underground, when you don't want to it!"

"I am sorry to hear this, Joey. I had even thought that you might join a singing-class in the house."

"Me, sir? No, no, Young Master Wilding, you won't catch Joey Ladle muddling the Armory. A pecking-machine, sir, is all that I am capable of proving myself, out of my cellars; but that you're welcome to, if you think it's worth your while to keep such a thing on your premises."

"I do, Joey."

"Say no more, sir. The Business's word is my law. And you're a going to take Young Master George Vendale partner into the old Business?"

"I am, Joey."

"More changes, you see! But don't change the name of the Firm again. Don't do it, Young Master Wilding. It was bad luck enough to make it Yourself and Co. Better by far have left it Pebbleson Nephew that good luck always stuck to. You should never change luck when it's good, sir."

"At all events, I have no intention of changing the name of the House again, Joey."

'Glad to hear it, and wish you good-day, Young Master Wilding. But you had better by half," muttered Joey Ladle inaudibly, as he closed the door and shook his head, "have let the name alone from the first. You had better by half have followed the luck instead of crossing it."

WANTED, A HOUSEKEEPER

The wine-merchant sat in his dining-room next morning, to receive the personal applicants for the vacant post in his establishment. It was an old-fashioned wainscoted room; the panels ornamented with festoons of flowers carved in wood; with an oaken floor, a well-worn Turkey carpet, and dark mahogany furniture, all of which had seen service and polish under Pebbleson Nephew. The great sideboard had assisted at many business-dinners given by Pebbleson Nephew to their connection, on the principle of throwing sprats overboard to catch whales; and Pebbleson Nephew's comprehensive three-sided plate-warmer, made to fit the whole front of the large fireplace, kept watch beneath it over a sarcophagus-shaped cellaret that had in its time held many a dozen of Pebbleson Nephew's wine. But the little rubicund old bachelor with a pigtail, whose portrait was over the sideboard (and who could easily be identified as decidedly Pebbleson and decidedly not Nephew), had retired into another sarcophagus, and the plate-warmer had grown as cold as he. So, the golden and black griffins that supported the candelabra, with black balls in their mouths at the end of gilded chains, looked as if in their old age they had lost all heart for playing at ball, and were dolefully exhibiting their chains in the Missionary line of inquiry, whether they had not earned emancipation by this time, and were not griffins and brothers.

Such a Columbus of a morning was the summer morning, that it discovered Cripple Corner. The light and warmth pierced in at the open windows, and irradiated the picture of a lady hanging over the chimney-piece, the only other decoration of the walls.

"My mother at five-and-twenty," said Mr. Wilding to himself, as his eyes enthusiastically followed the light to the portrait's face, "I hang up here, in order that visitors may admire my mother in the bloom of her youth and beauty.

223

My mother at fifty I hang in the seclusion of my own chamber, as a remembrance sacred to me. O! It's you, Jarvis!"

These latter words he addressed to a clerk who had tapped at the door, and now looked in.

"Yes, sir. I merely wished to mention that it's gone ten, sir, and that there are several females in the Counting-house."

"Dear me!" said the wine-merchant, deepening in the pink of his complexion and whitening in the white, "are there several? So many as several? I had better begin before there are more. I'll see them one by one, Jarvis, in the order of their arrival."

Hastily entrenching himself in his easy-chair at the table behind a great inkstand, having first placed a chair on the other side of the table opposite his own seat, Mr. Wilding entered on his task with considerable trepidation.

He ran the gauntlet that must be run on any such occasion. There were the usual species of profoundly unsympathetic women, and the usual species of much too sympathetic women. There were buccaneering widows who came to seize him, and who griped umbrellas under their arms, as if each umbrella were he, and each griper had got him. There were towering maiden ladies who had seen better days, and who came armed with clerical testimonials to their theology, as if he were Saint Peter with his keys. There were gentle maiden ladies who came to marry him. There were professional housekeepers, like non-commissioned officers, who put him through his domestic exercise, instead of submitting themselves to catechism. There were languid invalids, to whom salary was not so much an object as the comforts of a private hospital. There were sensitive creatures who burst into tears on being addressed, and had to be restored with glasses of cold water. There were some respondents who came two together, a highly promising one and a wholly unpromising one: of whom the promising one answered all questions charmingly, until it would at last appear that

she was not a candidate at all, but only the friend of the
unpromising one, who had glowered in absolute silence and
apparent injury.

At last, when the good wine-merchant's simple heart was
failing him, there entered an applicant quite different from
all the rest. A woman, perhaps fifty, but looking younger,
with a face remarkable for placid cheerfulness, and a manner
no less remarkable for its quiet expression of equability of
temper. Nothing in her dress could have been changed to
her advantage. Nothing in the noiseless self-possession of
her manner could have been changed to her advantage.
Nothing could have been in better unison with both, than
her voice when she answered the question : "What name
shall I have the pleasure of noting down?" with the words,
"My name is Sarah Goldstraw. Mrs. Goldstraw. My
husband has been dead many years, and we had no family."

Half a dozen questions had scarcely extracted as much to
the purpose from any one else. The voice dwelt so agreeably
on Mr. Wilding's ear as he made his note, that he was
rather long about it. When he looked up again, Mrs.
Goldstraw's glance had naturally gone round the room, and
now returned to him from the chimney-piece. Its expression
was one of frank readiness to be questioned, and to answer
straight.

"You will excuse my asking you a few questions?" said
the modest wine-merchant.

"O, surely, sir. Or I should have no business here."

"Have you filled the station of housekeeper before?"

"Only once. I have lived with the same widow lady for
twelve years. Ever since I lost my husband. She was an
invalid, and is lately dead : which is the occasion of my now
wearing black."

"I do not doubt that she has left you the best credentials?"
said Mr. Wilding.

"I hope I may say, the very best. I thought it would
save trouble, sir, if I wrote down the name and address of

her representatives, and brought it with me." Laying a card
on the table.

"You singularly remind me, Mrs. Goldstraw," said Wilding,
taking the card beside him, "of a manner and tone of voice
that I was once acquainted with. Not of an individual—I
feel sure of that, though I cannot recall what it is I have in
my mind—but of a general bearing. I ought to add, it was
a kind and pleasant one."

She smiled, as she rejoined: "At least, I am very glad of
that, sir."

"Yes," said the wine-merchant, thoughtfully repeating his
last phrase, with a momentary glance at his future housekeeper,
"it was a kind and pleasant one. But that is the most I
can make of it. Memory is sometimes like a half-forgotten
dream. I don't know how it may appear to you, Mrs.
Goldstraw, but so it appears to me."

Probably it appeared to Mrs. Goldstraw in a similar light,
for she quietly assented to the proposition. Mr. Wilding
then offered to put himself at once in communication with
the gentlemen named upon the card: a firm of proctors in
Doctors' Commons. To this, Mrs. Goldstraw thankfully
assented. Doctors' Commons not being far off, Mr. Wilding
suggested the feasibility of Mrs. Goldstraw's looking in again,
say in three hours' time. Mrs. Goldstraw readily undertook
to do so. In fine, the result of Mr. Wilding's inquiries being
eminently satisfactory, Mrs. Goldstraw was that afternoon
engaged (on her own perfectly fair terms) to come to-morrow
and set up her rest as housekeeper in Cripple Corner.

THE HOUSEKEEPER SPEAKS

On the next day Mrs. Goldstraw arrived, to enter on her
domestic duties.

Having settled herself in her own room, without troubling
the servants, and without wasting time, the new housekeeper
announced herself as waiting to be favoured with any

instructions which her master might wish to give her. The wine-merchant received Mrs. Goldstraw in the dining-room, in which he had seen her on the previous day; and, the usual preliminary civilities having passed on either side, the two sat down to take counsel together on the affairs of the house.

"About the meals, sir?" said Mrs. Goldstraw. "Have I a large, or a small, number to provide for?"

"If I can carry out a certain old-fashioned plan of mine," replied Mr. Wilding, "you will have a large number to provide for. I am a lonely single man, Mrs. Goldstraw; and I hope to live with all the persons in my employment as if they were members of my family. Until that time comes, you will only have me, and the new partner whom I expect immediately, to provide for. What my partner's habits may be, I cannot yet say. But I may describe myself as a man of regular hours, with an invariable appetite that you may depend upon to an ounce."

"About breakfast, sir?" asked Mrs. Goldstraw. "Is there anything particular——?"

She hesitated, and left the sentence unfinished. Her eyes turned slowly away from her master, and looked towards the chimney-piece. If she had been a less excellent and experienced housekeeper, Mr. Wilding might have fancied that her attention was beginning to wander at the very outset of the interview.

"Eight o'clock is my breakfast-hour," he resumed. "It is one of my virtues to be never tired of broiled bacon, and it is one of my vices to be habitually suspicious of the freshness of eggs." Mrs. Goldstraw looked back at him, still a little divided between her master's chimney-piece and her master. "I take tea," Mr. Wilding went on; "and I am perhaps rather nervous and fidgety about drinking it, within a certain time after it is made. If my tea stands too long——"

He hesitated, on his side, and left the sentence unfinished. If he had not been engaged in discussing a subject of such paramount interest to himself as his breakfast, Mrs. Goldstraw might have fancied that his attention was beginning to wander at the very outset of the interview.

"If your tea stands too long, sir——?" said the house-keeper, politely taking up her master's lost thread.

"If my tea stands too long," repeated the wine-merchant mechanically, his mind getting farther and farther away from his breakfast, and his eyes fixing themselves more and more inquiringly on his housekeeper's face. "If my tea—— Dear, dear me, Mrs. Goldstraw! what *is* the manner and tone of voice that you remind me of? It strikes me even more strongly to-day, than it did when I saw you yesterday. What can it be?"

"What can it be?" repeated Mrs. Goldstraw.

She said the words, evidently thinking while she spoke them of something else. The wine-merchant, still looking at her inquiringly, observed that her eyes wandered towards the chimney-piece once more. They fixed on the portrait of his mother, which hung there, and looked at it with that slight contraction of the brow which accompanies a scarcely conscious effort of memory. Mr. Wilding remarked:

"My late dear mother, when she was five-and-twenty."

Mrs. Goldstraw thanked him with a movement of the head for being at the pains to explain the picture, and said, with a cleared brow, that it was the portrait of a very beautiful lady.

Mr. Wilding, falling back into his former perplexity, tried once more to recover that lost recollection, associated so closely, and yet so undiscoverably, with his new housekeeper's voice and manner.

"Excuse my asking you a question which has nothing to do with me or my breakfast," he said. "May I inquire if you have ever occupied any other situation than the situation of housekeeper?"

"O yes, sir. I began life as one of the nurses at the Foundling."

"Why, that's it!" cried the wine-merchant, pushing back

his chair. "By heaven! Their manner is the manner you remind me of!"

In an astonished look at him, Mrs. Goldstraw changed colour, checked herself, turned her eyes upon the ground, and sat still and silent.

"What is the matter?" asked Mr. Wilding.

"Do I understand that you were in the Foundling, sir?"

"Certainly. I am not ashamed to own it."

"Under the name you now bear?"

"Under the name of Walter Wilding."

"And the lady——?" Mrs. Goldstraw stopped short with a look at the portrait which was now unmistakably a look of alarm.

"You mean my mother," interrupted Mr. Wilding.

"Your—mother," repeated the housekeeper, a little constrainedly, "removed you from the Foundling? At what age, sir?"

"At between eleven and twelve years old. It's quite a romantic adventure, Mrs. Goldstraw."

He told the story of the lady having spoken to him, while he sat at dinner with the other boys in the Foundling, and of all that had followed in his innocently communicative way. "My poor mother could never have discovered me," he added, "if she had not met with one of the matrons who pitied her. The matron consented to touch the boy whose name was 'Walter Wilding' as she went round the dinner-tables—and so my mother discovered me again, after having parted from me as an infant at the Foundling doors."

At those words Mrs. Goldstraw's hand, resting on the table, dropped helplessly into her lap. She sat, looking at her new master, with a face that had turned deadly pale, and with eyes that expressed an unutterable dismay.

"What does this mean?" asked the wine-merchant. "Stop!" he cried. "Is there something else in the past time which I ought to associate with you? I remember my mother telling me of another person at the Foundling, to whose kindness she owed a debt of gratitude. When she first parted with me, as an infant, one of the nurses informed her of the name that had been given to me in the institution. You were that nurse?"

"God forgive me, sir—I was that nurse!"

"God forgive you?"

"We had better get back, sir (if I may make so bold as to say so), to my duties in the house," said Mrs. Goldstraw. "Your breakfast-hour is eight. Do you lunch, or dine, in the middle of the day?"

The excessive pinkness which Mr. Bintrey had noticed in his client's face began to appear there once more. Mr. Wilding put his hand to his head, and mastered some momentary confusion in that quarter, before he spoke again.

"Mrs. Goldstraw," he said, "you are concealing something from me!"

The housekeeper obstinately repeated, "Please to favour me, sir, by saying whether you lunch, or dine, in the middle of the day?"

"I don't know what I do in the middle of the day. I can't enter into my household affairs, Mrs. Goldstraw, till I know why you regret an act of kindness to my mother, which she always spoke of gratefully to the end of her life. You are not doing me a service by your silence. You are agitating me, you are alarming me, you are bringing on the singing in my head."

His hand went up to his head again, and the pink in his face deepened by a shade or two.

"It's hard, sir, on just entering your service," said the housekeeper, "to say what may cost me the loss of your good will. Please to remember, end how it may, that I only speak because you have insisted on my speaking, and because I see that I am alarming you by my silence. When I told the poor lady, whose portrait you have got there, the name by which her infant was christened in the Foundling, I allowed myself to forget my duty, and dreadful consequences, I am afraid, have followed from it. I'll tell you the truth, as plainly as I can. A few months from the time when I had informed the lady of her baby's name, there came to our institution in the country another lady (a stranger), whose object was to adopt one of our children. She brought the needful permission with her, and after looking at a great many of the children, without being able to make up her mind, she took a sudden fancy to one of the babies—a boy —under my care. Try, pray try, to compose yourself, sir! It's no use disguising it any longer. The child the stranger took away was the child of that lady whose portrait hangs there!"

Mr. Wilding started to his feet. "Impossible!" he cried out, vehemently. "What are you talking about? What absurd story are you telling me now? There's her portrait! Haven't I told you so already? The portrait of my mother!"

"When that unhappy lady removed you from the Foundling, in after years," said Mrs. Goldstraw, gently, "she was the victim, and you were the victim, sir, of a dreadful mistake."

He dropped back into his chair. "The room goes round with me," he said. "My head! my head!" The housekeeper rose in alarm, and opened the windows. Before she could get to the door to call for help, a sudden burst of tears relieved the oppression which had at first almost appeared to threaten his life. He signed entreatingly to Mrs. Goldstraw not to leave him. She waited until the paroxysm of weeping had worn itself out. He raised his head as he recovered himself, and looked at her with the angry, unreasoning suspicion of a weak man.

"Mistake?" he said, wildly repeating her last word. "How do I know you are not mistaken yourself?"

"There is no hope that I am mistaken, sir. I will tell you why, when you are better fit to hear it."

"Now! now!"

The tone in which he spoke warned Mrs. Goldstraw that it would be cruel kindness to let him comfort himself a moment longer with the vain hope that she might be wrong. A few words more would end it, and those few words she determined to speak.

"I have told you," she said, "that the child of the lady whose portrait hangs there, was adopted in its infancy, and taken away by a stranger. I am as certain of what I say as that I am now sitting here, obliged to distress you, sir, sorely against my will. Please to carry your mind on, now, to about three months after that time. I was then at the Foundling, in London, waiting to take some children to our institution in the country. There was a question that day about naming an infant—a boy—who had just been received. We generally named them out of the Directory. On this occasion, one of the gentlemen who managed the Hospital happened to be looking over the Register. He noticed that the name of the baby who had been adopted ('Walter Wilding') was scratched out—for the reason, of course, that the child had been removed for good from our care. 'Here's a name to let,' he said. 'Give it to the new foundling who has been received to-day.' The name was given, and the child was christened. You, sir, were that child."

The wine-merchant's head dropped on his breast. "I was that child!" he said to himself, trying helplessly to fix the idea in his mind. "I was that child!"

"Not very long after you had been received into the Institution, sir," pursued Mrs. Goldstraw, "I left my situation there, to be married. If you will remember that, and if you can give your mind to it, you will see for yourself how the mistake happened. Between eleven and twelve years passed before the lady, whom you have believed to be your mother, returned to the Foundling, to find her son, and to remove him to her own home. The lady only knew that her infant had been called 'Walter Wilding.' The matron who took pity on her, could but point out the only 'Walter Wilding' known in the Institution. I, who might have set the matter right, was far away from the Foundling and all that belonged to it. There was nothing—there was really nothing that could prevent this terrible mistake from taking place. I feel for you—I do indeed, sir! You must think —and with reason—that it was in an evil hour that I came here (innocently enough, I'm sure), to apply for your house-keeper's place. I feel as if I was to blame—I feel as if I ought to have had more self-command. If I had only been able to keep my face from showing you what that portrait and what your own words put into my mind, you need never, to your dying day, have known what you know now."

Mr. Wilding looked up suddenly. The inbred honesty of the man rose in protest against the housekeeper's last words. His mind seemed to steady itself, for the moment, under the shock that had fallen on it.

"Do you mean to say that you would have concealed this from me if you could?" he exclaimed.

"I hope I should always tell the truth, sir, if I was asked," said Mrs. Goldstraw. "And I know it is better for *me* that I should not have a secret of this sort weighing on my mind. But is it better for *you*? What use can it serve now——?"

"What use? Why, good Lord! if your story is true——"

"Should I have told it, sir, as I am now situated, if it had not been true?"

"I beg your pardon," said the wine-merchant. "You must make allowance for me. This dreadful discovery is something I can't realise even yet. We loved each other so dearly—I felt so fondly that I was her son. She died, Mrs. Goldstraw, in my arms—she died blessing me as only a mother *could* have blessed me. And now, after all these years, to be told she was *not* my mother! O me, O me! I don't know what I am saying!" he cried, as the impulse of self-control under which he had spoken a moment since, flickered, and died out. "It was not this dreadful grief—it was something else that I had it in my mind to speak of. Yes, yes. You surprised me—you wounded me just now. You talked as if you would have hidden this from me, if you could. Don't talk in that way again. It would have been a crime to have hidden it. You mean well, I know. I don't want to distress you—you are a kind-hearted woman. But you don't remember what my position is. She left me all that I possess, in the firm persuasion that I was her son. I am not her son. I have taken the place, I have innocently got the inheritance of another man. He must be found! How do I know he is not at this moment in misery, without bread to eat? He must be found! My only hope of bearing up against the shock that has fallen on me, is the hope of doing something which *she* would have approved. You must know more, Mrs. Goldstraw, than you have told me yet. Who was the stranger who adopted the child? You must have heard the lady's name?"

"I never heard it, sir. I have never seen her, or heard of her, since."

"Did she say nothing when she took the child away? Search your memory. She must have said something."

"Only one thing, sir, that I can remember. It was a miserably bad season, that year; and many of the children were suffering from it. When she took the baby away, the lady said to me, laughing, 'Don't be alarmed about his health. He will be brought up in a better climate than this—I am going to take him to Switzerland.'"

"To Switzerland? What part of Switzerland?"

"She didn't say, sir."

"Only that faint clue!" said Mr. Wilding. "And a quarter of a century has passed since the child was taken away! What am I to do?"

"I hope you won't take offence at my freedom, sir," said Mrs. Goldstraw; "but why should you distress yourself about what is to be done? He may not be alive now, for anything you know. And, if he is alive, it's not likely he can be in any distress. The lady who adopted him was a bred and born lady—it was easy to see that. And she must have satisfied them at the Foundling that she could provide for the child, or they would never have let her take him away. If I was in your place, sir—please to excuse my saying so—I should comfort myself with remembering that I had loved that poor lady whose portrait you have got there—truly loved her as my mother, and that she had truly loved me as her son. All she gave to you, she gave for the sake of that love. It never altered while she lived; and it won't alter, I'm sure, as long as *you* live. How can you have a better right, sir, to keep what you have got than that?"

Mr. Wilding's immovable honesty saw the fallacy in his housekeeper's point of view at a glance.

"You don't understand me," he said. "It's *because* I loved her that I feel it a duty—a sacred duty—to do justice to her son. If he is a living man, I must find him: for my own sake, as well as for his. I shall break down under this dreadful trial, unless I employ myself—actively, instantly employ myself—in doing what my conscience tells me ought to be done. I must speak to my lawyer; I must set my lawyer at work before I sleep to-night." He approached a tube in the wall of the room, and called down through it to the office below. "Leave me for a little, Mrs. Goldstraw," he resumed; "I shall be more composed, I shall be better able to speak to you later in the day. We shall get on well —I hope we shall get on well together—in spite of what has happened. It isn't your fault; I know it isn't your fault. There! there! shake hands; and—and do the best you can in the house—I can't talk about it now."

The door opened as Mrs. Goldstraw advanced towards it; and Mr. Jarvis appeared.

"Send for Mr. Bintrey," said the wine-merchant. "Say I want to see him directly."

The clerk unconsciously suspended the execution of the order, by announcing "Mr. Vendale," and showing in the new partner in the firm of Wilding and Co.

"Pray excuse me for one moment, George Vendale," said

Wilding. "I have a word to say to Jarvis. Send for Mr. Bintrey," he repeated—"send at once."

Mr. Jarvis laid a letter on the table before he left the room. "From our correspondents at Neuchâtel, I think, sir. The letter has got the Swiss postmark."

NEW CHARACTERS ON THE SCENE

The words, "The Swiss Postmark," following so soon upon the housekeeper's reference to Switzerland, wrought Mr. Wilding's agitation to such a remarkable height, that his new partner could not decently make a pretence of letting it pass unnoticed.

"Wilding," he asked hurriedly, and yet stopping short and glancing around as if for some visible cause of his state of mind: "what is the matter?"

"My good George Vendale," returned the wine-merchant, giving his hand with an appealing look, rather as if he wanted help to get over some obstacle, than as if he gave it in welcome or salutation: "my good George Vendale, so much is the matter, that I shall never be myself again. It is impossible that I can ever be myself again. For, in fact, I am not myself."

The new partner, a brown-cheeked handsome fellow, of about his own age, with a quick determined eye and an impulsive manner, retorted with natural astonishment: "Not yourself?"

"Not what I supposed myself to be," said Wilding.

"What, in the name of wonder, *did* you suppose yourself to be that you are not?" was the rejoinder, delivered with a cheerful frankness, inviting confidence from a more reticent man. "I may ask without impertinence, now that we are partners."

"There again!" cried Wilding, leaning back in his chair, with a lost look at the other. "Partners! I had no right to come into this business. It was never meant for me. My mother never meant it should be mine. I mean, his mother meant it should be his—if I mean anything—or if I am anybody."

"Come, come," urged his partner, after a moment's pause, and taking possession of him with that calm confidence which inspires a strong nature when it honestly desires to aid a weak one. "Whatever has gone wrong, has gone wrong through no fault of yours, I am very sure. I was not in this counting-house with you, under the old *régime*, for three years, to doubt you, Wilding. We were not younger men than we are, together, for that. Let me begin our partner-ship by being a serviceable partner, and setting right whatever is wrong. Has that letter anything to do with it?"

"Hah!" said Wilding, with his hand to his temple. "There again! My head! I was forgetting the coincidence. The Swiss postmark."

"At a second glance I see that the letter is unopened, so it is not very likely to have much to do with the matter," said Vendale, with comforting composure. "Is it for you, or for us?"

"For us," said Wilding.

"Suppose I open it and read it aloud, to get it out of our way?"

"Thank you, thank you."

"The letter is only from our champagne-making friends, the house at Neuchâtel. 'Dear Sir. We are in receipt of yours of the 28th ult., informing us that you have taken your Mr. Vendale into partnership, whereon we beg you to receive the assurance of our felicitations. Permit us to embrace the occasion of specially commending to you M. Jules Obenreizer.' Impossible!"

Wilding looked up in quick apprehension, and cried, "Eh?"

"Impossible sort of name," returned his partner, slightly— "Obenreizer. '—Of specially commending to you M. Jules Obenreizer, of Soho-square, London (north side), henceforth fully accredited as our agent, and who has already had the

237

honour of making the acquaintance of your Mr. Vendale, in his (said M. Obenreizer's) native country, Switzerland.' To be sure! pooh pooh, what have I been thinking of! I remember now; ' when travelling with his niece.' "

" With his——? " Vendale had so slurred the last word, that Wilding had not heard it.

" When travelling with his Niece. Obenreizer's Niece," said Vendale, in a somewhat superfluously lucid manner. " Niece of Obenreizer. (I met them in my first Swiss tour, travelled a little with them, and lost them for two years; met them again, my Swiss tour before last, and have lost them ever since.) Obenreizer. Niece of Obenreizer. To be sure! Possible sort of name, after all! 'M. Obenreizer is in possession of our absolute confidence, and we do not doubt you will esteem his merits.' Duly signed by the House, ' Defresnier et Cie.' Very well. I undertake to see M. Obenreizer presently, and clear him out of the way. That clears the Swiss postmark out of the way. So now, my dear Wilding, tell me what I can clear out of *your* way, and I'll find a way to clear it."

More than ready and grateful to be thus taken charge of, the honest wine-merchant wrung his partner's hand, and, beginning his tale by pathetically declaring himself an Impostor, told it.

" It was on this matter, no doubt, that you were sending for Bintrey when I came in ? " said his partner, after reflecting.

" It was."

" He has experience and a shrewd head; I shall be anxious to know his opinion. It is bold and hazardous in me to give you mine before I know his, but I am not good at holding back. Plainly, then, I do not see these circumstances as you see them. I do not see your position as you see it. As to your being an Impostor, my dear Wilding, that is simply absurd, because no man can be that without being a consenting party to an imposition. Clearly you never were

so. As to your enrichment by the lady who believed you to
be her son, and whom you were forced to believe, on her
showing, to be your mother, consider whether that did
not arise out of the personal relations between you. You
gradually became much attached to her; she gradually
became much attached to you. It was on you, personally
you, as I see the case, that she conferred these worldly
advantages; it was from her, personally her, that you
took them."

"She supposed me," objected Wilding, shaking his head,
"to have a natural claim upon her, which I had not."

"I must admit that," replied his partner, "to be true.
But if she had made the discovery that you have made, six
months before she died, do you think it would have cancelled
the years you were together, and the tenderness that each
of you had conceived for the other, each on increasing
knowledge of the other?"

"What I think," said Wilding, simply but stoutly holding
to the bare fact, "can no more change the truth than it can
bring down the sky. The truth is that I stand possessed of
what was meant for another man."

"He may be dead," said Vendale.

"He may be alive," said Wilding. "And if he is alive,
have I not—innocently, I grant you innocently—robbed him
of enough? Have I not robbed him of all the happy time
that I enjoyed in his stead? Have I not robbed him of the
exquisite delight that filled my soul when that dear lady,"
stretching his hand towards the picture, "told me she was
my mother? Have I not robbed him of all the care she
lavished on me? Have I not even robbed him of all the
devotion and duty that I so proudly gave to her? Therefore
it is that I ask myself, George Vendale, and I ask you, where
is he? What has become of him?"

"Who can tell!"

"I must try to find out who can tell. I must institute
inquiries. I must never desist from prosecuting inquiries. I

will live upon the interest of my share—I ought to say his share—in this business, and will lay up the rest for him. When I find him, I may perhaps throw myself upon his generosity; but I will yield up all to him. I will, I swear. As I loved and honoured her," said Wilding, reverently kissing his hand towards the picture, and then covering his eyes with it. "As I loved and honoured her, and have a world of reasons to be grateful to her!" And so broke down again.

His partner rose from the chair he had occupied, and stood beside him with a hand softly laid upon his shoulder. "Walter, I knew you before to-day to be an upright man, with a pure conscience and a fine heart. It is very fortunate for me that I have the privilege to travel on in life so near to so trustworthy a man. I am thankful for it. Use me as your right hand, and rely upon me to the death. Don't think the worse of me if I protest to you that my uppermost feeling at present is a confused, you may call it an unreasonable, one. I feel far more pity for the lady and for you, because you did not stand in your supposed relations, than I can feel for the unknown man (if he ever became a man), because he was unconsciously displaced. You have done well in sending for Mr. Bintrey. What I think will be a part of his advice, I know is the whole of mine. Do not move a step in this serious matter precipitately. The secret must be kept among us with great strictness, for to part with it lightly would be to invite fraudulent claims, to encourage a host of knaves, to let loose a flood of perjury and plotting. I have no more to say now, Walter, than to remind you that you sold me a share in your business, expressly to save yourself from more work than your present health is fit for, and that I bought it expressly to do work, and mean to do it."

With these words, and a parting grip of his partner's shoulder that gave them the best emphasis they could have had, George Vendale betook himself presently to the counting-house, and presently afterwards to the address of M. Jules Obenreizer.

As he turned into Soho-square, and directed his steps towards its north side, a deepened colour shot across his sun-browned face, which Wilding, if he had been a better observer, or had been less occupied with his own trouble, might have noticed when his partner read aloud a certain passage in their Swiss correspondent's letter, which he had not read so distinctly as the rest.

A curious colony of mountaineers has long been enclosed within that small flat London district of Soho. Swiss watch-makers, Swiss silver-chasers, Swiss jewellers, Swiss importers of Swiss musical boxes and Swiss toys of various kinds, draw close together there. Swiss professors of music, painting, and languages; Swiss artificers in steady work; Swiss couriers, and other Swiss servants chronically out of place; industrious Swiss laundresses and clear-starchers; mysteriously existing Swiss of both sexes; Swiss creditable and Swiss discreditable; Swiss to be trusted by all means, and Swiss to be trusted by no means; these diverse Swiss particles are attracted to a centre in the district of Soho. Shabby Swiss eating-houses, coffee-houses, and lodging-houses, Swiss drinks and dishes, Swiss service for Sundays, and Swiss schools for week-days, are all to be found there. Even the native-born English taverns drive a sort of broken-English trade; announcing in their windows Swiss whets and drams, and sheltering in their bars Swiss skirmishes of love and animosity on most nights in the year.

When the new partner in Wilding and Co. rang the bell of a door bearing the blunt inscription OBENREIZER on a brass plate—the inner door of a substantial house, whose ground story was devoted to the sale of Swiss clocks—he passed at once into domestic Switzerland. A white-tiled stove for winter-time filled the fireplace of the room into which he was shown, the room's bare floor was laid together in a neat pattern of several ordinary woods, the room had a prevalent air of surface bareness and much scrubbing; and the little square of flowery carpet by the sofa, and the velvet chimney-board with its capacious clock and vases of artificial flowers, contended with that tone, as if, in bringing out the whole effect, a Parisian had adapted a dairy to domestic purposes.

Mimic water was dropping off a mill-wheel under the clock. The visitor had not stood before it, following it with his eyes, a minute, when M. Obenreizer, at his elbow, startled him by saying, in very good English, very slightly clipped: "How do you do? So glad!"

"I beg your pardon. I didn't hear you come in."

"Not at all! Sit, please."

Releasing his visitor's two arms, which he had lightly pinioned at the elbows by way of embrace, M. Obenreizer also sat, remarking, with a smile: "You are well? So glad!" and touching his elbows again.

"I don't know," said Vendale, after exchange of salutations, "whether you may yet have heard of me from your House at Neuchâtel?"

"Ah, yes!"

"In connection with Wilding and Co.?"

"Ah, surely!"

"Is it not odd that I should come to you, in London here, as one of the Firm of Wilding and Co., to pay the Firm's respects?"

"Not at all! What did I always observe when we were on the mountains? We call them vast; but the world is so little. So little is the world, that one cannot keep away from persons. There are so few persons in the world, that they continually cross and re-cross. So very little is the world, that one cannot get rid of a person. Not," touching his elbows again, with an ingratiatory smile, "that one would desire to get rid of you."

"I hope not, M. Obenreizer."

"Please call me, in your country, Mr. I call myself so, for I love your country. If I *could* be English! But I am born.

And you? Though descended from so fine a family, you have had the condescension to come into trade? Stop though. Wines? Is it trade in England or profession? Not fine art?"

"Mr. Obenreizer," returned Vendale, somewhat out of countenance, "I was but a silly young fellow, just of age, when I first had the pleasure of travelling with you, and when you and I and Mademoiselle your niece—who is well?"

"Thank you. Who is well."

"—Shared some slight glacier dangers together. If, with a boy's vanity, I rather vaunted my family, I hope I did so as a kind of introduction of myself. It was very weak, and in very bad taste; but perhaps you know our English proverb, 'Live and Learn.'"

"You make too much of it," returned the Swiss. "And what the devil! After all, yours *was* a fine family."

George Vendale's laugh betrayed a little vexation as he rejoined: "Well! I was strongly attached to my parents, and when we first travelled together, Mr. Obenreizer, I was in the first flush of coming into what my father and mother left me. So I hope it may have been, after all, more youthful openness of speech and heart than boastfulness."

"All openness of speech and heart! No boastfulness!" cried Obenreizer. "You tax yourself too heavily. You tax yourself, my faith! as if you was your Government taxing you! Besides, it commenced with me. I remember, that evening in the boat upon the lake, floating among the reflections of the mountains and valleys, the crags and pine woods, which were my earliest remembrance, I drew a word-picture of my sordid childhood. Of our poor hut, by the waterfall which my mother showed to travellers; of the cow-shed where I slept with the cow; of my idiot half-brother always sitting at the door, or limping down the Pass to beg; of my half-sister always spinning, and resting her enormous goître on a great stone; of my being a famished, naked little

243

wretch of two or three years, when they were men and women with hard hands to beat me, I, the only child of my father's second marriage—if it even was a marriage. What more natural than for you to compare notes with me, and say, 'We are as one by age; at that same time I sat upon my mother's lap in my father's carriage, rolling through the rich English streets, all luxury surrounding me, all squalid poverty kept far from me. Such is *my* earliest remembrance as opposed to yours!'"

Mr. Obenreizer was a black-haired young man of a dark complexion, through whose swarthy skin no red glow ever shone. When colour would have come into another cheek, a hardly discernible beat would come into his, as if the machinery for bringing up the ardent blood were there, but the machinery were dry. He was robustly made, well proportioned, and had handsome features. Many would have perceived that some surface change in him would have set them more at their ease with him, without being able to define what change. If his lips could have been made much thicker, and his neck much thinner, they would have found their want supplied.

But the great Obenreizer peculiarity was, that a certain nameless film would come over his eyes—apparently by the action of his own will—which would impenetrably veil, not only from those tellers of tales, but from his face at large, every expression save one of attention. It by no means followed that his attention should be wholly given to the person with whom he spoke, or even wholly bestowed on present sounds and objects. Rather, it was a comprehensive watchfulness of everything he had in his own mind, and everything that he knew to be, or suspected to be, in the minds of other men.

At this stage of the conversation, Mr. Obenreizer's film came over him.

"The object of my present visit," said Vendale, "is, I need hardly say, to assure you of the friendliness of Wilding and

Co., and of the goodness of your credit with us, and of our desire to be of service to you. We hope shortly to offer you our hospitality. Things are not quite in train with us yet, for my partner, Mr. Wilding, is reorganising the domestic part of our establishment, and is interrupted by some private affairs. You don't know Mr. Wilding, I believe ? "

Mr. Obenreizer did not.

"You must come together soon. He will be glad to have made your acquaintance, and I think I may predict that you will be glad to have made his. You have not been long established in London, I suppose, Mr. Obenreizer ? "

"It is only now that I have undertaken this agency."

"Mademoiselle your niece—is—not married ? "

"Not married."

George Vendale glanced about him, as if for any tokens of her.

"She has been in London ? "

"She *is* in London."

"When, and where, might I have the honour of recalling myself to her remembrance ? "

Mr. Obenreizer, discarding his film and touching his visitor's elbows as before, said lightly : "Come up-stairs."

Fluttered enough by the suddenness with which the interview he had sought was coming upon him after all, George Vendale followed up-stairs. In a room over the chamber he had just quitted—a room also Swiss-appointed—a young lady sat near one of three windows, working at an embroidery-frame ; and an older lady sat with her face turned close to another white-tiled stove (though it was summer, and the stove was not lighted), cleaning gloves. The young lady wore an unusual quantity of fair bright hair, very prettily braided about a rather rounder white forehead than the average English type, and so her face might have been a shade—or say a light— rounder than the average English face, and her figure slightly rounder than the figure of the average English girl at nineteen. A remarkable indication of freedom and grace of limb, in

245

her quiet attitude, and a wonderful purity and freshness of
colour in her dimpled face and bright gray eyes, seemed
fraught with mountain air. Switzerland too, though the
general fashion of her dress was English, peeped out of the
fanciful bodice she wore, and lurked in the curious clocked
red stocking, and in its little silver-buckled shoe. As to the
elder lady, sitting with her feet apart upon the lower brass
ledge of the stove, supporting a lap-full of gloves while she
cleaned one stretched on her left hand, she was a true Swiss
impersonation of another kind; from the breadth of her cushion-
like back, and the ponderosity of her respectable legs (if the
word be admissible), to the black velvet band tied tightly
round her throat for the repression of a rising tendency to
goître; or, higher still, to her great copper-coloured gold ear-
rings; or, higher still, to her head-dress of black gauze
stretched on wire.

"Miss Marguerite," said Obenreizer to the young lady,
"do you recollect this gentleman?"

"I think," she answered, rising from her seat, surprised
and a little confused : "it is Mr. Vendale?"

"I think it is," said Obenreizer, dryly. "Permit me, Mr.
Vendale. Madame Dor."

The elder lady by the stove, with the glove stretched on
her left hand, like a glover's sign, half got up, half looked
over her broad shoulder, and wholly plumped down again and
rubbed away.

"Madame Dor," said Obenreizer, smiling, "is so kind as to
keep me free from stain or tear. Madame Dor humours my
weakness for being always neat, and devotes her time to
removing every one of my specks and spots."

Madame Dor, with the stretched glove in the air, and her
eyes closely scrutinizing its palm, discovered a tough spot in
Mr. Obenreizer at that instant, and rubbed hard at him.
George Vendale took his seat by the embroidery-frame (having
first taken the fair right hand that his entrance had checked),
and glanced at the gold cross that dipped into the bodice,

with something of the devotion of a pilgrim who had reached his shrine at last. Obenreizer stood in the middle of the room with his thumbs in his waistcoat-pockets, and became filmy.

"He was saying down-stairs, Miss Obenreizer," observed Vendale, "that the world is so small a place, that people cannot escape one another. I have found it much too large for me since I saw you last."

"Have you travelled so far, then?" she inquired.

"Not so far, for I have only gone back to Switzerland each year; but I could have wished—and indeed I have wished very often—that the little world did not afford such opportunities for long escapes as it does. If it had been less, I might have found my fellow-travellers sooner, you know."

The pretty Marguerite coloured, and very slightly glanced in the direction of Madame Dor.

"You find us at length, Mr. Vendale. Perhaps you may lose us again."

"I trust not. The curious coincidence that has enabled me to find you, encourages me to hope not."

"What is that coincidence, sir, if you please?" A dainty little native touch in this turn of speech, and in its tone, made it perfectly captivating, thought George Vendale, when again he noticed an instantaneous glance towards Madame Dor. A caution seemed to be conveyed in it, rapid flash though it was; so he quietly took heed of Madame Dor from that time forth.

"It is that I happen to have become a partner in a House of business in London, to which Mr. Obenreizer happens this very day to be expressly recommended: and that, too, by another house of business in Switzerland, in which (as it turns out) we both have a commercial interest. He has not told you?"

"Ah!" cried Obenreizer, striking in, filmless. "No. I had not told Miss Marguerite. The world is so small and so monotonous that a surprise is worth having in such a little

247

jog-trot place. It is as he tells you, Miss Marguerite. He, of so fine a family, and so proudly bred, has condescended to trade. To trade! Like us poor peasants who have risen from ditches!"

A cloud crept over the fair brow, and she cast down her eyes.

"Why, it is good for trade!" pursued Obenreizer, enthusiastically. "It ennobles trade! It is the misfortune of trade, it is its vulgarity, that any low people—for example, we poor peasants—may take to it and climb by it. See you, my dear Vendale!" He spoke with great energy. "The father of Miss Marguerite, my eldest half-brother, more than two times your age or mine, if living now, wandered without shoes, almost without rags, from that wretched Pass—wandered —wandered—got to be fed with the mules and dogs at an Inn in the main valley far away—got to be Boy there—got to be Ostler—got to be Waiter—got to be Cook—got to be Landlord. As Landlord, he took me (could he take the idiot beggar his brother, or the spinning monstrosity his sister?) to put as pupil to the famous watchmaker, his neighbour and friend. His wife dies when Miss Marguerite is born. What is his will, and what are his words to me, when *he* dies, she being between girl and woman? 'All for Marguerite, except so much by the year for you. You are young, but I make her your ward, for you were of the obscurest and the poorest peasantry, and so was I, and so was her mother; we were abject peasants all, and you will remember it.' The thing is equally true of most of my countrymen, now in trade in this your London quarter of Soho. Peasants once; low-born drudging Swiss Peasants. Then how good and great for trade:" here, from having been warm, he became playfully jubilant, and touched the young wine-merchant's elbows again with his light embrace: "to be exalted by gentlemen."

"I do not think so," said Marguerite, with a flushed cheek, and a look away from the visitor, that was almost defiant. "I think it is as much exalted by us peasants."

248

"Fie, fie, Miss Marguerite," said Obenreizer. "You speak in proud England."

"I speak in proud earnest," she answered, quietly resuming her work, "and I am not English, but a Swiss peasant's daughter."

There was a dismissal of the subject in her words, which Vendale could not contend against. He only said in an earnest manner, "I most heartily agree with you, Miss Obenreizer, and I have already said so, as Mr. Obenreizer will bear witness," which he by no means did, "in this house."

Now, Vendale's eyes were quick eyes, and sharply watching Madame Dor by times, noted something in the broad back view of that lady. There was considerable pantomimic expression in her glove-cleaning. It had been very softly done when he spoke with Marguerite, or it had altogether stopped, like the action of a listener. When Obenreizer's peasant-speech came to an end, she rubbed most vigorously, as if applauding it. And once or twice, as the glove (which she always held before her a little above her face) turned in the air, or as this finger went down, or that went up, he even fancied that it made some telegraphic communication to Obenreizer: whose back was certainly never turned upon it, though he did not seem at all to heed it.

Vendale observed too, that in Marguerite's dismissal of the subject twice forced upon him to his misrepresentation, there was an indignant treatment of her guardian which she tried to check: as though she would have flamed out against him, but for the influence of fear. He also observed—though this was not much—that he never advanced within the distance of her at which he first placed himself: as though there were limits fixed between them. Neither had he ever spoken of her without the prefix "Miss," though whenever he uttered it, it was with the faintest trace of an air of mockery. And now it occurred to Vendale for the first time that something curious in the man, which he had never before been able to define, was definable as a certain subtle essence of mockery that eluded touch or analysis. He felt convinced that Marguerite was in some sort a prisoner as to her free-will—though she held her own against those two combined, by the force of her character, which was nevertheless inadequate to her release. To feel convinced of this, was not to feel less disposed to love her than he had always been. In a word, he was desperately in love with her, and thoroughly determined to pursue the opportunity which had opened at last.

For the present, he merely touched upon the pleasure that Wilding and Co. would soon have in entreating Miss Obenreizer to honour their establishment with her presence—a curious old place, though a bachelor house withal—and so did not protract his visit beyond such a visit's ordinary length. Going down-stairs, conducted by his host, he found the Obenreizer counting-house at the back of the entrance-hall, and several shabby men in outlandish garments hanging about, whom Obenreizer put aside that he might pass, with a few words in *patois*.

"Countrymen," he explained, as he attended Vendale to the door. "Poor compatriots. Grateful and attached, like dogs! Good-bye. To meet again. So glad!"

Two more light touches on his elbows dismissed him into the street.

Sweet Marguerite at her frame, and Madame Dor's broad back at her telegraph, floated before him to Cripple Corner. On his arrival there, Wilding was closeted with Bintrey. The cellar doors happening to be open, Vendale lighted a candle in a cleft stick, and went down for a cellarous stroll. Graceful Marguerite floated before him faithfully, but Madame Dor's broad back remained outside.

The vaults were very spacious, and very old. There had been a stone crypt down there, when bygones were not bygones; some said, part of a monkish refectory; some said, of a chapel; some said, of a Pagan temple. It was all one now. Let who would make what he liked of a crumbled pillar and a broken arch or so. Old Time had made what *he* liked of it, and was quite indifferent to contradiction.

The close air, the musty smell, and the thunderous rumbling in the streets above, as being out of the routine of ordinary life, went well enough with the picture of pretty Marguerite holding her own against those two. So Vendale went on until, at a turning in the vaults, he saw a light like the light he carried.

"O! You are here, are you, Joey?"

"Oughtn't it rather to go, 'O! *You*'re here, are you, Master George?' For it's my business to be here. But it ain't yourn."

"Don't grumble, Joey."

"O! *I* don't grumble," returned the Cellarman. "If any-thing grumbles, it's what I've took in through the pores; it ain't me. Have a care as something in *you* don't begin a grumbling, Master George. Stop here long enough for the wapours to work, and they'll be at it."

His present occupation consisted of poking his head into the bins, making measurements and mental calculations, and entering them in a rhinoceros-hide-looking note-book, like a piece of himself.

"They'll be at it," he resumed, laying the wooden rod that he measured with across two casks, entering his last calculation, and straightening his back, "trust 'em! And so you've regularly come into the business, Master George?"

"Regularly. I hope you don't object, Joey?"

"*I* don't, bless you. But Wapours objects that you're too young. You're both on you too young."

"We shall get over that objection day by day, Joey."

"Ay, Master George; but I shall day by day get over the objection that I'm too old, and so I shan't be capable of seeing much improvement in you."

The retort so tickled Joey Ladle that he grunted forth a

laugh and delivered it again, grunting forth another laugh after the second edition of "improvement in you."

"But what's no laughing matter, Master George," he resumed, straightening his back once more, "is, that young Master Wilding has gone and changed the luck. Mark my words. He has changed the luck, and he'll find it out. *I* ain't been down here all my life for nothing! *I* know by what I notices down here, when it's a-going to rain, when it's a-going to hold up, when it's a-going to blow, when it's a-going to be calm. *I* know, by what I notices down here, when the luck's changed, quite as well."

"Has this growth on the roof anything to do with your divination?" asked Vendale, holding his light towards a gloomy ragged growth of dark fungus, pendent from the arches with a very disagreeable and repellent effect. "We are famous for this growth in this vault, aren't we?"

"We are, Master George," replied Joey Ladle, moving a step or two away, "and if you'll be advised by me, you'll let it alone."

Taking up the rod just now laid across the two casks, and faintly moving the languid fungus with it, Vendale asked, "Ay, indeed? Why so?"

"Why, not so much because it rises from the casks of wine, and may leave you to judge what sort of stuff a Cellarman takes into himself when he walks in the same all the days of his life, nor yet so much because at a stage of its growth it's maggots, and you'll fetch 'em down upon you," returned Joey Ladle, still keeping away, "as for another reason, Master George."

"What other reason?"

"(I wouldn't keep on touchin' it, if I was you, sir.) I'll tell you if you'll come out of the place. First, take a look at its colour, Master George."

"I am doing so."

"Done, sir. Now, come out of the place."

He moved away with his light, and Vendale followed with

his. When Vendale came up with him, and they were going back together, Vendale, eyeing him as they walked through the arches, said: "Well, Joey? The colour."

"Is it like clotted blood, Master George?"

"Like enough, perhaps."

"More than enough, I think," muttered Joey Ladle, shaking his head solemnly.

"Well, say it is like; say it is exactly like. What then?"

"Master George, they do say——"

"Who?"

"How should I know who?" rejoined the Cellarman, apparently much exasperated by the unreasonable nature of the question. "Them! Them as says pretty well everything, you know. How should I know who They are, if you don't?"

"True. Go on."

"They do say that the man that gets by any accident a piece of that dark growth right upon his breast, will, for sure and certain, die by murder."

As Vendale laughingly stopped to meet the Cellarman's eyes, which he had fastened on his light while dreamily saying those words, he suddenly became conscious of being struck upon his own breast by a heavy hand. Instantly following with his eyes the action of the hand that struck him—which was his companion's—he saw that it had beaten off his breast a web or clot of the fungus even then floating to the ground.

For a moment he turned upon the Cellarman almost as scared a look as the Cellarman turned upon him. But in another moment they had reached the daylight at the foot of the cellar-steps, and before he cheerfully sprang up them, he blew out his candle and the superstition together.

EXIT WILDING

On the morning of the next day, Wilding went out alone, after leaving a message with his clerk. "If Mr. Vendale should ask for me," he said, "or if Mr. Bintrey should call, tell them I am gone to the Foundling." All that his partner had said to him, all that his lawyer, following on the same side, could urge, had left him persisting unshaken in his own point of view. To find the lost man, whose place he had usurped, was now the paramount interest of his life, and to inquire at the Foundling was plainly to take the first step in the direction of discovery. To the Foundling, accordingly, the wine-merchant now went.

The once familiar aspect of the building was altered to him, as the look of the portrait over the chimney-piece was altered to him. His one dearest association with the place which had sheltered his childhood had been broken away from it for ever. A strange reluctance possessed him, when he stated his business at the door. His heart ached as he sat alone in the waiting-room while the Treasurer of the institution was being sent for to see him. When the interview began, it was only by a painful effort that he could compose himself sufficiently to mention the nature of his errand.

The Treasurer listened with a face which promised all needful attention, and promised nothing more.

"We are obliged to be cautious," he said, when it came to his turn to speak, "about all inquiries which are made by strangers."

"You can hardly consider me a stranger," answered Wilding, simply. "I was one of your poor lost children here, in the bygone time."

The Treasurer politely rejoined that this circumstance inspired him with a special interest in his visitor. But he pressed, nevertheless, for that visitor's motive in making his inquiry. Without further preface, Wilding told him his motive, suppressing nothing. The Treasurer rose, and led the way into the room in which the registers of the institution were kept. "All the information which our books can give is heartily at your service," he said. "After the time that has elapsed I am afraid it is the only information we have to offer you."

A JOURNEY OF INVESTIGATION

The books were consulted, and the entry was found expressed as follows:—

"3d March, 1836. Adopted, and removed from the Foundling Hospital, a male infant, named Walter Wilding. Name and condition of the person adopting the child— Mrs. Jane Ann Miller, widow. Address—Lime-Tree Lodge, Groombridge Wells. References—the Reverend John Harker, Groombridge Wells; and Messrs. Giles, Jeremie, and Giles, bankers, Lombard-street."

"Is that all?" asked the wine-merchant. "Had you no after-communication with Mrs. Miller?"

"None—or some reference to it must have appeared in this book."

"May I take a copy of the entry?"

"Certainly! You are a little agitated. Let me make a copy for you."

"My only chance, I suppose," said Wilding, looking sadly at the copy, "is to inquire at Mrs. Miller's residence, and to try if her references can help me?"

"That is the only chance I see at present," answered the Treasurer. "I heartily wish I could have been of some further assistance to you."

With those farewell words to comfort him, Wilding set forth on the journey of investigation which began from the Foundling doors. The first stage to make for, was plainly the house of business of the bankers in Lombard-street. Two of the partners in the firm were inaccessible to chance-visitors when he asked for them. The third, after raising certain inevitable difficulties, consented to let a clerk examine the Ledger marked with the initial letter "M." The account of Mrs. Miller, widow, of Groombridge Wells, was found. Two long lines, in faded ink, were drawn across it; and at the bottom of the page there appeared this note: "Account closed, September 30th, 1837."

So the first stage of the journey was reached—and so it ended in No Thoroughfare! After sending a note to Cripple

Corner to inform his partner that his absence might be prolonged for some hours, Wilding took his place in the train, and started for the second stage on the journey—Mrs. Miller's residence at Groombridge Wells.

Mothers and children travelled with him; mothers and children met each other at the station; mothers and children were in the shops when he entered them to inquire for Lime-Tree Lodge. Everywhere, the nearest and dearest of human relations showed itself happily in the happy light of day. Everywhere, he was reminded of the treasured delusion from which he had been awakened so cruelly—of the lost memory which had passed from him like a reflection from a glass.

Inquiring here, inquiring there, he could hear of no such place as Lime-Tree Lodge. Passing a house-agent's office, he went in wearily, and put the question for the last time. The house-agent pointed across the street to a dreary mansion of many windows, which might have been a manufactory, but which was an hotel. "That's where Lime-Tree Lodge stood, sir," said the man, "ten years ago."

The second stage reached, and No Thoroughfare again!

But one chance was left. The clerical reference, Mr. Harker, still remained to be found. Customers coming in at the moment to occupy the house-agent's attention, Wilding went down the street, and entering a bookseller's shop, asked if he could be informed of the Reverend John Harker's present address.

The bookseller looked unaffectedly shocked and astonished, and made no answer.

Wilding repeated his question.

The bookseller took up from his counter a prim little volume in a binding of sober gray. He handed it to his visitor, open at the title-page. Wilding read:

"The martyrdom of the Reverend John Harker in New Zealand. Related by a former member of his flock."

Wilding put the book down on the counter. "I beg your pardon," he said, thinking a little, perhaps, of his own present martyrdom while he spoke. The silent bookseller acknowledged the apology by a bow. Wilding went out.

Third and last stage, and No Thoroughfare for the third and last time.

There was nothing more to be done; there was absolutely no choice but to go back to London, defeated at all points. From time to time on the return journey, the wine-merchant looked at his copy of the entry in the Foundling Register. There is one among the many forms of despair—perhaps the most pitiable of all—which persists in disguising itself as Hope. Wilding checked himself in the act of throwing the useless morsel of paper out of the carriage window. "It may lead to something yet," he thought. "While I live, I won't part with it. When I die, my executors shall find it sealed up with my will."

Now, the mention of his will set the good wine-merchant on a new track of thought, without diverting his mind from its engrossing subject. He must make his will immediately.

The application of the phrase No Thoroughfare to the case had originated with Mr. Bintrey. In their first long conference following the discovery, that sagacious personage had a hundred times repeated, with an obstructive shake of the head, "No Thoroughfare, Sir, No Thoroughfare. My belief is that there is no way out of this at this time of day, and my advice is, make yourself comfortable where you are."

In the course of the protracted consultation, a magnum of the forty-five year old port-wine had been produced for the wetting of Mr. Bintrey's legal whistle; but the more clearly he saw his way through the wine, the more emphatically he did not see his way through the case; repeating as often as he set his glass down empty, "Mr. Wilding, No Thoroughfare. Rest and be thankful."

It is certain that the honest wine-merchant's anxiety to make a will originated in profound conscientiousness; though it is possible (and quite consistent with his rectitude) that he may unconsciously have derived some feeling of relief from

257

the prospect of delegating his own difficulty to two other men who were to come after him. Be that as it may, he pursued his new track of thought with great ardour, and lost no time in begging George Vendale and Mr. Bintrey to meet him in Cripple Corner and share his confidence.

"Being all three assembled with closed doors," said Mr. Bintrey, addressing the new partner on the occasion, "I wish to observe, before our friend (and my client) entrusts us with his further views, that I have endorsed what I understand from him to have been your advice, Mr. Vendale, and what would be the advice of every sensible man. I have told him that he positively must keep his secret. I have spoken with Mrs. Goldstraw, both in his presence and in his absence; and if anybody is to be trusted (which is a very large IF), I think she is to be trusted to that extent. I have pointed out to our friend (and my client), that to set on foot random inquiries would not only be to raise the Devil, in the likeness of all the swindlers in the kingdom, but would also be to waste the estate. Now, you see, Mr. Vendale, our friend (and my client) does not desire to waste the estate, but, on the contrary, desires to husband it for what he considers— but I can't say I do—the rightful owner, if such rightful owner should ever be found. I am very much mistaken if he ever will be, but never mind that. Mr. Wilding and I are, at least, agreed that the estate is not to be wasted. Now, I have yielded to Mr. Wilding's desire to keep an advertisement at intervals flowing through the newspapers, cautiously inviting any person who may know anything about that adopted infant, taken from the Foundling Hospital, to come to my office; and I have pledged myself that such advertisement shall regularly appear. I have gathered from our friend (and my client) that I meet you here to-day to take his instructions, not to give him advice. I am prepared to receive his instructions, and to respect his wishes; but you will please observe that this does not imply my approval of either as a matter of professional opinion."

MR. WILDING MAKES HIS WILL

Thus Mr. Bintrey; talking quite as much *at* Wilding as *to* Vendale. And yet, in spite of his care for his client, he was so amused by his client's Quixotic conduct, as to eye him from time to time with twinkling eyes, in the light of a highly comical curiosity.

"Nothing," observed Wilding, "can be clearer. I only wish my head were as clear as yours, Mr. Bintrey."

"If you feel that singing in it coming on," hinted the lawyer, with an alarmed glance, "put it off.—I mean the interview."

"Not at all, I thank you," said Wilding. "What was I going to—— "

"Don't excite yourself, Mr. Wilding," urged the lawyer.

"No; I *wasn't* going to," said the wine-merchant. "Mr. Bintrey and George Vendale, would you have any hesitation or objection to become my joint trustees and executors, or can you at once consent?"

"*I* consent," replied George Vendale, readily.

"*I* consent," said Bintrey, not so readily.

"Thank you both. Mr. Bintrey, my instructions for my last will and testament are short and plain. Perhaps you will now have the goodness to take them down. I leave the whole of my real and personal estate, without any exception or reservation whatsoever, to you two, my joint trustees and executors, in trust to pay over the whole to the true Walter Wilding, if he shall be found and identified within two years after the day of my death. Failing that, in trust to you two to pay over the whole as a benefaction and legacy to the Foundling Hospital."

"Those are all your instructions, are they, Mr. Wilding?" demanded Bintrey, after a blank silence, during which nobody had looked at anybody.

"The whole."

"And as to those instructions, you have absolutely made up your mind, Mr. Wilding?"

"Absolutely, decidedly, finally."

259

"It only remains," said the lawyer, with one shrug of his shoulders, "to get them into technical and binding form, and to execute and attest. Now, does that press? Is there any hurry about it? You are not going to die yet, sir."

"Mr. Bintrey," answered Wilding, gravely, "when I am going to die is within other knowledge than yours or mine. I shall be glad to have this matter off my mind, if you please."

"We are lawyer and client again," rejoined Bintrey, who, for the nonce, had become almost sympathetic. "If this day week—here, at the same hour—will suit Mr. Vendale and yourself, I will enter in my Diary that I attend you accordingly."

The appointment was made, and in due sequence kept. The will was formally signed, sealed, delivered, and witnessed, and was carried off by Mr. Bintrey for safe storage among the papers of his clients, ranged in their respective iron boxes, with their respective owners' names outside, on iron tiers in his consulting-room, as if that legal sanctuary were a condensed Family Vault of Clients.

With more heart than he had lately had for former subjects of interest, Wilding then set about completing his patriarchal establishment, being much assisted not only by Mrs. Goldstraw but by Vendale too: who, perhaps, had in his mind the giving of an Obenreizer dinner as soon as possible. Anyhow, the establishment being reported in sound working order, the Obenreizers, Guardian and Ward, were asked to dinner, and Madame Dor was included in the invitation. If Vendale had been over head and ears in love before—a phrase not to be taken as implying the faintest doubt about it—this dinner plunged him down in love ten thousand fathoms deep. Yet, for the life of him, he could not get one word alone with charming Marguerite. So surely as a blessed moment seemed to come, Obenreizer, in his filmy state, would stand at Vendale's elbow, or the broad back of Madame Dor would appear before his eyes. That speechless matron was never seen in a front view, from the moment of her arrival to that of her departure—except at dinner. And from the instant of her retirement to the drawing-room, after a hearty participation in that meal, she turned her face to the wall again.

Yet, through four or five delightful though distracting hours, Marguerite was to be seen, Marguerite was to be heard, Marguerite was to be occasionally touched. When they made the round of the old dark cellars, Vendale led her by the hand; when she sang to him in the lighted room at night, Vendale, standing by her, held her relinquished gloves, and would have bartered against them every drop of the forty-five year old, though it had been forty-five times forty-five years old, and its nett price forty-five times forty-five pounds per dozen. And still, when she was gone, and a great gap of an extinguisher was clapped on Cripple Corner, he tormented himself by wondering, Did she think that he admired her! Did she think that he adored her! Did she suspect that she had won him, heart and soul! Did she care to think at all about it! And so, Did she and Didn't she, up and down the gamut, and above the line and below the line, dear, dear! Poor restless heart of humanity! To think that the men who were mummies thousands of years ago, did the same, and ever found the secret how to be quiet after it!

"What do you think, George," Wilding asked him next day, "of Mr. Obenreizer? (I won't ask you what you think of Miss Obenreizer.)"

"I don't know," said Vendale, "and I never did know, what to think of him."

"He is well informed and clever," said Wilding.

"Certainly clever."

"A good musician." (He had played very well, and sung very well, overnight.)

"Unquestionably a good musician."

"And talks well."

"Yes," said George Vendale, ruminating, "and talks well. Do you know, Wilding, it oddly occurs to me, as I think about him, that he doesn't keep silence well!"

"How do you mean? He is not obtrusively talkative."

"No, and I don't mean that. But when he is silent, you can hardly help vaguely, though perhaps most unjustly, mistrusting him. Take people whom you know and like. Take any one you know and like."

"Soon done, my good fellow," said Wilding. "I take you."

"I didn't bargain for that, or foresee it," returned Vendale, laughing. "However, take me. Reflect for a moment. Is your approving knowledge of my interesting face mainly founded (however various the momentary expressions it may include) on my face when I am silent?"

"I think it is," said Wilding.

"I think so too. Now, you see, when Obenreizer speaks— in other words, when he is allowed to explain himself away —he comes out right enough; but when he has not the opportunity of explaining himself away, he comes out rather wrong. Therefore it is, that I say he does not keep silence well. And passing hastily in review such faces as I know, and don't trust, I am inclined to think, now I give my mind to it, that none of them keep silence well."

This proposition in Physiognomy being new to Wilding, he was at first slow to admit it, until asking himself the question whether Mrs. Goldstraw kept silence well, and remembering that her face in repose decidedly invited trustfulness, he was as glad as men usually are to believe what they desire to believe.

But, as he was very slow to regain his spirits or his health, his partner, as another means of setting him up—and perhaps also with contingent Obenreizer views—reminded him of those musical schemes of his in connection with his family, and how a singing-class was to be formed in the house, and a Choir in a neighbouring church. The class was established speedily, and, two or three of the people having already some musical knowledge, and singing tolerably, the Choir soon followed. The latter was led, and chiefly taught, by Wilding himself: who had hopes of converting his dependents into so many Foundlings, in respect of their capacity to sing sacred choruses.

Now, the Obenreizers being skilled musicians, it was easily brought to pass that they should be asked to join these musical unions. Guardian and Ward consenting, or Guardian consenting for both, it was necessarily brought to pass that Vendale's life became a life of absolute thraldom and enchantment. For, in the mouldy Christopher-Wren church on Sundays, with its dearly beloved brethren assembled and met together, five-and-twenty strong, was not that Her voice that shot like light into the darkest places, thrilling the walls and pillars as though they were pieces of his heart! What time, too, Madame Dor in a corner of the high pew, turning her back upon everybody and everything, could not fail to be Ritualistically right at some moment of the service; like the man whom the doctors recommended to get drunk once a month, and who, that he might not overlook it, got drunk every day.

But, even those seraphic Sundays were surpassed by the Wednesday concerts established for the patriarchal family. At those concerts she would sit down to the piano and sing them, in her own tongue, songs of her own land, songs calling from the mountain-tops to Vendale, " Rise above the grovelling level country; come far away from the crowd; pursue me as I mount higher; higher, higher, melting into the azure distance; rise to my supremest height of all, and love me here!" Then would the pretty bodice, the clocked stocking, and the silver-buckled shoe be, like the broad forehead and the bright eyes, fraught with the spring of a very chamois, until the strain was over.

Not even over Vendale himself did these songs of hers cast a more potent spell than over Joey Ladle in his different way. Steadily refusing to muddle the harmony by taking any share in it, and evincing the supremest contempt for scales and such-like rudiments of music—which, indeed, seldom

captivate mere listeners—Joey did at first give up the whole
business for a bad job, and the whole of the performers
for a set of howling Dervishes. But, descrying traces of
unmuddled harmony in a part-song one day, he gave his
two under cellarmen faint hopes of getting on towards
something in course of time. An anthem of Handel's led to
further encouragement from him: though he objected that
that great musician must have been down in some of them
foreign cellars pretty much, for to go and say the same thing
so many times over; which, took it in how you might, he
considered a certain sign of your having took it in somehow.
On a third occasion, the public appearance of Mr. Jarvis
with a flute, and of an odd man with a violin, and the performance of a duet by the two, did so astonish him that,
solely of his own impulse and motion, he became inspired
with the words, "Ann Koar!" repeatedly pronouncing them
as if calling in a familiar manner for some lady who had
distinguished herself in the orchestra. But this was his
final testimony to the merits of his mates, for, the instrumental
duet being performed at the first Wednesday concert, and
being presently followed by the voice of Marguerite Obenreizer,
he sat with his mouth wide open, entranced, until she had
finished; when, rising in his place with much solemnity, and
prefacing what he was about to say with a bow that specially
included Mr. Wilding in it, he delivered himself of the
gratifying sentiment: "Arter that, ye may all on ye get to
bed!" And ever afterwards declined to render homage in
any other words to the musical powers of the family.

Thus began a separate personal acquaintance between
Marguerite Obenreizer and Joey Ladle. She laughed so
heartily at his compliment, and yet was so abashed by it,
that Joey made bold to say to her, after the concert was
over, he hoped he wasn't so muddled in his head as to have
took a liberty? She made him a gracious reply, and Joey
ducked in return.

"You'll change the luck time about, Miss," said Joey,

ducking again. "It's such as you in the place that can bring round the luck of the place."

"Can I? Round the luck?" she answered, in her pretty English, and with a pretty wonder. "I fear I do not understand. I am so stupid."

"Young Master Wilding, Miss," Joey explained confidentially, though not much to her enlightenment, "changed the luck, afore he took in young Master George. So I say, and so they'll find. Lord! Only come into the place and sing over the luck a few times, Miss, and it won't be able to help itself!"

With this, and with a whole brood of ducks, Joey backed out of the presence. But Joey being a privileged person, and even an involuntary conquest being pleasant to youth and beauty, Marguerite merrily looked out for him next time.

"Where is my Mr. Joey, please?" she asked Vendale.

So Joey was produced and shaken hands with, and that became an Institution.

Another Institution arose in this wise. Joey was a little hard of hearing. He himself said it was "Wapours," and perhaps it might have been; but whatever the cause of the effect, there the effect was, upon him. On this first occasion he had been seen to sidle along the wall, with his left hand to his left ear, until he had sidled himself into a seat pretty near the singer, in which place and position he had remained, until addressing to his friends the amateurs the compliment before mentioned. It was observed on the following Wednesday that Joey's action as a Pecking Machine was impaired at dinner, and it was rumoured about the table that this was explainable by his high-strung expectations of Miss Obenreizer's singing, and his fears of not getting a place where he could hear every note and syllable. The rumour reaching Wilding's ears, he in his good nature called Joey to the front at night before Marguerite began. Thus the Institution came into being that on succeeding nights,

Marguerite, running her hands over the keys before singing, always said to Vendale, "Where is my Mr. Joey, please?" and that Vendale always brought him forth, and stationed him near by. That he should then, when all eyes were upon him, express in his face the utmost contempt for the exertions of his friends and confidence in Marguerite alone, whom he would stand contemplating, not unlike the rhinoceros out of the spelling-book, tamed and on his hind legs, was a part of the Institution. Also that when he remained after the singing in his most ecstatic state, some bold spirit from the back should say, "What do you think of it, Joey?" and he should be goaded to reply, as having that instant conceived the retort, "Arter that, ye may all on ye get to bed!" These were other parts of the Institution.

But, the simple pleasures and small jests of Cripple Corner were not destined to have a long life. Underlying them from the first was a serious matter, which every member of the patriarchal family knew of, but which, by tacit agreement, all forbore to speak of. Mr. Wilding's health was in a bad way.

He might have overcome the shock he had sustained in the one great affection of his life, or he might have overcome his consciousness of being in the enjoyment of another man's property; but the two together were too much for him. A man haunted by twin ghosts, he became deeply depressed. The inseparable spectres sat at the board with him, ate from his platter, drank from his cup, and stood by his bedside at night. When he recalled his supposed mother's love, he felt as though he had stolen it. When he rallied a little under the respect and attachment of his dependants, he felt as though he were even fraudulent in making them happy, for that should have been the unknown man's duty and gratification.

Gradually, under the pressure of his brooding mind, his body stooped, his step lost its elasticity, his eyes were seldom lifted from the ground. He knew he could not help the deplorable mistake that had been made, but he knew he

266

could not mend it; for the days and weeks went by and no one claimed his name or his possessions. And now there began to creep over him a cloudy consciousness of often-recurring confusion in his head. He would unaccountably lose, sometimes whole hours, sometimes a whole day and night. Once, his remembrance stopped as he sat at the head of the dinner-table, and was blank until daybreak. Another time, it stopped as he was beating time to their singing, and went on again when he and his partner were walking in the courtyard by the light of the moon, half the night later. He asked Vendale (always full of consideration, work, and help) how this was? Vendale only replied, "You have not been quite well; that's all." He looked for explanation into the faces of his people. But they would put it off with, "Glad to see you looking so much better, sir;" or "Hope you're doing nicely now, sir;" in which was no information at all.

At length, when the partnership was but five months old, Walter Wilding took to his bed, and his housekeeper became his nurse.

"Lying here, perhaps you will not mind my calling you Sally, Mrs. Goldstraw?" said the poor wine-merchant.

"It sounds more natural to me, sir, than any other name, and I like it better."

"Thank you, Sally. I think, Sally, I must of late have been subject to fits. Is that so, Sally? Don't mind telling me now."

"It has happened, sir."

"Ah! That is the explanation!" he quietly remarked. "Mr. Obenreizer, Sally, talks of the world being so small that it is not strange how often the same people come together, and come together at various places, and in various stages of life. But it does seem strange, Sally, that I should, as I may say, come round to the Foundling to die."

He extended his hand to her, and she gently took it.

"You are not going to die, dear Mr. Wilding."

"So Mr. Bintrey said, but I think he was wrong. The old child-feeling is coming back upon me, Sally. The old hush and rest, as I used to fall asleep."

After an interval he said, in a placid voice, "Please kiss me, Nurse," and, it was evident, believed himself to be lying in the old Dormitory.

As she had been used to bend over the fatherless and motherless children, Sally bent over the fatherless and motherless man, and put her lips to his forehead, murmuring:

"God bless you!"

"God bless you!" he replied, in the same tone.

After another interval, he opened his eyes in his own character, and said: "Don't move me, Sally, because of what I am going to say; I lie quite easily. I think my time is come. I don't know how it may appear to you, Sally, but—— "

Insensibility fell upon him for a few minutes; he emerged from it once more.

"—I don't know how it may appear to you, Sally, but so it appears to me."

When he had thus conscientiously finished his favourite sentence, his time came, and he died.

ACT II

THE summer and the autumn had passed. Christmas and the New Year were at hand.

As executors honestly bent on performing their duty towards the dead, Vendale and Bintrey had held more than one anxious consultation on the subject of Wilding's will. The lawyer had declared, from the first, that it was simply impossible to take any useful action in the matter at all. The only obvious inquiries to make, in relation to the lost man, had been made already by Wilding himself; with this result, that time and death together had not left a trace of him discoverable. To advertise for the claimant to the property, it would be necessary to mention particulars—a course of proceeding which would invite half the impostors in England to present themselves in the character of the true Walter Wilding. "If we find a chance of tracing the lost man, we will take it. If we don't, let us meet for another consultation on the first anniversary of Wilding's death." So Bintrey advised. And so, with the most earnest desire to fulfil his dead friend's wishes, Vendale was fain to let the matter rest for the present.

Turning from his interest in the past to his interest in the future, Vendale still found himself confronting a doubtful prospect. Months on months had passed since his first visit to Soho-square—and through all that time, the one language

269

in which he had told Marguerite that he loved her was the language of the eyes, assisted, at convenient opportunities, by the language of the hand.

What was the obstacle in his way? The one immovable obstacle which had been in his way from the first. No matter how fairly the opportunities looked, Vendale's efforts to speak with Marguerite alone ended invariably in one and the same result. Under the most accidental circumstances, in the most innocent manner possible, Obenreizer was always in the way.

With the last days of the old year came an unexpected chance of spending an evening with Marguerite, which Vendale resolved should be a chance of speaking privately to her as well. A cordial note from Obenreizer invited him, on New Year's Day, to a little family dinner in Soho-square. "We shall be only four," the note said. "We shall be only two," Vendale determined, "before the evening is out!"

New Year's Day, among the English, is associated with the giving and receiving of dinners, and with nothing more. New Year's Day, among the foreigners, is the grand opportunity of the year for the giving and receiving of presents. It is occasionally possible to acclimatise a foreign custom. In this instance Vendale felt no hesitation about making the attempt. His one difficulty was to decide what his New Year's gift to Marguerite should be. The defensive pride of the peasant's daughter—morbidly sensitive to the inequality between her social position and his—would be secretly roused against him if he ventured on a rich offering. A gift, which a poor man's purse might purchase, was the one gift that could be trusted to find its way to her heart, for the giver's sake. Stoutly resisting temptation, in the form of diamonds and rubies, Vendale bought a brooch of the filigree-work of Genoa—the simplest and most unpretending ornament that he could find in the jeweller's shop.

He slipped his gift into Marguerite's hand as she held it out to welcome him on the day of the dinner.

A NEW YEAR'S GIFT

"This is your first New Year's Day in England," he said. "Will you let me help to make it like a New Year's Day at home?"

She thanked him, a little constrainedly, as she looked at the jeweller's box, uncertain what it might contain. Opening the box, and discovering the studiously simple form under which Vendale's little keepsake offered itself to her, she penetrated his motive on the spot. Her face turned on him brightly, with a look which said, "I own you have pleased and flattered me." Never had she been so charming, in Vendale's eyes, as she was at that moment. Her winter dress—a petticoat of dark silk, with a bodice of black velvet rising to her neck, and enclosing it softly in a little circle of swansdown—heightened, by all the force of contrast, the dazzling fairness of her hair and her complexion. It was only when she turned aside from him to the glass, and, taking out the brooch that she wore, put his New Year's gift in its place, that Vendale's attention wandered far enough away from her to discover the presence of other persons in the room. He now became conscious that the hands of Obenreizer were affectionately in possession of his elbows. He now heard the voice of Obenreizer thanking him for his attention to Marguerite, with the faintest possible ring of mockery in its tone. ("Such a simple present, dear sir! and showing such nice tact!") He now discovered, for the first time, that there was one other guest, and but one, besides himself, whom Obenreizer presented as a compatriot and friend. The friend's face was mouldy, and the friend's figure was fat. His age was suggestive of the autumnal period of human life. In the course of the evening he developed two extraordinary capacities. One was a capacity for silence; the other was a capacity for emptying bottles.

Madame Dor was not in the room. Neither was there any visible place reserved for her when they sat down to table. Obenreizer explained that it was "the good Dor's simple habit to dine always in the middle of the day. She would make her excuses later in the evening." Vendale wondered whether the good Dor had, on this occasion, varied her domestic employment from cleaning Obenreizer's gloves to cooking Obenreizer's dinner. This at least was certain—the dishes served were, one and all, as achievements in cookery, high above the reach of the rude elementary art of England. The dinner was unobtrusively perfect. As for the wine, the eyes of the speechless friend rolled over it, as in solemn ecstasy. Sometimes he said "Good!" when a bottle came in full; and sometimes he said "Ah!" when a bottle went out empty—and there his contributions to the gaiety of the evening ended.

Silence is occasionally infectious. Oppressed by private anxieties of their own, Marguerite and Vendale appeared to feel the influence of the speechless friend. The whole responsibility of keeping the talk going rested on Obenreizer's shoulders, and manfully did Obenreizer sustain it. He opened his heart in the character of an enlightened foreigner, and sang the praises of England. When other topics ran dry, he returned to this inexhaustible source, and always set the stream running again as copiously as ever. Obenreizer would have given an arm, an eye, or a leg to have been born an Englishman. Out of England there was no such institution as a home, no such thing as a fireside, no such object as a beautiful woman. His dear Miss Marguerite would excuse him, if he accounted for *her* attractions on the theory that English blood must have mixed at some former time with their obscure and unknown ancestry. Survey this English nation, and behold a tall, clean, plump, and solid people! Look at their cities! What magnificence in their public buildings! What admirable order and propriety in their streets! Admire their laws, combining the eternal principle of justice with the other eternal principle of pounds, shillings, and pence; and applying the product to all civil injuries, from an injury to a man's honour, to an injury to a man's nose! You have ruined my daughter—pounds, shillings, and pence!

A NOTE FOR MR. OBENREIZER

You have knocked me down with a blow in my face—pounds, shillings, and pence! Where was the material prosperity of such a country as *that* to stop? Obenreizer, projecting himself into the future, failed to see the end of it. Obenreizer's enthusiasm entreated permission to exhale itself, English fashion, in a toast. Here is our modest little dinner over, here is our frugal dessert on the table, and here is the admirer of England conforming to national customs, and making a speech! A toast to your white cliffs of Albion, Mr. Vendale! to your national virtues, your charming climate, and your fascinating women! to your Hearths, to your Homes, to your Habeas Corpus, and to all your other institutions! In one word—to England! Heep-heep-heep! hooray!

Obenreizer's voice had barely chanted the last note of the English cheer, the speechless friend had barely drained the last drop out of his glass, when the festive proceedings were interrupted by a modest tap at the door. A woman-servant came in, and approached her master with a little note in her hand. Obenreizer opened the note with a frown; and, after reading it with an expression of genuine annoyance, passed it on to his compatriot and friend. Vendale's spirits rose as he watched these proceedings. Had he found an ally in the annoying little note? Was the long-looked-for chance actually coming at last?

"I am afraid there is no help for it?" said Obenreizer, addressing his fellow-countryman. "I am afraid we must go."

The speechless friend handed back the letter, shrugged his heavy shoulders, and poured himself out a last glass of wine. His fat fingers lingered fondly round the neck of the bottle. They pressed it with a little amatory squeeze at parting. His globular eyes looked dimly, as through an intervening haze, at Vendale and Marguerite. His heavy articulation laboured, and brought forth a whole sentence at a birth. "I think," he said, "I should have liked a little more wine." His breath failed him after that effort; he gasped, and walked to the door.

Obenreizer addressed himself to Vendale with an appearance of the deepest distress.

"I am so shocked, so confused, so distressed," he began. "A misfortune has happened to one of my compatriots. He is alone, he is ignorant of your language—I and my good friend, here, have no choice but to go and help him. What can I say in my excuse? How can I describe my affliction at depriving myself in this way of the honour of your company?"

He paused, evidently expecting to see Vendale take up his hat and retire. Discerning his opportunity at last, Vendale determined to do nothing of the kind. He met Obenreizer dexterously, with Obenreizer's own weapons.

"Pray don't distress yourself," he said. "I'll wait here with the greatest pleasure till you come back."

Marguerite blushed deeply, and turned away to her embroidery-frame in a corner by the window. The film showed itself in Obenreizer's eyes, and the smile came something sourly to Obenreizer's lips. To have told Vendale that there was no reasonable prospect of his coming back in good time, would have been to risk offending a man whose favourable opinion was of solid commercial importance to him. Accepting his defeat with the best possible grace, he declared himself to be equally honoured and delighted by Vendale's proposal. "So frank, so friendly, so English!" He bustled about, apparently looking for something he wanted, disappeared for a moment through the folding-doors communicating with the next room, came back with his hat and coat, and protesting that he would return at the earliest possible moment, embraced Vendale's elbows, and vanished from the scene in company with the speechless friend.

Vendale turned to the corner by the window, in which Marguerite had placed herself with her work. There, as if she had dropped from the ceiling, or come up through the floor—there, in the old attitude, with her face to the stove —sat an Obstacle that had not been foreseen, in the person of Madame Dor! She half got up, half looked over her broad shoulder at Vendale, and plumped down again. Was she at work? Yes. Cleaning Obenreizer's gloves, as before? No; darning Obenreizer's stockings.

The case was now desperate. Two serious considerations presented themselves to Vendale. Was it possible to put Madame Dor into the stove? The stove wouldn't hold her. Was it possible to treat Madame Dor, not as a living woman, but as an article of furniture? Could the mind be brought to contemplate this respectable matron purely in the light of a chest of drawers, with a black gauze head-dress accidentally left on the top of it? Yes, the mind could be brought to do that. With a comparatively trifling effort, Vendale's mind did it. As he took his place on the old-fashioned window-seat, close by Marguerite and her embroidery, a slight movement appeared in the chest of drawers, but no remark issued from it. Let it be remembered that solid furniture is not easy to move, and that it has this advantage in consequence—there is no fear of upsetting it.

Unusually silent and unusually constrained—with the bright colour fast fading from her face, with a feverish energy possessing her fingers—the pretty Marguerite bent over her embroidery, and worked as if her life depended on it. Hardly less agitated himself, Vendale felt the importance of leading her very gently to the avowal which he was eager to make— to the other sweeter avowal still, which he was longing to hear. A woman's love is never to be taken by storm; it yields insensibly to a system of gradual approach. It ventures by the roundabout way, and listens to the low voice. Vendale led her memory back to their past meetings when they were travelling together in Switzerland. They revived the impressions, they recalled the events, of the happy bygone time. Little by little, Marguerite's constraint vanished. She smiled, she was interested, she looked at Vendale, she grew idle with her needle, she made false stitches in her work. Their voices sank lower and lower; their faces bent nearer and nearer to each other as they spoke. And Madame Dor? Madame Dor behaved like an angel. She never looked round; she never said a word; she went on with Obenreizer's stockings. Pulling each stocking up tight over her left arm, and holding that arm aloft from time to time, to catch the light on her work, there were moments—delicate and indescribable moments—when Madame Dor appeared to be sitting upside down, and contemplating one of her own respectable legs, elevated in the air. As the minutes wore on, these elevations followed each other at longer and longer intervals. Now and again, the black gauze head-dress nodded, dropped forward, recovered itself. A little heap of stockings slid softly from Madame Dor's lap, and remained unnoticed on the floor. A prodigious ball of worsted followed the stockings, and rolled lazily under the table. The black gauze head-dress nodded, dropped forward, recovered itself, nodded again, dropped forward again, and recovered itself no more. A composite sound, partly as of the purring of an immense cat, partly as of the planing of a soft board, rose over the hushed voices of the lovers, and hummed at regular intervals through the room. Nature and Madame Dor had combined together in Vendale's interests. The best of women was asleep.

Marguerite rose to stop—not the snoring—let us say, the audible repose of Madame Dor. Vendale laid his hand on her arm, and pressed her back gently into her chair.

"Don't disturb her," he whispered. "I have been waiting to tell you a secret. Let me tell it now."

Marguerite resumed her seat. She tried to resume her needle. It was useless; her eyes failed her; her hand failed her; she could find nothing.

"We have been talking," said Vendale, "of the happy time when we first met, and first travelled together. I have a confession to make. I have been concealing something. When we spoke of my first visit to Switzerland, I told you of all the impressions I had brought back with me to England—except one. Can you guess what that one is?"

Her eyes looked steadfastly at the embroidery, and her face turned a little away from him. Signs of disturbance began to appear in her neat velvet bodice, round the region of the brooch. She made no reply. Vendale pressed the question without mercy.

"Can you guess what the one Swiss impression is, which I have not told you yet?"

Her face turned back towards him, and a faint smile trembled on her lips.

"An impression of the mountains, perhaps?" she said slyly.

"No; a much more precious impression than that."

"Of the lakes?"

"No. The lakes have not grown dearer and dearer in remembrance to me every day. The lakes are not associated with my happiness in the present, and my hopes in the future. Marguerite! all that makes life worth having hangs, for me, on a word from your lips. Marguerite! I love you!"

Her head drooped as he took her hand. He drew her to him, and looked at her. The tears escaped from her downcast eyes, and fell slowly over her cheeks.

"O, Mr. Vendale," she said sadly, "it would have been kinder to have kept your secret. Have you forgotten the distance between us? It can never, never be!"

"There can be but one distance between us, Marguerite— a distance of your making. My love, my darling, there is no higher rank in goodness, there is no higher rank in beauty, than yours! Come! whisper the one little word which tells me you will be my wife!"

She sighed bitterly. "Think of your family," she murmured; "and think of mine!"

Vendale drew her a little nearer to him.

"If you dwell on such an obstacle as that," he said, "I shall think but one thought—I shall think I have offended you."

She started, and looked up. "O, no!" she exclaimed innocently. The instant the words passed her lips, she saw

277

the construction that might be placed on them. Her confession had escaped her in spite of herself. A lovely flush of colour overspread her face. She made a momentary effort to disengage herself from her lover's embrace. She looked up at him entreatingly. She tried to speak. The words died on her lips in the kiss that Vendale pressed on them. "Let me go, Mr. Vendale!" she said faintly.

"Call me George."

She laid her head on his bosom. All her heart went out to him at last. "George!" she whispered.

"Say you love me!"

Her arms twined themselves gently round his neck. Her lips, timidly touching his cheek, murmured the delicious words —"I love you!"

In the moment of silence that followed, the sound of the opening and closing of the house-door came clear to them through the wintry stillness of the street.

Marguerite started to her feet.

"Let me go!" she said. "He has come back!"

She hurried from the room, and touched Madame Dor's shoulder in passing. Madame Dor woke up with a loud snort, looked first over one shoulder and then over the other, peered down into her lap, and discovered neither stockings, worsted, nor darning-needle in it. At the same moment, footsteps became audible ascending the stairs. "Mon Dieu!" said Madame Dor, addressing herself to the stove, and trembling violently. Vendale picked up the stockings and the ball, and huddled them all back in a heap over her shoulder. "Mon Dieu!" said Madame Dor, for the second time, as the avalanche of worsted poured into her capacious lap.

The door opened, and Obenreizer came in. His first glance round the room showed him that Marguerite was absent.

"What!" he exclaimed, "my niece is away? My niece is not here to entertain you in my absence? This is unpardonable. I shall bring her back instantly."

A WORD IN PRIVATE

Vendale stopped him.

"I beg you will not disturb Miss Obenreizer," he said. "You have returned, I see, without your friend?"

"My friend remains, and consoles our afflicted compatriot. A heart-rending scene, Mr. Vendale! The household gods at the pawnbroker's—the family immersed in tears. We all embraced in silence. My admirable friend alone possessed his composure. He sent out, on the spot, for a bottle of wine."

"Can I say a word to you in private, Mr. Obenreizer?"

"Assuredly." He turned to Madame Dor. "My good creature, you are sinking for want of repose. Mr. Vendale will excuse you."

Madame Dor rose, and set forth sideways on her journey from the stove to bed. She dropped a stocking. Vendale picked it up for her, and opened one of the folding-doors. She advanced a step, and dropped three more stockings. Vendale, stooping to recover them as before, Obenreizer interfered with profuse apologies, and with a warning look at Madame Dor. Madame Dor acknowledged the look by dropping the whole of the stockings in a heap, and then shuffling away panic-stricken from the scene of disaster. Obenreizer swept up the complete collection fiercely in both hands. "Go!" he cried, giving his prodigious handful a preparatory swing in the air. Madame Dor said, "Mon Dieu," and vanished into the next room, pursued by a shower of stockings.

"What must you think, Mr. Vendale," said Obenreizer, closing the door, "of this deplorable intrusion of domestic details? For myself, I blush at it. We are beginning the New Year as badly as possible; everything has gone wrong to-night. Be seated, pray—and say, what may I offer you? Shall we pay our best respects to another of your noble English institutions? It is my study to be, what you call, jolly. I propose a grog."

Vendale declined the grog with all needful respect for that noble institution.

"I wish to speak to you on a subject in which I am deeply interested," he said. "You must have observed, Mr. Obenreizer, that I have, from the first, felt no ordinary admiration for your charming niece?"

"You are very good. In my niece's name, I thank you."

"Perhaps you may have noticed, latterly, that my admiration for Miss Obenreizer has grown into a tenderer and deeper feeling——?"

"Shall we say friendship, Mr. Vendale?"

"Say love—and we shall be nearer to the truth."

Obenreizer started out of his chair. The faintly discernible beat, which was his nearest approach to a change of colour, showed itself suddenly in his cheeks.

"You are Miss Obenreizer's guardian," pursued Vendale. "I ask you to confer upon me the greatest of all favours—I ask you to give me her hand in marriage."

Obenreizer dropped back into his chair. "Mr. Vendale," he said, "you petrify me."

"I will wait," rejoined Vendale, "until you have recovered yourself."

"One word before I recover myself. You have said nothing about this to my niece?"

"I have opened my whole heart to your niece. And I have reason to hope——"

"What!" interposed Obenreizer. "You have made a proposal to my niece, without first asking for my authority to pay your addresses to her?" He struck his hand on the table, and lost his hold over himself for the first time in Vendale's experience of him. "Sir!" he exclaimed, indignantly, "what sort of conduct is this? As a man of honour, speaking to a man of honour, how can you justify it?"

"I can only justify it as one of our English institutions," said Vendale quietly. "You admire our English institutions. I can't honestly tell you, Mr. Obenreizer, that I regret what I have done. I can only assure you that I have not acted in the matter with any intentional disrespect towards yourself. This said, may I ask you to tell me plainly what objection you see to favouring my suit?"

"I see this immense objection," answered Obenreizer, "that my niece and you are not on a social equality together. My niece is the daughter of a poor peasant; and you are the son of a gentleman. You do us an honour," he added, lowering himself again gradually to his customary polite level, "which deserves, and has, our most grateful acknowledgments. But the inequality is too glaring; the sacrifice is too great. You English are a proud people, Mr. Vendale. I have observed enough of this country to see that such a marriage as you propose would be a scandal here. Not a hand would be held out to your peasant-wife; and all your best friends would desert you."

"One moment," said Vendale, interposing on his side. "I may claim, without any great arrogance, to know more of my country people in general, and of my own friends in particular, than you do. In the estimation of everybody whose opinion is worth having, my wife herself would be the one sufficient justification of my marriage. If I did not feel certain—observe, I say certain—that I am offering her a position which she can accept without so much as the shadow of a humiliation—I would never (cost me what it might) have asked her to be my wife. Is there any other obstacle that you see? Have you any personal objection to me?"

Obenreizer spread out both his hands in courteous protest. "Personal objection!" he exclaimed. "Dear sir, the bare question is painful to me."

"We are both men of business," pursued Vendale, "and you naturally expect me to satisfy you that I have the means of supporting a wife. I can explain my pecuniary position in two words. I inherit from my parents a fortune of twenty thousand pounds. In half of that sum I have only a life-interest, to which, if I die, leaving a widow, my widow succeeds. If I die, leaving children, the money itself is divided among them, as they come of age. The other half of my fortune is at my own disposal, and is invested in the wine-business. I see my way to greatly improving that business. As it stands at present, I cannot state my return from my capital embarked at more than twelve hundred a year. Add the yearly value of my life-interest—and the total reaches a present annual income of fifteen hundred pounds. I have the fairest prospect of soon making it more. In the meantime, do you object to me on pecuniary grounds?"

Driven back to his last entrenchment, Obenreizer rose, and took a turn backwards and forwards in the room. For the moment, he was plainly at a loss what to say or do next.

"Before I answer that last question," he said, after a little close consideration with himself, "I beg leave to revert for a moment to Miss Marguerite. You said something just now which seemed to imply that she returns the sentiment with which you are pleased to regard her?"

"I have the inestimable happiness," said Vendale, "of knowing that she loves me."

Obenreizer stood silent for a moment, with the film over his eyes, and the faintly perceptible beat becoming visible again in his cheeks.

"If you will excuse me for a few minutes," he said, with ceremonious politeness, "I should like to have the opportunity of speaking to my niece." With those words, he bowed, and quitted the room.

Left by himself, Vendale's thoughts (as a necessary result of the interview, thus far) turned instinctively to the consideration of Obenreizer's motives. He had put obstacles in the way of the courtship; he was now putting obstacles in the way of the marriage—a marriage offering advantages which even his ingenuity could not dispute. On the face of it, his conduct was incomprehensible. What did it mean?

Seeking, under the surface, for the answer to that question —and remembering that Obenreizer was a man of about his own age; also, that Marguerite was, strictly speaking, his

half-niece only—Vendale asked himself, with a lover's ready
jealousy, whether he had a rival to fear, as well as a
guardian to conciliate. The thought just crossed his mind,
and no more. The sense of Marguerite's kiss still lingering
on his cheek reminded him gently that even the jealousy of a
moment was now a treason to *her*.

On reflection, it seemed most likely that a personal motive
of another kind might suggest the true explanation of
Obenreizer's conduct. Marguerite's grace and beauty were
precious ornaments in that little household. They gave it a
special social attraction and a special social importance. They
armed Obenreizer with a certain influence in reserve, which
he could always depend upon to make his house attractive,
and which he might always bring more or less to bear on the
forwarding of his own private ends. Was he the sort of
man to resign such advantages as were here implied, without
obtaining the fullest possible compensation for the loss? A
connection by marriage with Vendale offered him solid advantages, beyond all doubt. But there were hundreds of men in
London with far greater power and far wider influence than
Vendale possessed. Was it possible that this man's ambition
secretly looked higher than the highest prospects that could
be offered to him by the alliance now proposed for his niece?
As the question passed through Vendale's mind, the man
himself reappeared—to answer it, or not to answer it, as the
event might prove.

A marked change was visible in Obenreizer when he
resumed his place. His manner was less assured, and there
were plain traces about his mouth of recent agitation which
had not been successfully composed. Had he said something,
referring either to Vendale or to himself, which had raised
Marguerite's spirit, and which had placed him, for the first
time, face to face with a resolute assertion of his niece's will?
It might or might not be. This only was certain—he looked
like a man who had met with a repulse.

"I have spoken to my niece," he began. "I find, Mr.

Vendale, that even your influence has not entirely blinded her to the social objections to your proposal."

"May I ask," returned Vendale, "if that is the only result of your interview with Miss Obenreizer?"

A momentary flash leapt out through the Obenreizer film.

"You are master of the situation," he answered, in a tone of sardonic submission. "If you insist on my admitting it, I do admit it in those words. My niece's will and mine used to be one, Mr. Vendale. You have come between us, and her will is now yours. In my country, we know when we are beaten, and we submit with our best grace. I submit, with my best grace, on certain conditions. Let us revert to the statement of your pecuniary position. I have an objection to you, my dear sir—a most amazing, a most audacious objection, from a man in my position to a man in yours."

"What is it?"

"You have honoured me by making a proposal for my niece's hand. For the present (with best thanks and respects), I beg to decline it."

"Why?"

"Because you are not rich enough."

The objection, as the speaker had foreseen, took Vendale completely by surprise. For the moment he was speechless.

"Your income is fifteen hundred a year," pursued Obenreizer. "In my miserable country I should fall on my knees before your income, and say, 'What a princely fortune!' In wealthy England, I sit as I am, and say, 'A modest independence, dear sir; nothing more. Enough, perhaps, for a wife in your own rank of life, who has no social prejudices to conquer. Not more than half enough for a wife who is a meanly born foreigner, and who has all your social prejudices against her.' Sir! if my niece is ever to marry you, she will have what you call uphill work of it in taking her place at starting. Yes, yes; this is not your view, but it remains, immovably remains, my view for all that. For my niece's sake, I claim that this uphill work shall be made as smooth as possible.

284

Whatever material advantages she can have to help her, ought, in common justice, to be hers. Now, tell me, Mr. Vendale, on your fifteen hundred a year can your wife have a house in a fashionable quarter, a footman to open her door, a butler to wait at her table, and a carriage and horses to drive about in? I see the answer in your face—your face says, No. Very good. Tell me one more thing, and I have done. Take the mass of your educated, accomplished, and lovely country-women, is it, or is it not, the fact that a lady who has a house in a fashionable quarter, a footman to open her door, a butler to wait at her table, and a carriage and horses to drive about in, is a lady who has gained four steps, in female estimation, at starting? Yes? or No?"

"Come to the point," said Vendale. "You view this question as a question of terms. What are your terms?"

"The lowest terms, dear sir, on which you can provide your wife with those four steps at starting. Double your present income—the most rigid economy cannot do it in England on less. You said just now that you expected greatly to increase the value of your business. To work— and increase it! I am a good devil after all! On the day when you satisfy me, by plain proofs, that your income has risen to three thousand a year, ask me for my niece's hand, and it is yours."

"May I inquire if you have mentioned this arrangement to Miss Obenreizer?"

"Certainly. She has a last little morsel of regard still left for me, Mr. Vendale, which is not yours yet; and she accepts my terms. In other words, she submits to be guided by her guardian's regard for her welfare, and by her guardian's superior knowledge of the world." He threw himself back in his chair, in firm reliance on his position, and in full possession of his excellent temper.

Any open assertion of his own interests, in the situation in which Vendale was now placed, seemed to be (for the present at least) hopeless. He found himself literally left with no ground to stand on. Whether Obenreizer's objections were the genuine product of Obenreizer's own view of the case, or whether he was simply delaying the marriage in the hope of ultimately breaking it off altogether—in either of these events, any present resistance on Vendale's part would be equally useless. There was no help for it but to yield, making the best terms that he could on his own side.

"I protest against the conditions you impose on me," he began.

"Naturally," said Obenreizer; "I dare say I should protest, myself, in your place."

"Say, however," pursued Vendale, "that I accept your terms. In that case, I must be permitted to make two stipulations on my part. In the first place, I shall expect to be allowed to see your niece."

"Aha! to see my niece? and to make her in as great a hurry to be married as you are yourself? Suppose I say, No? you would see her perhaps without my permission?"

"Decidedly!"

"How delightfully frank! How exquisitely English! You shall see her, Mr. Vendale, on certain days, which we will appoint together. What next?"

"Your objection to my income," proceeded Vendale, "has taken me completely by surprise. I wish to be assured against any repetition of that surprise. Your present views of my qualification for marriage require me to have an income of three thousand a year. Can I be certain, in the future, as your experience of England enlarges, that your estimate will rise no higher?"

"In plain English," said Obenreizer, "you doubt my word?"

"Do you purpose to take *my* word for it when I inform you that I have doubled my income?" asked Vendale. "If my memory does not deceive me, you stipulated, a minute since, for plain proofs?"

"Well played, Mr. Vendale! You combine the foreign

quickness with the English solidity. Accept my best congratulations. Accept, also, my written guarantee."

He rose; seated himself at a writing-desk at a side-table, wrote a few lines, and presented them to Vendale with a low bow. The engagement was perfectly explicit, and was signed and dated with scrupulous care.

"Are you satisfied with your guarantee?"

"I am satisfied."

"Charmed to hear it, I am sure. We have had our little skirmish—we have really been wonderfully clever on both sides. For the present our affairs are settled. I bear no malice. You bear no malice. Come, Mr. Vendale, a good English shake hands."

Vendale gave his hand, a little bewildered by Obenreizer's sudden transitions from one humour to another.

"When may I expect to see Miss Obenreizer again?" he asked, as he rose to go.

"Honour me with a visit to-morrow," said Obenreizer, "and we will settle it then. Do have a grog before you go! No? Well! well! we will reserve the grog till you have your three thousand a year, and are ready to be married. Aha! When will that be?"

"I made an estimate, some months since, of the capacities of my business," said Vendale. "If that estimate is correct, I shall double my present income——"

"And be married!" added Obenreizer.

"And be married," repeated Vendale, "within a year from this time. Good night."

VENDALE MAKES MISCHIEF

When Vendale entered his office the next morning, the dull commercial routine at Cripple Corner met him with a new face. Marguerite had an interest in it now! The whole machinery which Wilding's death had set in motion, to realise the value of the business—the balancing of ledgers, the estimating of debts, the taking of stock, and the rest of it—was now transformed into machinery which indicated the chances for and against a speedy marriage. After looking over results, as presented by his accountant, and checking additions and subtractions, as rendered by the clerks, Vendale turned his attention to the stock-taking department next, and sent a message to the cellars, desiring to see the report.

The Cellarman's appearance, the moment he put his head in at the door of his master's private room, suggested that something very extraordinary must have happened that morning. There was an approach to alacrity in Joey Ladle's movements! There was something which actually simulated cheerfulness in Joey Ladle's face!

"What's the matter?" asked Vendale. "Anything wrong?"

"I should wish to mention one thing," answered Joey. "Young Mr. Vendale, I have never set myself up for a prophet."

"Who ever said you did?"

"No prophet, as far as I've heard tell of that profession," proceeded Joey, "ever lived principally underground. No prophet, whatever else he might take in at the pores, ever took in wine from morning to night, for a number of years together. When I said to Young Master Wilding, respecting his changing the name of the firm, that one of these days he might find he'd changed the luck of the firm—did I put myself forward as a prophet? No, I didn't. Has what I said to him come true? Yes, it has. In the time of Pebbleson Nephew, Young Mr. Vendale, no such thing was ever known as a mistake made in a consignment delivered at these doors. There's a mistake been made now. Please to remark that it happened before Miss Margaret came here. For which reason it don't go against what I've said respecting Miss Margaret singing round the luck. Read that, sir," concluded Joey, pointing attention to a special passage in the report, with a forefinger which appeared to be in process of taking in through the pores nothing more remarkable than dirt. "It's foreign to my nature to crow over the house I serve, but I feel it a kind of a solemn duty to ask you to read that."

Vendale read as follows:—"Note, respecting the Swiss champagne. An irregularity has been discovered in the last consignment received from the firm of Defresnier and Co." Vendale stopped, and referred to a memorandum-book by his side. "That was in Mr. Wilding's time," he said. "The vintage was a particularly good one, and he took the whole of it. The Swiss champagne has done very well, hasn't it?"

"I don't say it's done badly," answered the Cellarman. "It may have got sick in our customers' bins, or it may have bust in our customers' hands. But I don't say it's done badly with *us*."

Vendale resumed the reading of the note: "We find the number of the cases to be quite correct by the books. But six of them, which present a slight difference from the rest in the brand, have been opened, and have been found to contain a red wine instead of champagne. The similarity in the brands, we suppose, caused a mistake to be made in sending the consignment from Neuchâtel. The error has not been found to extend beyond six cases."

"Is that all!" exclaimed Vendale, tossing the note away from him.

Joey Ladle's eye followed the flying morsel of paper drearily. "I'm glad to see you take it easy, sir," he said. "Whatever happens, it will be always a comfort to you to remember that you took it easy at first. Sometimes one mistake leads to another. A man drops a bit of orange-peel on the pavement by mistake, and another man treads on it by mistake, and there's a job at the hospital, and a party crippled for life. I'm glad you take it easy, sir. In Pebbleson Nephew's time we shouldn't have taken it easy till we had seen the end of it. Without desiring to crow over the house, Young Mr. Vendale, I wish you well through it. No offence, sir," said the Cellarman, opening the door to go out, and looking in again ominously before he shut it. "I'm muddled and molloncolly, I grant you. But I'm an old servant of Pebbleson Nephew, and I wish you well through them six cases of red wine."

Left by himself, Vendale laughed, and took up his pen. "I may as well send a line to Defresnier and Company," he thought, "before I forget it." He wrote at once in these terms:

"Dear Sirs. We are taking stock, and a trifling mistake has been discovered in the last consignment of champagne sent by your house to ours. Six of the cases contain red wine—which we hereby return to you. The matter can easily be set right, either by your sending us six cases of the champagne, if they can be produced, or, if not, by your crediting us with the value of six cases on the amount last paid (five hundred pounds) by our firm to yours. Your faithful servants,

"WILDING AND Co."

This letter despatched to the post, the subject dropped at once out of Vendale's mind. He had other and far more interesting matters to think of. Later in the day he paid the visit to Obenreizer which had been agreed on between them. Certain evenings in the week were set apart which he was privileged to spend with Marguerite—always, however, in the presence of a third person. On this stipulation Obenreizer politely but positively insisted. The one concession he made was to give Vendale his choice of who the third person should be. Confiding in past experience, his choice fell unhesitatingly upon the excellent woman who mended Obenreizer's stockings. On hearing of the responsibility entrusted to her, Madame Dor's intellectual nature burst suddenly into a new stage of development. She waited till Obenreizer's eye was off her—and then she looked at Vendale, and dimly winked.

BAD NEWS

The time passed—the happy evenings with Marguerite came and went. It was the tenth morning since Vendale had written to the Swiss firm, when the answer appeared on his desk, with the other letters of the day:

"Dear Sirs. We beg to offer our excuses for the little mistake which has happened. At the same time, we regret to add that the statement of our error, with which you have favoured us, has led to a very unexpected discovery. The affair is a most serious one for you and for us. The particulars are as follows:

"Having no more champagne of the vintage last sent to you, we made arrangements to credit your firm with the value of the six cases, as suggested by yourself. On taking this step, certain forms observed in our mode of doing business necessitated a reference to our bankers' book, as well as to our ledger. The result is a moral certainty that no such remittance as you mention can have reached our house, and a literal certainty that no such remittance has been paid to our account at the bank.

"It is needless, at this stage of the proceedings, to trouble you with details. The money has unquestionably been stolen in the course of its transit from you to us. Certain peculiarities which we observe, relating to the manner in which the fraud has been perpetrated, lead us to conclude that the thief may have calculated on being able to pay the missing sum to our bankers, before an inevitable discovery followed the annual striking of our balance. This would not have happened, in the usual course, for another three months. During that period, but for your letter, we might have remained perfectly unconscious of the robbery that has been committed.

"We mention this last circumstance, as it may help to show you that we have to do, in this case, with no ordinary thief. Thus far we have not even a suspicion of who that thief is. But we believe you will assist us in making some advance towards discovery, by examining the receipt (forged,

291

of course) which has no doubt purported to come to you
from our house. Be pleased to look and see whether it is a
receipt entirely in manuscript, or whether it is a numbered
and printed form which merely requires the filling in of the
amount. The settlement of this apparently trivial question
is, we assure you, a matter of vital importance. Anxiously
awaiting your reply, we remain, with high esteem and
consideration,

"Defresnier & CIE."

Vendale had the letter on his desk, and waited a moment
to steady his mind under the shock that had fallen on it.
At the time of all others when it was most important to
him to increase the value of his business, that business was
threatened with a loss of five hundred pounds. He thought
of Marguerite, as he took the key from his pocket and opened
the iron chamber in the wall in which the books and papers
of the firm were kept.

He was still in the chamber, searching for the forged receipt,
when he was startled by a voice speaking close behind him.

"A thousand pardons," said the voice; "I am afraid I
disturb you."

He turned, and found himself face to face with Marguerite's
guardian.

"I have called," pursued Obenreizer, "to know if I can be
of any use. Business of my own takes me away for some days
to Manchester and Liverpool. Can I combine any business
of yours with it? I am entirely at your disposal, in the
character of commercial traveller for the firm of Wilding
and Co."

"Excuse me for one moment," said Vendale; "I will speak
to you directly." He turned round again, and continued his
search among the papers. "You come at a time when
friendly offers are more than usually precious to me," he
resumed. "I have had very bad news this morning from
Neuchâtel."

"Bad news!" exclaimed Obenreizer. "From Defresnier and Company?"

"Yes. A remittance we sent to them has been stolen. I am threatened with a loss of five hundred pounds. What's that?"

Turning sharply, and looking into the room for the second time, Vendale discovered his envelope-case overthrown on the floor, and Obenreizer on his knees picking up the contents.

"All my awkwardness," said Obenreizer. "This dreadful news of yours startled me; I stepped back——" He became too deeply interested in collecting the scattered envelopes to finish the sentence.

"Don't trouble yourself," said Vendale. "The clerk will pick the things up."

"This dreadful news!" repeated Obenreizer, persisting in collecting the envelopes. "This dreadful news!"

"If you will read the letter," said Vendale, "you will find I have exaggerated nothing. There it is, open on my desk."

He resumed his search, and in a moment more discovered the forged receipt. It was on the numbered and printed form, described by the Swiss firm. Vendale made a memorandum of the number and the date. Having replaced the receipt and locked up the iron chamber, he had leisure to notice Obenreizer, reading the letter in the recess of a window at the far end of the room.

"Come to the fire," said Vendale. "You look perished with the cold out there. I will ring for some more coals."

Obenreizer rose, and came slowly back to the desk. "Marguerite will be as sorry to hear of this as I am," he said, kindly. "What do you mean to do?"

"I am in the hands of Defresnier and Company," answered Vendale. "In my total ignorance of the circumstances, I can only do what they recommend. The receipt which I have just found, turns out to be the numbered and printed form. They seem to attach some special importance to its discovery.

You have had experience, when you were in the Swiss house, of their way of doing business. Can you guess what object they have in view?"

Obenreizer offered a suggestion.

"Suppose I examine the receipt?" he said.

"Are you ill?" asked Vendale, startled by the change in his face, which now showed itself plainly for the first time. "Pray go to the fire. You seem to be shivering—I hope you are not going to be ill?"

"Not I!" said Obenreizer. "Perhaps I have caught cold. Your English climate might have spared an admirer of your English institutions. Let me look at the receipt."

Vendale opened the iron chamber. Obenreizer took a chair, and drew it close to the fire. He held both hands over the flames. "Let me look at the receipt," he repeated, eagerly, as Vendale reappeared with the paper in his hand. At the same moment a porter entered the room with a fresh supply of coals. Vendale told him to make a good fire. The man obeyed the order with a disastrous alacrity. As he stepped forward and raised the scuttle, his foot caught in a fold of the rug, and he discharged his entire cargo of coals into the grate. The result was an instant smothering of the flame, and the production of a stream of yellow smoke, without a visible morsel of fire to account for it.

"Imbecile!" whispered Obenreizer to himself, with a look at the man which the man remembered for many a long day afterwards.

"Will you come into the clerks' room?" asked Vendale. "They have a stove there."

"No, no. No matter."

Vendale handed him the receipt. Obenreizer's interest in examining it appeared to have been quenched as suddenly and as effectually as the fire itself. He just glanced over the document, and said, "No; I don't understand it! I am sorry to be of no use."

"I will write to Neuchâtel by to-night's post," said Vendale, putting away the receipt for the second time. "We must wait, and see what comes of it."

"By to-night's post," repeated Obenreizer. "Let me see. You will get the answer in eight or nine days' time. I shall be back before that. If I can be of any service, as commercial traveller, perhaps you will let me know between this and then. You will send me written instructions? My best thanks. I shall be most anxious for your answer from Neuchâtel. Who knows? It may be a mistake, my dear friend, after all. Courage! courage! courage!" He had entered the room with no appearance of being pressed for time. He now snatched up his hat, and took his leave with the air of a man who had not another moment to lose.

Left by himself, Vendale took a turn thoughtfully in the room.

His previous impression of Obenreizer was shaken by what he had heard and seen at the interview which had just taken place. He was disposed, for the first time, to doubt whether, in this case, he had not been a little hasty and hard in his judgment on another man. Obenreizer's surprise and regret, on hearing the news from Neuchâtel, bore the plainest marks of being honestly felt—not politely assumed for the occasion. With troubles of his own to encounter, suffering, to all appearance, from the first insidious attack of a serious illness, he had looked and spoken like a man who really deplored the disaster that had fallen on his friend. Hitherto Vendale had tried vainly to alter his first opinion of Marguerite's guardian, for Marguerite's sake. All the generous instincts in his nature now combined together and shook the evidence which had seemed unanswerable up to this time. "Who knows?" he thought. "I may have read that man's face wrongly, after all."

The time passed—the happy evenings with Marguerite came and went. It was again the tenth morning since Vendale had written to the Swiss firm; and again the answer appeared on his desk with the other letters of the day:

"Dear Sir. My senior partner, M. Defresnier, has been called away, by urgent business, to Milan. In his absence (and with his full concurrence and authority), I now write to you again on the subject of the missing five hundred pounds.

"Your discovery that the forged receipt is executed upon one of our numbered and printed forms has caused inexpressible surprise and distress to my partner and to myself. At the time when your remittance was stolen, but three keys were in existence opening the strong-box in which our receipt-forms are invariably kept. My partner had one key; I had the other. The third was in the possession of a gentleman who, at that period, occupied a position of trust in our house. We should as soon have thought of suspecting one of ourselves as of suspecting this person. Suspicion now points at him, nevertheless. I cannot prevail on myself to inform you who the person is, so long as there is the shadow of a chance that he may come innocently out of the inquiry which must now be instituted. Forgive my silence; the motive of it is good.

"The form our investigation must now take is simple enough. The handwriting on your receipt must be compared, by competent persons whom we have at our disposal, with certain specimens of handwriting in our possession. I cannot send you the specimens for business reasons, which, when you hear them, you are sure to approve. I must beg you to send me the receipt to Neuchâtel—and, in making this request, I must accompany it by a word of necessary warning.

"If the person, at whom suspicion now points, really proves to be the person who has committed this forgery and theft, I have reason to fear that circumstances may have already put him on his guard. The only evidence against him is the evidence in your hands, and he will move heaven and earth to obtain and destroy it. I strongly urge you not to trust the receipt to the post. Send it to me, without loss of time, by a private hand, and choose nobody for your messenger but a person long established in your own employment, accustomed to travelling, capable of speaking French; a man of courage, a man of honesty, and, above all things, a man who can be trusted to let no stranger scrape acquaintance with him on the route. Tell no one—absolutely no one—but your messenger of the turn this matter has now taken. The safe transit of the receipt may depend on your interpreting *literally* the advice which I give you at the end of this letter.

"I have only to add that every possible saving of time is now of the last importance. More than one of our receipt-forms is missing—and it is impossible to say what new frauds may not be committed, if we fail to lay our hands on the thief.

"Your faithful servant,   " ROLLAND,

"(Signing for Defresnier and Cie.)"

Who was the suspected man? In Vendale's position, it seemed useless to inquire.

Who was to be sent to Neuchâtel with the receipt? Men of courage and men of honesty were to be had at Cripple Corner for the asking. But where was the man who was accustomed to foreign travelling, who could speak the French language, and who could be really relied on to let no stranger scrape acquaintance with him on his route? There was but one man at hand who combined all those requisites in his own person, and that man was Vendale himself.

It was a sacrifice to leave his business; it was a greater sacrifice to leave Marguerite. But a matter of five hundred pounds was involved in the pending inquiry; and a literal interpretation of M. Rolland's advice was insisted on in terms which there was no trifling with. The more Vendale thought of it, the more plainly the necessity faced him, and said, "Go!"

As he locked up the letter with the receipt, the association of ideas reminded him of Obenreizer. A guess at the identity of the suspected man looked more possible now. Obenreizer might know.

The thought had barely passed through his mind, when the door opened, and Obenreizer entered the room.

"They told me at Soho-square you were expected back last night," said Vendale, greeting him. "Have you done well in the country? Are you better?"

A thousand thanks. Obenreizer had done admirably well; Obenreizer was infinitely better. And now, what news? Any letter from Neuchâtel?

"A very strange letter," answered Vendale. "The matter has taken a new turn, and the letter insists—without excepting anybody—on my keeping our next proceedings a profound secret."

"Without excepting anybody?" repeated Obenreizer. As he said the words, he walked away again, thoughtfully, to the window at the other end of the room, looked out for a moment, and suddenly came back to Vendale. "Surely they must have forgotten?" he resumed, "or they would have excepted *me?*"

"It is Monsieur Rolland who writes," said Vendale. "And, as you say, he must certainly have forgotten. That view of the matter quite escaped me. I was just wishing I had you to consult, when you came into the room. And here I am tied by a formal prohibition, which cannot possibly have been intended to include you. How very annoying!"

Obenreizer's filmy eyes fixed on Vendale attentively.

"Perhaps it is more than annoying!" he said. "I came this morning not only to hear the news, but to offer myself as messenger, negotiator—what you will. Would you believe it? I have letters which oblige me to go to Switzerland immediately. Messages, documents, anything—I could have taken them all to Defresnier and Rolland for you."

"You are the very man I wanted," returned Vendale. "I had decided, most unwillingly, on going to Neuchâtel myself, not five minutes since, because I could find no one here capable of taking my place. Let me look at the letter again."

He opened the strong room to get at the letter. Obenreizer,

after first glancing round him to make sure that they were alone, followed a step or two and waited, measuring Vendale with his eye. Vendale was the tallest man, and unmistakably the strongest man also of the two. Obenreizer turned away, and warmed himself at the fire.

Meanwhile, Vendale read the last paragraph in the letter for the third time. There was the plain warning—there was the closing sentence, which insisted on a literal interpretation of it. The hand, which was leading Vendale in the dark, led him on that condition only. A large sum was at stake: a terrible suspicion remained to be verified. If he acted on his own responsibility, and if anything happened to defeat the object in view, who would be blamed? As a man of business, Vendale had but one course to follow. He locked the letter up again.

"It is most annoying," he said to Obenreizer—"it is a piece of forgetfulness on Monsieur Rolland's part which puts me to serious inconvenience, and places me in an absurdly false position towards you. What am I to do? I am acting in a very serious matter, and acting entirely in the dark. I have no choice but to be guided, not by the spirit, but by the letter of my instructions. You understand me, I am sure? You know, if I had not been fettered in this way, how gladly I should have accepted your services?"

"Say no more!" returned Obenreizer. "In your place I should have done the same. My good friend, I take no offence. I thank you for your compliment. We shall be travelling companions, at any rate," added Obenreizer. "You go, as I go, at once?"

"At once. I must speak to Marguerite first, of course!"

"Surely! surely! Speak to her this evening. Come, and pick me up on the way to the station. We go together by the mail train to-night?"

"By the mail train to-night."

It was later than Vendale had anticipated when he drove

up to the house in Soho-square. Business difficulties, occasioned by his sudden departure, had presented themselves by dozens. A cruelly large share of the time which he had hoped to devote to Marguerite had been claimed by duties at his office which it was impossible to neglect.

To his surprise and delight, she was alone in the drawing-room when he entered it.

"We have only a few minutes, George," she said. "But Madame Dor has been good to me—and we can have those few minutes alone." She threw her arms round his neck, and whispered eagerly, "Have you done anything to offend Mr. Obenreizer?"

"I!" exclaimed Vendale, in amazement.

"Hush!" she said, "I want to whisper it. You know the little photograph I have got of you. This afternoon it happened to be on the chimney-piece. He took it up and looked at it—and I saw his face in the glass. I know you have offended him! He is merciless; he is revengeful; he is as secret as the grave. Don't go with him, George—don't go with him!"

"My own love," returned Vendale, "you are letting your fancy frighten you! Obenreizer and I were never better friends than we are at this moment."

Before a word more could be said, the sudden movement of some ponderous body shook the floor of the next room. The shock was followed by the appearance of Madame Dor. "Obenreizer!" exclaimed this excellent person in a whisper, and plumped down instantly in her regular place by the stove.

Obenreizer came in with a courier's bag strapped over his shoulder.

"Are you ready?" he asked, addressing Vendale. "Can I take anything for you? You have no travelling-bag. I have got one. Here is the compartment for papers, open at your service."

"Thank you," said Vendale. "I have only one paper of importance with me; and that paper I am bound to take charge of myself. Here it is," he added, touching the breast-pocket of his coat, "and here it must remain till we get to Neuchâtel."

As he said those words, Marguerite's hand caught his, and pressed it significantly. She was looking towards Obenreizer. Before Vendale could look, in his turn, Obenreizer had wheeled round, and was taking leave of Madame Dor.

"Adieu, my charming niece!" he said, turning to Marguerite next. "En route, my friend, for Neuchâtel!" He tapped Vendale lightly over the breast-pocket of his coat, and led the way to the door.

Vendale's last look was for Marguerite. Marguerite's last words to him were, "Don't go!"

I⊤ was about the middle of the month of February when Vendale and Obenreizer set forth on their expedition. The winter being a hard one, the time was bad for travellers. So bad was it that these two travellers, coming to Strasbourg, found its great inns almost empty. And even the few people they did encounter in that city, who had started from England or from Paris on business journeys towards the interior of Switzerland, were turning back.

Many of the railroads in Switzerland that tourists pass easily enough now, were almost or quite impracticable then. Some were not begun; more were not completed. On such as were open, there were still large gaps of old road where communication in the winter season was often stopped; on others, there were weak points where the new work was not safe, either under conditions of severe frost, or of rapid thaw. The running of trains on this last class was not to be counted on in the worst time of the year, was contingent upon weather, or was wholly abandoned through the months considered the most dangerous.

At Strasbourg there were more travellers' stories afloat, respecting the difficulties of the way further on, than there were travellers to relate them. Many of these tales were as wild as usual; but the more modestly marvellous did derive some colour from the circumstance that people were indisputably turning back. However, as the road to Basle was open, Vendale's resolution to push on was in no wise disturbed. Obenreizer's resolution was necessarily Vendale's, seeing that he stood at bay thus desperately: He must be ruined, or must destroy the evidence that Vendale carried about him, even if he destroyed Vendale with it.

The state of mind of each of these two fellow-travellers towards the other was this. Obenreizer, encircled by impending ruin through Vendale's quickness of action, and seeing the circle narrowed every hour by Vendale's energy, hated him with the animosity of a fierce, cunning lower animal. He had always had instinctive movements in his breast against him; perhaps, because of that old sore of gentleman and peasant; perhaps, because of the openness of his nature; perhaps, because of his better looks; perhaps, because of his success with Marguerite; perhaps, on all those grounds, the two last not the least. And now he saw in him, besides, the hunter who was tracking him down. Vendale, on the other hand, always contending generously against his first vague mistrust, now felt bound to contend against it more than ever: reminding himself, " He is Marguerite's guardian. We are on perfectly friendly terms; he is my companion of his own proposal, and can have no interested motive in sharing this undesirable journey." To which pleas in behalf of Obenreizer, chance added one consideration more, when they came to Basle after a journey of more than twice the average duration.

They had had a late dinner, and were alone in an inn room there, overhanging the Rhine: at that place rapid and deep, swollen and loud. Vendale lounged upon a couch, and Obenreizer walked to and fro: now, stopping at the window, looking at the crooked reflection of the town lights in the dark water (and peradventure thinking, " If I could fling him into it!"); now, resuming his walk with his eyes upon the floor.

" Where shall I rob him, if I can? Where shall I murder him, if I must?" So, as he paced the room, ran the river, ran the river, ran the river.

The burden seemed to him, at last, to be growing so plain, that he stopped; thinking it as well to suggest another burden to his companion.

"The Rhine sounds to-night," he said with a smile, "like the old waterfall at home. That waterfall which my mother showed to travellers (I told you of it once). The sound of it changed with the weather, as does the sound of all falling waters and flowing waters. When I was pupil of the watchmaker, I remembered it as sometimes saying to me for whole days, 'Who are you, my little wretch? Who are you, my little wretch?' I remembered it as saying, other times, when its sound was hollow, and storm was coming up the Pass: 'Boom, boom, boom. Beat him, beat him, beat him.' Like my mother enraged—if she was my mother."

"If she was?" said Vendale, gradually changing his attitude to a sitting one. "If she was? Why do you say 'if'?"

"What do I know?" replied the other negligently, throwing up his hands and letting them fall as they would. "What would you have? I am so obscurely born, that how can I say? I was very young, and all the rest of the family were men and women, and my so-called parents were old. Anything is possible of a case like that."

"Did you ever doubt—— ?"

"I told you once, I doubt the marriage of those two," he replied, throwing up his hands again, as if he were throwing the unprofitable subject away. "But here I am in Creation. *I* come of no fine family. What does it matter?"

"At least you are Swiss," said Vendale, after following him with his eyes to and fro.

"How do I know?" he retorted abruptly, and stopping to look back over his shoulder. "I say to you, at least you are English. How do you know?"

"By what I have been told from infancy."

"Ah! I know of myself that way."

"And," added Vendale, pursuing the thought that he could not drive back, "by my earliest recollections."

"I also. I know of myself that way—if that way satisfies."

"Does it not satisfy you?"

"It must. There is nothing like 'it must' in this little world. It must. Two short words those, but stronger than long proof or reasoning."

"You and poor Wilding were born in the same year. You were nearly of an age," said Vendale, again thoughtfully looking after him as he resumed his pacing up and down.

"Yes. Very nearly."

Could Obenreizer be the missing man? In the unknown associations of things, was there a subtler meaning than he himself thought, in that theory so often on his lips about the smallness of the world? Had the Swiss letter presenting him followed so close on Mrs. Goldstraw's revelation concerning the infant who had been taken away to Switzerland, because he was that infant grown a man? In a world where so many depths lie unsounded, it might be. The chances, or the laws—call them either—that had wrought out the revival of Vendale's own acquaintance with Obenreizer, and had ripened it into intimacy, and had brought them here together this present winter night, were hardly less curious; while read by such a light, they were seen to cohere towards the furtherance of a continuous and an intelligible purpose.

Vendale's awakened thoughts ran high while his eyes musingly followed Obenreizer pacing up and down the room, the river ever running to the tune: "Where shall I rob him, if I can? Where shall I murder him, if I must?" The secret of his dead friend was in no hazard from Vendale's lips; but just as his friend had died of its weight, so did he in his lighter succession feel the burden of the trust, and the obligation to follow any clue, however obscure. He rapidly asked himself, would he like this man to be the real Wilding? No. Argue down his mistrust as he might, he was unwilling to put such a substitute in the place of his late guileless, outspoken, childlike partner. He rapidly asked himself, would he like this man to be rich? No. He had more power than enough over Marguerite as it was, and wealth might invest him with more. Would he like this man to be Marguerite's Guardian, and yet proved to stand in no degree of relationship towards her, however disconnected and distant? No. But these were not considerations to come between him and fidelity to the dead. Let him see to it that they passed him with no other notice than the knowledge that they *had* passed him, and left him bent on the discharge of a solemn duty. And he did see to it, so soon that he followed his companion with ungrudging eyes, while he still paced the room; that companion, whom he supposed to be moodily reflecting on his own birth, and not on another man's—least of all what man's—violent Death.

The road in advance from Basle to Neuchâtel was better than had been represented. The latest weather had done it good. Drivers, both of horses and mules, had come in that evening after dark, and had reported nothing more difficult to be overcome than trials of patience, harness, wheels, axles, and whipcord. A bargain was soon struck for a carriage and horses, to take them on in the morning, and to start before daylight.

"Do you lock your door at night when travelling?" asked Obenreizer, standing warming his hands by the wood fire in Vendale's chamber, before going to his own.

"Not I. I sleep too soundly."

"You are so sound a sleeper?" he retorted, with an admiring look. "What a blessing!"

"Anything but a blessing to the rest of the house," rejoined Vendale, "if I had to be knocked up in the morning from the outside of my bedroom door."

"I, too," said Obenreizer, "leave open my room. But let me advise you, as a Swiss who knows: always, when you travel in my country, put your papers—and, of course, your money—under your pillow. Always the same place."

"You are not complimentary to your countrymen," laughed Vendale.

"My countrymen," said Obenreizer, with that light touch of his friend's elbows by way of Good Night and benediction, "I suppose are like the majority of men. And the majority of men will take what they can get. Adieu! At four in the morning."

"Adieu! At four."

Left to himself, Vendale raked the logs together, sprinkled over them the white wood-ashes lying on the hearth, and sat down to compose his thoughts. But they still ran high on their latest theme, and the running of the river tended to agitate rather than to quiet them. As he sat thinking, what little disposition he had had to sleep departed. He felt it hopeless to lie down yet, and sat dressed by the fire. Marguerite, Wilding, Obenreizer, the business he was then upon, and a thousand hopes and doubts that had nothing to do with it, occupied his mind at once. Everything seemed to have power over him but slumber. The departed disposition to sleep kept far away.

He had sat for a long time thinking, on the hearth, when his candle burned down and its light went out. It was of little moment; there was light enough in the fire. He changed his attitude, and, leaning his arm on the chair-back, and his chin upon that hand, sat thinking still.

But he sat between the fire and the bed, and, as the fire flickered in the play of air from the fast-flowing river, his enlarged shadow fluttered on the white wall by the bedside. His attitude gave it an air, half of mourning and half of bending over the bed imploring. His eyes were observant of it, when he became troubled by the disagreeable fancy that it was like Wilding's shadow, and not his own.

A slight change of place would cause it to disappear. He made the change, and the apparition of his disturbed fancy vanished. He now sat in the shade of a little nook beside the fire, and the door of the room was before him.

It had a long, cumbrous iron latch. He saw the latch slowly and softly rise. The door opened a very little, and

307

came to again, as though only the air had moved it. But he saw that the latch was out of the hasp.

The door opened again very slowly, until it opened wide enough to admit some one. It afterwards remained still for a while, as though cautiously held open on the other side. The figure of a man then entered, with its face turned towards the bed, and stood quiet just within the door. Until it said, in a low half-whisper, at the same time taking one step forward: " Vendale ! "

"What now?" he answered, springing from his seat; "who is it?"

It was Obenreizer, and he uttered a cry of surprise as Vendale came upon him from that unexpected direction. "Not in bed?" he said, catching him by both shoulders with an instinctive tendency to a struggle. "Then something *is* wrong!"

"What do you mean?" said Vendale, releasing himself.

"First tell me; you are not ill?"

"Ill? No."

"I have had a bad dream about you. How is it that I see you up and dressed?"

"My good fellow, I may as well ask you how it is that I see *you* up and undressed?"

"I have told you why. I have had a bad dream about you. I tried to rest after it, but it was impossible. I could not make up my mind to stay where I was without knowing you were safe; and yet I could not make up my mind to come in here. I have been minutes hesitating at the door. It is so easy to laugh at a dream that you have not dreamed. Where is your candle?"

"Burnt out."

"I have a whole one in my room. Shall I fetch it?"

"Do so."

His room was very near, and he was absent for but a few seconds. Coming back with the candle in his hand, he kneeled down on the hearth and lighted it. As he blew with his breath a charred billet into flame for the purpose, Vendale, looking down at him, saw that his lips were white and not easy of control.

"Yes!" said Obenreizer, setting the lighted candle on the table, "it was a bad dream. Only look at me!"

His feet were bare; his red-flannel shirt was thrown back at the throat, and its sleeves were rolled above the elbows; his only other garment, a pair of under pantaloons or drawers, reaching to the ankles, fitted him close and tight. A certain lithe and savage appearance was on his figure, and his eyes were very bright.

"If there had been a wrestle with a robber, as I dreamed," said Obenreizer, "you see, I was stripped for it."

"And armed too," said Vendale, glancing at his girdle.

"A traveller's dagger, that I always carry on the road," he answered carelessly, half drawing it from its sheath with his left hand, and putting it back again. "Do you carry no such thing?"

"Nothing of the kind."

"No pistols?" said Obenreizer, glancing at the table, and from it to the untouched pillow.

"Nothing of the sort."

"You Englishmen are so confident! You wish to sleep?"

"I have wished to sleep this long time, but I can't do it."

"I neither, after the bad dream. My fire has gone the way of your candle. May I come and sit by yours? Two o'clock! It will so soon be four, that it is not worth the trouble to go to bed again."

"I shall not take the trouble to go to bed at all, now," said Vendale; "sit here and keep me company, and welcome."

Going back to his room to arrange his dress, Obenreizer soon returned in a loose cloak and slippers, and they sat down on opposite sides of the hearth. In the interval Vendale had replenished the fire from the wood-basket in his room, and Obenreizer had put upon the table a flask and cup from his.

"Common cabaret brandy, I am afraid," he said, pouring out; "bought upon the road, and not like yours from Cripple Corner. But yours is exhausted; so much the worse. A cold night, a cold time of night, a cold country, and a cold house. This may be better than nothing; try it."

Vendale took the cup, and did so.

"How do you find it?"

"It has a coarse after-flavour," said Vendale, giving back the cup with a slight shudder, " and I don't like it."

"You are right," said Obenreizer, tasting, and smacking his lips; "it *has* a coarse after-flavour, and *I* don't like it. Booh! It burns, though!" He had flung what remained in the cup upon the fire.

Each of them leaned an elbow on the table, reclined his head upon his hand, and sat looking at the flaring logs. Obenreizer remained watchful and still; but Vendale, after certain nervous twitches and starts, in one of which he rose to his feet and looked wildly about him, fell into the strangest confusion of dreams. He carried his papers in a leather case or pocket-book, in an inner breast-pocket of his buttoned travelling-coat; and whatever he dreamed of, in the lethargy that got possession of him, something importunate in these papers called him out of that dream, though he could not wake from it. He was belated on the steppes of Russia (some shadowy person gave that name to the place) with Marguerite; and yet the sensation of a hand at his breast, softly feeling the outline of the pocket-book as he lay asleep before the fire, was present to him. He was ship-wrecked in an open boat at sea, and having lost his clothes, had no other covering than an old sail; and yet a creeping hand, tracing outside all the other pockets of the dress he actually wore, for papers, and finding none answer its touch, warned him to rouse himself. He was in the ancient vault at Cripple Corner, to which was transferred the very bed substantial and present in that very room at Basle; and Wilding (not dead, as he had supposed, and yet he did not

310

wonder much) shook him, and whispered, "Look at that man! Don't you see he has risen, and is turning the pillow? Why should he turn the pillow, if not to seek those papers that are in your breast? Awake!" And yet he slept, and wandered off into other dreams.

Watchful and still, with his elbow on the table, and his head upon that hand, his companion at length said: "Vendale! We are called. Past Four!" Then, opening his eyes, he saw, turned sideways on him, the filmy face of Obenreizer.

"You have been in a heavy sleep," he said. "The fatigue of constant travelling and the cold!"

"I am broad awake now," cried Vendale, springing up, but with an unsteady footing. "Haven't you slept at all?"

"I may have dozed, but I seem to have been patiently looking at the fire. Whether or no, we must wash, and breakfast, and turn out. Past four, Vendale; past four!"

It was said in a tone to rouse him, for already he was half asleep again. In his preparation for the day, too, and at his breakfast, he was often virtually asleep while in mechanical action. It was not until the cold dark day was closing in, that he had any distincter impressions of the ride than jingling bells, bitter weather, slipping horses, frowning hill-sides, bleak woods, and a stoppage at some wayside house of entertainment, where they had passed through a cowhouse to reach the travellers' room above. He had been conscious of little more, except of Obenreizer sitting thoughtful at his side all day, and eyeing him much.

But when he shook off his stupor, Obenreizer was not at his side. The carriage was stopping to bait at another way-side house; and a line of long narrow carts, laden with casks of wine, and drawn by horses with a quantity of blue collar and head-gear, were baiting too. These came from the direction in which the travellers were going, and Obenreizer (not thoughtful now, but cheerful and alert) was talking with the foremost driver. As Vendale stretched his limbs, circulated his blood, and cleared off the lees of his lethargy, with a sharp run to and fro in the bracing air, the line of carts moved on : the drivers all saluting Obenreizer as they passed him.

"Who are those?" asked Vendale.

"They are our carriers—Defresnier and Company's," replied Obenreizer. "Those are our casks of wine." He was singing to himself, and lighting a cigar.

"I have been drearily dull company to-day," said Vendale. "I don't know what has been the matter with me."

"You had no sleep last night; and a kind of brain-congestion frequently comes, at first, of such cold," said Obenreizer. "I have seen it often. After all, we shall have our journey for nothing, it seems."

"How for nothing?"

"The House is at Milan. You know, we are a Wine House at Neuchâtel, and a Silk House at Milan? Well, Silk happening to press of a sudden, more than Wine, Defresnier was summoned to Milan. Rolland, the other partner, has been taken ill since his departure, and the doctors will allow him to see no one. A letter awaits you at Neuchâtel to tell you so. I have it from our chief carrier whom you saw me talking with. He was surprised to see me, and said he had that word for you if he met you. What do you do? Go back?"

"Go on," said Vendale.

"On?"

"On? Yes. Across the Alps, and down to Milan."

Obenreizer stopped in his smoking to look at Vendale, and then smoked heavily, looked up the road, looked down the road, looked down at the stones in the road at his feet.

"I have a very serious matter in charge," said Vendale; "more of these missing forms may be turned to as bad account, or worse; I am urged to lose no time in helping the House to take the thief; and nothing shall turn me back."

"No?" cried Obenreizer, taking out his cigar to smile, and giving his hand to his fellow-traveller. "Then nothing shall turn *me* back. Ho, driver! Despatch. Quick there! Let us push on!"

They travelled through the night. There had been snow, and there was a partial thaw, and they mostly travelled at a foot-pace, and always with many stoppages to breathe the splashed and floundering horses. After an hour's broad daylight, they drew rein at the inn-door at Neuchâtel, having been some eight-and-twenty hours in conquering some eighty English miles.

When they had hurriedly refreshed and changed, they went together to the house of business of Defresnier and Company. There they found the letter which the wine-carrier had described, enclosing the tests and comparisons of handwriting essential to the discovery of the Forger. Vendale's determination to press forward, without resting, being already taken, the only question to delay them was by what Pass could they cross the Alps? Respecting the state of the two Passes of the St. Gotthard and the Simplon, the guides and mule-drivers differed greatly; and both passes were still far enough off, to prevent the travellers from having the benefit of any recent experience of either. Besides which, they well know that a fall of snow might altogether change the described conditions in a single hour, even if they were correctly stated. But, on the whole, the Simplon appearing to be the hope-fuller route, Vendale decided to take it. Obenreizer bore little or no part in the discussion, and scarcely spoke.

To Geneva, to Lausanne, along the level margin of the lake to Vevey, so into the winding valley between the spurs of the mountains, and into the valley of the Rhone. The sound of the carriage-wheels, as they rattled on, through the day, through the night, became as the wheels of a great clock, recording the hours. No change of weather varied the journey, after it had hardened into a sullen frost. In a sombre-yellow sky, they saw the Alpine ranges; and they saw enough of snow on nearer and much lower hill-tops and hill-sides, to sully, by contrast, the purity of lake, torrent, and waterfall, and make the villages look discoloured and dirty. But no snow fell, nor was there any snow-drift on the road. The stalking along the valley of more or less of white mist, changing on their hair and dress into icicles, was the only variety between them and the gloomy sky. And still by day, and still by night, the wheels. And still they rolled, in the hearing of one of them, to the burden, altered from the burden of the Rhine: "The time is gone for robbing him alive, and I must murder him."

They came, at length, to the poor little town of Brieg, at the foot of the Simplon. They came there after dark, but yet could see how dwarfed men's works and men became with the immense mountains towering over them. Here they must lie for the night; and here was warmth of fire, and lamp, and dinner, and wine, and after-conference resounding, with guides and drivers. No human creature had come across the Pass for four days. The snow above the snow-line was too soft for wheeled carriage, and not hard enough for sledge. There was snow in the sky. There had been snow in the sky for days past, and the marvel was that it had not fallen, and the certainty was that it must fall. No vehicle could cross. The journey might be tried on mules, or it might be tried on foot; but the best guides must be paid danger-price in either case, and that, too, whether they succeeded in taking the two travellers across, or turned for safety and brought them back.

In this discussion, Obenreizer bore no part whatever. He sat silently smoking by the fire until the room was cleared and Vendale referred to him.

"Bah! I am weary of these poor devils and their trade," he said, in reply. "Always the same story. It is the story of their trade to-day, as it was the story of their trade when I was a ragged boy. What do you and I want? We want a knapsack each, and a mountain-staff each. We want no guide; we should guide him; he would not guide us. We leave our portmanteaus here, and we cross together. We have been on the mountains together before now, and I am mountain-born, and I know this Pass—Pass!—rather High Road!—by heart. We will leave these poor devils, in pity, to trade with others; but they must not delay us to make a pretence of earning money. Which is all they mean."

Vendale, glad to be quit of the dispute, and to cut the knot: active, adventurous, bent on getting forward, and therefore very susceptible to the last hint: readily assented. Within two hours, they had purchased what they wanted for the expedition, had packed their knapsacks, and lay down to sleep.

At break of day, they found half the town collected in the narrow street to see them depart. The people talked together in groups; the guides and drivers whispered apart, and looked up at the sky; no one wished them a good journey.

As they began the ascent, a gleam of sun shone from the otherwise unaltered sky, and for a moment turned the tin spires of the town to silver.

"A good omen!" said Vendale (though it died out while he spoke). "Perhaps our example will open the Pass on this side."

"No; we shall not be followed," returned Obenreizer, looking up at the sky and back at the valley. "We shall be alone up yonder."

ON THE MOUNTAIN

The road was fair enough for stout walkers, and the air grew lighter and easier to breathe as the two ascended. But the settled gloom remained as it had remained for days back. Nature seemed to have come to a pause. The sense of hearing, no less than the sense of sight, was troubled by having to wait so long for the change, whatever it might be, that impended. The silence was as palpable and heavy as

315

the lowering clouds—or rather cloud, for there seemed to be but one in all the sky, and that one covering the whole of it.

Although the light was thus dismally shrouded, the prospect was not obscured. Down in the valley of the Rhone behind them, the stream could be traced through all its many windings, oppressively sombre and solemn in its one leaden hue, a colourless waste. Far and high above them, glaciers and suspended avalanches overhung the spots where they must pass, by and by; deep and dark below them on their right, were awful precipice and roaring torrent; tremendous mountains arose in every vista. The gigantic landscape, uncheered by a touch of changing light or a solitary ray of sun, was yet terribly distinct in its ferocity. The hearts of two lonely men might shrink a little, if they had to win their way for miles and hours among a legion of silent and motion-less men—mere men like themselves—all looking at them with fixed and frowning front. But how much more, when the legion is of Nature's mightiest works, and the frown may turn to fury in an instant!

As they ascended, the road became gradually more rugged and difficult. But the spirits of Vendale rose as they mounted higher, leaving so much more of the road behind them conquered. Obenreizer spoke little, and held on with a determined purpose. Both, in respect of agility and endurance, were well qualified for the expedition. Whatever the born mountaineer read in the weather-tokens that was illegible to the other, he kept to himself.

"Shall we get across to-day?" asked Vendale.

"No," replied the other. "You see how much deeper the snow lies here than it lay half a league lower. The higher we mount the deeper the snow will lie. Walking is half wading even now. And the days are so short! If we get as high as the fifth Refuge, and lie to-night at the Hospice, we shall do well."

"Is there no danger of the weather rising in the night," asked Vendale, anxiously, "and snowing us up?"

"There is danger enough about us," said Obenreizer, with a cautious glance onward and upward, "to render silence our best policy. You have heard of the Bridge of the Ganther?"

"I have crossed it once."

"In the summer?"

"Yes; in the travelling season."

"Yes; but it is another thing at this season;" with a sneer, as though he were out of temper. "This is not a time of year, or a state of things, on an Alpine Pass, that you gentlemen holiday-travellers know much about."

"You are my Guide," said Vendale, good humouredly. "I trust to you."

"I am your Guide," said Obenreizer, "and I will guide you to your journey's end. There is the Bridge before us."

They had made a turn into a desolate and dismal ravine, where the snow lay deep below them, deep above them, deep on every side. While speaking, Obenreizer stood pointing at the Bridge, and observing Vendale's face, with a very singular expression on his own.

"If I, as Guide, had sent you over there, in advance, and encouraged you to give a shout or two, you might have brought down upon yourself tons and tons and tons of snow, that would not only have struck you dead, but buried you deep, at a blow."

"No doubt," said Vendale.

"No doubt. But that is not what I have to do, as Guide. So pass silently. Or, going as we go, our indiscretion might else crush and bury *me*. Let us get on!"

There was a great accumulation of snow on the Bridge; and such enormous accumulations of snow overhung them from projecting masses of rock, that they might have been making their way through a stormy sky of white clouds. Using his staff skilfully, sounding as he went, and looking upward, with bent shoulders, as it were to resist the mere idea of a fall from above, Obenreizer softly led. Vendale closely followed. They were yet in the midst of their

317

dangerous way, when there came a mighty rush, followed by a sound as of thunder. Obenreizer clapped his hand on Vendale's mouth and pointed to the track behind them. Its aspect had been wholly changed in a moment. An avalanche had swept over it, and plunged into the torrent at the bottom of the gulf below.

Their appearance at the solitary Inn not far beyond this terrible Bridge, elicited many expressions of astonishment from the people shut up in the house. "We stay but to rest," said Obenreizer, shaking the snow from his dress at the fire. "This gentleman has very pressing occasion to get across; tell them, Vendale."

"Assuredly, I have very pressing occasion. I must cross."

"You hear, all of you. My friend has very pressing occasion to get across, and we want no advice and no help. I am as good a guide, my fellow-countrymen, as any of you. Now, give us to eat and drink."

In exactly the same way, and in nearly the same words, when it was coming on dark and they had struggled through the greatly increased difficulties of the road, and had at last reached their destination for the night, Obenreizer said to the astonished people of the Hospice, gathering about them at the fire, while they were yet in the act of getting their wet shoes off, and shaking the snow from their clothes:

"It is well to understand one another, friends all. This gentleman——"

"—Has," said Vendale, readily taking him up with a smile, "very pressing occasion to get across. Must cross."

"You hear?—has very pressing occasion to get across, must cross. We want no advice and no help. I am mountain-born, and act as Guide. Do not worry us by talking about it, but let us have supper, and wine, and bed."

All through the intense cold of the night, the same awful stillness. Again at sunrise, no sunny tinge to gild or redden the snow. The same interminable waste of deathly white; the same immovable air; the same monotonous gloom in the sky.

"Travellers!" a friendly voice called to them from the door, after they were afoot, knapsack on back and staff in hand, as yesterday; "recollect! There are five places of shelter, near together, on the dangerous road before you; and there is the wooden cross, and there is the next Hospice. Do not stray from the track. If the *Tourmente* comes on, take shelter instantly!"

"The trade of these poor devils!" said Obenreizer to his friend, with a contemptuous backward wave of his hand towards the voice. "How they stick to their trade! You Englishmen say we Swiss are mercenary. Truly, it does look like it."

They had divided between the two knapsacks such refreshments as they had been able to obtain that morning, and as they deemed it prudent to take. Obenreizer carried the wine as his share of the burden; Vendale, the bread and meat and cheese, and the flask of brandy.

They had for some time laboured upward and onward through the snow—which was now above their knees in the track, and of unknown depth elsewhere—and they were still labouring upward and onward through the most frightful part of that tremendous desolation, when snow began to fall. At first, but a few flakes descended slowly and steadily. After a little while the fall grew much denser, and suddenly it began without apparent cause to whirl itself into spiral shapes. Instantly ensuing upon this last change, an icy blast came roaring at them, and every sound and force imprisoned until now was let loose.

One of the dismal galleries through which the road is carried at that perilous point, a cave eked out by arches of great strength, was near at hand. They struggled into it, and the storm raged wildly. The noise of the wind, the noise of the water, the thundering down of displaced masses of rock and snow, the awful voices with which not only that gorge but every gorge in the whole monstrous range seemed to be suddenly endowed, the darkness as of night, the violent

319

revolving of the snow which beat and broke it into spray and blinded them, the madness of everything around insatiate for destruction, the rapid substitution of furious violence for unnatural calm, and hosts of appalling sounds for silence: these were things, on the edge of a deep abyss, to chill the blood, though the fierce wind, made actually solid by ice and snow, had failed to chill it.

Obenreizer, walking to and fro in the gallery without ceasing, signed to Vendale to help him unbuckle his knapsack. They could see each other, but could not have heard each other speak. Vendale complying, Obenreizer produced his bottle of wine, and poured some out, motioning Vendale to take that for warmth's sake, and not brandy. Vendale again complying, Obenreizer seemed to drink after him, and the two walked backwards and forwards side by side; both well knowing that to rest or sleep would be to die.

The snow came driving heavily into the gallery by the upper end at which they would pass out of it, if they ever passed out; for greater dangers lay on the road behind them than before. The snow soon began to choke the arch. An hour more, and it lay so high as to block out half the returning daylight. But it froze hard now, as it fell, and could be clambered through or over. The violence of the mountain storm was gradually yielding to a steady snowfall. The wind still raged at intervals, but not incessantly; and when it paused, the snow fell in heavy flakes.

They might have been two hours in their frightful prison, when Obenreizer, now crunching into the mound, now creeping over it with his head bowed down and his body touching the top of the arch, made his way out. Vendale followed close upon him, but followed without clear motive or calculation. For the lethargy of Basle was creeping over him again, and mastering his senses.

How far he had followed out of the gallery, or with what obstacles he had since contended, he knew not. He became roused to the knowledge that Obenreizer had set upon him, and that they were struggling desperately in the snow. He became roused to the remembrance of what his assailant carried in a girdle. He felt for it, drew it, struck at him, struggled again, struck at him again, cast him off, and stood face to face with him.

"I promised to guide you to your journey's end," said Obenreizer, "and I have kept my promise. The journey of your life ends here. Nothing can prolong it. You are sleeping as you stand."

"You are a villain. What have you done to me?"

"You are a fool. I have drugged you. You are doubly a fool, for I drugged you once before upon the journey, to try you. You are trebly a fool, for I am the thief and forger, and in a few moments I shall take those proofs against the thief and forger from your insensible body."

The entrapped man tried to throw off the lethargy, but its fatal hold upon him was so sure that, even while he heard those words, he stupidly wondered which of them had been wounded, and whose blood it was that he saw sprinkled on the snow.

"What have I done to you," he asked, heavily and thickly, "that you should be—so base—a murderer?"

"Done to me? You would have destroyed me, but that you have come to your journey's end. Your cursed activity interposed between me, and the time I had counted on in which I might have replaced the money. Done to me? You have come in my way—not once, not twice, but again and again and again. Did I try to shake you off in the beginning, or no? You were not to be shaken off. Therefore you die here."

Vendale tried to think coherently, tried to speak coherently, tried to pick up the iron-shod staff he had let fall; failing to touch it, tried to stagger on without its aid. All in vain, all in vain! He stumbled, and fell heavily forward on the brink of the deep chasm.

Stupefied, dozing, unable to stand upon his feet, a veil

before his eyes, his sense of hearing deadened, he made such a vigorous rally that, supporting himself on his hands, he saw his enemy standing calmly over him, and heard him speak.

"You call me murderer," said Obenreizer, with a grim laugh. "The name matters very little. But at least I have set my life against yours, for I am surrounded by dangers, and may never make my way out of this place. The *Tourmente* is rising again. The snow is on the whirl. I must have the papers now. Every moment has my life in it."

"Stop!" cried Vendale, in a terrible voice, staggering up with a last flash of fire breaking out of him, and clutching the thievish hands at his breast, in both of his. "Stop! Stand away from me! God bless my Marguerite! Happily she will never know how I died. Stand off from me, and let me look at your murderous face. Let it remind me—of something—left to say."

The sight of him fighting so hard for his senses, and the doubt whether he might not for the instant be possessed by the strength of a dozen men, kept his opponent still. Wildly glaring at him, Vendale faltered out the broken words:

"It shall not be—the trust—of the dead—betrayed by me —reputed parents—misinherited fortune—see to it!"

As his head dropped on his breast, and he stumbled on the brink of the chasm as before, the thievish hands went once more, quick and busy, to his breast. He made a convulsive attempt to cry "No!" desperately rolled himself over into the gulf; and sank away from his enemy's touch, like a phantom in a dreadful dream.

The mountain storm raged again, and passed again. The awful mountain-voices died away, the moon rose, and the soft and silent snow fell.

Two men and two large dogs came out at the door of the Hospice. The men looked carefully around them, and up at the sky. The dogs rolled in the snow, and took it into their mouths, and cast it up with their paws.

No Thoroughfare

One of the men said to the other: "We may venture now. We may find them in one of the five Refuges." Each fastened on his back a basket; each took in his hand a strong spiked pole; each girded under his arms a looped end of a stout rope, so that they were tied together.

Suddenly the dogs desisted from their gambols in the snow, stood looking down the ascent, put their noses up, put their noses down, became greatly excited, and broke into a deep loud bay together.

The two men looked in the faces of the two dogs. The two dogs looked, with at least equal intelligence, in the faces of the two men.

"Au· secours, then! Help! To the rescue!" cried the two men. The two dogs, with a glad, deep, generous bark, bounded away.

"Two more mad ones!" said the men, stricken motionless, and looking away in the moonlight. "Is it possible in such weather! And one of them a woman!"

Each of the dogs had the corner of a woman's dress in its mouth, and drew her along. She fondled their heads as she came up, and she came up through the snow with an accustomed tread. Not so the large man with her, who was spent and winded.

"Dear guides, dear friends of travellers! I am of your country. We seek two gentlemen crossing the Pass, who should have reached the Hospice this evening."

"They have reached it, ma'amselle."

"Thank Heaven! O thank Heaven!"

"But, unhappily, they have gone on again. We are setting forth to seek them even now. We had to wait until the *Tourmente* passed. It has been fearful up here."

"Dear guides, dear friends of travellers! Let me go with you. Let me go with you for the love of GOD! One of those gentlemen is to be my husband. I love him, O, so dearly. O so dearly! You see I am not faint, you see I am not tired. I am born a peasant girl. I will show you

323

that I know well how to fasten myself to your ropes. I will do it with my own hands. I will swear to be brave and good. But let me go with you, let me go with you! If any mischance should have befallen him, my love would find him, when nothing else could. On my knees, dear friends of travellers! By the love your dear mothers had for your fathers!"

The good, rough fellows were moved. "After all," they murmured to one another, "she speaks but the truth. She knows the ways of the mountains. See how marvellously she has come here. But as to Monsieur there, ma'amselle?"

"Dear Mr. Joey," said Marguerite, addressing him in his own tongue, "you will remain at the house, and wait for me; will you not?"

"If I know'd which o' you two recommended it," growled Joey Ladle, eyeing the two men with great indignation, "I'd fight you for sixpence, and give you half-a-crown towards your expenses. No, Miss. I'll stick by you as long as there's any sticking left in me, and I'll die for you when I can't do better."

The state of the moon rendering it highly important that no time should be lost, and the dogs showing signs of great uneasiness, the two men quickly took their resolution. The rope that yoked them together was exchanged for a longer one; the party were secured, Marguerite second, and the Cellarman last; and they set out for the Refuges. The actual distance of those places was nothing; the whole five, and the next Hospice to boot, being within two miles; but the ghastly way was whitened out and sheeted over.

They made no miss in reaching the Gallery where the two had taken shelter. The second storm of wind and snow had so wildly swept over it since, that their tracks were gone. But the dogs went to and fro with their noses down, and were confident. The party stopping, however, at the further arch, where the second storm had been especially furious, and where the drift was deep, the dogs became troubled, and went about and about, in quest of a lost purpose.

The great abyss being known to lie on the right, they wandered too much to the left, and had to regain the way with infinite labour through a deep field of snow. The leader of the line had stopped it, and was taking note of the landmarks, when one of the dogs fell to tearing up the snow a little before them. Advancing and stooping to look at it, thinking that some one might be overwhelmed there, they saw that it was stained, and that the stain was red.

The other dog was now seen to look over the brink of the gulf, with his fore legs straightened out, lest he should fall into it, and to tremble in every limb. Then the dog who had found the stained snow joined him, and then they ran to and fro, distressed and whining. Finally, they both stopped on the brink together, and setting up their heads, howled dolefully.

"There is some one lying below," said Marguerite.

"I think so," said the foremost man. "Stand well inward, the two last, and let us look over."

The last man kindled two torches from his basket, and handed them forward. The leader taking one, and Marguerite the other, they looked down; now shading the torches, now moving them to the right or left, now raising them, now depressing them, as moonlight far below contended with black shadows. A piercing cry from Marguerite broke a long silence.

"My God! On a projecting point, where a wall of ice stretches forward over the torrent, I see a human form!"

"Where, ma'amselle, where?"

"See, there! On the shelf of ice below the dogs!"

The leader, with a sickened aspect, drew inward, and they were all silent. But they were not all inactive, for Marguerite, with swift and skilful fingers, had detached both herself and him from the rope in a few seconds.

"Show me the baskets. These two are the only ropes?"

"The only ropes here, ma'amselle; but at the Hospice——"

"If he is alive—I know it is my lover—he will be dead before you can return. Dear Guides! Blessed friends of travellers! Look at me. Watch my hands. If they falter or go wrong, make me your prisoner by force. If they are steady and go right, help me to save him!"

She girded herself with a cord under the breast and arms, she formed it into a kind of jacket, she drew it into knots, she laid its end side by side with the end of the other cord, she twisted and twined the two together, she knotted them together, she set her foot upon the knots, she strained them, she held them for the two men to strain at.

"She is inspired," they said to one another.

"By the Almighty's mercy!" she exclaimed. "You both know that I am by far the lightest here. Give me the brandy and the wine, and lower me down to him. Then go for assistance and a stronger rope. You see that when it is lowered to me—look at this about me now—I can make it fast and safe to his body. Alive or dead, I will bring him up, or die with him. I love him passionately. Can I say more?"

They turned to her companion, but he was lying senseless on the snow.

"Lower me down to him," she said, taking two little kegs they had brought, and hanging them about her, "or I will dash myself to pieces! I am a peasant, and I know no giddiness or fear; and this is nothing to me, and I passionately love him. Lower me down!"

"Ma'amselle, ma'amselle, he must be dying or dead."

"Dying or dead, my husband's head shall lie upon my breast, or I will dash myself to pieces."

They yielded, overborne. With such precautions as their skill and the circumstances admitted, they let her slip from the summit, guiding herself down the precipitous icy wall with her hand, and they lowered down, and lowered down, and lowered down, until the cry came up: "Enough!"

"Is it really he, and is he dead?" they called down, looking over.

The cry came up: "He is insensible; but his heart beats. It beats against mine."

"How does he lie?"

The cry came up: "Upon a ledge of ice. It has thawed beneath him, and it will thaw beneath me. Hasten. If we die, I am content."

One of the two men hurried off with the dogs at such topmost speed as he could make; the other set up the lighted torches in the snow, and applied himself to recovering the Englishman. Much snow-chafing and some brandy got him on his legs, but delirious and quite unconscious where he was.

The watch remained upon the brink, and his cry went down continually: "Courage! They will soon be here. How goes it?" And the cry came up: "His heart still beats against mine. I warm him in my arms. I have cast off the rope, for the ice melts under us, and the rope would separate me from him; but I am not afraid."

The moon went down behind the mountain tops, and all the abyss lay in darkness. The cry went down: "How goes it?" The cry came up: "We are sinking lower, but his heart still beats against mine."

At length the eager barking of the dogs, and a flare of light upon the snow, proclaimed that help was coming on. Twenty or thirty men, lamps, torches, litters, ropes, blankets, wood to kindle a great fire, restoratives and stimulants, came in fast. The dogs ran from one man to another, and from this thing to that, and ran to the edge of the abyss, dumbly entreating Speed, speed, speed!

The cry went down: "Thanks to God, all is ready. How goes it?"

The cry came up: "We are sinking still, and we are deadly cold. His heart no longer beats against mine. Let no one come down, to add to our weight. Lower the rope only."

The fire was kindled high, a great glare of torches lighted

the sides of the precipice, lamps were lowered, a strong rope was lowered. She could be seen passing it round him, and making it secure.

The cry came up into a deathly silence: "Raise! Softly!" They could see her diminished figure shrink, as he was swung into the air.

They gave no shout when some of them laid him on a litter, and others lowered another strong rope. The cry again came up into a deathly silence: "Raise! Softly!" But when they caught her at the brink, then they shouted, then they wept, then they gave thanks to Heaven, then they kissed her feet, then they kissed her dress, then the dogs caressed her, licked her icy hands, and with their honest faces warmed her frozen bosom!

She broke from them all, and sank over him on his litter, with both her loving hands upon the heart that stood still.

THE CLOCK-LOCK

THE pleasant scene was Neuchâtel; the pleasant month was April; the pleasant place was a notary's office; the pleasant person in it was the notary: a rosy, hearty, handsome old man, chief notary of Neuchâtel, known far and wide in the canton as Maître Voigt. Professionally and personally, the notary was a popular citizen. His innumerable kindnesses and his innumerable oddities had for years made him one of the recognised public characters of the pleasant Swiss town. His long brown frock-coat and his black skull-cap, were among the institutions of the place: and he carried a snuff-box which, in point of size, was popularly believed to be without a parallel in Europe.

There was another person in the notary's office, not so pleasant as the notary. This was Obenreizer.

An oddly pastoral kind of office it was, and one that would never have answered in England. It stood in a neat back yard, fenced off from a pretty flower-garden. Goats browsed in the doorway, and a cow was within half-a-dozen feet of keeping company with the clerk. Maître Voigt's room was a bright and varnished little room, with panelled walls, like a toy-chamber. According to the seasons of the year, roses, sunflowers, hollyhocks, peeped in at the windows. Maître Voigt's bees hummed through the office all the summer, in at this window and out at that, taking it frequently in their day's work, as if honey were to be made from Maître

329

Voigt's sweet disposition. A large musical box on the chimney-piece often trilled away at the Overture to Fra Diavolo, or a Selection from William Tell, with a chirruping liveliness that had to be stopped by force on the entrance of a client, and irrepressibly broke out again the moment his back was turned.

"Courage, courage, my good fellow!" said Maître Voigt, patting Obenreizer on the knee, in a fatherly and comforting way. "You will begin a new life to-morrow morning in my office here."

Obenreizer—dressed in mourning, and subdued in manner —lifted his hand, with a white handkerchief in it, to the region of his heart. "The gratitude is here," he said. "But the words to express it are not here."

"Ta-ta-ta! Don't talk to me about gratitude!" said Maître Voigt. "I hate to see a man oppressed. I see you oppressed, and I hold out my hand to you by instinct. Besides, I am not too old yet, to remember my young days. Your father sent me my first client. (It was on a question of half an acre of vineyard that seldom bore any grapes.) Do I owe nothing to your father's son? I owe him a debt of friendly obligation, and I pay it to you. That's rather neatly expressed, I think," added Maître Voigt, in high good humour with himself. "Permit me to reward my own merit with a pinch of snuff!"

Obenreizer dropped his eyes to the ground, as though he were not even worthy to see the notary take snuff.

"Do me one last favour, sir," he said, when he raised his eyes. "Do not act on impulse. Thus far, you have only a general knowledge of my position. Hear the case for and against me, in its details, before you take me into your office. Let my claim on your benevolence be recognised by your sound reason as well as by your excellent heart. In *that* case, I may hold up my head against the bitterest of my enemies, and build myself a new reputation on the ruins of the character I have lost."

MR. OBENREIZER EXPLAINS

"As you will," said Maître Voigt. "You speak well, my son. You will be a fine lawyer one of these days."

"The details are not many," pursued Obenreizer. "My troubles begin with the accidental death of my late travelling companion, my lost dear friend Mr. Vendale."

"Mr. Vendale," repeated the notary. "Just so. I have heard and read of the name, several times within these two months. The name of the unfortunate English gentleman who was killed on the Simplon. When you got that scar upon your cheek and neck."

"—From my own knife," said Obenreizer, touching what must have been an ugly gash at the time of its infliction.

"From your own knife," assented the notary, "and in trying to save him. Good, good, good. That was very good. Vendale. Yes. I have several times, lately, thought it droll that I should once have had a client of that name."

"But the world, sir," returned Obenreizer, "is *so* small!" Nevertheless he made a mental note that the notary had once had a client of that name.

"As I was saying, sir, the death of that dear travelling comrade begins my troubles. What follows? I save myself. I go down to Milan. I am received with coldness by Defresnier and Company. Shortly afterwards, I am discharged by Defresnier and Company. Why? They give no reason why. I ask, do they assail my honour? No answer. I ask, what is the imputation against me? No answer. I ask, where are their proofs against me? No answer. I ask, what am I to think? The reply is, 'M. Obenreizer is free to think what he will. What M. Obenreizer thinks, is of no importance to Defresnier and Company.' And that is all."

"Perfectly. That is all," assented the notary, taking a large pinch of snuff.

"But is that enough, sir?"

"That is not enough," said Maître Voigt. "The House of Defresnier are my fellow-townsmen—much respected, much esteemed—but the House of Defresnier must not silently

331

destroy a man's character. You can rebut assertion. But how can you rebut silence?"

"Your sense of justice, my dear patron," answered Obenreizer, "states in a word the cruelty of the case. Does it stop there? No. For, what follows upon that?"

"True, my poor boy," said the notary, with a comforting nod or two; "your ward rebels upon that."

"Rebels is too soft a word," retorted Obenreizer. "My ward revolts from me with horror. My ward defies me. My ward withdraws herself from my authority, and takes shelter (Madame Dor with her) in the house of that English lawyer, Mr. Bintrey, who replies to your summons to her to submit herself to my authority, that she will not do so."

"—And who afterwards writes," said the notary, moving his large snuff-box to look among the papers underneath it for the letter, "that he is coming to confer with me."

"Indeed?" replied Obenreizer, rather checked. "Well, sir. Have I no legal rights?"

"Assuredly, my poor boy," returned the notary. "All but felons have their legal rights."

"And who calls me felon?" said Obenreizer, fiercely.

"No one. Be calm under your wrongs. If the House of Defresnier would call you felon, indeed, we should know how to deal with them."

While saying these words, he had handed Bintrey's very short letter to Obenreizer, who now read it and gave it back.

"In saying," observed Obenreizer, with recovered composure, "that he is coming to confer with you, this English lawyer means that he is coming to deny my authority over my ward."

"You think so?"

"I am sure of it. I know him. He is obstinate and contentious. You will tell me, my dear sir, whether my authority is unassailable, until my ward is of age?"

"Absolutely unassailable."

"I will enforce it. I will make her submit herself to it. For," said Obenreizer, changing his angry tone to one of

332

grateful submission, "I owe it to you, sir; to you, who have so confidingly taken an injured man under your protection, and into your employment."

"Make your mind easy," said Maître Voigt. "No more of this now, and no thanks! Be here to-morrow morning, before the other clerk comes—between seven and eight. You will find me in this room; and I will myself initiate you in your work. Go away! go away! I have letters to write. I won't hear a word more."

Dismissed with this generous abruptness, and satisfied with the favourable impression he had left on the old man's mind, Obenreizer was at leisure to revert to the mental note he had made that Maître Voigt once had a client whose name was Vendale.

"I ought to know England well enough by this time;" so his meditations ran, as he sat on a bench in the yard; "and it is not a name I ever encountered there, except"—he looked involuntarily over his shoulder—"as *his* name. Is the world so small that I cannot get away from him, even now when he is dead? He confessed at the last that he had betrayed the trust of the dead, and misinherited a fortune. And I was to see to it. And I was to stand off, that my face might remind him of it. Why *my* face, unless it concerned *me?* I am sure of his words, for they have been in my ears ever since. Can there be anything bearing on them, in the keeping of this old idiot? Anything to repair my fortunes, and blacken his memory? He dwelt upon my earliest remembrances, that night at Basle. Why, unless he had a purpose in it?"

Maître Voigt's two largest he-goats were butting at him to butt him out of the place, as if for that disrespectful mention of their master. So he got up and left the place. But he walked alone for a long time on the border of the lake, with his head drooped in deep thought.

Between seven and eight next morning, he presented himself again at the office. He found the notary ready for him, at

work on some papers which had come in on the previous
evening. In a few clear words, Maître Voigt explained the
routine of the office, and the duties Obenreizer would be
expected to perform. It still wanted five minutes to eight,
when the preliminary instructions were declared to be complete.

"I will show you over the house and the offices," said
Maître Voigt, "but I must put away these papers first.
They come from the municipal authorities, and they must be
taken special care of."

Obenreizer saw his chance, here, of finding out the repository
in which his employer's private papers were kept.

"Can't I save you the trouble, sir?" he asked. "Can't I
put those documents away under your directions?"

Maître Voigt laughed softly to himself; closed the portfolio
in which the papers had been sent to him; handed it to
Obenreizer.

"Suppose you try," he said. "All my papers of importance
are kept yonder."

He pointed to a heavy oaken door, thickly studded with nails,
at the lower end of the room. Approaching the door, with
the portfolio, Obenreizer discovered, to his astonishment, that
there were no means whatever of opening it from the outside.
There was no handle, no bolt, no key, and (climax of passive
obstruction!) no keyhole.

"There is a second door to this room?" said Obenreizer,
appealing to the notary.

"No," said Maître Voigt. "Guess again."

"There is a window?"

"Nothing of the sort. The window has been bricked up.
The only way in, is the way by that door. Do you give it
up?" cried Maître Voigt, in high triumph. "Listen, my good
fellow, and tell me if you hear nothing inside?"

Obenreizer listened for a moment, and started back from
the door.

"I know!" he exclaimed. "I heard of this when I was
apprenticed here at the watchmaker's. Perrin Brothers have

334

finished their famous clock-lock at last—and you have got it?"

"Bravo!" said Maître Voigt. "The clock-lock it is! There, my son! There you have one more of what the good people of this town call, 'Daddy Voigt's follies.' With all my heart! Let those laugh who win. No thief can steal *my* keys. No burglar can pick *my* lock. No power on earth, short of a battering-ram or a barrel of gunpowder, can move that door, till my little sentinel inside—my worthy friend who goes 'Tick, Tick,' as I tell him—says 'Open!' The big door obeys the little Tick, Tick, and the little Tick, Tick, obeys *me*. That!" cried Daddy Voigt, snapping his fingers, "for all the thieves in Christendom!"

"May I see it in action?" asked Obenreizer. "Pardon my curiosity, dear sir! You know that I was once a tolerable worker in the clock trade."

"Certainly you shall see it in action," said Maître Voigt. "What is the time now? One minute to eight. Watch, and in one minute you will see the door open of itself."

In one minute, smoothly and slowly and silently, as if invisible hands had set it free, the heavy door opened inward, and disclosed a dark chamber beyond. On three sides, shelves filled the walls, from floor to ceiling. Arranged on the shelves, were rows upon rows of boxes made in the pretty inlaid woodwork of Switzerland, and bearing inscribed on their fronts (for the most part in fanciful coloured letters) the names of the notary's clients.

Maître Voigt lighted a taper, and led the way into the room. "You shall see the clock," he said proudly. "I possess the greatest curiosity in Europe. It is only a privileged few whose eyes can look at it. I give the privilege to your good father's son—you shall be one of the favoured few who enter the room with me. See! here it is, on the right-hand wall at the side of the door."

"An ordinary clock," exclaimed Obenreizer. "No! Not an ordinary clock. It has only one hand."

335

"Aha!" said Maître Voigt. "Not an ordinary clock, my friend. No, no. That one hand goes round the dial. As I put it, so it regulates the hour at which the door shall open. See! The hand points to eight. At eight the door opened, as you saw for yourself."

"Does it open more than once in the four-and-twenty hours?" asked Obenreizer.

"More than once?" repeated the notary, with great scorn. "You don't know, my good friend, Tick-Tick! He will open the door as often as I ask him. All he wants is his directions, and he gets them here. Look below the dial. Here is a half-circle of steel let into the wall, and here is a hand (called the regulator) that travels round it, just as *my* hand chooses. Notice, if you please, that there are figures to guide me on the half-circle of steel. Figure I. means: Open once in the four-and-twenty hours. Figure II. means: Open twice; and so on to the end. I set the regulator every morning, after I have read my letters, and when I know what my day's work is to be. Would you like to see me set it now? What is to-day? Wednesday. Good! This is the day of our rifle-club; there is little business to do; I grant a half-holiday. No work here to-day, after three o'clock. Let us first put away this portfolio of municipal papers. There! No need to trouble Tick-Tick to open the door until eight to-morrow. Good! I leave the dial-hand at eight; I put back the regulator to I.; I close the door; and closed the door remains, past all opening by anybody, till to-morrow morning at eight."

Obenreizer's quickness instantly saw the means by which he might make the clock-lock betray its master's confidence, and place its master's papers at his disposal.

"Stop, sir!" he cried, at the moment when the notary was closing the door. "Don't I see something moving among the boxes—on the floor there?"

(Maître Voigt turned his back for a moment to look. In that moment, Obenreizer's ready hand put the regulator on,

from the figure " I." to the figure " II." Unless the notary
looked again at the half-circle of steel, the door would open
at eight that evening, as well as at eight next morning, and
nobody but Obenreizer would know it.)

"There is nothing!" said Maître Voigt. "Your troubles
have shaken your nerves, my son. Some shadow thrown by
my taper; or some poor little beetle, who lives among the
old lawyer's secrets, running away from the light. Hark! I
hear your fellow-clerk in the office. To work! to work! and
build to-day the first step that leads to your new fortunes!"

He good-humouredly pushed Obenreizer out before him;
extinguished the taper, with a last fond glance at his clock
which passed harmlessly over the regulator beneath; and
closed the oaken door.

At three, the office was shut up. The notary and everybody
in the notary's employment, with one exception, went to see
the rifle-shooting. Obenreizer had pleaded that he was not in
spirits for a public festival. Nobody knew what had become
of him. It was believed that he had slipped away for a
solitary walk.

The house and offices had been closed but a few minutes,
when the door of a shining wardrobe in the notary's shining
room opened, and Obenreizer stepped out. He walked to a
window, unclosed the shutters, satisfied himself that he could
escape unseen by way of the garden, turned back into the
room, and took his place in the notary's easy chair. He was
locked up in the house, and there were five hours to wait
before eight o'clock came.

He wore his way through the five hours: sometimes reading
the books and newspapers that lay on the table: sometimes
thinking: sometimes walking to and fro. Sunset came on.
He closed the window-shutters before he kindled a light.
The candle lighted, and the time drawing nearer and nearer,
he sat, watch in hand, with his eyes on the oaken door.

At eight, smoothly and softly and silently the door opened.
One after another, he read the names on the outer rows of

boxes. No such name as Vendale! He removed the outer row, and looked at the row behind. These were older boxes, and shabbier boxes. The four first that he examined, were inscribed with French and German names. The fifth bore a name which was almost illegible. He brought it out into the room, and examined it closely. There, covered thickly with time-stains and dust, was the name: "Vendale."

The key hung to the box by a string. He unlocked the box, took out four loose papers that were in it, spread them open on the table, and began to read them. He had not so occupied a minute, when his face fell from its expression of eagerness and avidity, to one of haggard astonishment and disappointment. But, after a little consideration, he copied the papers. He then replaced the papers, replaced the box, closed the door, extinguished the candle, and stole away.

As his murderous and thievish footfall passed out of the garden, the steps of the notary and some one accompanying him stopped at the front door of the house. The lamps were lighted in the little street, and the notary had his door-key in his hand.

"Pray do not pass my house, Mr. Bintrey," he said. "Do me the honour to come in. It is one of our town half-holidays—our Tir—but my people will be back directly. It is droll that you should ask your way to the Hotel of me. Let us eat and drink before you go there."

"Thank you; not to-night," said Bintrey. "Shall I come to you at ten to-morrow?"

"I shall be enchanted, sir, to take so early an opportunity of redressing the wrongs of my injured client," returned the good notary.

"Yes," retorted Bintrey; "your injured client is all very well—but—a word in your ear."

He whispered to the notary and walked off. When the notary's housekeeper came home, she found him standing at his door motionless, with the key still in his hand, and the door unopened.

AN INFRACTION OF THE LAW

The scene shifts again—to the foot of the Simplon, on the Swiss side.

In one of the dreary rooms of the dreary little inn at Brieg, Mr. Bintrey and Maître Voigt sat together at a professional council of two. Mr. Bintrey was searching in his despatch-box. Maître Voigt was looking towards a closed door, painted brown to imitate mahogany, and communicating ·with an inner room.

"Isn't it time·he was here?" asked the notary, shifting his position, and glancing at a second door at the other end of the room, painted yellow to imitate deal.

"He *is* here," answered Bintrey, after listening for a moment.

The yellow door was opened by a waiter, and Obenreizer walked in.

After greeting Maître Voigt with a cordiality which appeared to cause the notary no little embarrassment, Obenreizer bowed with grave and distant politeness to Bintrey. "For what reason have I been brought from Neuchâtel to the foot of the mountain?" he inquired, taking the seat which the English lawyer had indicated to him.

"You shall be quite satisfied on that head before our interview is over," returned Bintrey. "For the present, permit me to suggest proceeding at once to business. There has been a correspondence, Mr. Obenreizer, between you and your niece. I am here to represent your niece."

"In other words, you, a lawyer, are here to represent an infraction of the law."

"Admirably put!" said Bintrey. "If all the people I have to deal with were only like you, what an easy profession mine would be! I am here to represent an infraction of the law—that is your point of view. I am here to make a compromise between you and your niece—that is my point of view."

339

"There must be two parties to a compromise," rejoined Obenreizer. "I decline, in this case, to be one of them. The law gives me authority to control my niece's actions, until she comes of age. She is not yet of age; and I claim my authority."

At this point Maître Voigt attempted to speak. Bintrey silenced him with a compassionate indulgence of tone and manner, as if he was silencing a favourite child.

"No, my worthy friend, not a word. Don't excite yourself unnecessarily; leave it to me." He turned, and addressed himself again to Obenreizer. "I can think of nothing comparable to you, Mr. Obenreizer, but granite—and even that wears out in course of time. In the interests of peace and quietness—for the sake of your own dignity—relax a little. If you will only delegate your authority to another person whom I know of, that person may be trusted never to lose sight of your niece, night or day!"

"You are wasting your time and mine," returned Obenreizer. "If my niece is not rendered up to my authority within one week from this day, I invoke the law. If you resist the law, I take her by force."

He rose to his feet as he said the last word. Maître Voigt looked round again towards the brown door which led into the inner room.

"Have some pity on the poor girl," pleaded Bintrey. "Remember how lately she lost her lover by a dreadful death! Will nothing move you?"

"Nothing."

Bintrey, in his turn, rose to his feet, and looked at Maître Voigt. Maître Voigt's hand, resting on the table, began to tremble. Maître Voigt's eyes remained fixed, as if by irresistible fascination, on the brown door. Obenreizer, suspiciously observing him, looked that way too.

"There is somebody listening in there!" he exclaimed, with a sharp backward glance at Bintrey.

"There are two people listening," answered Bintrey.

" Who are they ? "

" You shall see."

With that answer, he raised his voice and spoke the next words—the two common words which are on everybody's lips, at every hour of the day : " Come in ! "

The brown door opened. Supported on Marguerite's arm —his sunburnt colour gone, his right arm bandaged and slung over his breast—Vendale stood before the murderer, a man risen from the dead.

In the moment of silence that followed, the singing of a caged bird in the courtyard outside was the one sound stirring in the room. Maître Voigt touched Bintrey, and pointed to Obenreizer. " Look at him ! " said the notary, in a whisper.

The shock had paralyzed every movement in the villain's body, but the movement of the blood. His face was like the face of a corpse. The one vestige of colour left in it was a livid purple streak which marked the course of the scar where his victim had wounded him on the cheek and neck. Speechless, breathless, motionless alike in eye and limb, it seemed as if, at the sight of Vendale, the death to which he had doomed Vendale had struck him where he stood.

" Somebody ought to speak to him," said Maître Voigt. " Shall I ? "

Even at that moment Bintrey persisted in silencing the notary, and in keeping the lead in the proceedings to himself. Checking Maître Voigt by a gesture, he dismissed Marguerite and Vendale in these words :—" The object of your appearance here is answered," he said. " If you will withdraw for the present, it may help Mr. Obenreizer to recover himself."

It did help him. As the two passed through the door and closed it behind them, he drew a deep breath of relief. He looked round him for the chair from which he had risen, and dropped into it.

" Give him time ! " pleaded Maître Voigt.

" No," said Bintrey. " I don't know what use he may make

of it if I do." He turned once more to Obenreizer, and
went on. " I owe it to myself," he said—" I don't admit,
mind, that I owe it to *you*—to account for my appearance
in these proceedings, and to state what has been done under
my advice, and on my sole responsibility. Can you listen
to me ? "

" I can listen to you."

" Recall the time when you started for Switzerland with
Mr. Vendale," Bintrey began. " You had not left England
four-and-twenty hours before your niece committed an act
of imprudence which not even your penetration could foresee.
She followed her promised husband on his journey, without
asking anybody's advice or permission, and without any better
companion to protect her than a Cellarman in Mr. Vendale's
employment."

" Why did she follow me on the journey ? and how came
the Cellarman to be the person who accompanied her ? "

" She followed you on the journey," answered Bintrey,
" because she suspected there had been some serious collision
between you and Mr. Vendale, which had been kept secret
from her ; and because she rightly believed you to be capable
of serving your interests, or of satisfying your enmity, at the
price of a crime. As for the Cellarman, he was one, among
the other people in Mr. Vendale's establishment, to whom
she had applied (the moment your back was turned) to know
if anything had happened between their master and you.
The Cellarman alone had something to tell her. A senseless
superstition, and a common accident which had happened to
his master, in his master's cellar, had connected Mr. Vendale
in this man's mind with the idea of danger by murder. Your
niece surprised him into a confession, which aggravated ten-
fold the terrors that possessed her. Aroused to a sense of
the mischief he had done, the man, of his own accord, made
the one atonement in his power. ' If my master is in danger,
miss,' he said, ' it's my duty to follow him, too ; and it's more
than my duty to take care of *you*.' The two set forth

together—and, for once, a superstition has had its use. It decided your niece on taking the journey; and it led the way to saving a man's life. Do you understand me, so far?"

"I understand you, so far."

"My first knowledge of the crime that you had committed," pursued Bintrey, "came to me in the form of a letter from your niece. All you need know is that her love and her courage recovered the body of your victim, and aided the after-efforts which brought him back to life. While he lay helpless at Brieg, under her care, she wrote to me to come out to him. Before starting, I informed Madame Dor that I knew Miss Obenreizer to be safe, and knew where she was. Madame Dor informed me, in return, that a letter had come for your niece, which she knew to be in your handwriting. I took possession of it, and arranged for the forwarding of any other letters which might follow. Arrived at Brieg, I found Mr. Vendale out of danger, and at once devoted myself to hastening the day of reckoning with you. Defresnier and Company turned you off on suspicion; acting on information privately supplied by me. Having stripped you of your false character, the next thing to do was to strip you of your authority over your niece. To reach this end, I not only had no scruple in digging the pitfall under your feet in the dark—I felt a certain professional pleasure in fighting you with your own weapons. By my advice the truth has been carefully concealed from you up to this day. By my advice the trap into which you have walked was set for you (you know why, now, as well as I do) in this place. There was but one certain way of shaking the devilish self-control which has hitherto made you a formidable man. That way has been tried, and (look at me as you may) that way has succeeded. The last thing that remains to be done," concluded Bintrey, producing two little slips of manuscript from his despatch-box, "is to set your niece free. You have attempted murder, and you have committed forgery and theft. We have the evidence ready against you in both cases. If you are convicted as a felon, you know as well as I do what becomes of your authority over your niece. Personally, I should have preferred taking that way out of it. But considerations are pressed on me which I am not able to resist, and this interview must end, as I have told you already, in a compromise. Sign those lines, resigning all authority over Miss Obenreizer, and pledging yourself never to be seen in England or in Switzerland again; and I will sign an indemnity which secures you against further proceedings on our part."

Obenreizer took the pen, in silence, and signed his niece's release. On receiving the indemnity in return, he rose, but made no movement to leave the room. He stood looking at Maître Voigt with a strange smile gathering at his lips, and a strange light flashing in his filmy eyes.

"What are you waiting for?" asked Bintrey.

Obenreizer pointed to the brown door. "Call them back," he answered. "I have something to say in their presence before I go."

"Say it in my presence," retorted Bintrey. "I decline to call them back."

Obenreizer turned to Maître Voigt. "Do you remember telling me that you once had an English client named Vendale?" he asked.

"Well," answered the notary. "And what of that?"

"Maître Voigt, your clock-lock has betrayed you."

"What do you mean?"

"I have read the letters and certificates in your client's box. I have taken copies of them. I have got the copies here. Is there, or is there not, a reason for calling them back?"

For a moment the notary looked to and fro, between Obenreizer and Bintrey, in helpless astonishment. Recovering himself, he drew his brother-lawyer aside, and hurriedly spoke a few words close at his ear. The face of Bintrey—after first faithfully reflecting the astonishment on the face of Maître Voigt—suddenly altered its expression. He sprang, with the activity of a young man, to the door of the inner room, entered it, remained inside for a minute, and returned followed by Marguerite and Vendale. "Now, Mr. Obenreizer," said Bintrey, "the last move in the game is yours. Play it."

"Before I resign my position as that young lady's guardian," said Obenreizer, "I have a secret to reveal in which she is interested. In making my disclosure, I am not claiming her attention for a narrative which she, or any other person present, is expected to take on trust. I am possessed of written proofs, copies of originals, the authenticity of which Maître Voigt himself can attest. Bear that in mind, and permit me to refer you, at starting, to a date long past—the month of February, in the year one thousand eight hundred and thirty-six."

"Mark the date, Mr. Vendale," said Bintrey.

"My first proof," said Obenreizer, taking a paper from his pocket-book. "Copy of a letter, written by an English lady (married) to her sister, a widow. The name of the person writing the letter I shall keep suppressed until I have done. The name of the person to whom the letter is written I am willing to reveal. It is addressed to 'Mrs. Jane Anne Miller, of Groombridge-wells, England.'"

Vendale started, and opened his lips to speak. Bintrey instantly stopped him, as he had stopped Maître Voigt. "No," said the pertinacious lawyer. "Leave it to me."

Obenreizer went on:

"It is needless to trouble you with the first half of the letter," he said. "I can give the substance of it in two words. The writer's position at the time is this. She has been long living in Switzerland with her husband—obliged to live there for the sake of her husband's health. They are about to move to a new residence on the Lake of Neuchâtel in a week, and they will be ready to receive Mrs. Miller as visitor in a fortnight from that time. This said, the writer next enters into an important domestic detail. She has been childless for years—she and her husband have now no hope

345

of children; they are lonely; they want an interest in life; they have decided on adopting a child. Here the important part of the letter begins; and here, therefore, I read it to you word for word."

He folded back the first page of the letter and read as follows:

" * * * Will you help us, my dear sister, to realise our new project? As English people, we wish to adopt an English child. This may be done, I believe, at the Foundling: my husband's lawyers in London will tell you how. I leave the choice to you, with only these conditions attached to it—that the child is to be an infant under a year old, and is to be a boy. Will you pardon the trouble I am giving you, for my sake; and will you bring our adopted child to us, with your own children, when you come to Neuchâtel?

"I must add a word as to my husband's wishes in this matter. He is resolved to spare the child whom we make our own any future mortification and loss of self-respect which might be caused by a discovery of his true origin. He will bear my husband's name, and he will be brought up in the belief that he is really our son. His inheritance of what we have to leave will be secured to him—not only according to the laws of England in such cases, but according to the laws of Switzerland also; for we have lived so long in this country, that there is a doubt whether we may not be considered as 'domiciled' in Switzerland. The one precaution left to take is to prevent any after-discovery at the Foundling. Now, our name is a very uncommon one; and if we appear on the Register of the Institution as the persons adopting the child, there is just a chance that something might result from it. Your name, my dear, is the name of thousands of other people; and if *you* will consent to appear on the Register, there need be no fear of any discoveries in that quarter. We are moving, by the doctor's orders, to a part of Switzerland in which our circumstances are quite unknown; and you, as I understand, are about to engage a new nurse for the journey when you come to see us. Under these circumstances, the child may appear as my child, brought back to me under my sister's care. The only servant we take with us from our old home is my own maid, who can be safely trusted. As for the lawyers in England and in Switzerland, it is their profession to keep secrets—and we may feel quite easy in that direction. So there you have our harmless little conspiracy! Write by return of post, my love, and tell me you will join it." * * *

"Do you still conceal the name of the writer of that letter?" asked Vendale.

"I keep the name of the writer till the last," answered Obenreizer, "and I proceed to my second proof—a mere slip of paper this time, as you see. Memorandum given to the Swiss lawyer, who drew the documents referred to in the letter I have just read, expressed as follows:—'Adopted from the Foundling Hospital of England, 3d March, 1836, a male infant, called, in the Institution, Walter Wilding. Person appearing on the register, as adopting the child, Mrs. Jane Anne Miller, widow, acting in this matter for her married sister, domiciled in Switzerland.' Patience!" resumed Obenreizer, as Vendale, breaking loose from Bintrey, started to his feet. "I shall not keep the name concealed much longer. Two more little slips of paper, and I have done. Third proof! Certificate of Doctor Ganz, still living in practice at Neuchâtel, dated July, 1838. The doctor certifies (you shall read it for yourselves directly), first, that he attended the adopted child in its infant maladies; second, that, three months before the date of the certificate, the gentleman adopting the child as his son died; third, that *on* the date of the certificate, his widow and her maid, taking the adopted child with them, left Neuchâtel on their return to England. One more link now added to this, and my chain of evidence

347

is complete. The maid remained with her mistress till her mistress's death, only a few years since. The maid can swear to the identity of the adopted infant, from his childhood to his youth—from his youth to his manhood, as he is now. There is her address in England—and there, Mr. Vendale, is the fourth, and final proof!"

"Why do you address yourself to *me?*" said Vendale, as Obenreizer threw the written address on the table.

Obenreizer turned on him, in a sudden frenzy of triumph.

"*Because you are the man!* If my niece marries you, she marries a bastard, brought up by public charity. If my niece marries you, she marries an impostor, without name or lineage, disguised in the character of a gentleman of rank and family."

"Bravo!" cried Bintrey. "Admirably put, Mr. Obenreizer! It only wants one word more to complete it. She marries— thanks entirely to your exertions—a man who inherits a handsome fortune, and a man whose origin will make him prouder than ever of his peasant-wife. George Vendale, as brother-executors, let us congratulate each other! Our dear dead friend's last wish on earth is accomplished. We have found the lost Walter Wilding. As Mr. Obenreizer said just now—you are the man!"

The words passed by Vendale unheeded. For the moment he was conscious of but one sensation; he heard but one voice. Marguerite's hand was clasping his. Marguerite's voice was whispering to him: "I never loved you, George, as I love you now!"

THE CURTAIN FALLS

May-day. There is merry-making in Cripple Corner, the chimneys smoke, the patriarchal dining-hall is hung with garlands, and Mrs. Goldstraw, the respected housekeeper, is very busy. For, on this bright morning the young master of Cripple Corner is married to its young mistress, far away:

to wit, in the little town of Brieg, in Switzerland, lying at the foot of the Simplon Pass where she saved his life.

The bells ring gaily in the little town of Brieg, and flags are stretched across the street, and rifle shots are heard, and sounding music from brass instruments. Streamer-decorated casks of wine have been rolled out under a gay awning in the public way before the Inn, and there will be free feasting and revelry. What with bells and banners, draperies hanging from windows, explosion of gunpowder, and reverberation of brass music, the little town of Brieg is all in a flutter, like the hearts of its simple people.

It was a stormy night last night, and the mountains are covered with snow. But the sun is bright to-day, the sweet air is fresh, the tin spires of the little town of Brieg are burnished silver, and the Alps are ranges of far-off white cloud in a deep blue sky.

The primitive people of the little town of Brieg have built a greenwood arch across the street, under which the newly married pair shall pass in triumph from the church. It is inscribed, on that side, "HONOUR AND LOVE TO MARGUERITE VENDALE!" for the people are proud of her to enthusiasm. This greeting of the bride under her new name is affectionately meant as a surprise, and therefore the arrangement has been made that she, unconscious why, shall be taken to the church by a tortuous back way. A scheme not difficult to carry into execution in the crooked little town of Brieg.

So, all things are in readiness, and they are to go and come on foot. Assembled in the Inn's best chamber, festively adorned, are the bride and bridegroom, the Neuchâtel notary, the London lawyer, Madame Dor, and a certain large mysterious Englishman, popularly known as Monsieur Zhoé-Ladelle. And behold Madame Dor, arrayed in a spotless pair of gloves of her own, with no hand in the air, but both hands clasped round the neck of the bride; to embrace whom Madame Dor has turned her broad back on the company, consistent to the last.

"Forgive me, my beautiful," pleads Madame Dor, "for that I ever was his she-cat!"

"She-cat, Madame Dor?"

"Engaged to sit watching my so charming mouse," are the explanatory words of Madame Dor, delivered with a penitential sob.

"Why, you were our best friend! George, dearest, tell Madame Dor. Was she not our best friend?"

"Undoubtedly, darling. What should we have done without her?"

"You are both so generous," cries Madame Dor, accepting consolation, and immediately relapsing. "But I commenced as a she-cat."

"Ah! But like the cat in the fairy-story, good Madame Dor," says Vendale, saluting her cheek, "you were a true woman. And, being a true woman, the sympathy of your heart was with true love."

"I don't wish to deprive Madame Dor of her share in the embraces that are going on," Mr. Bintrey puts in, watch in hand, "and I don't presume to offer any objection to your having got yourselves mixed together, in the corner there, like the three Graces. I merely remark that I think it's time we were moving. What are *your* sentiments on that subject, Mr. Ladle?"

"Clear, sir," replies Joey, with a gracious grin. "I'm clearer altogether, sir, for having lived so many weeks upon the surface. I never was half so long upon the surface afore, and it's done me a power of good. At Cripple Corner, I was too much below it. Atop of the Simpleton, I was a deal too high above it. I've found the medium here, sir. And if ever I take it in convivial, in all the rest of my days, I mean to do it this day, to the toast of 'Bless 'em both.'"

"I, too!" says Bintrey. "And now, Monsieur Voigt, let you and me be two men of Marseilles, and allons, marchons, arm-in-arm!"

They go down to the door, where others are waiting for

them, and they go quietly to the church, and the happy marriage takes place. While the ceremony is yet in progress, the notary is called out. When it is finished, he has returned, is standing behind Vendale, and touches him on the shoulder.

"Go to the side door, one moment, Monsieur Vendale. Alone. Leave Madame to me."

At the side door of the church, are the same two men from the Hospice. They are snow-stained and travel-worn. They wish him joy, and then each lays his broad hand upon Vendale's breast, and one says in a low voice, while the other steadfastly regards him :

"It is here, Monsieur. Your litter. The very same."

"My litter is here? Why?"

"Hush! For the sake of Madame. Your companion of that day——"

"What of him?"

The man looks at his comrade, and his comrade takes him up. Each keeps his hand laid earnestly on Vendale's breast.

"He had been living at the first Refuge, monsieur, for some days. The weather was now good, now bad."

"Yes?"

"He arrived at our Hospice the day before yesterday, and, having refreshed himself with sleep on the floor before the fire, wrapped in his cloak, was resolute to go on, before dark, to the next Hospice. He had a great fear of that part of the way, and thought it would be worse to-morrow."

"Yes?"

"He went on alone. He had passed the gallery when an avalanche—like that which fell behind you near the Bridge of the Ganther——"

"Killed him?"

"We dug him out, suffocated and broken all to pieces! But, monsieur, as to Madame. We have brought him here on the litter, to be buried. We must ascend the street outside. Madame must not see. It would be an accursed thing to bring the litter through the arch across the street, until Madame has passed through. As you descend, we who accompany the litter will set it down on the stones of the street the second to the right, and will stand before it. But do not let Madame turn her head towards the street the second to the right. There is no time to lose. Madame will be alarmed by your absence. Adieu!"

Vendale returns to his bride, and draws her hand through his unmaimed arm. A pretty procession awaits them at the main door of the church. They take their station in it, and descend the street amidst the ringing of the bells, the firing of the guns, the waving of the flags, the playing of the music, the shouts, the smiles, and tears, of the excited town. Heads are uncovered as she passes, hands are kissed to her, all the people bless her. "Heaven's benediction on the dear girl! See where she goes in her youth and beauty; she who so nobly saved his life!"

Near the corner of the street the second to the right, he speaks to her, and calls her attention to the windows on the opposite side. The corner well passed, he says: "Do not look round, my darling, for a reason that I have," and turns his head. Then, looking back along the street, he sees the litter and its bearers passing up alone under the arch, as he and she and their marriage train go down towards the shining valley.

THE LAZY TOUR OF TWO IDLE APPRENTICES

CHAPTER I

In the autumn month of September, eighteen hundred and fifty-seven, wherein these presents bear date, two idle apprentices, exhausted by the long, hot summer, and the long, hot work it had brought with it, ran away from their employer. They were bound to a highly meritorious lady (named Literature), of fair credit and repute, though, it must be acknowledged, not quite so highly esteemed in the City as she might be. This is the more remarkable, as there is nothing against the respectable lady in that quarter, but quite the contrary; her family having rendered eminent service to many famous citizens of London. It may be sufficient to name Sir William Walworth, Lord Mayor under King Richard II., at the time of Wat Tyler's insurrection, and Sir Richard Whittington: which latter distinguished man and magistrate was doubtless indebted to the lady's family for the gift of his celebrated cat. There is also strong reason to suppose that they rang the Highgate bells for him with their own hands.

The misguided young men who thus shirked their duty to the mistress from whom they had received many favours, were actuated by the low idea of making a perfectly idle trip, in any direction. They had no intention of going anywhere in particular; they wanted to see nothing, they wanted to know nothing, they wanted to learn nothing, they wanted to do nothing. They wanted only to be idle. They took to themselves (after HOGARTH), the names of Mr. Thomas Idle and Mr. Francis Goodchild; but there was not a moral pin to choose between them, and they were both idle in the last degree.

Between Francis and Thomas, however, there was this difference of character: Goodchild was laboriously idle, and would take upon himself any amount of pains and labour to assure himself that he was idle; in short, had no better idea of idleness than that it was useless industry. Thomas Idle, on the other hand, was an idler of the unmixed Irish or Neapolitan type; a passive idler, a born-and-bred idler, a consistent idler, who practised what he would have preached if he had not been too idle to preach; a one entire and perfect chrysolite of idleness.

The two idle apprentices found themselves, within a few hours of their escape, walking down into the North of England, that is to say, Thomas was lying in a meadow, looking at the railway trains as they passed over a distant viaduct—which was *his* idea of walking down into the North; while Francis was walking a mile due South against time—which was *his* idea of walking down into the North. In the meantime the day waned, and the milestones remained unconquered.

"Tom," said Goodchild, "the sun is getting low. Up, and let us go forward!"

"Nay," quoth Thomas Idle, "I have not done with Annie Laurie yet." And he proceeded with that idle but popular ballad, to the effect that for the bonnie young person of that name he would "lay him doon and dee"—equivalent, in prose, to lay him down and die.

"What an ass that fellow was!" cried Goodchild, with the bitter emphasis of contempt.

"Which fellow?" asked Thomas Idle.

" The fellow in your song. Lay him doon and dee ! Finely he'd show off before the girl by doing *that*. A sniveller ! Why couldn't he get up, and punch somebody's head ! "

" Whose ? " asked Thomas Idle.

" Anybody's. Everybody's would be better than nobody's ! If I fell into that state of mind about a girl, do you think I'd lay me doon and dee? No, sir," proceeded Goodchild, with a disparaging assumption of the Scottish accent, " I'd get me oop and peetch into somebody. Wouldn't you ? "

" I wouldn't have anything to do with her," yawned Thomas Idle. " Why should I take the trouble ? "

" It's no trouble, Tom, to fall in love," said Goodchild, shaking his head.

" It's trouble enough to fall out of it, once you're in it," retorted Tom. " So I keep out of it altogether. It would be better for you, if you did the same."

Mr. Goodchild, who is always in love with somebody, and not unfrequently with several objects at once, made no reply. He heaved a sigh of the kind which is termed by the lower orders " a bellowser," and then, heaving Mr. Idle on his feet (who was not half so heavy as the sigh), urged him north-ward.

These two had sent their personal baggage on by train : only retaining each a knapsack. Idle now applied himself to constantly regretting the train, to tracking it through the intricacies of Bradshaw's Guide, and finding out where it is now—and where now—and where now—and to asking what was the use of walking, when you could ride at such a pace as that. Was it to see the country ? If that was the object, look at it out of the carriage windows. There was a great deal more of it to be seen there than here. Besides, who wanted to see the country ? Nobody. And again, whoever did walk ? Nobody. Fellows set off to walk, but they never did it. They came back and said they did, but they didn't. Then why should he walk ? He wouldn't walk. He swore it by this milestone !

It was the fifth from London, so far had they penetrated into the North. Submitting to the powerful chain of argument, Goodchild proposed a return to the Metropolis, and a falling back upon Euston Square Terminus. Thomas assented with alacrity, and so they walked down into the North by the next morning's express, and carried their knapsacks in the luggage-van.

It was like all other expresses, as every express is and must be. It bore through the harvest country a smell like a large washing-day, and a sharp issue of steam as from a huge brazen tea-urn. The greatest power in nature and art combined, it yet glided over dangerous heights in the sight of people looking up from fields and roads, as smoothly and unreally as a light miniature plaything. Now, the engine shrieked in hysterics of such intensity, that it seemed desirable that the men who had her in charge should hold her feet, slap her hands, and bring her to; now, burrowed into tunnels with a stubborn and undemonstrative energy so confusing that the train seemed to be flying back into leagues of darkness. Here, were station after station, swallowed up by the express without stopping; here, stations where it fired itself in like a volley of cannon-balls, swooped away four country-people with nosegays, and three men of business with portmanteaus, and fired itself off again, bang, bang, bang! At long intervals were uncomfortable refreshment-rooms, made more uncomfortable by the scorn of Beauty towards Beast, the public (but to whom she never relented, as Beauty did in the story, towards the other Beast), and where sensitive stomachs were fed, with a contemptuous sharpness occasioning indigestion. Here, again, were stations with nothing going but a bell, and wonderful wooden razors set aloft on great posts, shaving the air. In these fields, the horses, sheep, and cattle were well used to the thundering meteor, and didn't mind; in those, they were all set scampering together, and a herd of pigs scoured after them. The pastoral country darkened, became coaly, became smoky, became

358

infernal, got better, got worse, improved again, grew rugged, turned romantic; was a wood, a stream, a chain of hills, a gorge, a moor, a cathedral town, a fortified place, a waste. Now, miserable black dwellings, a black canal, and sick black towers of chimneys; now, a trim garden, where the flowers were bright and fair; now, a wilderness of hideous altars all a-blaze; now, the water meadows with their fairy rings; now, the mangy patch of unlet building ground outside the stagnant town, with the larger ring where the Circus was last week. The temperature changed, the dialect changed, the people changed, faces got sharper, manner got shorter, eyes got shrewder and harder; yet all so quickly, that the spruce guard in the London uniform and silver lace, had not yet rumpled his shirt-collar, delivered half the dispatches in his shiny little pouch, or read his newspaper.

Carlisle! Idle and Goodchild had got to Carlisle. It looked congenially and delightfully idle. Something in the way of public amusement had happened last month, and something else was going to happen before Christmas; and, in the meantime there was a lecture on India for those who liked it—which Idle and Goodchild did not. Likewise, by those who liked them, there were impressions to be bought of all the vapid prints, going and gone, and of nearly all the vapid books. For those who wanted to put anything in missionary boxes, here were the boxes. For those who wanted the Reverend Mr. Podgers (artist's proofs, thirty shillings), here was Mr. Podgers to any amount. Not less gracious and abundant, Mr. Codgers also of the vineyard, but opposed to Mr. Podgers, brotherly tooth and nail. Here, were guide-books to the neighbouring antiquities, and eke the Lake country, in several dry and husky sorts; here, many physically and morally impossible heads of both sexes, for young ladies to copy, in the exercise of the art of drawing; here, further, a large impression of MR. SPURGEON, solid as to the flesh, not to say even something gross. The working young men of Carlisle were drawn up, with their hands in their pockets, across the pavements, four and six abreast, and appeared (much to the satisfaction of Mr. Idle) to have nothing else to do. The working and growing young women of Carlisle, from the age of twelve upwards, promenaded the streets in the cool of the evening, and rallied the said young men. Sometimes the young men rallied the young women, as in the case of a group gathered round an accordion-player, from among whom a young man advanced behind a young woman for whom he appeared to have a tenderness, and hinted to her that he was there and playful, by giving her (he wore clogs) a kick.

On market morning, Carlisle woke up amazingly, and became (to the two Idle Apprentices) disagreeably and reproachfully busy. There were its cattle market, its sheep market, and its pig market down by the river, with raw-boned and shock-headed Rob Roys hiding their Lowland dresses beneath heavy plaids, prowling in and out among the animals, and flavouring the air with fumes of whiskey. There was its corn market down the main street, with hum of chaffering over open sacks. There was its general market in the street too, with heather brooms on which the purple flower still flourished, and heather baskets primitive and fresh to behold. With women trying on clogs and caps at open stalls, and "Bible stalls" adjoining. With "Doctor Mantle's Dispensary for the cure of all Human Maladies and no charge for advice," and with Doctor Mantle's "Laboratory of Medical, Chemical, and Botanical Science"—both healing institutions established on one pair of trestles, one board, and one sun-blind. With the renowned phrenologist from London, begging to be favoured (at sixpence each) with the company of clients of both sexes, to whom, on examination of their heads, he would make revelations "enabling him or her to know themselves." Through all these bargains and blessings, the recruiting-sergeant watchfully elbowed his way, a thread of War in the peaceful skein. Likewise on the walls were printed hints that the Oxford Blues might not be indisposed to hear of a few fine active young men; and that whereas the standard of that distinguished corps is full six feet, "growing lads of five feet eleven" need not absolutely despair of being accepted.

Scenting the morning air more pleasantly than the buried majesty of Denmark did, Messrs. Idle and Goodchild rode away from Carlisle at eight o'clock one forenoon, bound for the village of Hesket, Newmarket, some fourteen miles distant. Goodchild (who had already begun to doubt whether he was idle: as his way always is when he has nothing to do) had read of a certain black old Cumberland hill or mountain, called Carrock, or Carrock Fell; and had arrived at the conclusion that it would be the culminating triumph of Idleness to ascend the same. Thomas Idle, dwelling on the pains inseparable from that achievement, had expressed the strongest doubts of the expediency, and even of the sanity, of the enterprise; but Goodchild had carried his point, and they rode away.

Up hill and down hill, and twisting to the right, and twisting to the left, and with old Skiddaw (who has vaunted himself a great deal more than his merits deserve; but that is rather the way of the Lake country), dodging the apprentices in a picturesque and pleasant manner. Good, weather-proof, warm, pleasant houses, well white-limed, scantily dotting the road. Clean children coming out to look, carrying other clean children as big as themselves. Harvest still lying out and much rained upon; here and there, harvest still unreaped. Well-cultivated gardens attached to the cottages, with plenty of produce forced out of their hard soil. Lonely nooks, and wild; but people can be born, and married, and buried in such nooks, and can live and love, and be loved, there as elsewhere, thank God! (Mr. Goodchild's remark.) By-and-by, the village. Black, coarse-stoned, rough-windowed houses; some with outer staircases, like Swiss houses; a sinuous and stony gutter winding up hill and round the corner, by way of street. All the children running out directly. Women pausing in washing, to peep from doorways and very little windows. Such were the observations of Messrs. Idle and Goodchild, as their conveyance stopped at the village shoemaker's. Old Carrock gloomed down upon it all in a very ill-tempered state; and rain was beginning.

The village shoemaker declined to have anything to do with Carrock. No visitors went up Carrock. No visitors came there at all. Aa' the world ganged awa' yon. The driver appealed to the Innkeeper. The Innkeeper had two men working in the fields, and one of them should be called in, to go up Carrock as guide. Messrs. Idle and Goodchild, highly approving, entered the Innkeeper's house, to drink whiskey and eat oatcake.

The Innkeeper was not idle enough—was not idle at all, which was a great fault in him—but was a fine specimen of a north-country man, or any kind of man. He had a ruddy cheek, a bright eye, a well-knit frame, an immense hand, a cheery, outspeaking voice, and a straight, bright, broad look. He had a drawing-room, too, upstairs, which was worth a visit to the Cumberland Fells. (This was Mr. Francis Goodchild's opinion, in which Mr. Thomas Idle did not concur.)

The ceiling of this drawing-room was so crossed and re-crossed by beams of unequal lengths, radiating from a centre, in a corner, that it looked like a broken star-fish. The room was comfortably and solidly furnished with good mahogany and horsehair. It had a snug fireside, and a couple of well-curtained windows, looking out upon the wild country behind the house. What it most developed was, an unexpected taste for little ornaments and nick-nacks, of which it contained a most surprising number. They were not very various, consisting in great part of waxen babies with their limbs more or less mutilated, appealing on one leg to the parental affections from under little cupping glasses; but, Uncle Tom was there, in crockery, receiving theological instructions from

362

A CURIOUS ROOM

Miss Eva, who grew out of his side like a wen, in an exceedingly rough state of profile propagandism. Engravings
of Mr. Hunt's country boy, before and after his pie, were on
the wall, divided by a highly-coloured nautical piece, the
subject of which had all her colours (and more) flying, and
was making great way through a sea of a regular pattern,
like a lady's collar. A benevolent, elderly gentleman of the
last century, with a powdered head, kept guard, in oil and
varnish, over a most perplexing piece of furniture on a table;
in appearance between a driving seat and an angular knife-
box, but, when opened, a musical instrument of tinkling wires,
exactly like David's harp packed for travelling. Everything
became a nick-nack in this curious room. The copper tea-
kettle, burnished up to the highest point of glory, took his
station on a stand of his own at the greatest possible distance
from the fireplace, and said: "By your leave, not a kettle,
but a bijou." The Staffordshire-ware butter-dish with the
cover on, got upon a little round occasional table in a window,
with a worked top, and announced itself to the two chairs
accidentally placed there, as an aid to polite conversation, a
graceful trifle in china to be chatted over by callers, as they
airily trifled away the visiting moments of a butterfly existence, in that rugged old village on the Cumberland Fells.
The very footstool could not keep the floor, but got upon a
sofa, and therefrom proclaimed itself, in high relief of white
and liver-coloured wool, a favourite spaniel coiled up for
repose. Though, truly, in spite of its bright glass eyes, the
spaniel was the least successful assumption in the collection:
being perfectly flat, and dismally suggestive of a recent mistake in sitting down on the part of some corpulent member
of the family.

There were books, too, in this room; books on the table,
books on the chimney-piece, books in an open press in the
corner. Fielding was there, and Smollett was there, and
Steele and Addison were there, in dispersed volumes; and
there were tales of those who go down to the sea in ships,

363

for windy nights; and there was really a choice of good books for rainy days or fine. It was so very pleasant to see these things in such a lonesome by-place—so very agreeable to find these evidences of a taste, however homely, that went beyond the beautiful cleanliness and trimness of the house—so fanciful to imagine what a wonder a room must be to the little children born in the gloomy village—what grand impressions of it those of them who became wanderers over the earth would carry away; and how, at distant ends of the world, some old voyagers would die, cherishing the belief that the finest apartment known to men was once in the Hesket-Newmarket Inn, in rare old Cumberland—it was such a charmingly lazy pursuit to entertain these rambling thoughts over the choice oatcake and the genial whiskey, that Mr. Idle and Mr. Goodchild never asked themselves how it came to pass that the men in the fields were never heard of more, how the stalwart landlord replaced them without explanation, how his dog-cart came to be waiting at the door, and how everything was arranged without the least arrangement for climbing to old Carrock's shoulders, and standing on his head.

Without a word of inquiry, therefore, the Two Idle Apprentices drifted out resignedly into a fine, soft, close, drowsy, penetrating rain; got into the landlord's light dog-cart, and rattled off through the village for the foot of Carrock. The journey at the outset was not remarkable. The Cumberland road went up and down like all other roads; the Cumberland curs burst out from backs of cottages and barked like other curs, and the Cumberland peasantry stared after the dog-cart amazedly, as long as it was in sight, like the rest of their race. The approach to the foot of the mountain resembled the approaches to the feet of most other mountains all over the world. The cultivation gradually ceased, the trees grew gradually rare, the road became gradually rougher, and the sides of the mountain looked gradually more and more lofty, and more and more difficult to get up. The dog-cart was left at a lonely farm-house. The landlord borrowed a large umbrella, and, assuming in an instant the character of the most cheerful and adventurous of guides, led the way to the ascent. Mr. Goodchild looked eagerly at the top of the mountain, and, feeling apparently that he was now going to be very lazy indeed, shone all over wonderfully to the eye, under the influence of the contentment within and the moisture without. Only in the bosom of Mr. Thomas Idle did Despondency now hold her gloomy state. He kept it a secret; but he would have given a very handsome sum, when the ascent began, to have been back again at the inn. The sides of Carrock looked fearfully steep, and the top of Carrock was hidden in mist. The rain was falling faster and faster. The knees of Mr. Idle—always weak on walking excursions—shivered and shook with fear and damp. The wet was already penetrating through the young man's outer coat to a brand-new shooting-jacket, for which he had reluctantly paid the large sum of two guineas on leaving town; he had no stimulating refreshment about him but a small packet of clammy gingerbread nuts; he had nobody to give him an arm, nobody to push him gently behind, nobody to pull him up tenderly in front, nobody to speak to who really felt the difficulties of the ascent, the dampness of the rain, the denseness of the mist, and the unutterable folly of climbing, undriven, up any steep place in the world, when there is level ground within reach to walk on instead. Was it for this that Thomas had left London? London, where there are nice short walks in level public gardens, with benches of repose set up at convenient distances for weary travellers —London, where rugged stone is humanely pounded into little lumps for the road, and intelligently shaped into smooth slabs for the pavement! No! it was not for the laborious ascent of the crags of Carrock that Idle had left his native city, and travelled to Cumberland. Never did he feel more disastrously convinced that he had committed a very grave error in judgment than when he found himself standing in the rain at the bottom of a steep mountain, and knew that the responsibility rested on his weak shoulders of actually getting to the top of it.

The honest landlord went first, the beaming Goodchild followed, the mournful Idle brought up the rear. From time to time, the two foremost members of the expedition changed places in the order of march; but the rearguard never altered his position. Up the mountain or down the mountain, in the water or out of it, over the rocks, through the bogs, skirting the heather, Mr. Thomas Idle was always the last, and was always the man who had to be looked after and waited for. At first the ascent was delusively easy, the sides of the mountain sloped gradually, and the material of which they were composed was a soft spongy turf, very tender and pleasant to walk upon. After a hundred yards or so, however, the verdant scene and the easy slope disappeared, and the rocks began. Not noble, massive rocks, standing upright, keeping a certain regularity in their positions, and possessing, now and then, flat tops to sit upon, but little irritating, comfortless rocks, littered about anyhow by Nature; treacherous, disheartening rocks of all sorts of small shapes and small sizes, bruisers of tender toes and trippers-up of wavering feet. When these impediments were passed, heather and slough followed. Here the steepness of the ascent was slightly mitigated; and here the exploring party of three turned round to look at the view below them. The scene of the moorland and the fields was like a feeble water-colour drawing half sponged out. The mist was darkening, the rain was thickening, the trees were dotted about like spots of faint shadow, the division-lines which mapped out the fields were all getting blurred together, and the lonely farm-house where the dog-cart had been left, loomed spectral in the grey light like the last human dwelling at the end of the habitable world. Was this a sight worth climbing to see? Surely—surely not!

Up again—for the top of Carrock is not reached yet. The landlord, just as good-tempered and obliging as he was at the bottom of the mountain. Mr. Goodchild brighter in the eyes and rosier in the face than ever; full of cheerful remarks and apt quotations; and walking with a springiness of step wonderful to behold. Mr. Idle, farther and farther in the rear, with the water squeaking in the toes of his boots, with his two-guinea shooting-jacket clinging damply to his aching sides, with his overcoat so full of rain, and standing out so pyramidically stiff, in consequence, from his shoulders downwards, that he felt as if he was walking in a gigantic extinguisher—the despairing spirit within him representing but too aptly the candle that had just been put out. Up and up and up again, till a ridge is reached and the outer edge of the mist on the summit of Carrock is darkly and drizzingly near. Is this the top? No, nothing like the top. It is an aggravating peculiarity of all mountains, that, although they have only one top when they are seen (as they ought always to be seen) from below, they turn out to have a perfect eruption of false tops whenever the traveller is sufficiently ill-advised to go out of his way for the purpose of ascending them. Carrock is but a trumpery little mountain of fifteen hundred feet, and it presumes to have false tops, and even precipices, as if it were Mont Blanc. No matter; Goodchild enjoys it, and will go on; and Idle, who is afraid of being left behind by himself, must follow. On entering the edge of the mist, the landlord stops, and says he hopes that it will not get any thicker. It is twenty years since he last ascended Carrock, and it is barely possible, if the mist increases, that the party may be lost on the mountain. Goodchild hears this dreadful intimation, and is not in the least impressed by it. He marches for the top that is never to be found, as if he was the Wandering Jew, bound to go on for ever, in defiance of everything. The landlord faithfully accompanies him. The two, to the dim eye of Idle, far below, look in the exaggerative mist, like a pair of friendly giants, mounting the steps of some invisible castle together. Up and up, and then down a little. and then up and then along a strip of level ground, and then up again. The wind, a wind unknown in the happy valley, blows keen and strong; the rain-mist gets impenetrable; a dreary little cairn of stones appears. The landlord adds one to the heap, first walking all round the cairn as if he were about to perform an incantation, then dropping the stone on to the top of the heap with the gesture of a magician adding an ingredient to a cauldron in full bubble. Goodchild sits down by the cairn as if it was his study-table at home; Idle, drenched and panting, stands up with his back to the wind, ascertains distinctly that this is the top at last, looks round with all the little curiosity that is left in him, and gets, in return, a magnificent view of —Nothing!

The effect of this sublime spectacle on the minds of the exploring party is a little injured by the nature of the direct conclusion to which the sight of it points—the said conclusion being that the mountain mist has actually gathered round them, as the landlord feared it would. It now becomes imperatively necessary to settle the exact situation of the farm-house in the valley at which the dog-cart has been left, before the travellers attempt to descend. While the landlord is endeavouring to make this discovery in his own way, Mr. Goodchild plunges his hand under his wet coat, draws out a little red morocco-case, opens it, and displays to the view of his companions a neat pocket-compass. The north is found, the point at which the farm-house is situated is settled, and the descent begins. After a little downward walking, Idle (behind as usual) sees his fellow-travellers turn aside sharply—tries to follow them—loses them in the mist—is shouted after, waited for, recovered—and then finds that a halt has been ordered, partly on his account, partly for the purpose of again consulting the compass.

The point in debate is settled as before between Goodchild and the landlord, and the expedition moves on, not down the mountain, but marching straight forward round the slope of it. The difficulty of following this new route is acutely felt by Thomas Idle. He finds the hardship of walking at all greatly increased by the fatigue of moving his feet straight forward along the side of a slope, when their natural tendency, at every step, is to turn off at a right angle, and go straight down the declivity. Let the reader imagine himself to be walking along the roof of a barn, instead of up or down it, and he will have an exact idea of the pedestrian difficulty in which the travellers had now involved themselves. In ten minutes more Idle was lost in the distance again, was shouted for, waited for, recovered as before; found Goodchild repeating his observation of the compass, and remonstrated warmly against the sideway route that his companions persisted in following. It appeared to the uninstructed mind of Thomas that when three men want to get to the bottom of a mountain, their business is to walk down it; and he put this view of the case, not only with emphasis, but even with some irritability. He was answered from the scientific eminence of the compass on which his companions were mounted, that there was a frightful chasm somewhere near the foot of Carrock, called The Black Arches, into which the travellers were sure to march in the mist, if they risked continuing the descent from the place where they had now halted. Idle received this answer with the silent respect which was due to the commanders of the expedition, and followed along the roof of the barn, or rather the side of the mountain, reflecting upon the assurance which he received on starting again, that the object of the party was only to gain " a certain point," and, this haven attained, to continue the descent afterwards until the foot of Carrock was reached. Though quite unexceptionable as an abstract form of expression, the phrase " a certain point " has the disadvantage of sounding rather vaguely when it is pronounced on unknown ground, under a canopy of mist much thicker than a London fog. Nevertheless, after the compass, this phrase was all the clue the party had to hold by, and Idle clung to the extreme end of it as hopefully as he could.

More sideway walking, thicker and thicker mist, all sorts of points reached except the "certain point;" third loss of Idle, third shouts for him, third recovery of him, third consultation of compass. Mr. Goodchild draws it tenderly from his pocket, and prepares to adjust it. on a stone. Something falls on the turf—it is the glass. Something else drops immediately after—it is the needle. The compass is broken, and the exploring party is lost!

It is the practice of the English portion of the human race to receive all great disasters in dead silence. Mr. Goodchild restored the useless compass to his pocket without saying a word, Mr. Idle looked at the landlord, and the landlord looked at Mr. Idle. There was nothing for it now but to go on blindfold, and trust to the chapter of chances. Accordingly, the lost travellers moved forward, still walking round the slope of the mountain, still desperately resolved to avoid the Black Arches, and to succeed in reaching the "certain point."

A quarter of an hour brought them to the brink of a ravine, at the bottom of which there flowed a muddy little stream. Here another halt was called, and another consultation took place. The landlord, still clinging pertinaciously to the idea of reaching the "point," voted for crossing the ravine, and going on round the slope of the mountain. Mr. Goodchild, to the great relief of his fellow-traveller, took another view of the case, and backed Mr. Idle's proposal to descend Carrock at once, at any hazard—the rather as the running stream was a sure guide to follow from the mountain to the valley. Accordingly, the party descended to the rugged and stony banks of the stream; and here again Thomas lost ground sadly, and fell far behind his travelling companions. Not much more than six weeks had elapsed since he had sprained one of his ankles, and he began to feel this same ankle getting rather weak when he found himself among the stones that were strewn about the running water. Goodchild and the landlord were getting farther and farther ahead of him. He saw them cross the stream and disappear round a projection on its banks. He heard them shout the moment after as a signal that they had halted and were waiting for him. Answering the shout, he mended his pace, crossed the stream where they had crossed it, and was within one step of the opposite bank, when his foot slipped on a wet stone, his weak ankle gave a twist outwards, a hot, rending, tearing pain ran through it at the same moment, and down fell the idlest of the Two Idle Apprentices, crippled in an instant.

The situation was now, in plain terms, one of absolute danger. There lay Mr. Idle writhing with pain, there was the mist as thick as ever, there was the landlord as completely lost as the strangers whom he was conducting, and there was the compass broken in Goodchild's pocket. To leave the wretched Thomas on unknown ground was plainly impossible; and to get him to walk with a badly sprained ankle seemed equally out of the question. However, Goodchild (brought back by his cry for help) bandaged the ankle with a pocket-handkerchief, and assisted by the landlord, raised the crippled Apprentice to his legs, offered him a shoulder to lean on, and exhorted him for the sake of the whole party to try if he could walk. Thomas, assisted by the shoulder on one side, and a stick on the other, did try, with what pain and difficulty those only can imagine who have sprained an ankle and have had to tread on it afterwards. At a pace adapted to the feeble hobbling of a newly-lamed man, the lost party moved on, perfectly ignorant whether they were on the right side of the mountain or the wrong, and equally uncertain how long Idle would be able to contend with the pain in his ankle, before he gave in altogether and fell down again, unable to stir another step.

Slowly and more slowly, as the clog of crippled Thomas weighed heavily and more heavily on the march of the expedition, the lost travellers followed the windings of the stream, till they came to a faintly-marked cart-track, branching

off nearly at right angles, to the left. After a little consultation it was resolved to follow this dim vestige of a road
in the hope that it might lead to some farm or cottage, at
which Idle could be left in safety It was now getting on
towards the afternoon, and it was fast becoming more than
doubtful whether the party, delayed in their progress as
they now were, might not be overtaken by the darkness
before the right route was found, and be condemned to pass
the night on the mountain, without bit or drop to comfort
them, in their wet clothes.

The cart-track grew fainter and fainter, until it was washed
out altogether by another little stream, dark, turbulent, and
rapid. The landlord suggested, judging by the colour of the
water, that it must be flowing from one of the lead mines in
the neighbourhood of Carrock; and the travellers accordingly
kept by the stream for a little while, in the hope of possibly
wandering towards help in that way. After walking forward
about two hundred yards, they came upon a mine indeed,
but a mine, exhausted and abandoned; a dismal, ruinous
place, with nothing but the wreck of its works and buildings
left to speak for it. Here, there were a few sheep feeding.
The landlord looked at them earnestly, thought he recognised
the marks on them—then thought he did not—finally gave
up the sheep in despair—and walked on just as ignorant of
the whereabouts of the party as ever.

The march in the dark, literally as well as metaphorically
in the dark, had now been continued for three-quarters of an
hour from the time when the crippled Apprentice had met
with his accident. Mr. Idle, with all the will to conquer
the pain in his ankle, and to hobble on, found the power
rapidly failing him, and felt that another ten minutes at
most would find him at the end of his last physical resources.
He had just made up his mind on this point, and was about
to communicate the dismal result of his reflections to his
companions, when the mist suddenly brightened, and begun
to lift straight ahead. In another minute, the landlord, who

372

was in advance, proclaimed that he saw a tree. Before long, other trees appeared—then a cottage—then a house beyond the cottage, and a familiar line of road rising behind it. Last of all, Carrock itself loomed darkly into view, far away to the right hand. The party had not only got down the mountain without knowing how, but had wandered away from it in the mist, without knowing why—away, far down on the very moor by which they had approached the base of Carrock that morning.

The happy lifting of the mist, and the still happier dis-covery that the travellers had groped their way, though by a very roundabout direction, to within a mile or so of the part of the valley in which the farm-house was situated, restored Mr. Idle's sinking spirits and reanimated his failing strength. While the landlord ran off to get the dog-cart, Thomas was assisted by Goodchild to the cottage which had been the first building seen when the darkness brightened, and was propped up against the garden wall, like an artist's lay figure waiting to be forwarded, until the dog-cart should arrive from the farm-house below. In due time—and a very long time it seemed to Mr. Idle—the rattle of wheels was heard, and the crippled Apprentice was lifted into the seat. As the dog-cart was driven back to the inn, the landlord related an anecdote which he had just heard at the farm-house, of an unhappy man who had been lost, like his two guests and himself, on Carrock ; who had passed the night there alone ; who had been found the next morning, " scared and starved ; " and who never went out afterwards, except on his way to the grave. Mr. Idle heard this sad story, and derived at least one useful impression from it. Bad as the pain in his ankle was, he contrived to bear it patiently, for he felt grateful that a worse accident had not befallen him in the wilds of Carrock.

CHAPTER II

The dog-cart, with Mr. Thomas Idle and his ankle on the hanging seat behind, Mr. Francis Goodchild and the Innkeeper in front, and the rain in spouts and splashes everywhere, made the best of its way back to the little inn; the broken moor country looking like miles upon miles of Pre-Adamite sop, or the ruins of some enormous jorum of antediluvian toast-and-water. The trees dripped; the eaves of the scattered cottages dripped; the barren stone walls dividing the land, dripped; the yelping dogs dripped; carts and waggons under ill-roofed penthouses, dripped; melancholy cocks and hens perching on their shafts, or seeking shelter underneath them, dripped; Mr. Goodchild dripped; Thomas Idle dripped; the Innkeeper dripped; the mare dripped; the vast curtains of mist and cloud passed before the shadowy forms of the hills, streamed water as they were drawn across the landscape. Down such steep pitches that the mare seemed to be trotting on her head, and up such steep pitches that she seemed to have a supplementary leg in her tail, the dog-cart jolted and tilted back to the village. It was too wet for the women to look out, it was too wet even for the children to look out; all the doors and windows were closed, and the only sign of life or motion was in the rain-punctured puddles.

Whiskey and oil to Thomas Idle's ankle, and whiskey without oil to Francis Goodchild's stomach, produced an agreeable change in the systems of both; soothing Mr. Idle's

374

pain, which was sharp before, and sweetening Mr. Goodchild's temper, which was sweet before. Portmanteaus being then opened and clothes changed, Mr. Goodchild, through having no change of outer garments but broadcloth and velvet, suddenly became a magnificent portent in the Innkeeper's house, a shining frontispiece to the fashions for the month, and a frightful anomaly in the Cumberland village.

Greatly ashamed of his splendid appearance, the conscious Goodchild quenched it as much as possible, in the shadow of Thomas Idle's ankle, and in a corner of the little covered carriage that started with them for Wigton—a most desirable carriage for any country, except for its having a flat roof and no sides; which caused the plumps of rain accumulating on the roof to play vigorous games of bagatelle into the interior all the way, and to score immensely. It was comfortable to see how the people coming back in open carts from Wigton market made no more of the rain than if it were sunshine; how the Wigton policeman taking a country walk of half-a-dozen miles (apparently for pleasure), in resplendent uniform, accepted saturation as his normal state; how clerks and schoolmasters in black, loitered along the road without umbrellas, getting varnished at every step; how the Cumberland girls, coming out to look after the Cumberland cows, shook the rain from their eyelashes and laughed it away; and how the rain continued to fall upon all, as it only does fall in hill countries.

Wigton market was over, and its bare booths were smoking with rain all down the street. Mr. Thomas Idle, melodramatically carried to the inn's first floor, and laid upon three chairs (he should have had the sofa, if there had been one), Mr. Goodchild went to the window to take an observation of Wigton, and report what he saw to his disabled companion.

"Brother Francis, brother Francis," cried Thomas Idle, "What do you see from the turret?"

"I see," said Brother Francis, "what I hope and believe

to be one of the most dismal places ever seen by eyes. I see the houses with their roofs of dull black, their stained fronts, and their dark-rimmed windows, looking as if they were all in mourning. As every little puff of wind comes down the street, I see a perfect train of rain let off along the wooden stalls in the market-place and exploded against me. I see a very big gas lamp in the centre which I know, by a secret instinct, will not be lighted to-night. I see a pump, with a trivet underneath its spout whereon to stand the vessels that are brought to be filled with water. I see a man come to pump, and he pumps very hard, but no water follows, and he strolls empty away."

"Brother Francis, brother Francis," cried Thomas Idle, "what more do you see from the turret, besides the man and the pump, and the trivet and the houses all in mourning and the rain?"

"I see," said Brother Francis, "one, two, three, four, five, linen-drapers' shops in front of me. I see a linen-draper's shop next door to the right—and there are five more linen-drapers' shops down the corner to the left. Eleven homicidal linen-drapers' shops within a short stone's throw, each with its hands at the throats of all the rest! Over the small first-floor of one of these linen-drapers' shops appears the wonderful inscription, BANK."

"Brother Francis, brother Francis," cried Thomas Idle, "what more do you see from the turret, besides the eleven homicidal linen-drapers' shops, and the wonderful inscription, 'Bank,' on the small first-floor, and the man and the pump and the trivet and the houses all in mourning and the rain?"

"I see," said Brother Francis, "the depository for Christian Knowledge, and through the dark vapour I think I again make out Mr. Spurgeon looming heavily. Her Majesty the Queen, God bless her, printed in colours, I am sure I see. I see the *Illustrated London News* of several years ago, and I see a sweetmeat shop—which the proprietor calls a 'Salt

Warehouse'—with one small female child in a cotton bonnet looking in on tip-toe, oblivious of rain. And I see a watchmaker's with only three great pale watches of a dull metal hanging in his window, each in a separate pane."

"Brother Francis, brother Francis," cried Thomas Idle, "what more do you see of Wigton, besides these objects, and the man and the pump and the trivet and the houses all in mourning and the rain?"

"I see nothing more," said Brother Francis, "and there is nothing more to see, except the curlpaper bill of the theatre, which was opened and shut last week (the manager's family played all the parts), and the short, square, chinky omnibus that goes to the railway, and leads too rattling a life over the stones to hold together long. O yes! Now, I see two men with their hands in their pockets and their backs towards me."

"Brother Francis, brother Francis," cried Thomas Idle, "what do you make out from the turret, of the expression of the two men with their hands in their pockets and their backs towards you?"

"They are mysterious men," said Brother Francis, "with inscrutable backs. They keep their backs towards me with persistency. If one turns an inch in any direction, the other turns an inch in the same direction, and no more. They turn very stiffly, on a very little pivot, in the middle of the market-place. Their appearance is partly of a mining, partly of a ploughing, partly of a stable, character. They are looking at nothing—very hard. Their backs are slouched, and their legs are curved with much standing about. Their pockets are loose and dog's-eared, on account of their hands being always in them. They stand to be rained upon, without any movement of impatience or dissatisfaction, and they keep so close together that an elbow of each jostles an elbow of the other, but they never speak. They spit at times, but speak not. I see it growing darker and darker, and still I see them, sole visible population of the place, standing to be

377

rained upon with their backs towards me, and looking at nothing very hard."

"Brother Francis, brother Francis," cried Thomas Idle, "before you draw down the blind of the turret and come in to have your head scorched by the hot gas, see if you can, and impart to me, something of the expression of those two amazing men."

"The murky shadows," said Francis Goodchild, "are gathering fast; and the wings of evening, and the wings of coal, are folding over Wigton. Still, they look at nothing very hard, with their backs towards me. Ah! Now, they turn, and I see——"

"Brother Francis, brother Francis," cried Thomas Idle, "tell me quickly what you see of the two men of Wigton!"

"I see," said Francis Goodchild, "that they have no expression at all. And now the town goes to sleep, undazzled by the large unlighted lamp in the market-place; and let no man wake it."

At the close of the next day's journey, Mr. Thomas Idle's ankle became much swollen and inflamed. There are reasons which will presently explain themselves for not publicly indicating the exact direction in which that journey lay, or the place in which it ended. It was a long day's shaking of Thomas Idle over the rough roads, and a long day's getting out and going on before the horses, and fagging up hills, and scouring down hills, on the part of Mr. Goodchild, who in the fatigues of such labours congratulated himself on attaining a high point of idleness. It was at a little town, still in Cumberland, that they halted for the night—a very little town, with the purple and brown moor close upon its one street; a curious little ancient market-cross set up in the midst of it; and the town itself looking much as if it were a collection of great stones piled on end by the Druids long ago, which a few recluse people had since hollowed out for habitations.

"Is there a doctor here?" asked Mr. Goodchild, on his

knee, of the motherly landlady of the little Inn : stopping in his examination of Mr. Idle's ankle, with the aid of a candle.

"Ey, my word!" said the landlady, glancing doubtfully at the ankle for herself; "there's Doctor Speddie."

"Is he a good Doctor?"

"Ey!" said the landlady, "I ca' him so. A' cooms efther nae doctor that I ken. Mair nor which, a's just THE doctor heer."

"Do you think he is at home?"

Her reply was, "Gang awa', Jock, and bring him."

Jock, a white-headed boy, who, under pretence of stirring up some bay salt in a basin of water for the laving of this unfortunate ankle, had greatly enjoyed himself for the last ten minutes in splashing the carpet, set off promptly. A very few minutes had elapsed when he showed the Doctor in, by tumbling against the door before him and bursting it open with his head.

"Gently, Jock, gently," said the Doctor as he advanced with a quiet step. "Gentlemen, a good evening. I am sorry that my presence is required here. A slight accident, I hope? A slip and a fall? Yes, yes, yes. Carrock, indeed? Hah! Does that pain you, sir? No doubt, it does. It is the great connecting ligament here, you see, that has been badly strained. Time and rest, sir! They are often the recipe in greater cases," with a slight sigh, "and often the recipe in small. I can send a lotion to relieve you, but we must leave the cure to time and rest."

This he said, holding Idle's foot on his knee between his two hands, as he sat over against him. He had touched it tenderly and skilfully in explanation of what he said, and, when his careful examination was completed, softly returned it to its former horizontal position on a chair.

He spoke with a little irresolution whenever he began, but afterwards fluently. He was a tall, thin, large-boned, old gentleman, with an appearance at first sight of being hard-featured; but, at a second glance, the mild expression of his face and some particular touches of sweetness and patience about his mouth, corrected this impression and assigned his long professional rides, by day and night, in the bleak hill-weather, as the true cause of that appearance. He stooped very little, though past seventy and very grey. His dress was more like that of a clergyman than a country doctor, being a plain black suit, and a plain white neck-kerchief tied behind like a band. His black was the worse for wear, and there were darns in his coat, and his linen was a little frayed at the hems and edges. He might have been poor—it was likely enough in that out-of-the-way spot—or he might have been a little self-forgetful and eccentric. Any one could have seen directly, that he had neither wife nor child at home. He had a scholarly air with him, and that kind of considerate humanity towards others which claimed a gentle consideration for himself. Mr. Goodchild made this study of him while he was examining the limb, and as he laid it down. Mr. Goodchild wishes to add that he considers it a very good likeness.

It came out in the course of a little conversation, that Doctor Speddie was acquainted with some friends of Thomas Idle's, and had, when a young man, passed some years in Thomas Idle's birthplace on the other side of England. Certain idle labours, the fruit of Mr. Goodchild's apprentice-ship, also happened to be well known to him. The lazy travellers were thus placed on a more intimate footing with the Doctor than the casual circumstances of the meeting would of themselves have established; and when Doctor Speddie rose to go home, remarking that he would send his assistant with the lotion, Francis Goodchild said that was unnecessary, for, by the Doctor's leave, he would accompany him, and bring it back. (Having done nothing to fatigue himself for a full quarter of an hour, Francis began to fear that he was not in a state of idleness.)

Doctor Speddie politely assented to the proposition of

Francis Goodchild, "as it would give him the pleasure of enjoying a few more minutes of Mr. Goodchild's society than he could otherwise have hoped for," and they went out together into the village street. The rain had nearly ceased, the clouds had broken before a cool wind from the north-east, and stars were shining from the peaceful heights beyond them.

Doctor Speddie's house was the last house in the place. Beyond it, lay the moor, all dark and lonesome. The wind moaned in a low, dull, shivering manner round the little garden, like a houseless creature that knew the winter was coming. It was exceedingly wild and solitary. "Roses," said the Doctor, when Goodchild touched some wet leaves overhanging the stone porch; "but they get cut to pieces."

The Doctor opened the door with a key he carried, and led the way into a low but pretty ample hall with rooms on either side. The door of one of these stood open, and the Doctor entered it, with a word of welcome to his guest. It, too, was a low room, half surgery and half parlour, with shelves of books and bottles against the walls, which were of a very dark hue. There was a fire in the grate, the night being damp and chill. Leaning against the chimney-piece looking down into it, stood the Doctor's Assistant.

A man of a most remarkable appearance. Much older than Mr. Goodchild had expected, for he was at least two-and-fifty; but, that was nothing. What was startling in him was his remarkable paleness. His large black eyes, his sunken cheeks, his long and heavy iron-grey hair, his wasted hands, and even the attenuation of his figure, were at first forgotten in his extraordinary pallor. There was no vestige of colour in the man. When he turned his face, Francis Goodchild started as if a stone figure had looked round at him.

"Mr. Lorn," said the Doctor. "Mr. Goodchild."

The Assistant, in a distraught way—as if he had forgotten something—as if he had forgotten everything, even to his own name and himself—acknowledged the visitor's presence, and stepped further back into the shadow of the wall behind him. But, he was so pale that his face stood out in relief against the dark wall, and really could not be hidden so.

"Mr. Goodchild's friend has met with an accident, Lorn," said Doctor Speddie. "We want the lotion for a bad sprain."

A pause.

"My dear fellow, you are more than usually absent to-night. The lotion for a bad sprain."

"Ah! yes! Directly."

He was evidently relieved to turn away, and to take his white face and his wild eyes to a table in a recess among the bottles. But, though he stood there, compounding the lotion with his back towards them, Goodchild could not, for many moments, withdraw his gaze from the man. When he at length did so, he found the Doctor observing him, with some trouble in his face. "He is absent," explained the Doctor, in a low voice. "Always absent. Very absent."

"Is he ill?"

"No, not ill."

"Unhappy?"

"I have my suspicions that he was," assented the Doctor, "once."

Francis Goodchild could not but observe that the Doctor accompanied these words with a benignant and protecting glance at their subject, in which there was much of the expression with which an attached father might have looked at a heavily afflicted son. Yet, that they were not father and son must have been plain to most eyes. The Assistant, on the other hand, turning presently to ask the Doctor some question, looked at him with a wan smile as if he were his whole reliance and sustainment in life.

It was in vain for the Doctor in his easy-chair, to try to lead the mind of Mr. Goodchild in the opposite easy-chair, away from what was before him. Let Mr. Goodchild do what he would to follow the Doctor, his eyes and thoughts reverted to the Assistant. The Doctor soon perceived it, and, after falling silent, and musing in a little perplexity, said:

" Lorn ! "

" My dear Doctor."

" Would you go to the Inn, and apply that lotion? You will show the best way of applying it, far better than Mr. Goodchild can."

" With pleasure."

The Assistant took his hat, and passed like a shadow to the door.

"Lorn !" said the Doctor, calling after him.

He returned.

" Mr. Goodchild will keep me company till you come home. Don't hurry. Excuse my calling you back."

"It is not," said the Assistant, with his former smile, " the first time you have called me back, dear Doctor." With those words he went away.

" Mr. Goodchild," said Doctor Speddie, in a low voice, and with his former troubled expression of face, "I have seen that your attention has been concentrated on my friend."

"He fascinates me. I must apologise to you, but he has quite bewildered and mastered me."

"I find that a lonely existence and a long secret," said the Doctor, drawing his chair a little nearer to Mr. Goodchild's, " become in the course of time very heavy. I will tell you something. You may make what use you will of it, under fictitious names. I know I may trust you. I am the more inclined to confidence to-night, through having been unexpectedly led back, by the current of our conversation at the Inn, to scenes in my early life. Will you please to draw a little nearer?"

Mr. Goodchild drew a little nearer, and the Doctor went on thus : speaking, for the most part, in so cautious a voice, that the wind, though it was far from high, occasionally got the better of him.

When this present nineteenth century was younger by a good many years than it is now, a certain friend of mine, named Arthur Holliday, happened to arrive in the town of Doncaster, exactly in the middle of a race-week, or, in other words, in the middle of the month of September. He was one of those reckless, rattle-pated, open-hearted, and open-mouthed young gentlemen, who possess the gift of familiarity in its highest perfection, and who scramble carelessly along the journey of life making friends, as the phrase is, wherever they go. His father was a rich manufacturer, and had bought landed property enough in one of the midland counties to make all the born squires in his neighbourhood thoroughly envious of him. Arthur was his only son, possessor in prospect of the great estate and the great business after his father's death; well supplied with money, and not too rigidly looked after, during his father's lifetime. Report, or scandal, whichever you please, said that the old gentleman had been rather wild in his youthful days, and that, unlike most parents, he was not disposed to be violently indignant when he found that his son took after him. This may be true or not. I myself only knew the elder Mr. Holliday when he was getting on in years; and then he was as quiet and as respectable a gentleman as ever I met with.

Well, one September, as I told you, young Arthur comes to Doncaster, having decided all of a sudden, in his hare-brained way, that he would go to the races. He did not reach the town till towards the close of the evening, and he went at once to see about his dinner and bed at the principal hotel. Dinner they were ready enough to give him; but as for a bed, they laughed when he mentioned it. In the race-week at Doncaster, it is no uncommon thing for visitors who have not bespoken apartments, to pass the night in their carriages at the inn doors. As for the lower sort of strangers, I myself have often seen them, at that full time, sleeping out on the doorsteps for want of a covered place to creep under. Rich as he was, Arthur's chance of getting a night's lodging (seeing

THE RACE-WEEK AT DONCASTER

that he had not written beforehand to secure one) was more than doubtful. He tried the second hotel, and the third hotel, and two of the inferior inns after that; and was met everywhere by the same form of answer. No accommodation for the night of any sort was left. All the bright golden sovereigns in his pocket would not buy him a bed at Doncaster in the race-week.

To a young fellow of Arthur's temperament, the novelty of being turned away into the street, like a penniless vagabond, at every house where he asked for a lodging, presented itself in the light of a new and highly amusing piece of experience. He went on, with his carpet-bag in his hand, applying for a bed at every place of entertainment for travellers that he could find in Doncaster, until he wandered into the outskirts of the town. By this time, the last glimmer of twilight had faded out, the moon was rising dimly in a mist, the wind was getting cold, the clouds were gathering heavily, and there was every prospect that it was soon going to rain.

The look of the night had rather a lowering effect on young Holliday's good spirits. He began to contemplate the houseless situation in which he was placed, from the serious rather than the humorous point of view; and he looked about him, for another public-house to inquire at, with something very like downright anxiety in his mind on the subject of a lodging for the night. The suburban part of the town towards which he had now strayed was hardly lighted at all, and he could see nothing of the houses as he passed them, except that they got progressively smaller and dirtier, the farther he went. Down the winding road before him shone the dull gleam of an oil lamp, the one faint, lonely light that struggled ineffectually with the foggy darkness all round him. He resolved to go on as far as this lamp, and then, if it showed him nothing in the shape of an Inn, to return to the central part of the town and to try if he could not at least secure a chair to sit down on, through the night, at one of the principal Hotels.

As he got near the lamp, he heard voices; and, walking close under it, found that it lighted the entrance to a narrow court, on the wall of which was painted a long hand in faded flesh-colour, pointing with a lean forefinger, to this inscription:—

THE TWO ROBINS

Arthur turned into the court without hesitation, to see what The Two Robins could do for him. Four or five men were standing together round the door of the house which was at the bottom of the court, facing the entrance from the street. The men were all listening to one other man, better dressed than the rest, who was telling his audience something, in a low voice, in which they were apparently very much interested.

On entering the passage, Arthur was passed by a stranger with a knapsack in his hand, who was evidently leaving the house.

"No," said the traveller with the knapsack, turning round and addressing himself cheerfully to a fat, sly-looking, bald-headed man, with a dirty white apron on, who had followed him down the passage. "No, Mr. Landlord, I am not easily scared by trifles; but, I don't mind confessing that I can't quite stand *that*."

It occurred to young Holliday, the moment he heard these words, that the stranger had been asked an exorbitant price for a bed at The Two Robins; and that he was unable or unwilling to pay it. The moment his back was turned, Arthur, comfortably conscious of his own well-filled pockets, addressed himself in a great hurry, for fear any other benighted traveller should slip in and forestall him, to the sly-looking landlord with the dirty apron and the bald head.

"If you have got a bed to let," he said, "and if that gentleman who has just gone out won't pay your price for it, I will."

The sly landlord looked hard at Arthur.

A DOUBLE-BEDDED ROOM

"Will you, sir?" he asked, in a meditative, doubtful way.

"Name your price," said young Holliday, thinking that the landlord's hesitation sprang from some boorish distrust of him. "Name your price, and I'll give you the money at once if you like?"

"Are you game for five shillings?" inquired the landlord, rubbing his stubbly double chin, and looking up thoughtfully at the ceiling above him.

Arthur nearly laughed in the man's face; but thinking it prudent to control himself, offered the five shillings as seriously as he could. The sly landlord held out his hand, then suddenly drew it back again.

"You're acting all fair and above-board by me," he said : "and, before I take your money, I'll do the same by you. Look here, this is how it stands. You can have a bed all to yourself for five shillings; but you can't have more than a half-share of the room it stands in. Do you see what I mean, young gentleman?"

"Of course I do," returned Arthur, a little irritably. "You mean that it is a double-bedded room, and that one of the beds is occupied?"

The landlord nodded his head, and rubbed his double chin harder than ever. Arthur hesitated, and mechanically moved back a step or two towards the door. The idea of sleeping in the same room with a total stranger, did not present an attractive prospect to him. He felt more than half inclined to drop his five shillings into his pocket, and to go out into the street once more.

"Is it yes, or no?" asked the landlord. "Settle it as quick as you can, because there's lots of people wanting a bed at Doncaster to-night, besides you."

Arthur looked towards the court, and heard the rain falling heavily in the street outside. He thought he would ask a question or two before he rashly decided on leaving the shelter of The Two Robins.

"What sort of a man is it who has got the other bed?"

387

he inquired. "Is he a gentleman? I mean, is he a quiet, well-behaved person?"

"The quietest man I ever came across," said the landlord, rubbing his fat hands stealthily one over the other. "As sober as a judge, and as regular as clock-work in his habits. It hasn't struck nine, not ten minutes ago, and he's in his bed already. I don't know whether that comes up to your notion of a quiet man: it goes a long way ahead of mine, I can tell you."

"Is he asleep, do you think?" asked Arthur.

"I know he's asleep," returned the landlord. "And what's more, he's gone off so fast, that I'll warrant you don't wake him. This way, sir," said the landlord, speaking over young Holliday's shoulder, as if he was addressing some new guest who was approaching the house.

"Here you are," said Arthur, determined to be beforehand with the stranger, whoever he might be. "I'll take the bed." And he handed the five shillings to the landlord, who nodded, dropped the money carelessly into his waistcoat-pocket, and lighted the candle.

"Come up and see the room," said the host of The Two Robins, leading the way to the staircase quite briskly, considering how fat he was.

They mounted to the second-floor of the house. The landlord half opened a door, fronting the landing, then stopped, and turned round to Arthur.

"It's a fair bargain, mind, on my side as well as on yours," he said. "You give me five shillings, I give you in return a clean, comfortable bed; and I warrant, beforehand, that you won't be interfered with, or annoyed in any way, by the man who sleeps in the same room as you." Saying those words, he looked hard, for a moment, in young Holliday's face, and then led the way into the room.

It was larger and cleaner than Arthur had expected it would be. The two beds stood parallel with each other—a space of about six feet intervening between them. They were both of the same medium size, and both had the same plain white curtains, made to draw, if necessary, all round them. The occupied bed was the bed nearest the window. The curtains were all drawn round this, except the half curtain at the bottom, on the side of the bed farthest from the window. Arthur saw the feet of the sleeping man raising the scanty clothes into a sharp little eminence, as if he was lying flat on his back. He took the candle, and advanced softly to draw the curtain—stopped half-way, and listened for a moment—then turned to the landlord.

"He's a very quiet sleeper," said Arthur.

"Yes," said the landlord, "very quiet."

Young·Holliday advanced with the candle, and looked in at the man cautiously.

"How pale he is!" said Arthur.

"Yes," returned the landlord, "pale enough, isn't he?"

Arthur looked closer at the man. The bedclothes were drawn up to his chin, and they lay perfectly still over the region of his chest. Surprised and vaguely startled, as he noticed this, Arthur stooped down closer over the stranger; looked at his ashy, parted lips; listened breathlessly for an instant; looked again at the strangely still face, and the motionless lips and chest; and turned round suddenly on the landlord, with his own cheeks as pale for the moment as the hollow cheeks of the man on the bed.

"Come here," he whispered, under his breath. "Come here, for God's sake! The man's not asleep—he is dead!"

"You have found that out sooner than I thought you would," said the landlord, composedly. "Yes, he's dead, sure enough. He died at five o'clock to-day."

"How did he die? Who is he?" asked Arthur, staggered, for a moment, by the audacious coolness of the answer.

"As to who is he," rejoined the landlord, "I know no more about him than you do. There are his books and letters and things, all sealed up in that brown-paper parcel, for the Coroner's inquest to open to-morrow or next day.

He's been here a week, paying his way fairly enough, and stopping in-doors, for the most part, as if he was ailing. My girl brought him up his tea at five to-day; and as he was pouring of it out, he fell down in a faint, or a fit, or a compound of both, for anything I know. We could not bring him to—and I said he was dead. And the doctor couldn't bring him to—and the doctor said he was dead. And there he is. And the Coroner's inquest's coming as soon as it can. And that's as much as I know about it."

Arthur held the candle close to the man's lips. The flame still burnt straight up, as steadily as before. There was a moment of silence; and the rain pattered drearily through it against the panes of the window.

"If you haven't got nothing more to say to me," continued the landlord, "I suppose I may go. You don't expect your five shillings back, do you? There's the bed I promised you, clean and comfortable. There's the man I warranted not to disturb you, quiet in this world for ever. If you're frightened to stop alone with him, that's not my look out. I've kept my part of the bargain, and I mean to keep the money. I'm not Yorkshire, myself, young gentleman; but I've lived long enough in these parts to have my wits sharpened; and I shouldn't wonder if you found out the way to brighten up yours, next time you come amongst us." With these words, the landlord turned towards the door, and laughed to himself softly, in high satisfaction at his own sharpness.

Startled and shocked as he was, Arthur had by this time sufficiently recovered himself to feel indignant at the trick that had been played on him, and at the insolent manner in which the landlord exulted in it.

"Don't laugh," he said sharply, "till you are quite sure you have got the laugh against me. You shan't have the five shillings for nothing, my man. I'll keep the bed."

"Will you?" said the landlord. "Then I wish you a good night's rest." With that brief farewell, he went out, and shut the door after him.

ALONE WITH THE DEAD MAN

A good night's rest! The words had hardly been spoken, the door had hardly been closed, before Arthur half-repented the hasty words that had just escaped him. Though not naturally over-sensitive, and not wanting in courage of the moral as well as the physical sort, the presence of the dead man had an instantaneously chilling effect on his mind when he found himself alone in the room—alone, and bound by his own rash words to stay there till the next morning. An older man would have thought nothing of those words, and would have acted, without reference to them, as his calmer sense suggested. But Arthur was too young to treat the ridicule, even of his inferiors, with contempt—too young not to fear the momentary humiliation of falsifying his own foolish boast, more than he feared the trial of watching out the long night in the same chamber with the dead.

"It is but a few hours," he thought to himself, "and I can get away the first thing in the morning."

He was looking towards the occupied bed as that idea passed through his mind, and the sharp, angular eminence made in the clothes by the dead man's upturned feet again caught his eye. He advanced and drew the curtains, purposely abstaining, as he did so, from looking at the face of the corpse, lest he might unnerve himself at the outset by fastening some ghastly impression of it on his mind. He drew the curtain very gently, and sighed involuntarily as he closed it. "Poor fellow," he said, almost as sadly as if he had known the man. "Ah, poor fellow!"

He went next to the window. The night was black, and he could see nothing from it. The rain still pattered heavily against the glass. He inferred, from hearing it, that the window was at the back of the house; remembering that the front was sheltered from the weather by the court and the buildings over it.

While he was still standing at the window—for even the dreary rain was a relief, because of the sound it made; a relief, also, because it moved, and had some faint suggestion, in consequence, of life and companionship in it—while he was standing at the window, and looking vacantly into the black darkness outside, he heard a distant church-clock strike ten. Only ten! How was he to pass the time till the house was astir the next morning?

Under any other circumstances, he would have gone down to the public-house parlour, would have called for his grog, and would have laughed and talked with the company assembled as familiarly as if he had known them all his life. But the very thought of whiling away the time in this manner was distasteful to him. The new situation in which he was placed seemed to have altered him to himself already. Thus far, his life had been the common, trifling, prosaic, surface-life of a prosperous young man, with no troubles to conquer, and no trials to face. He had lost no relation whom he loved, no friend whom he treasured. Till this night, what share he had of the immortal inheritance that is divided amongst us all, had laid dormant within him. Till this night, Death and he had not once met, even in thought.

He took a few turns up and down the room—then stopped. The noise made by his boots on the poorly carpeted floor, jarred on his ear. He hesitated a little, and ended by taking the boots off, and walking backwards and forwards noiselessly. All desire to sleep or to rest had left him. The bare thought of lying down on the unoccupied bed instantly drew the picture on his mind of a dreadful mimicry of the position of the dead man. Who was he? What was the story of his past life? Poor he must have been, or he would not have stopped at such a place as The Two Robins Inn—and weakened, probably, by long illness, or he could hardly have died in the manner in which the landlord had described. Poor, ill, lonely,—dead in a strange place; dead, with nobody but a stranger to pity him. A sad story: truly, on the mere face of it, a very sad story.

While these thoughts were passing through his mind, he

had stopped insensibly at the window, close to which stood the foot of the bed with the closed curtains. At first he looked at it absently; then he became conscious that his eyes were fixed on it; and then, a perverse desire took possession of him to do the very thing which he had resolved not to do, up to this time—to look at the dead man.

He stretched out his hand towards the curtains; but checked himself in the very act of undrawing them, turned his back sharply on the bed, and walked towards the chimney-piece, to see what things were placed on it, and to try if he could keep the dead man out of his mind in that way.

There was a pewter inkstand on the chimney-piece, with some mildewed remains of ink in the bottle. There were two coarse china ornaments of the commonest kind; and there was a square of embossed card, dirty and fly-blown, with a collection of wretched riddles printed on it, in all sorts of zig-zag directions, and in variously coloured inks. He took the card, and went away, to read it, to the table on which the candle was placed; sitting down, with his back resolutely turned to the curtained bed.

He read the first riddle, the second, the third, all in one corner of the card—then turned it round impatiently to look at another. Before he could begin reading the riddles printed here, the sound of the church-clock stopped him. Eleven. He had got through an hour of the time, in the room with the dead man.

Once more he looked at the card. It was not easy to make out the letters printed on it, in consequence of the dimness of the light which the landlord had left him—a common tallow candle, furnished with a pair of heavy old-fashioned steel snuffers. Up to this time, his mind had been too much occupied to think of the light. He had left the wick of the candle unsnuffed, till it had risen higher than the flame, and had burnt into an odd pent-house shape at the top, from which morsels of the charred cotton fell off, from time to time, in little flakes. He took up the snuffers now, and trimmed the wick. The light brightened directly, and the room became less dismal.

Again he turned to the riddles; reading them doggedly and resolutely, now in one corner of the card, now in another. All his efforts, however, could not fix his attention on them. He pursued his occupation mechanically, deriving no sort of impression from what he was reading. It was as if a shadow from the curtained bed had got between his mind and the gaily printed letters—a shadow that nothing could dispel. At last, he gave up the struggle, and threw the card from him impatiently, and took to walking softly up and down the room again.

The dead man, the dead man, the *hidden* dead man on the bed! There was the one persistent idea still haunting him. Hidden? Was it only the body being there, or was it the body being there, concealed, that was preying on his mind? He stopped at the window, with that doubt in him; once more listening to the pattering rain, once more looking out into the black darkness.

Still the dead man! The darkness forced his mind back upon itself, and set his memory at work, reviving, with a painfully-vivid distinctness the momentary impression it had received from the first sight of the corpse. Before long the face seemed to be hovering out in the middle of the darkness, confronting him through the window, with the paleness whiter, with the dreadful dull line of light between the imperfectly-closed eyelids broader than he had seen it—with the parted lips slowly dropping farther and farther away from each other —with the features growing larger and moving closer, till they seemed to fill the window and to silence the rain, and to shut out the night.

The sound of a voice, shouting below-stairs, woke him suddenly from the dream of his own distempered fancy. He recognised it as the voice of the landlord. "Shut up at twelve, Ben," he heard it say. "I'm off to bed."

He wiped away the damp that had gathered on his forehead,

reasoned with himself for a little while, and resolved to shake his mind free of the ghastly counterfeit which still clung to it, by forcing himself to confront, if it was only for a moment, the solemn reality. Without allowing himself an instant to hesitate, he parted the curtains at the foot of the bed, and looked through.

There was a sad, peaceful, white face, with the awful mystery of stillness on it, laid back upon the pillow. No stir, no change there! He only looked at it for a moment before he closed the curtains again—but that moment steadied him, calmed him, restored him—mind and body—to himself.

He returned to his old occupation of walking up and down the room; persevering in it, this time, till the clock struck again. Twelve.

As the sound of the clock-bell died away, it was succeeded by the confused noise, down-stairs, of the drinkers in the tap-room leaving the house. The next sound, after an interval of silence, was caused by the barring of the door, and the closing of the shutters, at the back of the Inn. Then the silence followed again, and was disturbed no more.

He was alone now—absolutely, utterly, alone with the dead man, till the next morning.

The wick of the candle wanted trimming again. He took up the snuffers—but paused suddenly on the very point of using them, and looked attentively at the candle—then back, over his shoulder, at the curtained bed—then again at the candle. It had been lighted, for the first time, to show him the way up-stairs, and three parts of it, at least, were already consumed. In another hour it would be burnt out. In another hour—unless he called at once to the man who had shut up the Inn, for a fresh candle—he would be left in the dark.

Strongly as his mind had been affected since he had entered his room, his unreasonable dread of encountering ridicule, and of exposing his courage to suspicion, had not altogether lost its influence over him, even yet. He lingered irresolutely by the table, waiting till he could prevail on himself to open the door, and call, from the landing, to the man who had shut up the Inn. In his present hesitating frame of mind, it was a kind of relief to gain a few moments only by engaging in the trifling occupation of snuffing the candle. His hand trembled a little, and the snuffers were heavy and awkward to use. When he closed them on the wick, he closed them a hair's breadth too low. In an instant the candle was out, and the room was plunged in pitch darkness.

The one impression which the absence of light immediately produced on his mind, was distrust of the curtained bed—distrust which shaped itself into no distinct idea, but which was powerful enough, in its very vagueness, to bind him down to his chair, to make his heart beat fast, and to set him listening intently. No sound stirred in the room but the familiar sound of the rain against the window, louder and sharper now than he had heard it yet.

Still the vague distrust, the inexpressible dread possessed him, and kept him to his chair. He had put his carpet-bag on the table, when he first entered the room; and he now took the key from his pocket, reached out his hand softly, opened .the bag, and groped in it for his travelling writing-case, in which he knew that there was a small store of matches. When he had got one of the matches, he waited before he struck it on the coarse wooden table, and listened intently again, without knowing why. Still there was no sound in the room but the steady, ceaseless, rattling sound of the rain.

He lighted the candle again, without another moment of delay; and, on the instant of its burning up, the first object in the room that his eyes sought for was the curtained bed.

Just before the light had been put out, he had looked in that direction, and had seen no change, no disarrangement of any sort, in the folds of the closely-drawn curtains.

THE HOUSE AROUSED

When he looked at the bed, now, he saw, hanging over the side of it, a long white hand.

It lay perfectly motionless, midway on the side of the bed, where the curtain at the head and the curtain at the foot met. Nothing more was visible. The clinging curtains hid everything but the long white hand.

He stood looking at it unable to stir, unable to call out; feeling nothing, knowing nothing, every faculty he possessed gathered up and lost in the one seeing faculty. How long that first panic held him he never could tell afterwards. It might have been only for a moment; it might have been for many minutes together. How he got to the bed—whether he ran to it headlong, or whether he approached it slowly— how he wrought himself up to unclose the curtains and look in, he never has remembered, and never will remember to his dying day. It is enough that he did go to the bed, and that he did look inside the curtains.

The man had moved. One of his arms was outside the clothes; his face was turned a little on the pillow; his eyelids were wide open. Changed as to position, and as to one of the features, the face was, otherwise, fearfully and wonderfully unaltered. The dead paleness and the dead quiet were on it still.

One glance showed Arthur this—one glance, before he flew breathlessly to the door, and alarmed the house.

The man whom the landlord called "Ben," was the first to appear on the stairs. In three words, Arthur told him what had happened, and sent him for the nearest doctor.

I, who tell you this story, was then staying with a medical friend of mine, in practice at Doncaster, taking care of his patients for him, during his absence in London; and I, for the time being, was the nearest doctor. They had sent for me from the Inn, when the stranger was taken ill in the afternoon; but I was not at home, and medical assistance was sought for elsewhere. When the man from The Two Robins rang the night-bell, I was just thinking of going to bed.

Naturally enough, I did not believe a word of his story about "a dead man who had come to life again." However, I put on my hat, armed myself with one or two bottles of restorative medicine, and ran to the Inn, expecting to find nothing more remarkable, when I got there, than a patient in a fit.

My surprise at finding that the man had spoken the literal truth was almost, if not quite, equalled by my astonishment at finding myself face to face with Arthur Holliday as soon as I entered the bedroom. It was no time then for giving or seeking explanations. We just shook hands amazedly; and then I ordered everybody but Arthur out of the room, and hurried to the man on the bed.

The kitchen fire had not been long out. There was plenty of hot water in the boiler, and plenty of flannel to be had. With these, with my medicines, and with such help as Arthur could render under my direction, I dragged the man, literally, out of the jaws of death. In less than an hour from the time when I had been called in, he was alive and talking in the bed on which he had been laid out to wait for the Coroner's inquest.

You will naturally ask me, what had been the matter with him; and I might treat you, in reply, to a long theory, plentifully sprinkled with, what the children call, hard words. I prefer telling you that, in this case, cause and effect could not be satisfactorily joined together by any theory whatever. There are mysteries in life, and the condition of it, which human science has not fathomed yet; and I candidly confess to you, that, in bringing that man back to existence, I was, morally speaking, groping hap-hazard in the dark. I know (from the testimony of the doctor who attended him in the afternoon) that the vital machinery, so far as its action is appreciable by our senses, had, in this case, unquestionably stopped; and I am equally certain (seeing that I recovered him) that the vital principle was not extinct. When I add, that he had suffered from a long and complicated illness, and that his whole nervous system was utterly deranged, I have

398

told you all I really know of the physical condition of my dead-alive patient at The Two Robins Inn.

When he " came to," as the phrase goes, he was a startling object to look at, with his colourless face, his sunken cheeks, his wild black eyes, and his long black hair. The first question he asked me about himself, when he could speak, made me suspect that I had been called in to a man in my own profession. I mentioned to him my surmise; and he told me that I was right.

He said he had come last from Paris, where he had been attached to a hospital. That he had lately returned to England, on his way to Edinburgh, to continue his studies; that he had been taken ill on the journey; and that he had stopped to rest and recover himself at Doncaster. He did not add a word about his name, or who he was: and, of course, I did not question him on the subject. All I inquired, when he ceased speaking, was what branch of the profession he intended to follow.

" Any branch," he said, bitterly, " which will put bread into the mouth of a poor man."

At this, Arthur, who had been hitherto watching him in silent curiosity, burst out impetuously in his usual good-humoured way :—

" My dear fellow ! " (everybody was " my dear fellow " with Arthur) " now you have come to life again, don't begin by being downhearted about your prospects. I'll answer for it, I can help you to some capital thing in the medical line—or, if I can't, I know my father can."

The medical student looked at him steadily.

" Thank you," he said, coldly. Then added, " May I ask who your father is ? "

" He's well enough known all about this part of the country," replied Arthur. " He is a great manufacturer, and his name is Holliday."

My hand was on the man's wrist during this brief conversation. The instant the name of Holliday was pronounced I felt the pulse under my fingers flutter, stop, go on suddenly with a bound, and beat afterwards, for a minute or two, at the fever rate.

"How did you come here?" asked the stranger, quickly, excitably, passionately almost.

Arthur related briefly what had happened from the time of his first taking the bed at the inn.

"I am indebted to Mr. Holliday's son then for the help that has saved my life," said the medical student, speaking to himself, with a singular sarcasm in his voice. "Come here!"

He held out, as he spoke, his long, white, bony, right hand.

"With all my heart," said Arthur, taking the hand cordially. "I may confess it now," he continued, laughing. "Upon my honour, you almost frightened me out of my wits."

The stranger did not seem to listen. His wild black eyes were fixed with a look of eager interest on Arthur's face, and his long bony fingers kept tight hold of Arthur's hand. Young Holliday, on his side, returned the gaze, amazed and puzzled by the medical student's odd language and manners. The two faces were close together; I looked at them; and, to my amazement, I was suddenly impressed by the sense of a likeness between them—not in features, or complexion, but solely in expression. It must have been a strong likeness, or I should certainly not have found it out, for I am naturally slow at detecting resemblances between faces.

"You have saved my life," said the strange man, still looking hard in Arthur's face, still holding tightly by his hand. "If you had been my own brother, you could not have done more for me than that."

He laid a singularly strong emphasis on those three words "my own brother," and a change passed over his face as he pronounced them,—a change that no language of mine is competent to describe.

"I hope I have not done being of service to you yet," said Arthur. "I'll speak to my father, as soon as I get home."

"You seem to be fond and proud of your father, said the medical student. "I suppose, in return, he is fond and proud of you?"

"Of course, he is!" answered Arthur, laughing. "Is there anything wonderful in that? Isn't *your* father fond——"

The stranger suddenly dropped young Holliday's hand, and turned his face away.

"I beg your pardon," said Arthur. "I hope I have not unintentionally pained you. I hope you have not lost your father."

"I can't well lose what I have never had," retorted the medical student, with a harsh, mocking laugh.

"What you have never had!"

The strange man suddenly caught Arthur's hand again, suddenly looked once more hard in his face.

"Yes," he said, with a repetition of the bitter laugh. "You have brought a poor devil back into the world, who has no business there. Do I astonish you? Well! I have a fancy of my own for telling you what men in my situation generally keep a secret. I have no name and no father. The merciful law of Society tells me I am Nobody's Son! Ask your father if he will be my father too, and help me on in life with the family name."

Arthur looked at me, more puzzled than ever. I signed to him to say nothing, and then laid my fingers again on the man's wrist. No! In spite of the extraordinary speech that he had just made, he was not, as I had been disposed to suspect, beginning to get light-headed. His pulse, by this time, had fallen back to a quiet, slow beat, and his skin was moist and cool. Not a symptom of fever or agitation about him.

Finding that neither of us answered him, he turned to me, and began talking of the extraordinary nature of his case, and asking my advice about the future course of medical treatment to which he ought to subject himself. I said the matter required careful thinking over, and suggested that I should submit certain prescriptions to him the next morning. He told me to write them at once, as he would, most likely, be leaving Doncaster, in the morning, before I was up. It was quite useless to represent to him the folly and danger of such a proceeding as this. He heard me politely and patiently, but held to his resolution, without offering any reasons or any explanations, and repeated to me, that if I wished to give him a chance of seeing my prescription, I must write it at once. Hearing this, Arthur volunteered the loan of a travelling writing-case, which, he said, he had with him; and, bringing it to the bed, shook the note-paper out of the pocket of the case forthwith in his usual careless way. With the paper, there fell out on the counterpane of the bed a small packet of sticking-plaster, and a little water-colour drawing of a landscape.

The medical student took up the drawing and looked at it. His eye fell on some initials neatly written, in cypher, in one corner. He started and trembled; his pale face grew whiter than ever; his wild black eyes turned on Arthur, and looked through and through him.

"A pretty drawing," he said in a remarkably quiet tone of voice.

"Ah! and done by such a pretty girl," said Arthur. "Oh, such a pretty girl! I wish it was not a landscape—I wish it was a portrait of her!"

"You admire her very much?"

Arthur, half in jest, half in earnest, kissed his hand for answer.

"Love at first sight!" he said, putting the drawing away again. "But the course of it doesn't run smooth. It's the old story. She's monopolised as usual. Trammelled by a rash engagement to some poor man who is never likely to get money enough to marry her. It was lucky I heard of it in time, or I should certainly have risked a declaration when she gave me that drawing. Here, doctor! Here is pen, ink, and paper all ready for you."

"When she gave you that drawing? Gave it. Gave it." He repeated the words slowly to himself, and suddenly closed his eyes. A momentary distortion passed across his face, and I saw one of his hands clutch up the bedclothes and squeeze them hard. I thought he was going to be ill again, and begged that there might be no more talking. He opened his eyes when I spoke, fixed them once more searchingly on Arthur, and said, slowly and distinctly, "You like her, and she likes you. The poor man may die out of your way. Who can tell that she may not give you herself as well as her drawing, after all?"

Before young Holliday could answer, he turned to me, and said in a whisper, "Now for the prescription." From that time, though he spoke to Arthur again, he never looked at him more.

When I had written the prescription, he examined it, approved of it, and then astonished us both by abruptly wishing us good night. I offered to sit up with him, and he shook his head. Arthur offered to sit up with him, and he said, shortly, with his face turned away, "No." I insisted on having somebody left to watch him. He gave way when he found I was determined, and said he would accept the services of the waiter at the Inn.

"Thank you, both," he said, as we rose to go. "I have one last favour to ask—not of you, doctor, for I leave you to exercise your professional discretion—but of Mr. Holliday." His eyes, while he spoke, still rested steadily on me, and never once turned towards Arthur. "I beg that Mr. Holliday will not mention to any one—least of all to his father—the events that have occurred, and the words that have passed, in this room. I entreat him to bury me in his memory, as, but for him, I might have been buried in my grave. I cannot give my reasons for making this strange request. I can only implore him to grant it."

His voice faltered for the first time, and he hid his face on the pillow. Arthur, completely bewildered, gave the

403

required pledge. I took young Holliday away with me, immediately afterwards, to the house of my friend; determining to go back to the Inn, and to see the medical student again before he had left in the morning.

I returned to the Inn at eight o'clock, purposely abstaining from waking Arthur, who was sleeping off the past night's excitement on one of my friend's sofas. A suspicion had occurred to me as soon as I was alone in my bedroom, which made me resolve that Holliday and the stranger whose life he had saved should not meet again, if I could prevent it. I have already alluded to certain reports, or scandals, which I knew of, relating to the early life of Arthur's father. While I was thinking, in my bed, of what had passed at the Inn— of the change in the student's pulse when he heard the name of Holliday; of the resemblance of expression that I had discovered between his face and Arthur's; of the emphasis he had laid on those three words, "my own brother;" and of his incomprehensible acknowledgment of his own illegitimacy —while I was thinking of these things, the reports I have mentioned suddenly flew into my mind, and linked themselves fast to the chain of my previous reflections. Something within me whispered, "It is best that those two young men should not meet again." I felt it before I slept; I felt it when I woke; and I went, as I told you, alone to the Inn the next morning.

I had missed my only opportunity of seeing my nameless patient again. He had been gone nearly an hour when I inquired for him.

I have now told you everything that I know for certain, in relation to the man whom I brought back to life in the double-bedded room of the Inn at Doncaster. What I have next to add is matter for inference and surmise, and is not, strictly speaking, matter of fact.

I have to tell you, first, that the medical student turned out to be strangely and unaccountably right in assuming it

as more than probable that Arthur Holliday would marry
the young lady who had given him the water-colour drawing
of the landscape. That marriage took place a little more
than a year after the events occurred which I have just been
relating. The young couple came to live in the neighbourhood
in which I was then established in practice. I was present
at the wedding, and was rather surprised to find that Arthur
was singularly reserved with me, both before and after his
marriage, on the subject of the young lady's prior engagement.
He only referred to it once, when we were alone, merely
telling me, on that occasion, that his wife had done all that
honour and duty required of her in the matter, and that the
engagement had been broken off with the full approval of her
parents. I never heard more from him than this. For three
years he and his wife lived together happily. At the expira-
tion of that time, the symptoms of a serious illness first
declared themselves in Mrs. Arthur Holliday. It turned out
to be a long, lingering, hopeless malady. I attended her
throughout. We had been great friends when she was well,
and we became more attached to each other than ever when
she was ill. I had many long and interesting conversations
with her in the intervals when she suffered least. The result
of one of these conversations I may briefly relate, leaving you
to draw any inferences from it that you please.

The interview to which I refer, occurred shortly before her
death. I called one evening, as usual, and found her alone,
with a look in her eyes which told me that she had been
crying. She only informed me at first, that she had been
depressed in spirits; but, by little and little, she became more
communicative, and confessed to me that she had been
looking over some old letters, which had been addressed to
her, before she had seen Arthur, by a man to whom she had
been engaged to be married. I asked her how the engagement
came to be broken off. She replied that it had not been
broken off, but that it had died out in a very mysterious way.
The person to whom she was engaged—her first love, she

called him—was very poor, and there was no immediate prospect of their being married. He followed my profession, and went abroad to study. They had corresponded regularly, until the time when, as she believed, he had returned to England. From that period she heard no more of him. He was of a fretful, sensitive temperament; and she feared that she might have inadvertently done or said something that offended him. However that might be, he had never written to her again; and, after waiting a year, she had married Arthur. I asked when the first estrangement had begun, and found that the time at which she ceased to hear anything of her first lover exactly corresponded with the time at which I had been called in to my mysterious patient at The Two Robins Inn.

A fortnight after that conversation, she died. In course of time, Arthur married again. Of late years, he has lived principally in London, and I have seen little or nothing of him.

I have many years to pass over before I can approach to anything like a conclusion of this fragmentary narrative. And even when that later period is reached, the little that I have to say will not occupy your attention for more than a few minutes. Between six and seven years ago, the gentleman to whom I introduced you in this room, came to me, with good professional recommendations, to fill the position of my assistant. We met, not like strangers, but like friends—the only difference between us being, that I was very much surprised to see him, and that he did not appear to be at all surprised to see me. If he was my son or my brother, I believe he could not be fonder of me than he is; but he has never volunteered any confidences since he has been here, on the subject of his past life. I saw something that was familiar to me in his face when we first met; and yet it was also something that suggested the idea of change. I had a notion once that my patient at the Inn might be a natural son of Mr. Holliday's; I had another idea that he might also have been the man who was engaged to Arthur's first wife; and I have a third idea, still clinging to me, that Mr. Lorn is the only man in England who could really enlighten me, if he chose, on both those doubtful points. His hair is not black, now, and his eyes are dimmer than the piercing eyes that I remember, but, for all that, he is very like the nameless medical student of my young days—very like him. And, sometimes, when I come home late at night, and find him asleep, and wake him, he looks, in coming to, wonderfully like the stranger at Doncaster, as he raised himself in the bed on that memorable night!

The Doctor paused. Mr. Goodchild, who had been following every word that fell from his lips up to this time, leaned forward eagerly to ask a question. Before he could say a word, the latch of the door was raised, without any warning sound of footsteps in the passage outside. A long, white, bony hand appeared through the opening, gently pushing the door, which was prevented from working freely on its hinges by a fold in the carpet under it.

"That hand! Look at that hand, Doctor!" said Mr. Goodchild, touching him.

At the same moment, the Doctor looked at Mr. Goodchild, and whispered to him, significantly:

"Hush! he has come back."

CHAPTER III

The Cumberland Doctor's mention of Doncaster Races, inspired Mr. Francis Goodchild with the idea of going down to Doncaster to see the races. Doncaster being a good way off, and quite out of the way of the Idle Apprentices (if anything could be out of their way, who had no way), it necessarily followed that Francis perceived Doncaster in the race-week to be, of all possible idlenesses, the particular idleness that would completely satisfy him.

Thomas, with an enforced idleness grafted on the natural and voluntary power of his disposition, was not of this mind; objecting that a man compelled to lie on his back on a floor, a sofa, a table, a line of chairs, or anything he could get to lie upon, was not in racing condition, and that he desired nothing better than to lie where he was, enjoying himself in looking at the flies on the ceiling. But, Francis Goodchild, who had been walking round his companion in a circuit of twelve miles for two days, and had begun to doubt whether it was reserved for him ever to be idle in his life, not only overpowered this objection, but even converted Thomas Idle to a scheme he formed (another idle inspiration), of conveying the said Thomas to the sea-coast, and putting his injured leg under a stream of salt-water.

Plunging into this happy conception headforemost, Mr. Goodchild immediately referred to the county-map, and ardently discovered that the most delicious piece of sea-coast to be found within the limits of England, Ireland, Scotland, Wales, the Isle of Man, and the Channel Islands, all summed up together, was Allonby on the coast of Cumberland. There was the coast of Scotland opposite to Allonby, said Mr. Goodchild with enthusiasm; there was a fine Scottish mountain on that Scottish coast; there were Scottish lights to be seen shining across the glorious Channel, and at Allonby itself there was every idle luxury (no doubt) that a watering-place could offer to the heart of idle man. Moreover, said Mr. Goodchild, with his finger on the map, this exquisite retreat was approached by a coach-road, from a railway-station called Aspatria—a name, in a manner, suggestive of the departed glories of Greece, associated with one of the most engaging and most famous of Greek women. On this point, Mr. Goodchild continued at intervals to breathe a vein of classic fancy and eloquence exceedingly irksome to Mr. Idle, until it appeared that the honest English pronunciation of that Cumberland country shortened Aspatria into "Spatter." After this supplementary discovery, Mr. Goodchild said no more about it.

By way of Spatter, the crippled Idle was carried, hoisted, pushed, poked, and packed, into and out of carriages, into and out of beds, into and out of tavern resting-places, until he was brought at length within sniff of the sea. And now, behold the apprentices gallantly riding into Allonby in a one-horse fly, bent upon staying in that peaceful marine valley until the turbulent Doncaster time shall come round upon the wheel, in its turn among what are in sporting registers called the "Fixtures" for the month.

"Do you see Allonby !" asked Thomas Idle.

"I don't see it yet," said Francis, looking out of window.

"It must be there," said Thomas Idle.

"I don't see it," returned Francis.

"It must be there," repeated Thomas Idle, fretfully.

"Lord bless me !" exclaimed Francis, drawing in his head, "I suppose this is it !"

"A watering-place," retorted Thomas Idle, with the pardonable sharpness of an invalid, "can't be five gentlemen in straw hats, on a form on one side of a door, and four ladies in hats and falls, on a form on another side of a door, and three geese in a dirty little brook before them, and a boy's legs hanging over a bridge (with a boy's body I suppose on the other side of the parapet), and a donkey running away. What are you talking about?"

"Allonby, gentlemen," said the most comfortable of land-ladies, as she opened one door of the carriage; "Allonby, gentlemen," said the most attentive of landlords, as he opened the other.

Thomas Idle yielded his arm to the ready Goodchild, and descended from the vehicle. Thomas, now just able to grope his way along, in a doubled-up condition, with the aid of two thick sticks, was no bad embodiment of Commodore Trunnion, or of one of those many gallant Admirals of the stage, who have all ample fortunes, gout, thick sticks, tempers, wards, and nephews. With this distinguished naval appearance upon him, Thomas made a crab-like progress up a clean little bulk-headed staircase, into a clean little bulk-headed room, where he slowly deposited himself on a sofa, with a stick on either hand of him, looking exceedingly grim.

"Francis," said Thomas Idle, "what do you think of this place?"

"I think," returned Mr. Goodchild, in a glowing way, "it is everything we expected."

"Hah!" said Thomas Idle.

"There is the sea," cried Mr. Goodchild, pointing out of window; "and here," pointing to the lunch on the table, "are shrimps. Let us——" here Mr. Goodchild looked out of window, as if in search of something, and looked in again, —"let us eat 'em."

The shrimps eaten and the dinner ordered, Mr. Goodchild went out to survey the watering-place. As Chorus of the Drama, without whom Thomas could make nothing of the scenery, he by-and-by returned, to have the following report screwed out of him.

410

In brief, it was the most delightful place ever seen.

"But," Thomas Idle asked, "where is it?"

"It's what you may call generally up and down the beach, here and there," said Mr. Goodchild, with a twist of his hand.

"Proceed," said Thomas Idle.

It was, Mr. Goodchild went on to say, in cross-examination, what you might call a primitive place. Large? No, it was not large. Who ever expected it would be large? Shape? What a question to ask! No shape. What sort of a street? Why, no street. Shops? Yes, of course (quite indignant). How many? Who ever went into a place to count the shops? Ever so many. Six? Perhaps. A library? Why, of course (indignant again). Good collection of books? Most likely —couldn't say—had seen nothing in it but a pair of scales. Any reading-room? Of course, there was a reading-room. Where? Where! why, over there. Where was over there? Why, *there!* Let Mr. Idle carry his eye to that bit of waste ground above high-water mark, where the rank grass and loose stones were most in a litter; and he would see a sort of a long, ruinous brick loft, next door to a ruinous brick out-house, which loft had a ladder outside, to get up by. That was the reading-room, and if Mr. Idle didn't like the idea of a weaver's shuttle throbbing under a reading-room, that was his look out. *He* was not to dictate, Mr. Goodchild supposed (indignant again), to the company.

"By-the-by," Thomas Idle observed; "the company?"

Well! (Mr. Goodchild went on to report) very nice company. Where were they? Why, there they were. Mr. Idle could see the tops of their hats, he supposed. What? Those nine straw hats again, five gentlemen's and four ladies'? Yes, to be sure. Mr. Goodchild hoped the company were not to be expected to wear helmets, to please Mr. Idle.

Beginning to recover his temper at about this point, Mr. Goodchild voluntarily reported that if you wanted to be primitive, you could be primitive here, and that if you wanted to be idle, you could be idle here. In the course of some

411

days, he added, that there were three fishing-boats, but no rigging, and that there were plenty of fishermen who never fished. That they got their living entirely by looking at the ocean. What nourishment they looked out of it to support their strength, he couldn't say; but, he supposed it was some sort of Iodine. The place was full of their children, who were always upside down on the public buildings (two small bridges over the brook), and always hurting themselves or one another, so that their wailings made more continual noise in the air than could have been got in a busy place. The houses people lodged in, were nowhere in particular, and were in capital accordance with the beach; being all more or less cracked and damaged as its shells were, and all empty—as its shells were. Among them, was an edifice of destitute appearance, with a number of wall-eyed windows in it, looking desperately out to Scotland as if for help, which said it was a Bazaar (and it ought to know), and where you might buy anything you wanted—supposing what you wanted, was a little camp-stool or a child's wheelbarrow. The brook crawled or stopped between the houses and the sea, and the donkey was always running away, and when he got into the brook he was pelted out with stones, which never hit him, and which always hit some of the children who were upside down on the public buildings, and made their lamentations louder. This donkey was the public excitement of Allonby, and was probably supported at the public expense.

The foregoing descriptions, delivered in separate items, on separate days of adventurous discovery, Mr. Goodchild severally wound up, by looking out of window, looking in again, and saying, "But there is the sea, and here are the shrimps—let us eat 'em."

There were fine sunsets at Allonby when the low flat beach, with its pools of water and its dry patches, changed into long bars of silver and gold in various states of burnishing, and there were fine views—on fine days—of the Scottish coast. But, when it rained at Allonby, Allonby thrown back upon its ragged self, became a kind of place which the donkey seemed to have found out, and to have his highly sagacious reasons for wishing to bolt from. Thomas Idle observed, too, that Mr. Goodchild, with a noble show of disinterestedness, became every day more ready to walk to Maryport and back, for letters; and suspicions began to harbour in the mind of Thomas, that his friend deceived him, and that Maryport was a preferable place.

Therefore, Thomas said to Francis on a day when they had looked at the sea and eaten the shrimps, "My mind misgives me, Goodchild, that you go to Maryport, like the boy in the story-book, to ask *it* to be idle with you."

"Judge, then," returned Francis, adopting the style of the story-book, "with what success. I go to a region which is a bit of water-side Bristol, with a slice of Wapping, a seasoning of Wolverhampton, and a garnish of Portsmouth, and I say, 'Will *you* come and be idle with me?' And it answers, 'No; for I am a great deal too vaporous, and a great deal too rusty, and a great deal too muddy, and a great deal too dirty altogether; and I have ships to load, and pitch and tar to boil, and iron to hammer, and steam to get up, and smoke to make, and stone to quarry, and fifty other disagreeable things to do, and I can't be idle with you.' Then I go into jagged up-hill and down-hill streets, where I am in the pastrycook's shop at one moment, and next moment in savage fastnesses of moor and morass, beyond the confines of civilisation, and I say to those murky and black-dusty streets, 'Will *you* come and be idle with me?' To which they reply, 'No, we can't, indeed, for we haven't the spirits, and we are startled by the echo of your feet on the sharp pavement, and we have so many goods in our shop-windows which nobody wants, and we have so much to do for a limited public which never comes to us to be done for, that we are altogether out of sorts and can't enjoy ourselves with any one.' So I go to the Post-office, and knock at the shutter, and I say to the Post-master, 'Will *you* come and be idle with me?' To which he rejoins, 'No, I really can't, for I live, as you may see, in such a very little Post-office, and pass my life behind such a very little shutter, that my hand, when I put it out, is as the hand of a giant crammed through the window of a dwarf's house at a fair, and I am a mere Post-office anchorite in a cell much too small for him, and I can't get out, and I can't get in, and I have no space to be idle in, even if I would.' So, the boy," said Mr. Goodchild, concluding the tale, "comes back with the letters after all, and lives happy never afterwards."

But it may, not unreasonably, be asked—while Francis Goodchild was wandering hither and thither, storing his mind with perpetual observation of men and things, and sincerely believing himself to be the laziest creature in existence all the time—how did Thomas Idle, crippled and confined to the house, contrive to get through the hours of the day?

Prone on the sofa, Thomas made no attempt to get through the hours, but passively allowed the hours to get through *him*. Where other men in his situation would have read books and improved their minds, Thomas slept and rested his body. Where other men would have pondered anxiously over their future prospects, Thomas dreamed lazily of his past life. The one solitary thing he did, which most other people would have done in his place, was to resolve on making certain alterations and improvements in his mode of existence, as soon as the effects of the misfortune that had overtaken him had all passed away. Remembering that the current of his life had hitherto oozed along in one smooth stream of laziness, occasionally troubled on the surface by a slight passing ripple of industry, his present ideas on the subject of self-reform, inclined him—not as the reader may be disposed to imagine, to project schemes for a new existence of enterprise and exertion—but, on the contrary, to resolve that he would never, if he could possibly help it, be active or industrious again, throughout the whole of his future career.

It is due to Mr. Idle to relate that his mind sauntered

towards this peculiar conclusion on distinct and logically-producible grounds. After reviewing, quite at his ease, and with many needful intervals of repose, the generally-placid spectacle of his past existence, he arrived at the discovery that all the great disasters which had tried his patience and equanimity in early life, had been caused by his having allowed himself to be deluded into imitating some pernicious example of activity and industry that had been set him by others. The trials to which he here alludes were three in number, and may be thus reckoned up: First, the disaster of being an unpopular and a thrashed boy at school; secondly, the disaster of falling seriously ill; thirdly, the disaster of becoming acquainted with a great bore.

The first disaster occurred after Thomas had been an idle and a popular boy at school, for some happy years. One Christmas-time, he was stimulated by the evil example of a companion, whom he had always trusted and liked, to be untrue to himself, and to try for a prize at the ensuing half-yearly examination. He did try, and he got a prize—how, he did not distinctly know at the moment, and cannot remember now. No sooner, however, had the book—Moral Hints to the Young on the Value of Time—been placed in his hands, than the first troubles of his life began. The idle boys deserted him, as a traitor to their cause. The industrious boys avoided him, as a dangerous interloper; one of their number, who had always won the prize on previous occasions, expressing just resentment at the invasion of his privileges by calling Thomas into the play-ground, and then and there administering to him the first sound and genuine thrashing that he had ever received in his life. Unpopular from that moment, as a beaten boy, who belonged to no side and was rejected by all parties, young Idle soon lost caste with his masters, as he had previously lost caste with his schoolfellows. He had forfeited the comfortable reputation of being the one lazy member of the youthful community whom it was quite hopeless to punish. Never again did he hear the headmaster say reproachfully to an industrious boy who had committed a fault, " I might have expected this in Thomas Idle, but it is inexcusable, sir, in you, who know better." Never more, after winning that fatal prize, did he escape the retributive imposition, or the avenging birch. From that time, the masters made him work, and the boys would not let him play. From that time his social position steadily declined, and his life at school became a perpetual burden to him.

So, again, with the second disaster. While Thomas was lazy, he was a model of health. His first attempt at active exertion and his first suffering from severe illness are connected together by the intimate relations of cause and effect. Shortly after leaving school, he accompanied a party of friends to a cricket-field, in his natural and appropriate character of spectator only. On the ground it was discovered that the players fell short of the required number, and facile Thomas was persuaded to assist in making up the complement. At a certain appointed time, he was roused from peaceful slumber in a dry ditch, and placed before three wickets with a bat in his hand. Opposite to him, behind three more wickets, stood one of his bosom friends, filling the situation (as he was informed) of bowler. No words can describe Mr. Idle's horror and amazement, when he saw this young man—on ordinary occasions, the meekest and mildest of human beings —suddenly contract his eyebrows, compress his lips, assume the aspect of an infuriated savage, run back a few steps, then run forward, and, without the slightest previous provocation, hurl a detestably hard ball with all his might straight at Thomas's legs. Stimulated to preternatural activity of body and sharpness of eye by the instinct of self-preservation, Mr. Idle contrived, by jumping deftly aside at the right moment, and by using his bat (ridiculously narrow as it was for the purpose) as a shield, to preserve his life and limbs from the dastardly attack that had been made on both, to leave the full force of the deadly missile to strike his wicket instead of his leg ; and to end the innings, so far as his side

was concerned, by being immediately bowled out. Grateful
for his escape, he was about to return to the dry ditch, when
he was peremptorily stopped, and told that the other side
was "going in," and that he was expected to "field." His
conception of the whole art and mystery of "fielding," may
be summed up in the three words of serious advice which he
privately administered to himself on that trying occasion—
avoid the ball. Fortified by this sound and salutary principle,
he took his own course, impervious alike to ridicule and abuse.
Whenever the ball came near him, he thought of his shins,
and got out of the way immediately. "Catch it!" "Stop
it!" "Pitch it up!" were cries that passed by him like the
idle wind that he regarded not. He ducked under it, he
jumped over it, he whisked himself away from it on either
side. Never once, through the whole innings did he and the
ball come together on anything approaching to intimate
terms. The unnatural activity of body which was necessarily
called forth for the accomplishment of this result threw
Thomas Idle, for the first time in his life, into a perspiration.
The perspiration, in consequence of his want of practice in
the management of that particular result of bodily activity,
was suddenly checked; the inevitable chill succeeded; and
that, in its turn, was followed by a fever. For the first time
since his birth, Mr. Idle found himself confined to his bed
for many weeks together, wasted and worn by a long illness,
of which his own disastrous muscular exertion had been the
sole first cause.

The third occasion on which Thomas found reason to
reproach himself bitterly for the mistake of having attempted
to be industrious, was connected with his choice of a calling
in life. Having no interest in the Church, he appropriately
selected the next best profession for a lazy man in England
—the Bar. Although the Benchers of the Inns of Court
have lately abandoned their good old principles, and oblige
their students to make some show of studying, in Mr. Idle's
time no such innovation as this existed. Young men who

aspired to the honourable title of barrister were, very properly, not asked to learn anything of the law, but were merely required to eat a certain number of dinners at the table of their Hall, and to pay a certain sum of money ; and were called to the Bar as soon as they could prove that they had sufficiently complied with these extremely sensible regulations. Never did Thomas move more harmoniously in concert with his elders and betters than when he was qualifying himself for admission among the barristers of his native country. Never did he feel more deeply what real laziness was in all the serene majesty of its nature, than on the memorable day when he was called to the Bar, after having carefully abstained from opening his law-books during his period of probation, except to fall asleep over them. How he could ever again have become industrious, even for the shortest period, after that great reward conferred upon his idleness, quite passes his comprehension. The kind Benchers did everything they could to show him the folly of exerting himself. They wrote out his probationary exercise for him, and never expected him even to take the trouble of reading it through when it was written. They invited him, with seven other choice spirits as lazy as himself, to come and be called to the Bar, while they were sitting over their wine and fruit after dinner. They put his oaths of allegiance, and his dreadful official denunciations of the Pope and the Pretender, so gently into his mouth, that he hardly knew how the words got there. They wheeled all their chairs softly round from the table, and sat surveying the young barristers with their backs to their bottles, rather than stand up, or adjourn to hear the exercises read. And when Mr. Idle and the seven unlabouring neophytes, ranged in order, as a class, with their backs considerately placed against a screen, had begun, in rotation, to read the exercises which they had not written, even then, each Bencher, true to the great lazy principle of the whole proceeding, stopped each neophyte before he had stammered through his first line, and bowed to him, and told him politely that he was a barrister from that moment. This was all the ceremony. It was followed by a social supper, and by the presentation, in accordance with ancient custom, of a pound of sweetmeats and a bottle of Madeira, offered in the way of needful refreshment, by each grateful neophyte to each beneficent Bencher. It may seem inconceivable that Thomas should ever have forgotten the great do-nothing principle instilled by such a ceremony as this; but it is, nevertheless, true, that certain designing students of industrious habits found him out, took advantage of his easy humour, persuaded him that it was discreditable to be a barrister and to know nothing whatever about the law, and lured him, by the force of their own evil example, into a conveyancer's chambers, to make up for lost time, and to qualify himself for practice at the Bar. After a fortnight of self-delusion, the curtain fell from his eyes; he resumed his natural character, and shut up his books. But the retribution which had hitherto always followed his little casual errors of industry followed them still. He could get away from the conveyancer's chambers, but he could not get away from one of the pupils, who had taken a fancy to him,—a tall, serious, raw-boned, hard-working, disputatious pupil, with ideas of his own about reforming the Law of Real Property, who has been the scourge of Mr. Idle's existence ever since the fatal day when he fell into the mistake of attempting to study the law. Before that time his friends were all sociable idlers like himself. Since that time the burden of bearing with a hard-working young man has become part of his lot in life. Go where he will now, he can never feel certain that the raw-boned pupil is not affectionately waiting for him round a corner, to tell him a little more about the Law of Real Property. Suffer as he may under the infliction, he can never complain, for he must always remember, with unavailing regret, that he has his own thoughtless industry to thank for first exposing him to the great social calamity of knowing a bore.

419

These events of his past life, with the significant results that they brought about, pass drowsily through Thomas Idle's memory, while he lies alone on the sofa at Allonby and elsewhere, dreaming away the time which his fellow-apprentice gets through so actively out of doors. Remembering the lesson of laziness which his past disasters teach, and bearing in mind also the fact that he is crippled in one leg because he exerted himself to go up a mountain, when he ought to have known that his proper course of conduct was to stop at the bottom of it, he holds now, and will for the future firmly continue to hold, by his new resolution never to be industrious again, on any pretence whatever, for the rest of his life. The physical results of his accident have been related in a previous chapter. The moral .results now stand on record; and, with the enumeration of these, that part of the present narrative which is occupied by the Episode of The Sprained Ankle may now perhaps be considered, in all its aspects, as finished and complete.

" How do you propose that we get through this present afternoon and evening ? " demanded Thomas Idle, after two or three hours of the foregoing reflections at Allonby.

Mr. Goodchild faltered, looked out of window, looked in again, and said, as he had so often said before, " There is the sea, and here are the shrimps ;—let us eat 'em ! "

But, the wise donkey was at that moment in the act of bolting : not with the irresolution of his previous efforts which had been wanting in sustained force of character, but with real vigour of purpose : shaking .the dust off his mane and hind-feet at Allonby, and tearing away from it, as if he had nobly made up his mind that he never would be taken alive. At sight of this inspiring spectacle, which was visible from his sofa, Thomas Idle stretched his neck and dwelt upon it rapturously.

" Francis Goodchild," he then said, turning to his companion with a solemn air, " this is a delightful little Inn, excellently kept by the most comfortable of landladies and the most attentive of landlords, but——the donkey's right!"

The words, "There is the sea, and here are the——" again trembled on the lips of Goodchild, unaccompanied however by any sound.

"Let us instantly pack the portmanteaus," said Thomas Idle, "pay the bill, and order a fly out, with instructions to the driver to follow the donkey!"

Mr. Goodchild, who had only wanted encouragement to disclose the real state of his feelings, and who had been pining beneath his weary secret, now burst into tears, and confessed that he thought another day in the place would be the death of him.

So, the two idle apprentices followed the donkey until the night was far advanced. Whether he was recaptured by the town-council, or is bolting at this hour through the United Kingdom, they know not. They hope he may be still bolting; if so, their best wishes are with him.

It entered Mr. Idle's head, on the borders of Cumberland, that there could be no idler place to stay at, except by snatches of a few minutes each, than a railway station. "An intermediate station on a line—a junction—anything of that sort," Thomas suggested. Mr. Goodchild approved of the idea as eccentric, and they journeyed on and on, until they came to such a station where there was an Inn.

"Here," said Thomas, "we may be luxuriously lazy; other people will travel for us, as it were, and we shall laugh at their folly."

It was a Junction-Station, where the wooden razors before mentioned shaved the air very often, and where the sharp electric-telegraph bell was in a very restless condition. All manner of cross-lines of rails came zig-zagging into it, like a Congress of iron vipers; and, a little way out of it, a pointsman in an elevated signal-box was constantly going through the motions of drawing immense quantities of beer at a public-house bar. In one direction, confused perspectives of embankments and arches were to be seen from the platform; in the other, the rails soon disentangled themselves into two tracks, and shot away under a bridge, and curved round a corner. Sidings were there, in which empty luggage-vans and cattle-boxes often butted against each other as if they couldn't agree; and warehouses were there, in which great quantities of goods seemed to have taken the veil (of the consistency of tarpaulin), and to have retired from the world without any hope of getting back to it. Refreshment-rooms were there; one, for the hungry and thirsty Iron Locomotives where their coke and water were ready, and of good quality, for they were dangerous to play tricks with; the other, for the hungry and thirsty human Locomotives, who might take what they could get, and whose chief consolation was provided in the form of three terrific urns or vases of white metal, containing nothing, each forming a breastwork for a defiant and apparently much-injured woman.

Established at this Station, Mr. Thomas Idle and Mr. Francis Goodchild resolved to enjoy it. But, its contrasts were very violent, and there was also an infection in it.

First, as to its contrasts. They were only two, but they were Lethargy and Madness. The Station was either totally unconscious, or wildly raving. By day, in its unconscious state, it looked as if no life could come to it,—as if it were all rust, dust, and ashes—as if the last train for ever, had gone without issuing any Return-Tickets—as if the last Engine had uttered its last shriek and burst. One awkward shave of the air from the wooden razor, and everything changed. Tight office-doors flew open, panels yielded, books, newspapers, travelling-caps and wrappers broke out of brick walls, money chinked, conveyances oppressed by nightmares of luggage came careering into the yard, porters started up from secret places, ditto the much-injured women, the shining bell, who lived in a little tray on stilts by himself, flew into a man's hand and clamoured violently. The pointsman aloft in the signal-box made the motions of drawing, with some difficulty, hogsheads of beer. Down Train! More beer! Up Train! More beer. Cross Junction Train! More beer! Cattle Train! More beer. Goods Train! Simmering, whistling, trembling, rumbling, thundering. Trains on the whole confusion of intersecting rails, crossing one another, bumping one another, hissing one another, backing to go forward, tearing into distance to come close. People frantic. Exiles seeking restoration to their native carriages, and banished to remoter climes. More beer and more bell. Then, in a minute, the Station relapsed into stupor as the stoker of the Cattle Train, the last to depart, went gliding out of it, wiping the long nose of his oil-can with a dirty pocket-handkerchief.

By night, in its unconscious state, the Station was not so much as visible. Something in the air, like an enterprising chemist's established in business on one of the boughs of Jack's beanstalk, was all that could be discerned of it under the stars. In a moment it would break out, a constellation of gas. In another moment, twenty rival chemists, on twenty rival beanstalks, came into existence. Then, the Furies would be seen, waving their lurid torches up and down the confused perspectives of embankments and arches—would be heard, too, wailing and shrieking. Then, the Station would be full of palpitating trains, as in the day; with the heightening difference that they were not so clearly seen as in the day, whereas the Station walls, starting forward under the gas, like a hippopotamus's eyes, dazzled the human locomotives with the sauce-bottle, the cheap music, the bedstead, the distorted range of buildings where the patent safes are made, the gentleman in the rain with the registered umbrella, the lady returning from the ball with the registered respirator, and all their other embellishments. And now, the human locomotives, creased as to their countenances and purblind as to their eyes, would swarm forth in a heap, addressing themselves to the mysterious urns and the much-injured women; while the iron locomotives, dripping fire and water, shed their steam about plentifully, making the dull oxen in their cages, with heads depressed, and foam hanging from their mouths as their red looks glanced fearfully at the surrounding terrors, seem as though they had been drinking at half-frozen waters and were hung with icicles. Through the same steam would be caught glimpses of their fellow-travellers, the sheep, getting their white kid faces together, away from the bars, and stuffing the interstices with trembling wool. Also, down among the wheels, of the man with the sledge-hammer, ringing the axles of the fast night-train; against whom the oxen have a misgiving that he is the man with the pole-axe who is to come by-and-by, and so the nearest of them try to get back, and get a purchase for a thrust at him through the bars. Suddenly, the bell would ring, the steam would stop with one hiss and a yell, the chemists on the beanstalks would be busy, the avenging Furies would bestir themselves, the fast night-train would melt from eye and ear, the other trains going their ways more slowly would be heard faintly rattling in the distance like old-fashioned watches running down, the sauce-bottle and cheap music retired from view, even the bedstead went to bed, and there was no such visible thing as the Station to vex the cool wind in its blowing, or perhaps the autumn lightning, as it found out the iron rails.

The infection of the Station was this:—When it was in its raving state, the Apprentices found it impossible to be there, without labouring under the delusion that they were in a hurry. To Mr. Goodchild, whose ideas of idleness were so imperfect, this was no unpleasant hallucination, and accordingly that gentleman went through great exertions in yielding to it, and running up and down the platform, jostling everybody, under the impression that he had a highly important mission somewhere, and had not a moment to lose. But, to Thomas Idle, this contagion was so very unacceptable an incident of the situation, that he struck on the fourth day, and requested to be moved.

"This place fills me with a dreadful sensation," said Thomas, "of having something to do. Remove me, Francis."

"Where would you like to go next?" was the question of the ever-engaging Goodchild.

"I have heard there is a good old Inn at Lancaster, established in a fine old house: an Inn where they give you Bride-cake every day after dinner," said Thomas Idle. "Let us eat Bride-cake without the trouble of being married, or of knowing anybody in that ridiculous dilemma."

Mr. Goodchild, with a lover's sigh, assented. They departed from the Station in a violent hurry (for which, it is unnecessary to observe, there was not the least occasion), and were delivered at the fine old house at Lancaster, on the same night.

It is Mr. Goodchild's opinion, that if a visitor on his arrival at Lancaster could be accommodated with a pole which would push the opposite side of the street some yards farther off, it would be better for all parties. Protesting against being required to live in a trench, and obliged to speculate all day upon what the people can possibly be doing within a mysterious opposite window, which is a shop-window to look at, but not a shop-window in respect of its offering nothing for sale and declining to give any account whatever of itself, Mr. Goodchild concedes Lancaster to be a pleasant place. A place dropped in the midst of a charming landscape, a place with a fine ancient fragment of castle, a place of lovely walks, a place possessing staid old houses richly fitted with old Honduras mahogany, which has grown so dark with time that it seems to have got something of a retrospective mirror-quality into itself, and to show the visitor, in the depth of its grain, through all its polish, the hue of the wretched slaves who groaned long ago under old Lancaster merchants. And Mr. Goodchild adds that the stones of Lancaster do sometimes whisper, even yet, of rich men passed away—upon whose great prosperity some of these old doorways frowned sullen in the brightest weather—that their slave-gain turned to curses, as the Arabian Wizard's money turned to leaves, and that no good ever came of it, even unto the third and fourth generations, until it was wasted and gone.

It was a gallant sight to behold, the Sunday procession of the Lancaster elders to Church—all in black, and looking fearfully like a funeral without the Body—under the escort of Three Beadles.

"Think," said Francis, as he stood at the Inn window, admiring, "of being taken to the sacred edifice by three Beadles! I have, in my early time, been taken out of it by one Beadle; but, to be taken into it by three, O Thomas, is a distinction I shall never enjoy!"

CHAPTER IV

WHEN Mr. Goodchild had looked out of the Lancaster Inn window for two hours on end, with great perseverance, he began to entertain a misgiving that he was growing industrious. He therefore set himself next, to explore the country from the tops of all the steep hills in the neighbourhood.

He came back at dinner-time, red and glowing, to tell Thomas Idle what he had seen. Thomas, on his back reading, listened with great composure, and asked him whether he really had gone up those hills, and bothered himself with those views, and walked all those miles?

"Because I want to know," added Thomas, "what you would say of it, if you were obliged to do it?"

"It would be different, then," said Francis. "It would be work, then; now, it's play."

"Play!" replied Thomas Idle, utterly repudiating the reply. "Play! Here is a man goes systematically tearing himself to pieces, and putting himself through an incessant course of training, as if he were always under articles to fight a match for the champion's belt, and he calls it Play! Play!" exclaimed Thomas Idle, scornfully contemplating his one boot in the air. "You *can't* play. You don't know what it is. You make work of everything."

The bright Goodchild amiably smiled.

"So you do," said Thomas. "I mean it. To me you are an absolutely terrible fellow. You do nothing like another man. Where another fellow would fall into a footbath of

427

action or emotion, you fall into a mine. Where any other fellow would be a painted butterfly, you are a fiery dragon. Where another man would stake a sixpence, you stake your existence. If you were to go up in a balloon, you would make for Heaven; and if you were to dive into the depths of the earth, nothing short of the other place would content you. What a fellow you are, Francis!"

The cheerful Goodchild laughed.

"It's all very well to laugh, but I wonder you don't feel it to be serious," said Idle. "A man who can do nothing by halves appears to me to be a fearful man."

"Tom, Tom," returned Goodchild, "if I can do nothing by halves, and be nothing by halves, it's pretty clear that you must take me as a whole, and make the best of me."

With this philosophical rejoinder, the airy Goodchild clapped Mr. Idle on the shoulder in a final manner, and they sat down to dinner.

"By-the-by," said Goodchild, "I have been over a lunatic asylum too, since I have been out."

"He has been," exclaimed Thomas Idle, casting up his eyes, "over a lunatic asylum! Not content with being as great an Ass as Captain Barclay in the pedestrian way, he makes a Lunacy Commissioner of himself—for nothing!"

"An immense place," said Goodchild, "admirable offices, very good arrangements, very good attendants; altogether a remarkable place."

"And what did you see there?" asked Mr. Idle, adapting Hamlet's advice to the occasion, and assuming the virtue of interest, though he had it not.

"The usual thing," said Francis Goodchild, with a sigh. "Long groves of blighted men-and-women-trees; interminable avenues of hopeless faces; numbers, without the slightest power of really combining for any earthly purpose; a society of human creatures who have nothing in common but that they have all lost the power of being humanly social with one another."

428

THE MADMAN

"Take a glass of wine with me," said Thomas Idle, "and let *us* be social."

"In one gallery, Tom," pursued Francis Goodchild, "which looked to me about the length of the Long Walk at Windsor, more or less——"

"Probably less," observed Thomas Idle.

"In one gallery, which was otherwise clear of patients (for they were all out), there was a poor little dark-chinned, meagre man, with a perplexed brow and a pensive face, stooping low over the matting on the floor, and picking out with his thumb and forefinger the course of its fibres. The afternoon sun was slanting in at the large end-window, and there were cross patches of light and shade all down the vista, made by the unseen windows and the open doors of the little sleeping-cells on either side. In about the centre of the perspective, under an arch, regardless of the pleasant weather, regardless of the solitude, regardless of approaching footsteps, was the poor little dark-chinned, meagre man, poring over the matting. 'What are you doing there?' said my conductor, when we came to him. He looked up, and pointed to the matting. 'I wouldn't do that, I think,' said my conductor, kindly; 'if I were you, I would go and read, or I would lie down if I felt tired; but I wouldn't do that.' The patient considered a moment, and vacantly answered, 'No, sir, I won't; I'll—I'll go and read,' and so he lamely shuffled away into one of the little rooms. I turned my head before we had gone many paces. He had already come out again, and was again poring over the matting, and tracking out its fibres with his thumb and forefinger. I stopped to look at him, and it came into my mind, that probably the course of those fibres as they plaited in and out, over and under, was the only course of things in the whole wide world that it was left to him to understand —that his darkening intellect had narrowed down to the small cleft of light which showed him, 'This piece was twisted this way, went in here, passed under, came out

429

there, was carried on away here to the right where I now put my finger on it, and in this progress of events, the thing was made and came to be here.' Then, I wondered whether he looked into the matting, next, to see if it could show him anything of the process through which *he* came to be there, so strangely poring over it. Then, I thought how all of us, GOD help us! in our different ways are poring over our bits of matting, blindly enough, and what confusions and mysteries we make in the pattern. I had a sadder fellow-feeling with the little dark-chinned, meagre man, by that time, and I came away."

Mr. Idle diverting the conversation to grouse, custards, and bride-cake, Mr. Goodchild followed in the same direction. The bride-cake was as bilious and indigestible as if a real Bride had cut it, and the dinner it completed was an admirable performance.

The house was a genuine old house of a very quaint description, teeming with old carvings, and beams, and panels, and having an excellent old staircase, with a gallery or upper staircase, cut off from it by a curious fence-work of old oak, or of the old Honduras Mahogany wood. It was, and is, and will be, for many a long year to come, a remarkably picturesque house; and a certain grave mystery lurking in the depth of the old mahogany panels, as if they were so many deep pools of dark water—such, indeed, as they had been much among when they were trees—gave it a very mysterious character after nightfall.

When Mr. Goodchild and Mr. Idle had first alighted at the door, and stepped into the sombre, handsome old hall, they had been received by half-a-dozen noiseless old men in black, all dressed exactly alike, who glided up the stairs with the obliging landlord and waiter—but without appearing to get into their way, or to mind whether they did or no—and who had filed off to the right and left on the old staircase, as the guests entered their sitting-room. It was then broad, bright day. But, Mr. Goodchild had said, when their door was shut, "Who on earth are those old men?" And afterwards, both on going out and coming in, he had noticed that there were no old men to be seen.

Neither, had the old men, or any one of the old men, reappeared since. The two friends had passed a night in the house, but had seen nothing more of the old men. Mr. Goodchild, in rambling about it, had looked along passages, and glanced in at doorways, but had encountered no old men; neither did it appear that any old men were, by any member of the establishment, missed or expected.

Another odd circumstance impressed itself on their attention. It was, that the door of their sitting-room was never left untouched for a quarter of an hour. It was opened with hesitation, opened with confidence, opened a little way, opened a good way,—always clapped-to again without a word of explanation. They were reading, they were writing, they were eating, they were drinking, they were talking, they were dozing; the door was always opened at an unexpected moment, and they looked towards it, and it was clapped-to again, and nobody was to be seen. When this had happened fifty times or so, Mr. Goodchild had said to his companion, jestingly: "I begin to think, Tom, there was something wrong with those six old men."

Night had come again, and they had been writing for two or three hours: writing, in short, a portion of the lazy notes from which these lazy sheets are taken. They had left off writing, and glasses were on the table between them. The house was closed and quiet. Around the head of Thomas Idle, as he lay upon his sofa, hovered light wreaths of fragrant smoke. The temples of Francis Goodchild, as he leaned back in his chair, with his two hands clasped behind his head, and his legs crossed, were similarly decorated.

They had been discussing several idle subjects of speculation, not omitting the strange old men, and were still so occupied, when Mr. Goodchild abruptly changed his attitude to wind up his watch. They were just becoming drowsy enough to be stopped in their talk by any such slight check. Thomas Idle, who was speaking at the moment, paused and said, "How goes it?"

"One," said Goodchild.

As if he had ordered One old man, and the order were promptly executed (truly, all orders were so, in that excellent hotel), the door opened, and One old man stood there.

He did not come in, but stood with the door in his hand.

"One of the six, Tom, at last!" said Mr. Goodchild, in a surprised whisper.—"Sir, your pleasure?"

"Sir, *your* pleasure?" said the One old man.

"I didn't ring."

"The bell did," said the One old man.

He said BELL, in a deep, strong way, that would have expressed the church Bell.

"I had the pleasure, I believe, of seeing you, yesterday?" said Goodchild.

"I cannot undertake to say for certain," was the grim reply of the One old man.

"I think you saw me? Did you not?"

"Saw *you*?" said the old man. "O yes, I saw *you*. But, I see many who never see me."

A chilled, slow, earthy, fixed old man. A cadaverous old man of measured speech. An old man who seemed as unable to wink, as if his eyelids had been nailed to his forehead. An old man whose eyes—two spots of fire—had no more motion than if they had been connected with the back of his skull by screws driven through it, and rivetted and bolted outside, among his grey hair.

The night had turned so cold, to Mr. Goodchild's sensations, that he shivered. He remarked lightly, and half apologetically, "I think somebody is walking over my grave."

"No," said the weird old man, "there is no one there."

Mr. Goodchild looked at Idle, but Idle lay with his head enwreathed in smoke.

"No one there?" said Goodchild.

"There is no one at your grave, I assure you," said the old man.

He had come in and shut the door, and he now sat down. He did not bend himself to sit, as other people do, but seemed to sink bolt upright, as if in water, until the chair stopped him.

"My friend, Mr. Idle," said Goodchild, extremely anxious to introduce a third person into the conversation.

"I am," said the old man, without looking at him, "at Mr. Idle's service."

"If you are an old inhabitant of this place," Francis Goodchild resumed:

"Yes."

"Perhaps you can decide a point my friend and I were in doubt upon, this morning. They hang condemned criminals at the Castle, I believe?"

"*I* believe so," said the old man.

"Are their faces turned towards that noble prospect?"

"Your face is turned," replied the old man, "to the Castle wall. When you are tied up, you see its stones expanding and contracting violently, and a similar expansion and contraction seem to take place in your own head and breast. Then, there is a rush of fire and an earthquake, and the Castle springs into the air, and you tumble down a precipice."

His cravat appeared to trouble him. He put his hand to his throat, and moved his neck from side to side. He was an old man of a swollen character of face, and his nose was immoveably hitched up on one side, as if by a little hook inserted in that nostril. Mr. Goodchild felt exceedingly uncomfortable, and began to think the night was hot, and not cold.

"A strong description, sir," he observed.

"A strong sensation," the old man rejoined.

Again, Mr. Goodchild looked to Mr. Thomas Idle; but Thomas lay on his back with his face attentively turned towards the One old man, and made no sign. At this time

Mr. Goodchild believed that he saw threads of fire stretch from the old man's eyes to his own, and there attach themselves. (Mr. Goodchild writes the present account of his experience, and, with the utmost solemnity, protests that he had the strongest sensation upon him of being forced to look at the old man along those two fiery films, from that moment.)

"I must tell it to you," said the old man, with a ghastly and a stony stare.

"What?" asked Francis Goodchild.

"You know where it took place. Yonder!"

Whether he pointed to the room above, or to the room below, or to any room in that old house, or to a room in some other old house in that old town, Mr. Goodchild was not, nor is, nor ever can be, sure. He was confused by the circumstance that the right forefinger of the One old man seemed to dip itself in one of the threads of fire, light itself, and make a fiery start in the air, as it pointed somewhere. Having pointed somewhere, it went out.

"You know she was a Bride," said the old man.

"I know they still send up Bride-cake," Mr. Goodchild faltered. "This is a very oppressive air."

"She was a Bride," said the old man. "She was a fair, flaxen-haired, large-eyed girl, who had no character, no purpose. A weak, credulous, incapable, helpless nothing. Not like her mother. No, no. It was her father whose character she reflected.

"Her mother had taken care to secure everything to herself, for her own life, when the father of this girl (a child at that time) died—of sheer helplessness; no other disorder— and then He renewed the acquaintance that had once subsisted between the mother and Him. He had been put aside for the flaxen-haired, large-eyed man (or nonentity) with Money. He could overlook that for Money. He wanted compensation in Money.

"So, he returned to the side of that woman the mother.

434

made love to her again, danced attendance on her, and submitted himself to her whims. She wreaked upon him every whim she had, or could invent. He bore it. And the more he bore, the more he wanted compensation in Money, and the more he was resolved to have it.

"But, lo! Before he got it, she cheated him. In one of her imperious states, she froze, and never thawed again. She put her hands to her head one night, uttered a cry, stiffened, lay in that attitude certain hours, and died. And he had got no compensation from her in Money, yet. Blight and Murrain on her! Not a penny.

"He had hated her throughout that second pursuit, and had longed for retaliation on her. He now counterfeited her signature to an instrument, leaving all she had to leave, to her daughter—ten years old then—to whom the property passed absolutely, and appointing himself the daughter's Guardian. When He slid it under the pillow of the bed on which she lay, He bent down in the deaf ear of Death, and whispered: 'Mistress Pride, I have determined a long time that, dead or alive, you must make me compensation in Money.'

"So, now there were only two left. Which two were, He, and the fair flaxen-haired, large-eyed foolish daughter, who afterwards became the Bride.

"He put her to school. In a secret, dark, oppressive, ancient house, he put her to school with a watchful and unscrupulous woman. 'My worthy lady,' he said, 'here is a mind to be formed; will you help me to form it?' She accepted the trust. For which she, too, wanted compensation in Money, and had it.

"The girl was formed in the fear of him, and in the conviction, that there was no escape from him. She was taught, from the first, to regard him as her future husband—the man who must marry her—the destiny that overshadowed her—the appointed certainty that could never be evaded. The poor fool was soft white wax in their hands, and took the

435

impression that they put upon her. It hardened with time. It became a part of herself. Inseparable from herself, and only to be torn away from her, by tearing life away from her.

"Eleven years she had lived in the dark house and its gloomy garden. He was jealous of the very light and air getting to her, and they kept her close. He stopped the wide chimneys, shaded the little windows, left the strong-stemmed ivy to wander where it would over the house-front, the moss to accumulate on the untrimmed fruit-trees in the red-walled garden, the weeds to over-run its green and yellow walks. He surrounded her with images of sorrow and desolation. He caused her to be filled with fears of the place and of the stories that were told of it, and then on pretext of correcting them, to be left in it in solitude, or made to shrink about it in the dark. When her mind was most depressed and fullest of terrors, then, he would come out of one of the hiding-places from which he overlooked her, and present himself as her sole resource.

"Thus, by being from her childhood the one embodiment her life presented to her of power to coerce and power to relieve, power to bind and power to loose, the ascendency over her weakness was secured. She was twenty-one years and twenty-one days old, when he brought her home to the gloomy house, his half-witted, frightened, and submissive Bride of three weeks.

"He had dismissed the governess by that time—what he had left to do, he could best do alone—and they came back, upon a rainy night, to the scene of her long preparation. She turned to him upon the threshold, as the rain was dripping from the porch, and said :

"'O sir, it is the Death-watch ticking for me!'

"'Well!' he answered. 'And if it were?'

"'O sir!' she returned to him, 'look kindly on me, and be merciful to me! I beg your pardon. I will do anything you wish, if you will only forgive me!'

436

"That had become the poor fool's constant song: 'I beg your pardon,' and 'Forgive me!'

"She was not worth hating; he felt nothing but contempt for her. But, she had long been in the way, and he had long been weary, and the work was near its end, and had to be worked out.

"'You fool,' he said. 'Go up the stairs!'

"She obeyed very quickly, murmuring, 'I will do anything you wish!' When he came into the Bride's Chamber, having been a little retarded by the heavy fastenings of the great door (for they were alone in the house, and he had arranged that the people who attended on them should come and go in the day), he found her withdrawn to the furthest corner, and there standing pressed against the paneling as if she would have shrunk through it: her flaxen hair all wild about her face, and her large eyes staring at him in vague terror.

"'What are you afraid of? Come and sit down by me.'

"'I will do anything you wish. I beg your pardon, sir. Forgive me!' Her monotonous tune as usual.

"'Ellen, here is a writing that you must write out to-morrow, in your own hand. You may as well be seen by others, busily engaged upon it. When you have written it all fairly, and corrected all mistakes, call in any two people there may be about the house, and sign your name to it before them. Then, put it in your bosom to keep it safe, and when I sit here again to-morrow night, give it to me.'

"'I will do it all, with the greatest care. I will do anything you wish.'

"'Don't shake and tremble, then.'

"'I will try my utmost not to do it—if you will only forgive me!'

"Next day, she sat down at her desk, and did as she had been told. He often passed in and out of the room, to observe her, and always saw her slowly and laboriously writing: repeating to herself the words she copied, in appearance quite mechanically, and without caring or endeavouring to comprehend them, so that she did her task. He saw her follow the directions she had received, in all particulars; and at night, when they were alone again in the same Bride's Chamber, and he drew his chair to the hearth, she timidly approached him from her distant seat, took the paper from her bosom, and gave it into his hand.

"It secured all her possessions to him, in the event of her death. He put her before him, face to face, that he might look at her steadily; and he asked her, in so many plain words, neither fewer nor more, did she know that?

"There were spots of ink upon the bosom of her white dress, and they made her face look whiter and her eyes look larger as she nodded her head. There were spots of ink upon the hand with which she stood before him, nervously plaiting and folding her white skirts.

"He took her by the arm, and looked her, yet more closely and steadily, in the face. 'Now, die! I have done with you.'

"She shrunk, and uttered a low, suppressed cry.

"'I am not going to kill you. I will not endanger my life for yours. Die!'

"He sat before her in the gloomy Bride's Chamber, day after day, night after night, looking the word at her when he did not utter it. As often as her large unmeaning eyes were raised from the hands in which she rocked her head, to the stern figure, sitting with crossed arms and knitted forehead, in the chair, they read in it, 'Die!' When she dropped asleep in exhaustion, she was called back to shuddering consciousness, by the whisper, 'Die!' When she fell upon her old entreaty to be pardoned, she was answered, 'Die!' When she had out-watched and out-suffered the long night, and the rising sun flamed into the sombre room, she heard it hailed with, 'Another day and not dead?—Die!'

"Shut up in the deserted mansion, aloof from all mankind, and engaged alone in such a struggle without any respite, it came to this—that either he must die, or she. He knew

438

Lazy Tour of Two Idle Apprentices

it very well, and concentrated his strength against her feeble-ness. Hours upon hours he held her by the arm when her arm was black where he held it, and bade her Die!

"It was done, upon a windy morning, before sunrise. He computed the time to be half-past four; but, his forgotten watch had run down, and he could not be sure. She had broken away from him in the night, with loud and sudden cries—the first of that kind to which she had given vent—and he had had to put his hands over her mouth. Since then, she had been quiet in the corner of the paneling where she had sunk down; and he had left her, and had gone back with his folded arms and his knitted forehead to his chair.

"Paler in the pale light, more colourless than ever in the leaden dawn, he saw her coming, trailing herself along the floor towards him—a white wreck of hair, and dress, and wild eyes, pushing itself on by an irresolute and bending hand.

"'O, forgive me! I will do anything. O, sir, pray tell me I may live!'

"'Die!'

"'Are you so resolved? Is there no hope for me?'

"'Die!'

"Her large eyes strained themselves with wonder and fear; wonder and fear changed to reproach; reproach to blank nothing. It was done. He was not at first so sure it was done, but that the morning sun was hanging jewels in her hair—he saw the diamond, emerald, and ruby, glittering among it in little points, as he stood looking down at her—when he lifted her and laid her on her bed.

"She was soon laid in the ground. And now they were all gone, and he had compensated himself well.

"He had a mind to travel. Not that he meant to waste his Money, for he was a pinching man and liked his Money dearly (liked nothing else, indeed), but, that he had grown tired of the desolate house and wished to turn his back upon it and have done with it. But, the house was worth Money, and Money must not be thrown away. He determined to sell it before he went. That it might look the less wretched and bring a better price, he hired some labourers to work in the overgrown garden; to cut out the dead wood, trim the ivy that drooped in heavy masses over the windows and gables, and clear the walks in which the weeds were growing mid-leg high.

"He worked, himself, along with them. He worked later than they did, and, one evening at dusk, was left working alone, with his bill-hook in his hand. One autumn evening, when the Bride was five weeks dead.

"'It grows too dark to work longer,' he said to himself, 'I must give over for the night.'

"He detested the house, and was loath to enter it. He looked at the dark porch waiting for him like a tomb, and felt that it was an accursed house. Near to the porch, and near to where he stood, was a tree whose branches waved before the old bay-window of the Bride's Chamber, where it had been done. The tree swung suddenly, and made him start. It swung again, although the night was still. Looking up into it, he saw a figure among the branches.

"It was the figure of a young man. The face looked down, as his looked up; the branches cracked and swayed; the figure rapidly descended, and slid upon its feet before him. A slender youth of about her age, with long light brown hair.

"'What thief are you?' he said, seizing the youth by the collar.

"The young man, in shaking himself free, swung him a blow with his arm across the face and throat. They closed, but the young man got from him and stepped back, crying, with great eagerness and horror, 'Don't touch me! I would as lieve be touched by the Devil!'

"He stood still, with his bill-hook in his hand, looking at the young man. For, the young man's look was the counterpart of her last look, and he had not expected ever to see that again.

"'I am no thief. Even if I were, I would not have a coin of your wealth, if it would buy me the Indies. You murderer!'

"'What!'

"'I climbed it,' said the young man, pointing up into the tree, 'for the first time, nigh four years ago. I climbed it, to look at her. I saw her. I spoke to her. I have climbed it, many a time, to watch and listen for her. I was a boy, hidden among its leaves, when from that bay-window she gave me this!'

"He showed a tress of flaxen hair, tied with a mourning ribbon.

"'Her life,' said the young man, 'was a life of mourning. She gave me this, as a token of it, and a sign that she was dead to every one but you. If I had been older, if I had seen her sooner, I might have saved her from you. But, she was fast in the web when I first climbed the tree, and what could I do then to break it!'

"In saying those words, he burst into a fit of sobbing and crying: weakly at first, then passionately.

"'Murderer! I climbed the tree on the night when you brought her back. I heard her, from the tree, speak of the Death-watch at the door. I was three times in the tree while you were shut up with her, slowly killing her. I saw her, from the tree, lie dead upon her bed. I have watched you, from the tree, for proofs and traces of your guilt. The manner of it, is a mystery to me yet, but I will pursue you until you have rendered up your life to the hangman. You shall never, until then, be rid of me. I loved her! I can know no relenting towards you. Murderer, I loved her!'

"The youth was bare-headed, his hat having fluttered away in his descent from the tree. He moved towards the gate. He had to pass—Him—to get to it. There was breadth for two old-fashioned carriages abreast; and the youth's abhorrence, openly expressed in every feature of his face and limb of his body, and very hard to bear, had verge enough to keep itself at a distance in. He (by which I mean the other) had not stirred hand or foot, since he had stood still to look at the boy. He faced round, now, to follow him with his eyes. As the back of the bare light-brown head was turned to him, he saw a red curve stretch from his hand to it. He knew, before he threw the bill-hook, where it had alighted—I say, had alighted, and not, would alight; for, to his clear perception the thing was done before he did it. It cleft the head, and it remained there, and the boy lay on his face.

"He buried the body in the night, at the foot of the tree. As soon as it was light in the morning, he worked at turning up all the ground near the tree, and hacking and hewing at the neighbouring bushes and undergrowth. When the labourers came, there was nothing suspicious, and nothing suspected.

"But, he had, in a moment, defeated all his precautions, and destroyed the triumph of the scheme he had so long concerted, and so successfully worked out. He had got rid of the Bride, and had acquired her fortune without endangering his life; but now, for a death by which he had gained nothing, he had evermore to live with a rope around his neck.

"Beyond this, he was chained to the house of gloom and horror, which he could not endure. Being afraid to sell it or to quit it, lest discovery should be made, he was forced to live in it. He hired two old people, man and wife, for his servants; and dwelt in it, and dreaded it. His great difficulty, for a long time, was the garden. Whether he should keep it trim, whether he should suffer it to fall into its former state of neglect, what would be the least likely way of attracting attention to it?

"He took the middle course of gardening, himself, in his evening leisure, and of then calling the old serving-man to help him; but, of never letting him work there alone. And he made himself an arbour over against the tree, where he could sit and see that it was safe.

THE TREE STRUCK BY LIGHTNING

" As the seasons changed, and the tree changed, his mind
perceived dangers that were always changing. In the leafy
time, he perceived that the upper boughs were growing into
the form of the young man—that they made the shape of
him exactly, sitting in a forked branch swinging in the wind.
In the time of the falling leaves, he perceived that they came
down from the tree, forming tell-tale letters on the path, or
that they had a tendency to heap themselves into a churchyard mound above the grave. In the winter, when the tree
was bare, he perceived that the boughs swung at him the
ghost of the blow the young man had given, and that they
threatened him openly. In the spring, when the sap was
mounting in the trunk, he asked himself, were the dried-up
particles of blood mounting with it : to make out more
obviously this year than last, the leaf-screened figure of the
young man, swinging in the wind ?

" However, he turned his Money over and over, and still
over. He was in the dark trade, the gold-dust trade, and
most secret trades that yielded great returns. In ten years,
he had turned his Money over, so many times, that the
traders and shippers who had dealings with him, absolutely
did not lie—for once—when they declared that he had
increased his fortune, Twelve Hundred Per Cent.

" He possessed his riches one hundred years ago, when
people could be lost easily. He had heard who the youth
was, from hearing of the search that was made after him ;
but, it died away, and the youth was forgotten.

" The annual round of changes in the tree had been repeated
ten times since the night of the burial at its foot, when there
was a great thunder-storm over this place. It broke at
midnight, and raged until morning. The first intelligence
he heard from his old serving-man that morning, was, that
the tree had been struck by Lightning.

" It had been riven down the stem, in a very surprising
manner, and the stem lay in two blighted shafts : one resting
against the house, and one against a portion of the old red

garden-wall in which its fall had made a gap. The fissure went down the tree to a little above the earth, and there stopped. There was great curiosity to see the tree, and, with most of his former fears revived, he sat in his arbour —grown quite an old man—watching the people who came to see it.

"They quickly began to come, in such dangerous numbers, that he closed his garden-gate and refused to admit any more. But, there were certain men of science who travelled from a distance to examine the tree, and, in an evil hour, he let them in—Blight and Murrain on them, let them in!

"They wanted to dig up the ruin by the roots, and closely examine it, and the earth about it. Never, while he lived! They offered money for it. They! Men of science, whom he could have bought by the gross, with a scratch of his pen! He showed them the garden-gate again, and locked and barred it.

"But they were bent on doing what they wanted to do, and they bribed the old serving-man—a thankless wretch who regularly complained when he received his wages, of being underpaid—and they stole into the garden by night with their lanterns, picks, and shovels, and fell to at the tree. He was lying in a turret-room on the other side of the house (the Bride's Chamber had been unoccupied ever since), but he soon dreamed of picks and shovels, and got up.

"He came to an upper window on that side, whence he could see their lanterns, and them, and the loose earth in a heap which he had himself disturbed and put back, when it was last turned to the air. It was found! They had that minute lighted on it. They were all bending over it. One of them said, 'The skull is fractured;' and another, 'See here the bones;' and another, 'See here the clothes;' and then the first struck in again, and said, 'A rusty bill-hook!'

"He became sensible, next day, that he was already put under a strict watch, and that he could go nowhere without being followed. Before a week was out, he was taken and laid in hold. The circumstances were gradually pieced together against him, with a desperate malignity, and an appalling ingenuity. But, see the justice of men, and how it was extended to him! He was further accused of having poisoned that girl in the Bride's Chamber. He, who had carefully and expressly avoided imperilling a hair of his head for her, and who had seen her die of her own incapacity!

"There was doubt for which of the two murders he should be first tried; but, the real one was chosen, and he was found Guilty, and cast for Death. Bloodthirsty wretches! They would have made him Guilty of anything, so set they were upon having his life.

"His money could do nothing to save him, and he was hanged. *I* am He, and I was hanged at Lancaster Castle with my face to the wall, a hundred years ago!"

At this terrific announcement, Mr. Goodchild tried to rise and cry out. But, the two fiery lines extending from the old man's eyes to his own, kept him down, and he could not utter a sound. His sense of hearing, however, was acute, and he could hear the clock strike Two. No sooner had he heard the clock strike Two, than he saw before him Two old men!

Two.

The eyes of each, connected with his eyes by two films of fire: each, exactly like the other: each, addressing him at precisely one and the same instant: each, gnashing the same teeth in the same head, with the same twitched nostril above them, and the same suffused expression around it. Two old men. Differing in nothing, equally distinct to the sight, the copy no fainter than the original, the second as real as the first.

"At what time," said the Two old men, "did you arrive at the door below?"

"At Six."

"And there were Six old men upon the stairs!"

445

Mr. Goodchild having wiped the perspiration from his brow, or tried to do it, the Two old men proceeded in one voice, and in the singular number:

"I had been anatomised, but had not yet had my skeleton put together and re-hung on an iron hook, when it began to be whispered that the Bride's Chamber was haunted. It *was* haunted, and I was there.

"*We* were there. She and I were there. I, in the chair upon the hearth; she, a white wreck again, trailing itself towards me on the floor. But, I was the speaker no more, and the one word that she said to me from midnight until dawn was, 'Live!'

"The youth was there, likewise. In the tree outside the window. Coming and going in the moonlight, as the tree bent and gave. He has, ever since, been there, peeping in at me in my torment; revealing to me by snatches, in the pale lights and slatey shadows where he comes and goes, bare-headed—a bill-hook, standing edgewise in his hair.

"In the Bride's Chamber, every night from midnight until dawn—one month in the year excepted, as I am going to tell you—he hides in the tree, and she comes towards me on the floor; always approaching; never coming nearer; always visible as if by moonlight, whether the moon shines or no; always saying, from midnight until dawn, her one word, 'Live!'

"But, in the month wherein I was forced out of this life —this present month of thirty days—the Bride's Chamber is empty and quiet. Not so my old dungeon. Not so the rooms where I was restless and afraid, ten years. Both are fitfully haunted then. At One in the morning, I am what you saw me when the clock struck that hour—One old man. At Two in the morning, I am Two old men. At Three, I am Three. By Twelve at noon, I am Twelve old men, One for every hundred per cent. of old gain. Every one of the Twelve, with Twelve times my old power of suffering and agony. From that hour until Twelve at night, I, Twelve old men in anguish and fearful foreboding, wait for the coming of the executioner. At Twelve at night, I, Twelve old men turned off, swing invisible outside Lancaster Castle, with Twelve faces to the wall!

"When the Bride's Chamber was first haunted, it was known to me that this punishment would never cease, until I could make its nature, and my story, known to two living men together. I waited for the coming of two living men together into the Bride's Chamber, years upon years. It was infused into my knowledge (of the means I am ignorant) that if two living men, with their eyes open, could be in the Bride's Chamber at One in the morning, they would see me sitting in my chair.

"At length, the whispers that the room was spiritually troubled, brought two men to try the adventure. I was scarcely struck upon the hearth at midnight (I come there as if the Lightning blasted me into being), when I heard them ascending the stairs. Next, I saw them enter. One of them was a bold, gay, active man, in the prime of life, some five and forty years of age; the other, a dozen years younger. They brought provisions with them in a basket, and bottles. A young woman accompanied them, with wood and coals for the lighting of the fire. When she had lighted it, the bold, gay, active man accompanied her along the gallery outside the room, to see her safely down the staircase, and came back laughing.

"He locked the door, examined the chamber, put out the contents of the basket on the table before the fire—little recking of me, in my appointed station on the hearth, close to him—and filled the glasses, and ate and drank. His companion did the same, and was as cheerful and confident as he: though he was the leader. When they had supped, they laid pistols on the table, turned to the fire, and began to smoke their pipes of foreign make.

"They had travelled together, and had been much together, and had an abundance of subjects in common. In

447

the midst of their talking and laughing, the younger man made a reference to the leader's being always ready for any adventure; that one, or any other. He replied in these words:

"'Not quite so, Dick; if I am afraid of nothing else, I am afraid of myself.'

"His companion seeming to grow a little dull, asked him, in what sense? How?

"'Why, thus,' he returned. 'Here is a Ghost to be disproved. Well! I cannot answer for what my fancy might do if I were alone here, or what tricks my senses might play with me if they had me to themselves. But, in company with another man, and especially with you, Dick, I would consent to outface all the Ghosts that were ever told of in the universe.'

"'I had not the vanity to suppose that I was of so much importance to-night,' said the other.

"'Of so much,' rejoined the leader, more seriously than he had spoken yet, 'that I would, for the reason I have given, on no account have undertaken to pass the night here alone.

"It was within a few minutes of One. The head of the younger man had drooped when he made his last remark, and it drooped lower now.

"'Keep awake, Dick!' said the leader, gaily. 'The small hours are the worst.'

"He tried, but his head drooped again.

"'Dick!' urged the leader. 'Keep awake!'

"'I can't,' he indistinctly muttered. 'I don't know what strange influence is stealing over me. I can't.'

"His companion looked at him with a sudden horror, and I, in my different way, felt a new horror also; for, it was on the stroke of One, and I felt that the second watcher was yielding to me, and that the curse was upon me that I must send him to sleep.

"'Get up and walk, Dick!' cried the leader. 'Try!'

"It was in vain to go behind the slumberer's chair and,

448

shake him. One o'clock sounded, and I was present to the elder man, and he stood transfixed before me.

"To him alone, I was obliged to relate my story, without hope of benefit. To him alone, I was an awful phantom making a quite useless confession. I foresee it will ever be the same. The two living men together will never come to release me. When I appear, the senses of one of the two will be locked in sleep; he will neither see nor hear me; my communication will ever be made to a solitary listener, and will ever be unserviceable. Woe! Woe! Woe!"

As the Two old men, with these words, wrung their hands, it shot into Mr. Goodchild's mind that he was in the terrible situation of being virtually alone with the spectre, and that Mr. Idle's immoveability was explained by his having been charmed asleep at One o'clock. In the terror of this sudden discovery which produced an indescribable dread, he struggled so hard to get free from the four fiery threads, that he snapped them, after he had pulled them out to a great width. Being then out of bonds, he caught up Mr. Idle from the sofa and rushed down-stairs with him.

"What are you about, Francis?" demanded Mr. Idle. "My bedroom is not down here. What the deuce are you carrying me at all for? I can walk with a stick now. I don't want to be carried. Put me down."

Mr. Goodchild put him down in the old hall, and looked about him wildly.

"What are you doing? Idiotically plunging at your own sex, and rescuing them or perishing in the attempt?" asked Mr. Idle, in a highly petulant state.

"The One old man!" cried Mr. Goodchild, distractedly, —"and the Two old men!"

Mr. Idle deigned no other reply than "The One old woman, I think you mean," as he began hobbling his way back up the staircase, with the assistance of its broad balustrade.

"I assure you, Tom," began Mr. Goodchild, attending at his side, "that since you fell asleep——"

"Come, I like that!" said Thomas Idle, "I haven't closed an eye!"

With the peculiar sensitiveness on the subject of the disgraceful action of going to sleep out of bed, which is the lot of all mankind, Mr. Idle persisted in this declaration. The same peculiar sensitiveness impelled Mr. Goodchild, on being taxed with the same crime, to repudiate it with honourable resentment. The settlement of the question of The One old man and The Two old men was thus presently complicated, and soon made quite impracticable. Mr. Idle said it was all Bride-cake, and fragments, newly arranged, of things seen and thought about in the day. Mr. Goodchild said how could that be, when he hadn't been asleep, and what right could Mr. Idle have to say so, who had been asleep? Mr. Idle said he had never been asleep, and never did go to sleep, and that Mr. Goodchild, as a general rule, was always asleep. They consequently parted for the rest of the night, at their bedroom doors, a little ruffled. Mr. Goodchild's last words were, that he had had, in that real and tangible old sitting-room of that real and tangible old Inn (he supposed Mr. Idle denied its existence?), every sensation and experience, the present record of which is now within a line or two of completion; and that he would write it out and print it every word. Mr. Idle returned that he might if he liked—and he did like, and has now done it.

CHAPTER V

Two of the many passengers by a certain late Sunday evening train, Mr. Thomas Idle and Mr. Francis Goodchild, yielded up their tickets at a little rotten platform (converted into artificial touchwood by smoke and ashes), deep in the manufacturing bosom of Yorkshire. A mysterious bosom it appeared, upon a damp, dark, Sunday night, dashed through in the train to the music of the whirling wheels, the panting of the engine, and the part-singing of hundreds of third-class excursionists, whose vocal efforts " bobbed arayound " from sacred to profane, from hymns, to our transatlantic sisters the Yankee Gal and Mairy Anne, in a remarkable way. There seemed to have been some large vocal gathering near to every lonely station on the line. No town was visible, no village was visible, no light was visible; but, a multitude got out singing, and a multitude got in singing, and the second multitude took up the hymns, and adopted our transatlantic sisters, and sang of their own egregious wickedness, and of their bobbing arayound, and of how the ship it was ready and the wind it was fair, and they were bayound for the sea, Mairy Anne, until they in their turn became a getting-out multitude, and were replaced by another getting-in multitude, who did the same. And at every station, the getting-in multitude, with an artistic reference to the completeness of their chorus, incessantly cried, as with one voice while scuffling into the carriages, " We mun aa' gang toogither ! "

The singing and the multitudes had trailed off as the lonely places were left and the great towns were neared, and the way had lain as silently as a train's way ever can, over the vague black streets of the great gulfs of towns, and among their branchless woods of vague black chimneys. These towns looked, in the cinderous wet, as though they had one and all been on fire and were just put out—a dreary and quenched panorama, many miles long.

Thus, Thomas and Francis got to Leeds ; of which enterprising and important commercial centre it may be observed with delicacy, that you must either like it very much or not at all. Next day, the first of the Race-Week, they took train to Doncaster.

And instantly the character, both of travellers and of luggage, entirely changed, and no other business than race-business any longer existed on the face of the earth. The talk was all of horses and "John Scott." Guards whispered behind their hands to station-masters, of horses and John Scott. Men in cut-away coats and speckled cravats fastened with peculiar pins, and with the large bones of their legs developed under tight trousers, so that they should look as much as possible like horses' legs, paced up and down by twos at junction-stations, speaking low and moodily of horses and John Scott. The young clergyman in the black strait-waist-coat, who occupied the middle seat of the carriage, expounded in his peculiar pulpit-accent to the young and lovely Reverend Mrs. Crinoline, who occupied the opposite middle-seat, a few passages of rumour relative to "Oartheth, my love, and Mithter John Eth-corr." A bandy vagabond, with a head like a Dutch cheese, in a fustian stable-suit, attending on a horse-box and going about the platforms with a halter hanging round his neck like a Calais burgher of the ancient period much degenerated, was courted by the best society, by reason of what he had to hint, when not engaged in eating straw, concerning "t'harses and Joon Scott." The engine-driver himself, as he applied one eye to his large stationary double-eye-glass on the engine, seemed to keep the other open, sideways, upon horses and John Scott.

Breaks and barriers at Doncaster Station to keep the crowd off; temporary wooden avenues of ingress and egress, to help the crowd on. Forty extra porters sent down for this present blessed Race-Week, and all of them making up their betting-books in the lamp-room or somewhere else, and none of them to come and touch the luggage. Travellers disgorged into an open space, a howling wilderness of idle men. All work but race-work at a stand-still; all men at a stand-still. "Ey my word! Deant ask noon o' us to help wi' t'luggage. Bock your opinion loike a mon. Coom! Dang it, coom, t'harses and Joon Scott!" In the midst of the idle men, all the fly horses and omnibus horses of Doncaster and parts adjacent, rampant, rearing, backing, plunging, shying—apparently the result of their hearing of nothing but their own order and John Scott.

Grand Dramatic Company from London for the Race-Week. Poses Plastiques in the Grand Assembly Room up the Stable-Yard at seven and nine each evening, for the Race-Week. Grand Alliance Circus in the field beyond the bridge, for the Race-Week. Grand Exhibition of Aztec Lilliputians, important to all who want to be horrified cheap, for the Race-Week. Lodgings, grand and not grand, but all at grand prices, ranging from ten pounds to twenty, for the Grand Race-Week!

Rendered giddy enough by these things, Messieurs Idle and Goodchild repaired to the quarters they had secured beforehand, and Mr. Goodchild looked down from the window into the surging street.

"By Heaven, Tom!" cried he, after contemplating it, "I am in the Lunatic Asylum again, and these are all mad people under the charge of a body of designing keepers!"

All through the Race-Week, Mr. Goodchild never divested himself of this idea. Every day he looked out of window, with something of the dread of Lemuel Gulliver looking down at men after he returned home from the horse-country; and every day he saw the Lunatics, horse-mad, betting-mad, drunken-mad, vice-mad, and the designing Keepers always after them. The idea pervaded, like the second colour in shot-silk, the whole of Mr. Goodchild's impressions. 'They were much as follows:

Monday, mid-day. Races not to begin until to-morrow, but all the mob-Lunatics out, crowding the pavements of the one main street of pretty and pleasant Doncaster, crowding the road, particularly crowding the outside of the Betting Rooms, whooping and shouting loudly after all passing vehicles. Frightened lunatic horses occasionally running away, with infinite clatter. All degrees of men, from peers to paupers, betting incessantly. Keepers very watchful, and taking all good chances. An awful family likeness among the Keepers, to Mr. Palmer and Mr. Thurtell. With some knowledge of expression and some acquaintance with heads (thus writes Mr. Goodchild), I never have seen anywhere, so many repetitions of one class of countenance and one character of head (both evil) as in this street at this time. Cunning, covetousness, secrecy, cold calculation, hard callousness and dire insensibility, are the uniform Keeper characteristics. Mr. Palmer passes me five times in five minutes, and, as I go down the street, the back of Mr. Thurtell's skull is always going on before me.

Monday evening. Town lighted up; more Lunatics out than ever; a complete choke and stoppage of the thoroughfare outside the Betting Rooms. Keepers, having dined, pervade the Betting Rooms, and sharply snap at the moneyed Lunatics. Some Keepers flushed with drink, and some not, but all close and calculating. A vague echoing roar of "t'harses" and "t'races" always rising in the air, until midnight, at about which period it dies away in occasional drunken songs and straggling yells. But, all night, some unmannerly drinking-house in the neighbourhood opens its mouth at intervals and spits out a man too drunk to be retained: who thereupon makes what uproarious protest may be left in him, and either falls asleep where he tumbles, or is carried off in custody.

Tuesday morning, at daybreak. A sudden rising, as it were out of the earth, of all the obscene creatures, who sell "correct cards of the races." They may have been coiled in corners, or sleeping on door-steps, and, having all passed the night under the same set of circumstances, may all want to circulate their blood at the same time; but, however that may be, they spring into existence all at once and together, as though a new Cadmus had sown a race-horse's teeth. There is nobody up, to buy the cards; but, the cards are madly cried. There is no patronage to quarrel for; but, they madly quarrel and fight. Conspicuous among these hyænas, as breakfast-time discloses, is a fearful creature in the general semblance of a man: shaken off his next-to-no legs by drink and devilry, bare-headed and bare-footed, with a great shock of hair like a horrible broom, and nothing on him but a ragged pair of trousers and a pink glazed-calico coat—made on him—so very tight that it is as evident that he could never take it off, as that he never does. This hideous apparition, inconceivably drunk, has a terrible power of making a gong-like imitation of the braying of an ass: which feat requires that he should lay his right jaw in, his begrimed right paw, double himself up, and shake his bray out of himself, with much staggering on his next-to-no legs, and much twirling of his horrible broom, as if it were a mop. From the present minute, when he comes in sight holding up his cards to the windows, and hoarsely proposing purchase to My Lord, Your Excellency, Colonel, the Noble Captain, and Your Honourable Worship—from the present minute until the Grand Race-Week is finished, at all hours of the morning, evening, day, and night, shall the town reverberate, at capricious intervals, to the brays of this frightful animal the Gong-donkey.

No very great racing to-day, so no very great amount of

vehicles: though there is a good sprinkling, too: from farmers' carts and gigs, to carriages with post-horses and to fours-in-hand, mostly coming by the road from York, and passing on straight through the main street to the Course. A walk in the wrong direction may be a better thing for Mr. Goodchild to-day than the Course, so he walks in the wrong direction. Everybody gone to the races. Only children in the street. Grand Alliance Circus deserted; not one Star-Rider left; omnibus which forms the Pay-Place, having on separate panels Pay here for the Boxes, Pay here for the Pit, Pay here for the Gallery, hove down in a corner and locked up; nobody near the tent but the man on his knees on the grass, who is making the paper balloons for the Star young gentlemen to jump through to-night. A pleasant road, pleasantly wooded. No labourers working in the fields; all gone " t'races." The few late wenders of their way " t'races," who are yet left driving on the road, stare in amazement at the recluse who is not going " t'race.." Roadside innkeeper has gone " t'races." Turnpike-man has gone " t'races." His thrifty wife, washing clothes at the toll-house door, is going " t'races " to-morrow. Perhaps there may be no one left to take the toll to-morrow; who knows? Though assuredly that would be neither turn-pike-like nor Yorkshire-like. The very wind and dust seem to be hurrying " t'races," as they briskly pass the only way-farer on the road. In the distance, the Railway Engine, waiting at the town-end, shrieks despairingly. Nothing but the difficulty of getting off the Line, restrains that Engine from going " t'races," too, it is very clear.

At night, more Lunatics out than last night—and more Keepers. The latter very active at the Betting Rooms, the street in front of which is now impassable. Mr. Palmer as before. Mr. Thurtell as before. Roar and uproar as before. Gradual subsidence as before. Unmannerly drinking-house expectorates as before. Drunken negro-melodists, Gong-donkey, and correct cards, in the night.

On Wednesday morning, the morning of the great St.

Leger, it becomes apparent that there has been a great influx since yesterday, both of Lunatics and Keepers. The families of the tradesmen over the way are no longer within human ken; their places know them no more; ten, fifteen, and twenty guinea-lodgers fill them. At the pastry-cook's second-floor window, a Keeper is brushing Mr. Thurtell's hair—thinking it his own. In the wax-chandler's attic, another Keeper is putting on Mr. Palmer's braces. In the gunsmith's nursery, a Lunatic is shaving himself. In the serious stationer's best sitting-room, three Lunatics are taking a combination-breakfast, praising the (cook's) devil, and drinking neat brandy in an atmosphere of last midnight's cigars. No family sanctuary is free from our Angelic messengers—we put up at the Angel —who in the guise of extra waiters for the grand Race-Week, rattle in and out of the most secret chambers of everybody's house, with dishes and tin covers, decanters, soda-water bottles, and glasses. An hour later. Down the street and up the street, as far as eyes can see and a good deal farther, there is a dense crowd; outside the Betting Rooms it is like a great struggle at a theatre door—in the days of theatres; or at the vestibule of the Spurgeon temple—in the days of Spurgeon. An hour later. Fusing into this crowd, and somehow getting through it, are all kinds of conveyances, and all kinds of foot-passengers; carts, with brick-makers and brick-makeresses jolting up and down on planks; drags, with the needful grooms behind, sitting cross-armed in the needful manner, and slanting themselves backward from the soles of their boots at the needful angle; postboys, in the shining hats and smart jackets of the olden time, when stokers were not; beautiful Yorkshire horses, gallantly driven by their own breeders and masters. Under every pole, and every shaft, and every horse, and every wheel as it would seem, the Gong-donkey—metallically braying, when not struggling for life, or whipped out of the way.

By one o'clock, all this stir has gone out of the streets, and there is no one left in them but Francis Goodchild. Francis

Goodchild will not be left in them long; for, he too is on his way "t'races."

A most beautiful sight, Francis Goodchild finds "t'races" to be, when he has left fair Doncaster behind him, and comes out on the free course, with its agreeable prospect, its quaint Red House oddly changing and turning as Francis turns, its green grass, and fresh heath. A free course and an easy one, where Francis can roll smoothly where he will, and can choose between the start, or the coming-in, or the turn behind the brow of the hill, or any out-of-the-way point where he lists to see the throbbing horses straining every nerve, and making the sympathetic earth throb as they come by. Francis much delights to be, not in the Grand Stand, but where he can see it, rising against the sky with its vast tiers of little white dots of faces, and its last high rows and corners of people, looking like pins stuck into an enormous pincushion—not quite so symmetrically as his orderly eye could wish, when people change or go away. When the race is nearly run out, it is as good as the race to him to see the flutter among the pins, and the change in them from dark to light, as hats are taken off and waved. Not less full of interest, the loud anticipation of the winner's name, the swelling, and the final, roar; then, the quick dropping of all the pins out of their places, the revelation of the shape of the bare pincushion, and the closing-in of the whole host of Lunatics and Keepers, in the rear of the three horses with bright-coloured riders, who have not yet quite subdued their gallop though the contest is over.

Mr. Goodchild would appear to have been by no means free from lunacy himself at "t'races," though not of the prevalent kind. He is suspected by Mr. Idle to have fallen into a dreadful state concerning a pair of little lilac gloves and a little bonnet that he saw there. Mr. Idle asserts, that he did afterwards repeat at the Angel, with an appearance of being lunatically seized, some rhapsody to the following effect : "O little lilac gloves! And O winning little bonnet, making in conjunction with her golden hair quite a Glory in the

458

LOSSES AND GAINS

sunlight round the pretty head, why anything in the world
but you and me! Why may not this day's running—of
horses, to all the rest: of precious sands of life to me—be
prolonged through an everlasting autumn-sunshine, without
a sunset! Slave of the Lamp, or Ring, strike me yonder
gallant equestrian Clerk of the Course, in the scarlet coat,
motionless on the green grass for ages! Friendly Devil on
Two Sticks, for ten times ten thousands years, keep Blink-
Bonny jibbing at the post, and let us have no start! Arab
drums, powerful of old to summon Genii in the desert, sound
of yourselves and raise a troop for me in the desert of my
heart, which shall so enchant this dusty barouche (with a
conspicuous excise-plate, resembling the Collector's door-plate
at a turnpike), that I, within it, loving the little lilac gloves,
the winning little bonnet, and the dear unknown-wearer with
the golden hair, may wait by her side for ever, to see a Great
St. Leger that shall never be run!"

Thursday morning. After a tremendous night of crowding, shouting, drinking-house expectoration, Gong-donkey, and
correct cards. Symptoms of yesterday's gains in the way of
drink, and of yesterday's losses in the way of money, abundant.
Money-losses very great. As usual, nobody seems to have
won; but, large losses and many losers are unquestionable
facts. Both Lunatics and Keepers, in general very low. Several
of both kinds look in at the chemist's while Mr. Goodchild
is making a purchase there, to be "picked up." One red-eyed
Lunatic, flushed, faded, and disordered, enters hurriedly and
cries savagely, "Hond us a gloss of sal volatile in wather, or
soom dommed thing o' thot sart!" Faces at the Betting
Rooms very long, and a tendency to bite nails observable.
Keepers likewise given this morning to standing about solitary,
with their hands in their pockets, looking down at their boots
as they fit them into cracks of the pavement, and then
looking up whistling and walking away. Grand Alliance
Circus out, in procession; buxom lady-member of Grand
Alliance, in crimson riding-habit, fresher to look at, even in

her paint under the day sky, than the cheeks of Lunatics or Keepers. Spanish Cavalier appears to have lost yesterday, and jingles his bossed bridle with disgust, as if he were paying. Reaction also apparent at the Guildhall opposite, whence certain pickpockets come out handcuffed together, with that peculiar walk which is never seen under any other circumstances—a walk expressive of going to jail, game, but still of jails being in bad taste and arbitrary, and how would *you* like it if it was you instead of me, as it ought to be! Mid-day. Town filled as yesterday, but not so full; and emptied as yesterday, but not so empty. In the evening, Angel ordinary where every Lunatic and Keeper has his modest daily meal of turtle, venison, and wine, not so crowded as yesterday, and not so noisy. At night, the theatre. More abstracted faces in it than one ever sees at public assemblies; such faces wearing an expression which strongly reminds Mr. Goodchild of the boys at school who were "going up next," with their arithmetic or mathematics. These boys are, no doubt, going up to-morrow with *their* sums and figures. Mr. Palmer and Mr. Thurtell in the boxes O. P. Mr. Thurtell and Mr. Palmer in the boxes P. S. The firm of Thurtell, Palmer, and Thurtell, in the boxes Centre. A most odious tendency observable in these distinguished gentlemen to put vile constructions on sufficiently innocent phrases in the play, and then to applaud them in a Satyr-like manner. Behind Mr. Goodchild, with a party of other Lunatics and one Keeper, the express incarnation of the thing called a "gent." A gentleman born; a gent manufactured. A something with a scarf round its neck, and a slipshod speech issuing from behind the scarf; more depraved, more foolish, more ignorant, more unable to believe in any noble or good thing of any kind, than the stupidest Bosjesman. The thing is but a boy in years, and is addled with drink. To do its company justice, even its company is ashamed of it, as it drawls its slang criticisms on the representation, and inflames Mr. Goodchild with a burning ardour to fling it into the pit. Its remarks are so horrible, that Mr.

Goodchild, for the moment, even doubts whether that *is* a wholesome Art, which sets women apart on a high floor before such a thing as this, though as good as its own sisters, or its own mother—whom Heaven forgive for bringing it into the world! But, the consideration that a low nature must make a low world of its own to live in, whatever the real materials, or it could no more exist than any of us could without the sense of touch, brings Mr. Goodchild to reason : the rather, because the thing soon drops its downy chin upon its scarf, and slobbers itself asleep.

Friday Morning. Early fights. Gong-donkey, and correct cards. Again, a great set towards the races, though not so great a set as on Wednesday. Much packing going on too, upstairs at the gunsmith's, the wax-chandler's, and the serious stationer's ; for there will be a heavy drift of Lunatics and Keepers to London by the afternoon train. The course as pretty as ever ; the great pincushion as like a pincushion, but not nearly so full of pins ; whole rows of pins wanting. On the great event of the day, both Lunatics and Keepers become inspired with rage ; and there is a violent scuffling, and a rushing at the losing jockey, and an emergence of the said jockey from a swaying and menacing crowd, protected by friends, and looking the worse for wear ; which is a rough proceeding, though animating to see from a pleasant distance. After the great event, rills begin to flow from the pincushion towards the railroad ; the rills swell into rivers ; the rivers soon unite into a lake. The lake floats Mr. Goodchild into Doncaster, past the Itinerant personage in black, by the way-side telling him from the vantage ground of a legibly printed placard on a pole that for all these things the Lord will bring him to judgment. No turtle and venison ordinary this evening ; that is all over. No Betting at the rooms ; nothing there but the plants in pots, which have, all the week, been stood about the entry to give it an innocent appearance, and which have sorely sickened by this time.

Saturday. Mr. Idle wishes to know at breakfast, what
were those dreadful groanings in his bedroom doorway in
the night? Mr. Goodchild answers, Nightmare. Mr. Idle
repels the calumny, and calls the waiter. The Angel is very
sorry—had intended to explain; but you see, gentlemen,
there was a gentleman dined down-stairs with two more, and
he had lost a deal of money, and he would drink a deal of
wine, and in the night he "took the horrors," and got up;
and as his friends could do nothing with him he laid himself
down and groaned at Mr. Idle's door. "And he DID groan
there," Mr. Idle says; "and you will please to imagine me
inside, 'taking the horrors' too!"

So far, the picture of Doncaster on the occasion of its
great sporting anniversary, offers probably a general representation of the social condition of the town, in the past as
well as in the present time. The sole local phenomenon of
the current year, which may be considered as entirely un-
precedented in its way, and which certainly claims, on that
account, some slight share of notice, consists in the actual
existence of one remarkable individual, who is sojourning
in Doncaster, and who, neither directly nor indirectly, has
anything at all to do, in any capacity whatever, with the
racing amusements of the week. Ranging throughout the
entire crowd that fills the town, and including the inhabi-
tants as well as the visitors, nobody is to be found altogether
disconnected with the business of the day, excepting this one
unparalleled man. He does not bet on the races, like the
sporting men. He does not assist the races, like the jockeys,
starters, judges, and grooms. He does not look on at the
races, like Mr. Goodchild and his fellow-spectators. He does
not profit by the races, like the hotel-keepers and the trades-
people. He does not minister to the necessities of the races,
like the booth-keepers, the postilions, the waiters, and the
hawkers of Lists. He does not assist the attractions of the
races, like the actors at the theatre, the riders at the circus,

or the posturers at the Poses Plastiques. Absolutely and literally, he is the only individual in Doncaster who stands by the brink of the full-flowing race-stream, and is not swept away by it in common with all the rest of his species. Who is this modern hermit, this recluse of the St. Leger-week, this inscrutably ungregarious being, who lives apart from the amusements and activities of his fellow-creatures? Surely, there is little difficulty in guessing that clearest and easiest of all riddles. Who could he be, but Mr. Thomas Idle?

Thomas had suffered himself to be taken to Doncaster, just as he would have suffered himself to be taken to any other place in the habitable globe which would guarantee him the temporary possession of a comfortable sofa to rest his ankle on. Once established at the hotel, with his leg on one cushion and his back against another, he formally declined taking the slightest interest in any circumstance whatever connected with the races, or with the people who were assembled to see them. Francis Goodchild, anxious that the hours should pass by his crippled travelling-companion as lightly as possible, suggested that his sofa should be moved to the window, and that he should amuse himself by looking out at the moving panorama of humanity, which the view from it of the principal street presented. Thomas, however, steadily declined profiting by the suggestion.

"The farther I am from the window," he said, "the better, Brother Francis, I shall be pleased. I have nothing in common with the one prevalent idea of all those people who are passing in the street. Why should I care to look at them?"

"I hope I have nothing in common with the prevalent idea of a great many of them, either," answered Goodchild, thinking of the sporting gentlemen whom he had met in the course of his wanderings about Doncaster. "But, surely, among all the people who are walking by the house, at this very moment, you may find——"

"Not one living creature," interposed Thomas, "who is

not, in one way or another, interested in horses, and who is not, in a greater or less degree, an admirer of them. Now, I hold opinions in reference to these particular members of the quadruped creation, which may lay claim (as I believe) to the disastrous distinction of being unpartaken by any other human being, civilised or savage, over the whole surface of the earth. Taking the horse as an animal in the abstract, Francis, I cordially despise him from every point of view."

"Thomas," said Goodchild, "confinement to the house has begun to affect your biliary secretions. I shall go to the chemist's and get you some physic."

"I object," continued Thomas, quietly possessing himself of his friend's hat, which stood on a table near him,—"I object, first, to the personal appearance of the horse. I protest against the conventional idea of beauty, as attached to that animal. I think his nose too long, his forehead too low, and his legs (except in the case of the cart-horse) ridiculously thin by comparison with the size of his body. Again, considering how big an animal he is, I object to the contemptible delicacy of his constitution. Is he not the sickliest creature in creation? Does any child catch cold as easily as a horse? Does he not sprain his fetlock, for all his appearance of superior strength, as easily as I sprained my ankle! Furthermore, to take him from another point of view, what a helpless wretch he is! No fine lady requires more constant waiting-on than a horse. Other animals can make their own toilette: he must have a groom. You will tell me that this is because we want to make his coat artificially glossy. Glossy! Come home with me, and see my cat,—my clever cat, who can groom herself! Look at your own dog! see how the intelligent creature curry-combs himself with his own honest teeth! Then, again, what a fool the horse is, what a poor, nervous fool! He will start at a piece of white paper in the road as if it was a lion. His one idea, when he hears a noise that he is not accustomed to, is to run away from it. What do you say to those two

464

common instances of the sense and courage of this absurdly overpraised animal? I might multiply them to two hundred, if I chose to exert my mind and waste my breath, which I never do. I prefer coming at once to my last charge against the horse, which is the most serious of all, because it affects his moral character. I accuse him boldly, in his capacity of servant to man, of slyness and treachery. I brand him publicly, no matter how mild he may look about the eyes, or how sleek he may be about the coat, as a systematic betrayer, whenever he can get the chance, of the confidence reposed in him. What do you mean by laughing and shaking your head at me?"

"Oh, Thomas, Thomas!" said Goodchild. "You had better give me my hat; you had better let me get you that physic."

"I will let you get anything you like, including a composing draught for yourself," said Thomas, irritably alluding to his fellow-apprentice's inexhaustible activity, "if you will only sit quiet for five minutes longer, and hear me out. I say again the horse is a betrayer of the confidence reposed in him; and that opinion, let me add, is drawn from my own personal experience, and is not based on any fanciful theory whatever. You shall have two instances, two over-whelming instances. Let me start the first of these by asking, what is the distinguishing quality which the Shetland Pony has arrogated to himself, and is still perpetually trumpeting through the world by means of popular report and books on Natural History? I see the answer in your face: it is the quality of being Sure-Footed. He professes to have other virtues, such as hardiness and strength, which you may discover on trial; but the one thing which he insists on your believing, when you get on his back, is that he may be safely depended on not to tumble down with you. Very good. Some years ago, I was in Shetland with a party of friends. They insisted on taking me with them to the top of a precipice that overhung the sea. It was a great distance off, but they all determined to walk to it except me. I was wiser then than I was with you at Carrock, and I determined to be carried to the precipice. There was no carriage-road in the island, and nobody offered (in consequence, as I suppose, of the imperfectly-civilised state of the country) to bring me a sedan-chair, which is naturally what I should have liked best. A Shetland pony was produced instead. I remembered my Natural History, I recalled popular report, and I got on the little beast's back, as any other man would have done in my position, placing implicit confidence in the sureness of his feet. And how did he repay that confidence? Brother Francis, carry your mind on from morning to noon. Picture to yourself a howling wilderness of grass and bog, bounded by low stony hills. Pick out one particular spot in that imaginary scene, and sketch me in it, with outstretched arms, curved back, and heels in the air, plunging headforemost into a black patch of water and mud. Place just behind me the legs, the body, and the head of a sure-footed Shetland pony, all stretched flat on the ground, and you will have produced an accurate representation of a very lamentable fact And the moral device, Francis, of this picture will be to testify that when gentlemen put confidence in the legs of Shetland ponies, they will find to their cost that they are leaning on nothing but broken reeds. There is my first instance—and what have you got to say to that?"

"Nothing, but that I want my hat," answered Goodchild, starting up and walking restlessly about the room.

"You shall have it in a minute," rejoined Thomas. "My second instance"—(Goodchild groaned, and sat down again)—"My second instance is more appropriate to the present time and place, for it refers to a race-horse. Two years ago an excellent friend of mine, who was desirous of prevailing on me to take regular exercise, and who was well enough acquainted with the weakness of my legs to expect no very active compliance with his wishes on their part, offered to make me a present of one of his horses. Hearing that the animal in question had started in life on the turf, I declined accepting the gift with many thanks; adding, by way of explanation, that I looked on a race-horse as a kind of embodied hurricane, upon which no sane man of my character and habits could be expected to seat himself. My friend replied that, however appropriate my metaphor might be as applied to race-horses in general, it was singularly unsuitable as applied to the particular horse which he proposed to give me. From a foal upwards this remarkable animal had been the idlest and most sluggish of his race. Whatever capacities for speed he might possess he had kept so strictly to himself, that no amount of training had ever brought them out. He had been found hopelessly slow as a racer, and hopelessly lazy as a hunter, and was fit for nothing but a quiet, easy life of it with an old gentleman or an invalid. When I heard this account of the horse, I don't mind confessing that my heart warmed to him. Visions of Thomas Idle ambling serenely on the back of a steed as lazy as himself, presenting to a restless world the soothing and composite spectacle of a kind of sluggardly Centaur, too peaceable in his habits to alarm anybody, swam attractively before my eyes. I went to look at the horse in the stable. Nice fellow! he was fast asleep with a kitten on his back. I saw him taken out for an airing by the groom. If he had had trousers on his legs I should not have known them from my own, so deliberately were they lifted up, so gently were they put down, so slowly did they get over the ground. From that moment I gratefully accepted my friend's offer. I went home; the horse followed me—by a slow train. Oh, Francis, how devoutly I believed in that horse! how carefully I looked after all his little comforts! I had never gone the length of hiring a man-servant to wait on myself; but I went to the expense of hiring one to wait upon him. If I thought a little of myself when I bought the softest saddle that could be had for money, I thought also of my horse. When the man at the shop afterwards offered me spurs and a whip, I turned from him with horror. When I sallied out for my first ride, I went purposely unarmed with the means of hurrying my steed. He proceeded at his own pace every step of the way; and when he stopped, at last, and blew out both his sides with a heavy sigh, and turned his sleepy head and looked behind him, I took him home again, as I might take home an artless child who said to me, 'If you please, sir, I am tired.' For a week this complete harmony between me and my horse lasted undisturbed. At the end of that time, when he had made quite sure of my friendly confidence in his laziness, when he had thoroughly acquainted himself with all the little weaknesses of my seat (and their name is Legion), the smouldering treachery and ingratitude of the equine nature blazed out in an instant. Without the slightest provocation from me, with nothing passing him at the time but a pony-chaise driven by an old lady, he started in one instant from a state of sluggish depression to a state of frantic high spirits. He kicked, he plunged, he shied, he pranced, he capered fearfully. I sat on him as long as I could, and when I could sit no longer, I fell off. No, Francis! this is not a circumstance to be laughed at, but to be wept over. What would be said of a Man who had requited my kindness in that way? Range over all the rest of the animal creation, and where will you find me an instance of treachery so black as this? The cow that kicks down the milking-pail may have some reason for it; she may think herself taxed too heavily to contribute to the dilution of human tea and the greasing of human bread. The tiger who springs out on me unawares has the excuse of being hungry at the time, to say nothing of the further justification of being a total stranger to me. The very flea who surprises me in my sleep may defend his act of assassination on the ground that I, in my turn, am always ready to murder him when I am awake. I defy the whole body of Natural Historians to move me, logically, off the ground that I have taken in regard to the horse. Receive back your hat, Brother Francis, and go to the chemist's, if you please; for I have now done. Ask me to take anything you like, except an interest in the Doncaster races. Ask me to look at anything you like, except an assemblage of people all animated by feelings of a friendly and admiring nature towards the horse. You are a remarkably well-informed man, and you have heard of hermits. Look upon me as a member of that ancient fraternity, and you will sensibly add to the many obligations which Thomas Idle is proud to owe to Francis Goodchild."

Here, fatigued by the effort of excessive talking, disputatious Thomas waved one hand languidly, laid his head back on the sofa-pillow, and calmly closed his eyes.

At a later period, Mr. Goodchild assailed his travelling companion boldly from the impregnable fortress of common sense. But Thomas, though tamed in body by drastic discipline, was still as mentally unapproachable as ever on the subject of his favourite delusion.

The view from the window after Saturday's breakfast is altogether changed. The tradesmen's families have all come back again. The serious stationer's young woman of all work is shaking a duster out of the window of the combination breakfast-room; a child is playing with a doll, where Mr. Thurtell's hair was brushed; a sanitary scrubbing is in progress on the spot where Mr. Palmer's braces were put on. No signs of the Races are in the streets, but the tramps and the tumble-down-carts and trucks laden with drinking-forms and tables and remnants of booths, that are making their way out of the town as fast as they can. The Angel, which has been cleared for action all the week, already begins restoring every neat and comfortable article of furniture to its own neat and comfortable place. The Angel's daughters (pleasanter angels Mr. Idle and Mr. Goodchild never saw, nor more quietly expert in their business, nor more superior to the common vice of being above it), have a little time to rest, and to air their cheerful faces among the flowers in the yard. It is market-day. The market looks unusually natural, comfortable, and wholesome; the market-people too. The town seems quite restored, when, hark! a metallic bray— The Gong-donkey!

The wretched animal has not cleared off with the rest, but is here, under the window. How much more inconceivably drunk now, how much more begrimed of paw, how much more tight of calico hide, how much more stained and daubed and dirty and dunghilly, from his horrible broom to his tender toes, who shall say! He cannot even shake the bray out of himself now, without laying his cheek so near to the mud of the street, that he pitches over after delivering it. Now, prone in the mud, and now backing himself up against shop-windows, the owners of which come out in terror to remove him; now, in the drinking-shop, and now in the tobacconist's, where he goes to buy tobacco, and makes his way into the parlour, and where he gets a cigar, which in half-a-minute he forgets to smoke; now dancing, now dozing, now cursing, and now complimenting My Lord, the Colonel, the Noble Captain, and Your Honourable Worship, the Gong-donkey kicks up his heels, occasionally braying, until suddenly, he beholds the dearest friend he has in the world coming down the street.

The dearest friend the Gong-donkey has in the world, is a sort of Jackall, in a dull, mangy, black hide, of such small pieces that it looks as if it were made of blacking bottles turned inside out and cobbled together. The dearest friend in the world (inconceivably drunk too) advances at the Gong-donkey, with a hand on each thigh, in a series of humorous springs and stops, wagging his head as he comes. The Gong-donkey regarding him with attention and with the warmest affection, suddenly perceives that he is the greatest enemy he has in the world, and hits him hard in the countenance. The astonished Jackall closes with the Donkey, and they roll over and over in the mud, pummelling one another. A Police Inspector, supernaturally endowed with patience, who has long been looking on from the Guildhall-steps, says, to a myrmidon, "Lock 'em up! Bring 'em in!"

Appropriate finish to the Grand Race-Week. The Gong-donkey, captive and last trace of it, conveyed into limbo, where they cannot do better than keep him until next Race-Week. The Jackall is wanted too, and is much looked for, over the way and up and down. But, having had the good fortune to be undermost at the time of the capture, he has vanished into air.

On Saturday afternoon, Mr. Goodchild walks out and looks at the Course. It is quite deserted; heaps of broken crockery and bottles are raised to its memory; and correct cards and other fragments of paper are blowing about it, as the regulation little paper-books, carried by the French soldiers in their breasts, were seen, soon after the battle was fought, blowing idly about the plains of Waterloo.

Where will these present idle leaves be blown by the idle winds, and where will the last of them be one day lost and forgotten? An idle question, and an idle thought; and with it Mr. Idle fitly makes his bow, and Mr. Goodchild his, and thus ends the Lazy Tour of Two Idle Apprentices.

NOTES ON CHRISTMAS STORIES

DOCTOR MARIGOLD

Chapter II

"I know the . . . Bookseller of Berlin."

This was Monsieur Nicolai, who, being in bad health, had a number of subjective hallucinations, on which he wrote a report. He occupies an illustrious placé in all the chapters on illusions, in Manuals of Psychology, in company with an uncertain Mrs. A. The usual argument has been that no hallucinations have an objective cause (as, for instance, in the action of another mind), because there was no such cause in the case of the Berlin bookseller. Dickens's bank manager contributes an instance on the other side ; but there is no reason to suppose that his narrative is founded on fact.

"The change in him was so startling when I touched him."

Dickens was probably acquainted with the very old Highland belief that a second-sighted man can communicate his vision by placing his hand on the shoulder, and his foot on the foot, of a companion. Dr. Stewart (Nether Lochaber) gives a recent instance ; and the belief is mentioned by Kirk (1690) in his *Secret Commonwealth*, and in earlier works. The experiment was unsuccessful when tried by a seer on the present annotator.

This book, designed by
William B. Taylor
is a production of
Edito-Service S.A., Geneva

Printed in France